PRAISE FOR SKELETON

"I loved this book from beginning to end. Peter Parkin and Alison Darby spin a tale of love, government corruption, and good overcoming evil. It had me on the edge of my seat wanting more. I highly recommend this book."

Linda S., Florida

"Great book. Couldn't put it down. Lots of action, twists and turns to keep you gripped all the way to the last page."

Clarice T., United Kingdom

"The great thing about these authors' yarns is that they skillfully take you to a fantasy world that could easily match real life. In the case of Skeleton, as with their other books, I sure hope I am wrong about that. But, who knows?"

Rae J., Alberta

"Loved this book. Great story line and characters. Fast-paced, action-packed. I hope to see more from these two authors. Obviously a great collaboration. This would make a great movie."

Marilyn C., Ontario

ALSO BY THE AUTHORS

SERPENTINE

MAJESTIC

HEADHUNTER

SKELETON

sands press
Brockville, Ontario

SKELETON

PETER PARKIN & ALISON DARBY

sands press

sands press

A Division of 10361976 Canada Inc.
300 Central Avenue West
Brockville, Ontario
K6V 5V2

Toll Free 1-800-563-0911 or 613-345-2687
http://www.sandspress.com

ISBN 978-1-988281-47-6
Copyright © 2018 Peter Parkin
http://www.peterparkin.com
All Rights Reserved

Cover Design by Kristine Barker and Wendy Treverton
Edited by Sparks Literary
Formatting by Renee Hare
Publisher Kristine Barker
Author Agent Sparks Literary Consultants

"Everyone's Gone To The Moon" - Music and Lyrics by Kenneth King, Published by Marquis Music Co.

For information on bulk purchases of this book or any book published by Sands Press, please call 1-800-563-0911.

1st Printing March 2018

To book an author for your live event, please call: 1-800-563-0911

Sands Press is a literary publisher interested in new and established authors wishing to develop and market their product. For more information please visit our website at www.sandspress.com.

CHAPTER ONE

Dennis Chambers shuffled down the hall toward his mother's room. Room 207 had been her home for the last five years, a place that could only be described as antiseptic; not the least bit conducive to any kind of creative thinking. However, he knew painfully well that there wasn't much chance of that kind of thinking going on anyway in a place like this, from any of its residents.

The place smelled like death.

He continued to drag his feet down the corridor, tracks he had made more times than he could count. This route always filled him with the same feelings: anguish, trepidation. No joy at seeing his mom. No shared laughter like they had enjoyed for so many years before this terrible disease had stolen her mind and her soul. Stolen at least at the conscious level anyway, and he had now pretty much convinced himself that there was nothing at the subconscious level either. But Dennis always prayed that somewhere deep down inside the labyrinth of her being that she still existed; still remembered who she was, still remembered him and his sister, and still remembered and cherished her long-dead husband.

But while Dennis prayed every day for that, he was sure it was a moot point. He was just going through the motions. There was no denying that the body of his mother was just a shell now, a vessel that reflected to loved ones the physical reminders of what had once been a full and good life.

The corridor seemed to get longer and longer on each visit. This time was no different. Nurses passed him along the way, nodding respectfully. But there was no warmth on their faces. Just the tepid expressions of realism and resignation. They knew the score and in their own day-to-day duties they received no gratification, no exhilaration—none of the feelings that a nurse on a normal care floor might experience. No feedback, no satisfaction in knowing that the care they provided was being appreciated by their patients.

Their patients didn't even know they were there most of the time. Nurses who dedicated themselves to geriatric care were somehow oddly doomed just like their patients were. It was a dead zone, no chance to recover, no possibility of getting better, only the guarantee of getting progressively worse. It took a very unique person to be able to do that job, Dennis thought wryly.

He opened the door to room 207, and he had mixed feelings knowing this was the last time. This nursing home was being closed permanently due to government funding cutbacks. It was an ancient structure that needed millions of dollars to bring it up to code. It was far cheaper to build new structures than renovate old ones. And for now, there was no other place for his mother to go—except to Dennis' home. All the nursing homes were filled to overflowing, with a healthy majority of patients suffering from the same affliction as his mother—Alzheimer's and Dementia. People's lives were being prolonged now beyond what nature had ever intended, causing the emergence of diseases like these that had probably never been seen back when the life expectancy was only sixty-five. Lives lasted longer now, but the memories and souls were already dead long before their bodies gave out. *What was the point?*

Dennis' mother was sitting on the edge of her bed when he came through the door. She looked up in surprise. "Who are you?"

Dennis was used to this by now, but it still hurt like hell. "Mom, it's me. Denny. You remember me."

She squinted her eyes and examined him. "Are you the doctor who gave me that needle the other day? I didn't like that, you know. It hurt."

Dennis knew she hadn't had a needle in years. Her exhaustive regimen of meds were all taken by mouth now. Ten pills a day. And he suspected that the nurses were probably at the point now where they didn't really care if she took them or not. He felt guilty admitting to himself that he wasn't even sure he cared anymore. What were they really prolonging, and why? Despite wishing and praying otherwise, he really didn't believe the soul of his mother was anywhere near planet earth any longer.

"I'm your son: Dennis. I'm not the doctor. Look at my face, look into my eyes. You and I have the same eyes—remember? You used to say our eyes were as blue as the deep blue sea."

His mother looked at him quizzically and for one exciting instant Dennis thought he had made a connection.

"That's a silly thing to say. Why would you and I have the same eyes? And my eyes are brown. You can easily see that, you silly man. Who are you again?"

One thing for sure, his mother hadn't lost her feistiness—a skill she had mastered practicing law and negotiating her way through the corridors of power at the Department of Defense. Lucy Chambers had been a force to be reckoned with back then. That was for sure. As one of the senior counsels at the DOD, she had been privy to most issues that the public never got to see in the news. The same issues that always prevented her from ever truly answering the question, 'What did you do at work today, mom?'

As he gazed at the shell of his once brilliant mother sitting on the edge of the bed, he reflected on how she used to be. And how surprised he was when she had abandoned her stellar career at the tender age of fifty. She was eighty-five years old now, but didn't look it. A stranger would never guess by looking at her that she was so far gone. And people like his mother—brilliant, feisty, vivacious—were the ones where Alzheimer's was the most noticeable. A slow brain with Alzheimer's was…well…still just a slow brain. Not such a shock to loved ones. But a brilliant brain was like a Roman candle fizzling out after its blazing burn. Noticeable to all, impossible to hide, painful to watch.

She didn't have Dennis until she was thirty. He was three years younger than his sister, Melissa. At fifty-five years old, Dennis was already beginning the countdown to when the disease might start appearing in him and he knew Mel was doing the same. They both knew there was no medical evidence linking Alzheimer's to heredity so their chances were as good…or as bad…as anyone else's of getting it. But since Dennis got to see the disease first-hand it was a worry that was still impossible to ignore. Every time he did things like forgetting where he'd placed his keys, or carelessly leaving the milk out on the counter to spoil, he would think about it. It was impossible not to. He was too close to it.

He was jarred out of his daydream by the sudden appearance of a burly nurse bursting through the doorway. "Well, Mrs. Chambers, are we ready to go to your son's house today?"

Lucy turned her head around with ease and glared at the intruder. "Don't you people believe in knocking? First this doctor fellow, and now you! Where are your manners?"

Dennis grinned at the nurse, and she smiled knowingly in return. His first smile of the day.

Geriatric nurses were trained to ignore these outbursts from patients, because in most cases the yellers forgot within a minute or two that they had even yelled. There was no point in arguing because there was no argument to win or lose. It was merely a moment in time, which was really all an Alzheimer's patient's life was anyway—brief moments in time that were quickly forgotten.

The nurse introduced herself to Dennis as Jennifer, after which she quickly went about her business of bundling up his mother's possessions into a single suitcase. A wealthy life had been reduced to one suitcase. Lucy's wealth was now spread between her two children, and she had most likely forgotten completely now that at one time she had been a woman of privilege.

Dennis went over to his mom and held her hand. "Mom, we have to go. Let me help you into the wheelchair, okay?"

Lucy scowled at him in a manner that only she could pull off, but reluctantly allowed Dennis to pull her up from the bed and ease her into the wheelchair. "I don't know why they insist I ride in this stupid thing. I can still outrun most of the incompetents in this stupid hotel."

Dennis just smiled, spun the chair around and headed out the door. There were several other old folks leaving today too, he noticed. The hallway was jam-packed with wheelchairs, patients, family members and suitcases. He had to do some fancy maneuvering to get around some of the obstacles. Nurse Jennifer was running interference in front of him. She was carrying the suitcase and a potted plant. Dennis had another plant in his free hand, steering the wheelchair with the other.

They rounded the corner and headed out the front door to the sound of several nurses calling out, "Goodbye, Mrs. Chambers!" Lucy ignored them; in fact, she seemed annoyed by them.

Once they reached the portico outside the entranceway, they stopped. Dennis' car was parked right down on the street in front. He was lucky to have found that spot—traffic in Washington, D.C. was horrible at the best of times, and parking spaces were nearly impossible to find. Even the nursing home's parking lot always seemed to be full.

Jennifer headed down the stairs and Dennis steered the wheelchair over to the handicapped ramp. He put down the potted plant, wanting to use both hands to guide the chair down to the sidewalk. He could hear his mother grumbling as he started on the downward slope.

Safely at the bottom, he popped the trunk of his Mercedes, took the suitcase and potted plant from Jennifer and placed them inside. Then he knelt in front of his mom. "Let me take your purse, mom. You'll need your hands free getting into the car—it's a tight squeeze."

"No one takes my purse, young man. Who do you think you are?" She grabbed onto her purse even tighter, seemingly protecting valuable treasures. Dennis knew there were only a few things in that purse—things that were of sentimental value to his mom, like jewelry. But he respected that they were important to her, even though she no longer remembered or felt any sentiment. While she didn't remember the significance of things, part of her brain just seemed to know that they were significant.

"Okay, mom. Hold onto it. I'll be back in a sec—have to go back up and get the other plant." He nodded at Jennifer, leaning his head in the direction of his mom. "Watch her for a second, will you?"

Then he started his walk back up the steps. Halfway to the top he heard the screams. He whirled around just in time to see his mother and the wheelchair topple over while a young thug dragged on the strap of her purse. Jennifer, while trying to intervene, received a kick in the stomach from the thug's partner, sending her down hard.

Dennis leaped off the steps and raced to the sidewalk. He drank in the scene: his mother holding onto her purse for dear life, being dragged out of the wheelchair and onto the sidewalk, finally mercifully letting go.

The thugs ran. Dennis took off after them as Jennifer rose to her feet and reached down to help Lucy back up into her chair.

Dennis was fast. The muggers were young, but he could tell they weren't athletic. They were probably hoping the purse contained money that they could use to buy drugs. Drug addicts generally didn't keep themselves in good shape, which was to Dennis' advantage. At fifty-five he had still retained some of the athleticism of his youth and he called on it now.

He carefully deked around several people while the thugs, about thirty yards in front, were callously knocking them out of the way. At the end of the street they turned the corner and headed east. Dennis saw his opportunity—he cut the corner off, leaping up onto a concrete statue base and running straight across to the sidewalk the thugs had just turned onto. He flung himself through the air in a perfectly timed tackle, taking the kid with the purse to the ground. He pulled the purse out of the squirming thug's hand, then grabbed his long hair in his fist and smashed the kid's head into the pavement.

The next thing Dennis saw was the sole of a foot coming straight toward his face. Impact. He slumped back onto the sidewalk but held tightly onto the purse. No one was going to get his mother's purse. Through his blurry eyes he watched one punk helping the other to his feet, then both running off like scared jackrabbits.

Dennis struggled to his feet, putting his hand up to his tender nose. Some blood, but it didn't seem broken. He shook it off and wearily headed back in the direction he had come. Scores of curious people watched him trudge along, bloodied face, purse in hand.

He had been hoping to hang onto the youth and arrest him, but he knew that would have been mainly just symbolic anyway. The kid would have been back on the street in a matter of hours, stealing more purses, buying more drugs. A misdemeanor at best. At least he had his mom's purse back, so victory was his. And his mother would be happy…well, as happy as her disease allowed.

Lucy and Jennifer were waiting for him beside his car, looking none too worse for the ordeal. Lucy smiled when she saw her purse and it warmed Dennis' heart to see that such a little thing like a purse could bring out a rare smile.

Dennis composed himself while Jennifer stared at his blood-streaked nose and lips. "Okay, let's get back to what we were doing. I'll get that plant, then help you into the car, okay Mom?" She frowned at him, then started fidgeting with her fingers. Dennis just shrugged and resumed his walk up the steps.

Another scream—this time more of a wail—caused him to whirl around once again. His mother had her head buried in her hands and Jennifer was rubbing her back, looking puzzled.

He called back to her. "Mom, what's wrong now?"

Lucy angrily shifted her body, just enough to make the wheelchair spin around so she could face her son. Her eyes were alert and she stared right up into his—for the first time in many years she held a gaze into his eyes. She raised her gnarled little fist and shook it furiously. Her regal face was now scrunched up in fear as she pleaded with her son in a strong authoritative voice, a voice that Dennis hadn't heard since she gave up her career.

"Denny, Denny, we can't leave without the package!"

All Dennis could do was stare back at her, his bloodied mouth hanging open in shock.

"Get the package, Denny! Please! You have to get it!"

CHAPTER TWO

Men don't cry. Or, at least, *most* men don't cry. Or, at the very least, most men don't let anyone *see* them cry.

Dennis was well aware of the stigma that was attached to the sight of tears pouring down a man's cheeks. But he didn't care. He had never cared about that, because he had always allowed himself to cry. Strong men cried. Confident men cried. Men who cared cried. And Dennis was all those things.

Standing on the steps of the nursing home watching his mother pleading with him, recognizing him, connecting with him for the first time in about five years—it simultaneously squeezed and caressed the crap out of his soul. He could feel it deep within and the tears now streaming down his cheeks were uncontrollable. And he loved the feeling: the warmth, the wetness, the cleansing.

He sprang from the steps and ran over to his mother. He knelt in front of her and cupped her cheeks in his hands. "Mom, you know me! You still know me!"

"Denny, don't be silly. Why wouldn't I know you? You're my baby!" She pursed her lips together and gestured a kiss. Dennis leaned forward and kissed her dry, chapped mouth.

She brought her tiny hands up to his face and wiped the tears away. "Why are you crying? I can see you've hurt yourself." She rubbed away at the dried bloodstains. "How did you do this? Does it hurt?"

Dennis shook his head and smiled. "No, mom, it doesn't hurt. I've actually never felt better."

Lucy leaned her head back and took a good look at him. "Are you getting those nosebleeds again, Denny? Do I need to take you to see the doctor? Knowing you, you'd never go on your own."

Dennis wiped at his nose with his hand. "I just banged myself, mom. No, I haven't had those nosebleeds since I was a little boy. Nothing to worry about."

She smiled. It was her old smile; a smile that Dennis thought had disappeared from his life forever, one he would never see again except in old family videos. It was one of those smiles that always made the world seem brighter, kinder, a happier place. It was a smile that also had a way of conveying safety—she had always been firmly in charge.

"A mother always worries, Denny. I'll always worry about you and Melissa. Don't you ever forget that. If you had ever taken the time in your busy life to have children, you would know what I mean." She flashed a mischievous teasing grin at him.

Dennis was astonished. He was actually having a conversation with his mother. He felt his stomach doing flip-flops with each little bit of familiarity she threw his way. Teasing him about having a busy professional life with no time for anything else, was something she had always done. Always—she had never ever let up on that point. While she had been blessed with two grandchildren from Melissa, that had never seemed to be enough for her. She wanted *his* grandchildren. She had never been happy with the reality that her son had ignored that part of life.

Not that he hadn't tried. Dennis had done the marriage thing, and the next step would have been kids if he and Cathy had stayed married. But the union had died after ten years. Both of them had had busy careers, especially in the early years, and sadly they had just grown further and further apart. His mom had never really liked Cathy—it was always easy to tell when Lucy didn't like someone. She never suffered fools gladly. He reckoned that she had only tolerated Cathy for one thing: the fact that she was a woman, with good strong loins, able to bear children.

Dennis had been divorced now for twenty years. Despite the nagging from his mom back then, he had never tried too hard to fall for anyone else. Lucy had just wanted him married again and pursuing a family. She didn't really care who he was with—but always interrogated him in her lawyerly way as to whether or not there was a future with this one…or that one…or could he just juggle several at once and then pick the best? His mother had been insufferable that way.

He smiled warmly at her. Caressed her cheek. Brushed a lock of hair away from her gray eyebrows. "I'm too old to worry about having kids now, mom. But remember, you do have two wonderful grandchildren. Melissa has two boys, remember? They're grown men now; soon they'll have their own kids. You should be ecstatic over that. Don't focus on what I *haven't* done—be glad for what Mel *has* done."

Lucy pouted. When Dennis was young he hated this childish little thing she did when she wanted to make a point, get attention, or win a battle. Now he adored her infamous pout, hoped he could see it every day now for the rest of his life.

Nurse Jennifer was watching the exchange between Dennis and Lucy with interest. Dennis looked up at her and noticed the tender smile on her face, eyes lit up with wonder. She had respectfully backed up several feet away from the two of them, allowing the mysterious exchange to take place without any disturbance. Dennis nodded appreciatively at her, then stood up to his full six foot, three inch frame. "Jennifer, help me here. What's going on?"

She grimaced and moved closer. In a whisper that only Dennis could hear, she said, "We see this once in a while. It's wondrous when it happens, but be warned that it usually doesn't last long. Sometimes we think something triggers the event. And 'event' is truly the right word to use right now for what has happened with your mom. We usually don't see such a level of lucidity as she's showing. This is quite remarkable."

Dennis looked down at Lucy and saw that she was now fidgeting again, pulling at her fingers, playing with her wedding ring. He returned his attention to Jennifer and whispered back. "What can I do? What should I do?"

Jennifer's eyes bore a sudden sadness. "Nothing, sorry to say. Just enjoy it while it's here. But don't get attached to it. There is no such thing as a reversal of Alzheimer's—can't happen, doesn't happen. It's almost sad when these moments happen because while they're exciting for the moment, they always disappear—sometimes never to return."

Dennis nodded and dropped his attention back to his mother. "Mom, are you ready to go home? To my home?"

She jerked her head up and glared at him, fire once again in her eyes. "You still don't listen to anything I say to you, Denny—after all these years, too. Very discouraging. I told you that we have to get the package. Do you remember me saying that?"

Dennis had to admit she had a point. In his elation at having her mind back, he completely forgot the outburst that had started it all. "What package are you talking about, mom?"

"Do you expect me to remember everything? I'm an old woman, or haven't you noticed that?"

Dennis scratched his chin and knelt back down to his mother's level again. He held her hand and spoke softly to her. "You don't remember at all what this package is?"

"No."

"Then why is it important?"

"I just know it is. I tremble when I think of it."

"Is it a surprise, a gift from someone?"

"No, it's not something nice—I know that from my trembling. Do you feel it in my hands? Do you feel it, Denny?"

He had noticed that as soon as he held his mother's hand. He wrote it off as just being the usual eighty-five year old shakes. But his mom seemed to be convinced it was something else. "If it's nothing nice, mom, then why do you want me to get it? Shouldn't we just forget about it?" He was trying hard to be gentle.

Lucy held eye contact with him for about four or five seconds, then the tears started to flow. Her lips started twitching and he could tell she wanted to say something else, but no words came. Then her eyes shifted upwards toward the sky. As Dennis wiped the tears from her cheeks and from around her eyes, she mumbled, "It looks like rain. We should get inside."

"Okay, mom. Let me help you into the car."

She suddenly raised her little fist once again and shook it at him. "I'm not going anywhere with you doctors! I know what you're going to do to me. Take me back inside the hotel. Now!"

Dennis was shocked to his core for the second time within just a few minutes. He had witnessed a virtual resurrection, and now he was watching the slinking of a human spirit back into the inaccessible shadows of the subconscious. It was eerie. And it was heartbreaking.

He felt a hand on his shoulder and looked up to see Jennifer's kind and knowing eyes pleading with him to let it go. He smiled at her, and he knew that his was probably just one of countless sad smiles the nurse had seen from family members of patients. Smiles of resignation.

"I'll help you get her into the car, Mr. Chambers. I'll calm her down, don't you worry."

True to her word, she did. And true to the horrible mind-sucking disease that was Alzheimer's, Lucy had forgotten her outburst within mere seconds.

Dennis stood on the sidewalk with Jennifer, his mother now safely strapped into the front seat of the Mercedes. He looked up at the nursing home that would soon be demolished. His curious mind pondered. "Jennifer, would you mind sitting in the car with my mom for a few minutes? I need to go back inside."

"Sure, you go right ahead, Mr. Chambers. I'll sit with her as long as you need me to."

Dennis nodded his thanks, then walked quickly up the ramp and back through the front doors of the depressing building that his mother referred to as the 'hotel.' He headed down the hall, and took the elevator up to the second floor. Then he retraced the familiar walk down to room 207, except that the walk was no longer slow and depressing. His mother wasn't living in that room anymore, so now it was just a room.

The hall was bustling with activity. There were dozens of old folks in wheelchairs accompanied by sad relatives holding suitcases and potted plants. Nurses were almost non-existent now except for the occasional one helping people gather their belongings. There were different workers here now—maintenance workers moving furniture out of the rooms, removing doors that presumably could be reclaimed elsewhere. Dennis knew that the building was scheduled to be demolished, but he was surprised to see that it was probably going to be sooner rather than later. This seemed to be the day that almost all residents would be leaving.

He dodged a couple of workers carrying a bed-frame, and continued on toward his mother's room. As he approached he noticed that the door was closed. Strange. He hesitated for just a second, then turned the handle and swung the door open.

What greeted him inside was a sight that his eyes didn't expect. There were no maintenance workers shifting furniture around. Instead there were three men in suits. One was on a ladder, his hands fiddling with something inside the ventilation duct. Another man had his mother's phone turned upside down with the bottom removed, twisting away inside with a tiny screwdriver. The third man was on the floor, his arm buried inside the material of his mother's freshly slit mattress.

It took only an instant for Dennis to take in the entire bizarre scene with his keen and finely honed powers of observation. The three suits looked back at him sheepishly, like little kids caught with their fingers in the cookie jar.

The man with the phone in his hand recovered quickly. "Please step back and leave this room, sir."

Dennis stepped forward instead of back. "I will not. This was my mother's room. Who are you and what on earth are you doing here?"

"We don't have to answer that, but I'll do you the courtesy of identifying myself." The man pulled out a laminated card and handed it to Dennis. He studied it—it was an identification card showing the man to be 'Joseph Banda, Investigator, Department of Defense.'

Dennis reached into the inside pocket of his suit jacket and pulled out a gold shield—then arrogantly clipped it to the belt of his pants. Then he shoved a business card at Banda. "This will identify me as 'Dennis Chambers, Chief of Detectives, City of Washington.' Now, are we going to stand here and compare penis sizes, or are you going to answer me as to what you're doing here? This building is within city jurisdiction, *my* jurisdiction."

Banda scrutinized the card with interest, then glanced up, nonplussed. "Mr. Chambers, *my* jurisdiction is the entire country, so please don't pretend you can pull rank on me. I outrank you in every possible way."

"We'll see about that. What is the DOD doing tearing apart my mother's room?"

Banda didn't blink. "Standard procedure for former security clearance DOD employees, to examine their abandoned residences."

"She didn't abandon it, she was kicked out."

Still no blink. "It's a matter of national security to always inspect former places of habitation."

Dennis moved one step closer to Banda, until their eyes were about six inches apart. "It looks to me as if you're removing things, not necessarily looking for things—with the possible exception of your mattress-fetish friend on the floor."

Silence.

"My mother left the DOD thirty-five years ago and has been living in an almost fairyland state for the last five years. I'm curious to know why she could still be on your radar."

Silence with a steely glare.

Dennis put his hands on his hips, pulling back his jacket to display once again the ominously impressive gold shield on his belt...and his gun.

"Did you assholes bug my mother's room?"

CHAPTER THREE

It was a familiar sound—one that triggered an instant sensation of being young, comforted, soothed. She had held him in that chair up until he was four or five years of age. Just the two of them together…rocking… whenever he was restless. Or, perhaps more likely at times when she was restless.

Five years ago, when his mother had moved into the nursing home, Dennis had had to dispose of most of her furniture—some went to Melissa, some he kept, but most went to charity. Even though his house was large, there was only so much room. It hurt to get rid of anything. Every piece had memories for him. But none so much as that old rocking chair. He didn't have the heart to let it go—even though he knew he'd never use it himself. It was rickety, but still remarkably stable. It still worked, it still rocked, it was still adorned with the same frilly pads his mother had sewn together sixty years ago.

And she seemed to remember it. Dennis had positioned it strategically in front of the round front window of the drawing room. She was looking out at the street, and God only knew what was going through her mind. But Dennis felt comforted by the fact that she seemed to find the old chair familiar, and still rocked in it with the same smooth motion as back when he had been a young lad.

Nostalgia—a wonderful thing, but a lonely and sad pursuit when there was no one to share it with.

He had tried to trigger a memory a few hours ago: "Do you remember, mom, when you used to rock me and Melissa in that chair?" For his efforts, Dennis' only reward was a steely glare, accompanied by a grunt of, "You're crazy. Explain to me again how I'm supposed to know you?"

He stood in the doorway now, just watching his mother rock—eyes staring out to the street. Not following cars, people or dogs. Just staring.

And rocking.

He knew that if his mother were in her right mind…or any kind of mind for that matter…she would love his house. Built in the early 1800s, it was a classic Georgian style. Quite a few homes in Georgetown bore that honor but there were few in as fine shape as Dennis' home. Homes built in the 18th and early 19th centuries were mainly of Georgian and Palladian style. The White House was a perfect example of the Palladian style, and his was a perfect example of the Georgian style. In the late 19th, and 20th centuries, the Greek Revival and Art Deco styles took over. In the 21st, Post-Modernism came in.

Dennis' home was located on N Street, adorning a terraced hill overlooking the harbor on the Potomac River. Georgetown was one of the most charming, elegant neighborhoods in all of America. Even though it was part of the metropolis of Washington, D.C., it had an identity all its own. It was established in 1751, and being located right on the Potomac brought it notoriety as a major shipping center—for tobacco products in particular. The city of Washington finally annexed Georgetown in 1871, swallowing it up as part of the larger center. But it didn't succeed in destroying its spirit or identity. It was still the place to be. The terraced area where Dennis lived had been the enclave of wealthy ship owners and merchants back in the heydays of the early 1800s. They had enough greenbacks in their pockets to build their homes to last…and last they did.

Dennis had owned his Georgian home for about five years—he purchased it right after his mother's wealth had been handed over to him and Melissa. They each had joint power of attorney over Lucy's affairs, and she had requested in a 'living will' years before that if she ever became of unsound mind she wanted her children to have her money. She didn't want them to have to wait until she died. The only proviso was that both children would be equally obligated to take care of her financially until the day she died. But as far as Dennis and Melissa were concerned, there was no need for that proviso—their hearts would guide the way. They both loved their mother. Even though she wasn't really herself any longer, there was no question in their minds that she would be taken care of.

The old house was unique, to say the least. It was smack on the corner of N Street and 7th Street, a perfect vantage point for viewing all the expensive cars winding their way down to the Capital center. Beautiful huge trees and narrow painted sidewalks all accented the attractive old homes that dominated the city scape.

Washington was an easy city to navigate by car—streets that traveled east/west were labeled by letters, and those that flowed north/south were numbered. The occasional street was named, such as famous Pennsylvania Avenue, but by coincidence—or perhaps not—most of those named streets didn't really aim in a particular direction. They were…aimless. Dennis wondered—did that say something about the types of decisions made at 1600 Pennsylvania Avenue?

Dennis' home was huge, much larger than he needed for just himself, but he had fallen in love with it and saw it as an important investment in Georgetown's history—he wanted to be a part of that history. Plus, he hadn't been suffering for money. The house bagged him $2.5 million in 2007—then the recession hit and the house value dipped. It had since rebounded and was probably worth now at least what he had originally paid for it. He didn't care anyway, he wasn't selling. And he had enough money in the bank that he didn't even need to work anymore…thanks to his mother.

The prominent feature of the house was the turreted front—forming a rounded effect for all three rooms that were lucky enough to be so situated in the home's three stories. Adjacent to the turret were a cozy front porch on the south side, and a main entrance way on the north side. A stone wall surrounded the property, with lush hedges providing six-foot high privacy. The house was enormous and most of the rooms were, although furnished, hardly ever used. Four bedrooms, large kitchen, drawing room, rear living room, formal dining room—and the one room that was used the most, the office on the third floor. That was Dennis' sanctuary, one of the round rooms in the turret, furnished in manly fashion with leather furniture and an ornate desk facing towards the round window. There was also an old wood-burning fireplace, one of four in the house, which only got lit about a dozen times a year due to Washington's temperate climate. It didn't matter—just the look of the old fireplace warmed Dennis' heart.

Filing cabinets wrapped around two corners of the room, containing souvenir copies of criminal cases Dennis had solved during his career. The two blank walls were adorned with several framed documents—his Master's degree in Criminology from the University of Maryland, his undergraduate degree from Princeton, and five citations from the Washington Metropolitan Police for 'performance above and beyond the call of duty,' including two testaments for bravery. While Dennis wasn't a braggart, he was proud of what he had accomplished and wanted reminders of those things to be in his private sanctuary. They were for him to see, no one else.

Dennis pulled himself away from the drawing room and wandered down the hall, stopping at the bedroom that was now his mom's. He was glad that he had this guest bedroom on the main floor. It would have been impossible for his mother to negotiate the narrow stairs to the upper floors. But, the room needed some womanly touches. It was spartan, as most of the house was if truth were told.

Dennis' home was clearly a man's home. He hadn't spent any time or energy decorating it, or adding those essential little touches that made a home feel homey. He made a mental note to phone Melissa and enlist her help. While his mom probably wouldn't notice anything anyway, he wanted to at least make the home comfortable and pleasant for her. Lucy had always been a woman of style—she might still remember that aspect of her life. Well, probably not...but it would make Dennis feel better at least.

He walked out to the front porch and took a moment to marvel at how spring was making his city forget the vicious snowstorms it had faced during the winter—one of the worst winters in memory. Flowers were blooming now, and the trees were full to overflowing.

He loved living in Washington—some hated it, but he loved it. It had one hell of a history, including being burned to the ground by the British during the War of 1812. That was in retaliation for the Americans invading Toronto, Canada—then known as York and before Canada was even known as 'Canada.' But the British had left most of the residential areas in Washington untouched, which was the blessing that the city enjoyed today with priceless architecture that could be enjoyed by residents and tourists alike.

And the fact that the city was the nation's capital made it all the more exciting. The power of Washington was palpable—poor Philadelphia probably still rued the day that it lost the capital city prestige back in 1800.

However, the city sure had its share of problems, not the least of which were political scandals. And most Americans didn't realize that at one time not too long ago, it was the most violent city in the nation. "Murder Capital." Dennis took some pride in knowing that the crime rate had dropped by half over the past decade. He knew in his heart that his own tenacious leadership had contributed something to that astounding turnaround.

And most Americans also didn't realize that 55% of the city's population was African-American, compared with the national average of only 12%. Racial strife was something that Washington always had to be aware of, and deal with front and center—it didn't take much to set it off.

But 46% of the population also held university degrees, contrasting starkly with the country's average of only 27%. The obvious reason for this was the political centric, which also produced a very high average income of $61,000. And women did better in Washington than elsewhere in the country, with 44% having at least a Bachelor's degree.

As Dennis sipped his coffee on the front porch, he admired the stately Scarlet Oak on his front lawn, one of a hundred or so beauties on his street. He was proud that he had one of the city's official symbols right on his own property. A tree that motivated him to actually do some gardening once in a while—but in all honesty, only on those days when his gardener was sick. Dennis was not a natural-born domestic.

He sighed. Today was a day off from the grind, but it didn't feel like a day off. He was preoccupied with his mother and worried about how she would settle in—and how he would settle in. He wasn't accustomed to having a house guest. His sister certainly hadn't been able to take mom in, having been saddled herself with her husband's elderly parents. So, it fell to him, and he didn't exactly consider himself a nurturer or caregiver. He had a housekeeper, who took care of most of his shopping and cleaning needs. Now he'd hired a nurse as well, who would see to his mom's health, diet, and bathing. Dennis was relieved about that part—he loved his mother but he really didn't want to see her naked, not if he could help it.

The nurse would be arriving this afternoon, and she would actually be moving right in. One of the upstairs bedrooms would be hers, and she'd have a monitor in her room connected to Lucy's room. Any groans, moans or cries for help in the middle of the night would be responded to by the nurse. Dennis could concentrate on just sleeping—an activity he treasured sometimes more than life itself.

Dennis hadn't met the nurse yet. His secretary had taken care of the arrangements for him. She contacted an agency that specialized in private nursing care, and it apparently had a reputation for servicing government employees and retirees: senators, congressmen, even the families of former presidents. It was a prestigious, discreet and expensive agency.

Discretion was an important quality for a government-favored nursing service. Dennis knew, from inside gossip, that many times in the past there had been the need for specialized medical and nursing care for some very famous politicians. If only the public knew how many times presidents had been treated for venereal diseases, or how many had needed a daily regimen of antidepressants or uppers just to open their eyes and smile for the cameras. Things like that didn't exactly inspire confidence in leaders.

The expense didn't bother Dennis; he wanted the best for his mom and didn't want to have to worry about the quality of the employees. One thing about government-favored businesses—they generally employed the best people.

He glanced down the street and noticed that traffic seemed kind of heavy—typical Monday morning. Thankfully, he lived close to his office, about a fifteen-minute drive to police headquarters at the Henry J. Daly Building, 300 Indiana Avenue NW. He never minded the drive—with his morning coffee in the cup holder and the Bang/Olufsen pleasantly assaulting his senses, it was a pleasant way to start the day, to crank up his sharp brain.

The pensive moment was broken by the sound of the phone ringing inside the house. Dennis reluctantly went back inside and walked down the hall to the phone in the rear living room.

"Hello?"

"Dennis, it's Barb. How are you?"

Dennis smiled in recognition. "Barb, so good to hear from you. And I think I know why you're calling."

"Yes, you do. Bad boy! You didn't tell me that Lucy was moving. I had to go to the nursing home to visit her—all that way by myself—only to find out that you'd kidnapped her! I didn't even know they were closing down the home—why didn't you tell me?"

Dennis grimaced. "I'm sorry, Barb. So much to think about, I just forgot. Not nice. Yes, she's home with me now. And I have a nurse moving in this afternoon."

"You're such a busy man to begin with, without having the worry of your mom—I understand why you forgot about little old me. But I am hurt, you need to know that."

Dennis smiled. Barb was a marvelous flirt, and she always teased him mercilessly. "Well, I'll have to make it up to you. Dinner sometime? Please?"

"My heart just fluttered. An old woman like me can't take this kind of excitement—but I'll try to endure. For a handsome man like you, I'll endure. Yes, pick a night and I'll be there."

Dennis sat down on the leather sofa. "Well, now that we have our next date established, I think I know why you're really calling. You want to visit Lucy, right?"

"Yes, handsome. I have some flowers that I've lugged back and forth from the now non-existent nursing home. Can I come over tomorrow?"

"Sure, she'd love to see you."

"Don't kid a kidder, Denny. She won't even know I'm there—but I'll know, and that's all that matters to me."

Dennis pulled at the tassels on a pillow. "Yeah, we both know that's true. But I do have something exciting to tell you about. You'll be shocked. Come over tomorrow night—I'm back to work during the day, but I want to be here when you come. Okay?"

"Okay—I'll be there with bells on, around 7:00. Does that work?"

"Works great—but leave the bells at home. I don't like it when you get that kinky!"

Dennis heard a sexy chuckle just before the line disconnected. Barb Jenkins was one of his favorite people in the entire world. She had worked closely with his mom at the Department of Defense. She was around sixty-five years old now and had retired from the DOD five years ago. She started working with Lucy as a legal intern at around the tender age of twenty-five. Then after a short time, Lucy made it permanent, bringing her on as her executive assistant. Barb had graduated from Harvard Law with an honors degree at a very young age—one of the youngest who had ever achieved a degree from Harvard. She had been ahead of everyone her entire life, no surprise to Dennis. She had been brilliant—and still was.

Even though Barb had been ten years older than Dennis, he'd developed a serious crush on her after his marriage ended. And he always suspected she had too. Or at least he always received those kinds of signals from her. But—they had just remained friends despite all that stuff. She was still beautiful even at sixty-five: the face and body of a fifty-year old. But her real beauty was in her brain and spirit. No age could be placed on the magic Barbara spread from her marvelous gray cells.

Dennis was looking forward to seeing Barb, but most of all he was looking forward to sharing with her about the brief re-awakening of her former mentor—her close confidant, the woman who had done everything to make Barb Jenkins a resounding success. The woman who Barb had idolized for what seemed like forever. She would be thrilled to know that

Lucy, for a fleeting moment in time, had come alive again.

Dennis leaned his head back against the soft leather of his sofa. He sighed. Tomorrow he'd head back to work, back to the grind—but also to one other task that couldn't wait. Something weird, something that had left a knot in his stomach. The DOD men. He'd look into that. Nothing would stop him. While a full day had passed now since he'd caught them tampering with his mother's room, his anger hadn't passed.

And Dennis knew that, for him, anger was not the kind of emotion that subsided too willingly. It always lingered. Until resolved. And he always resolved it.

CHAPTER FOUR

It was warm for a spring evening. Central air conditioning hadn't yet adjusted to the sudden change in temperatures. Brett Horton dragged the sleeve of his shirt across his forehead, and rubbed the sweat out of his eyes. Then he continued to stare in the direction of two men sitting at a table in the corner.

He tried to remember the name of the bar he was in—Blinking Owl? Blinking Eagle? Not that it mattered. He picked up the coaster and squinted in the faint light. Yep, he was right on the first guess.

He watched with a practiced gaze, studying his subjects with the intensity that only twenty years in the United States Secret Service could teach. His trained eyes also flicked alertly back and forth across the bar without losing a moment of surveillance over his marks.

They were both well dressed, as you would expect to see in downtown Washington. Leaning in close to each other, they spoke in hushed tones. Brett knew who they were. One was a reporter for a sleazy political tabloid, the other was the legislative assistant to a very prominent, but very indiscreet, Senator.

Each of these young men were trying to make it in the power world of D.C. in their own way; except that today they had chosen the wrong way.

Brett raised his hand, motioning to the waiter for another beer. It was so hot, easy to drink beer on a day like this. He pondered that maybe the bar had actually disabled the air conditioning for just that very reason.

The beer came, and went. Brett downed it in one long pull—the liquid was soothing, and the partially suppressed belch afterwards was surprisingly satisfying. He allowed his eyes to focus on the men once again.

It was happening. He saw the reporter reach into his pocket, pull out an envelope and pass it over to the legislator. He opened it, fingered the contents briefly and then smiled in triumph. The man reached under the table, pulled his briefcase up onto his lap, and flicked it open. He dropped the envelope in and brought out another one, passing it over to the reporter with a sly smirk on his face.

The reporter nervously glanced around before taking a glance at the contents. Brett quickly averted his gaze. The young man held the envelope on his lap and slid several of the items out for a look. Then he looked up at the legislator, giving the thumbs up sign. He stuffed the envelope into an inside pocket of his suit jacket. The co-conspirators shook hands.

Then Brett got the gift he had been hoping for—one that always made his job so easy. The reporter stood up, excused himself and walked toward the washroom at the rear of the bar. *This was far too easy.*

Brett got up and followed. Reaching the washroom he took a quick glance inside first. The reporter had just unzipped and was standing at one of the four urinals. Brett bent down and looked under the stalls. Empty. *Just you and me, kid.* He went back out into the hall, removed a roll from his inside pocket and peeled off a bright yellow sticker. He flattened it to the outside of the washroom door. It read: 'Out of Order.'

Back inside the washroom, he pulled a rubber stopper out of another pocket and slid it under the door. He chuckled to himself as he thought back to when his tailor had expressed dismay and horror at being asked to sew no less than six inside pockets of various sizes to Brett's handsome stable of Saville Row suits.

He moved quickly now, no hesitation, and crept up behind the tall figure who was preoccupied with shaking the last errant drops from his penis. Brett shoved the man's head like a spiked volleyball, banging it into the ceramic tiled wall in front of him. He winced as he heard the sickening thud—he'd done this trick a thousand times and still hadn't gotten used to the sound.

The man bounced backward and crumpled to the floor, blood streaming from his forehead, eyeballs swimming in utter confusion. Brett calmly reached down, opened the man's jacket, and removed the envelope. Then he wagged a scolding finger across the stunned reporter's face. "You've been a very naughty boy. And you just spent a lot of money for nothing. Well, not entirely true. It will go to my favorite charity—me."

Brett strode to the door, stuffed the rubber stopper back into one of his six inside pockets, and walked quickly back to the main part of the bar. The legislator was still sitting at the table sipping his beer, waiting patiently for his partner in crime. Instead, he got Brett.

Brett sat down in a chair next to the shocked man, pulling in as close beside him as he could. He smiled at him. Putting one hand on the table, he leaned in close, shoving his other hand under the table until it found its mark. He squeezed the little man's balls with such force that he knew a hard-on would be impossible for him for at least a month. Peeing might prove difficult too.

The man gasped and tears quickly formed in his eyes. Brett continued to smile. "Open up your briefcase and hand over that envelope that is apparently stuffed with ill-gotten cash." He patted the front of his suit coat. "I have the photos by the way. Your friend let me have them. He is so agreeable, don't you think?"

The legislator gingerly leaned over and picked up his briefcase. He quickly unsnapped it for the second time that afternoon. Brett reached in and grabbed the envelope with his free hand. With his otherwise occupied hand he gave the man's balls one last hard squeeze just to make sure he had something to remember him by. Another gasp, louder this time. Tears were now streaming down his cheeks. Brett laughed.

He reached into the envelope and withdrew a fifty-dollar bill, dropping it on the table. "The least I can do is pay for your beers."

Brett scraped his chair back and stood up. "Tell me, son. What's your favorite charity?" The man looked up at him with a puzzled expression. Brett persisted, "Well, tell me. What is it?"

"Heart…and Stroke…Foundation."

Brett nodded in appreciation. "Good choice. My father died of heart disease, so I like that one too. I'm going to give some of this money to that charity, okay?" He smirked. "Does that help make this day worthwhile in some way for you?"

The legislator grimaced. "Who…the fuck…are you?"

"Someone you don't want to meet again. And you probably won't, because there's one more thing I want you to do today. As soon as you get back to the office, you're going to hand in your resignation to the good Senator. And if you don't, I'll know about it. Get my drift, son?"

The man nodded furiously—either in agreement or in spasm—as Brett turned around and strode calmly out of the bar.

He was glad to be outside again. At least there was a breeze. It had been stifling in the Blinking Owl. He patted his jacket pocket and wondered for a brief moment what the photos would show. He always wondered whenever he had to retrieve these packages. But he never ever looked. He didn't need the complication of knowing; neither did he need the emotional conflict of trying to establish in his mind the good guys from the bad guys. He would deliver the photos to his client at the prearranged time at the prearranged place. But he would keep whatever money was left over after the charitable donation—a nice tip for a hot day's work.

His Secret Service training had drilled incredible discipline into his psyche. He was fully aware of how detached he was. Work was just work, he didn't judge. He served. Even now, in private practice, he served— served his clients. When he was Secret Service, his client had been the U.S. government. His job then had been to protect the President, his family and other politicians. And the sanctity of the U.S. Treasury.

He had been assigned to the Presidential detail on several occasions for three separate Presidents, but never as a permanent assignment. He had been glad about that. Presidential details were far too messy. He didn't like messy. And they were boring also. He felt his talents had been wasted whenever he guarded the President. He much preferred his specialty—counter terrorism. Brett had been one of only a handful of agents who had been trusted to oversee the security of every destination that the President visited. And in the last three years before he retired, he was in charge of investigating every credible threat that the federal government became aware of. Anything that involved national security, existence of government, or continuity of government. He loved that work—it teased his brain. His sometimes very overactive brain.

As he walked along Madison Drive, he glanced over at the National Gallery of Art to his left and recalled the time he had killed an assailant on the front steps. Shot him right through the forehead. Well, in reality, there wasn't much forehead left after Brett's magnum had done its job.

That time hadn't even been related to any kind of threat to the President. Brett was just lucky enough to have been there at the time a wing nut started brandishing a gun, threatening patrons coming out of the Gallery. Brett had been one of those patrons, enjoying the Gallery on his day off. He just pulled his gun and shot him, no warning, nothing. And no questions asked either by any of the authorities—one call from the White House stopped the Washington Police in their tracks. Brett was Secret Service after all—enough said.

He pulled his jacket back and admired that very same gun, resting in the brown leather holster on his hip. A Smith and Wesson .357 Magnum. It was the most beautiful gun he owned. It had a matte silver finish, with a handsome wooden grip. The front sight was gold-beaded and the beastly barrel could fire off eight destructive rounds before needing a reload. Although, with a magnum like his, usually only one round was needed to destroy a life.

Brett turned right onto 4th Street, walked four houses down and then up the steps to his beautifully restored row house. He lived close to what was known as the Capitol Hill neighborhood, the most prestigious address in Washington and the political center of the nation's capital. This was handy for Brett, since most of his work was still government-related. Usually he could just walk to meetings and avoid negotiating Washington's horrendous traffic—and then the proverbial hunt for non-existent parking spaces.

He had retired from the Secret Service three years ago—not because he was dissatisfied, but because he decided he wanted to make some real money for a change. He had joined the service after graduating from Berkeley with a law degree. He had never really wanted to practice law; he'd just been putting in time. Then he was recruited by the Service and his life got a shot of adrenaline. Over the twenty years spent protecting Uncle Sam, he had accumulated an arsenal of deadly skills. He was now a master sniper, martial arts expert, counter-terrorism specialist, and an explosives designer. Skills worth selling to the highest bidder.

So he decided to do just that. And a funny thing happened on the way to self-employment. The U.S. government became his biggest client, his highest bidder, paying him now twenty times more than what it had paid him before, to do a lot of the same things. He was a private contractor now, so he could name his price. Funny how government worked, he thought. Go private and get a massive raise. Taxpayers had a right to be confused.

He usually worked alone; he preferred that. But occasionally he drew in some other contractors on larger jobs, or when other skill sets were needed. He had a good team of people that he could count on, a tight circle that he trusted with his life. Most of them had been Secret Service or FBI during their government careers, so they were discreet and talented. And they all enjoyed money as much as Brett did.

He opened his front door and stepped into the hallway, forced to look at his image in the full-length mirror on the opposite wall. At forty-eight years old, he still looked good. He didn't look his age at all, and was blessed with a trim athletic frame. Not too tall, hovering around the six-foot mark. His features were handsome; he knew that. Those features and his confident, charming personality were great assets to have as a self-employed man. Those assets opened doors—whether the door handles were being held by women or men, it didn't matter. They just opened for him. His hair was sandy brown, and his eyes were a dreamy blue.

He looked too good to be a killer. But that's what he was.

Brett strolled through his living room, admiring the floor to ceiling stone fireplace that he had built with his own hands. It was a masterpiece. As he walked, his Italian leather shoes made a solid clip-clop sound on the cherry hardwood floor. He loved the sound of 'solid.'

He entered the kitchen, which was another room he was proud of. French country cabinets, nickel-plated fridge, and the centerpiece of the kitchen—a black 'AGA' cooker—manufactured in the Shropshire area of the U.K. and installed in his house just a few months ago. He still hadn't mastered how to cook with it yet, but he knew it would only be a matter of time. Patience and perseverance—two things Brett was good at.

He opened the fridge and took out a bottle of beer. He twisted the cap off and took a long swig. While the liquid was pouring down his throat, he heard the words, "Hello, Brett."

He simultaneously spun and dropped, gun in hand before his knee even touched the floor. Bottle of beer in one hand, magnum in the other, both of them pointing at the chest of a man standing in the dining room doorway.

"Whoa, buddy! Take it easy!"

Brett sighed with relief and lowered his pistol. "Geez, I could have killed you, Bill. What the hell are you doing in here—and more importantly, how did you get in here?"

"Just wanted to show you that the U.S. government can easily bypass your supposedly foolproof Israeli locks." Bill Charlton smiled at his friend.

Brett stepped forward and gave Bill a friendly punch on the shoulder. "I love you, but don't ever break into my place again, okay?"

Bill laughed. "No, I don't think I will. Those Secret Service skills are just as sharp and finely-tuned as ever. My God, you still move as fast as a cat!"

Brett opened the fridge again and tossed Bill a bottle of beer. "Here, use your teeth to open it. You guys in the Defense department are supposed to be pretty tough."

"No, I think I'll just twist it open like you did! Why show off if I don't have to?"

The two friends sat down at the kitchen table. Brett pulled the envelope of photos out of his pocket, and tossed them over to Bill. "Here's what you wanted. I hope this solves your problem. And, by the way, we were supposed to meet later tonight for this envelope exchange. Why didn't you wait?"

Bill stuffed the envelope into his pocket without looking inside. "I decided to move up the schedule. Yes, we wanted these photos desperately—the Senator is chair of the Armed Services Committee, so DOD is very worried. Thanks for doing this for us."

Brett took another sip of his beer, then held the cool bottle up against his sweating forehead. "No problem. Pleased to be of service. You'll be billed of course, at my usual exorbitant hourly rate! By the way, I'm curious. Did DOD want those photos to save his sorry ass, or to blackmail his sorry ass?"

Bill just smiled, then leaned back in his chair and crossed his legs. "We have another assignment for you. It's a delicate one, and very serious. And very challenging."

Brett leaned forward and rested his elbows on the table. "They're all delicate and serious, Bill. And 'challenging' is what I do. So, what makes this one more challenging than usual?"

"We need you to find something."

"So?"

"It's hidden in two separate places."

"Again, so?"

Bill walked over to the fridge and pulled out two more beers. He handed one to Brett, twisted the cap off his and took a long slow sip.

"One of the hiding places is the demented mind of an eighty-five year old woman."

CHAPTER FIVE

"I wouldn't touch that with a ten foot pole. Just leave it alone."

Dennis grimaced, and shook his head at his colleague. "How the hell can I do that? I saw it with my own eyes. Those creeps had bugged my mother's room."

Bart Davis put his hand on Dennis' shoulder and squeezed. "She's an old lady, and she used to have a high security clearance. We could never even pretend to understand how the wheels turn at the Department of Defense." He smiled grimly. "And you know what? We never *will* understand either. That's just the way of the world."

"It's an invasion of privacy."

"Bullshit! Anyone who agrees to work for those spooks gives up their right to privacy, in my view. Your mother knew the score way back when— she may not have a clue now, but she certainly knew it then."

Dennis just stared at his friend, trying to absorb the reality of what he was saying. Bart was about Dennis' age, a little on the stout side but solid as a rock. He was the Chief of Internal Affairs. Dennis figured that if anyone had contacts within the DOD that he could use, it would be Bart.

"So, you're not going to help me? Not going to give me a name?"

"No, Denny, I'm not. I have a name, but you can't have it. For your own good. Sticking your nose in over there can only lead to trouble for you here. I guarantee it."

"Thanks a hell of a lot, Bart. All the things we've been through together, I would've thought I could count on you."

"You can count on me. And don't pull that guilt shit on me. I'm not going to help you hang yourself. And guess what—if you got into trouble over there, I would be the one called upon to investigate you here. Internal Affairs, remember? Talk about a conflict of interest! I dangle the bone to chase, you get hung up, and I have to investigate you. Kinda silly, don't you think?"

Dennis rubbed his forehead. "Yeah, when you put it that way."

"Okay, then. Do what you need to do, but don't use the department and don't tell me what you're doing. My advice—just forget about it. She's an old lady and those spooks were just doing their jobs. If they bugged her, so what."

"She told me something, Bart. Something that I'm losing sleep over trying to figure out what she meant."

Bart held up his hand in the stop sign. "Don't tell me anything else. I don't want to hear it." He wagged his finger at Dennis as he headed back down the hall toward the elevators.

Dennis swiveled in his chair and stared out the window onto Indiana Avenue. His office was on the 6th floor of the seven-storey building. The Henry J. Daly Building was an old structure, built in 1941, but still in marvelous shape. Dennis had a nice corner office and his department took up the entire 6th floor. He had a team of forty detectives working under him; a great team, but not nearly large enough to handle the crime that plagued Washington. Even though the crime rate had improved dramatically, it was still substantial. And complicated cases took forever to solve just due to the manpower issue.

The Daly Building was the headquarters for the Washington Metropolitan Police. The name was changed to its present moniker after a shocking incident that took place back in 1992. An armed man entered the building and shot a detective sergeant and two FBI agents to death—then turned the gun on himself. The detective killed was Hank Daly, a "cop's cop," and a well-loved father of two.

Now, any member of the public entering the building had to pass through metal detectors—an extra measure of security that most police departments throughout the United States implemented after that 1992 incident.

Dennis hadn't been there when it happened, having taken a leave of absence for a year after the collapse of his marriage—and the death of his father. Backpacking through China, he read about it in the papers. Wishing he was back in Washington. Wishing he'd been there to shoot the scum dead before he had been able to do it to himself. Dennis would have also made him suffer a bit first.

He pondered his next move, while calmly twisting and bending backwards the forefinger of his right hand, then reversing the move to the forefinger of his left hand. He slid his loafers off, put his feet up on the desk and began doing backward bending exercises with his toes.

"Dennis, I can always tell when you're thinking hard—those fingers and toes get the brunt."

He spun in his chair at hearing the singsong voice of his secretary, Nancy. He smiled—she had a mug of steaming coffee in her hand and he knew it was for him. She took good care of him and had been doing it for fifteen years. Nancy was around forty years old, blonde and pretty. And she was a class act—a dignified lady who was able to keep confidences. A job prerequisite for the shocking things she had to read every day.

"Yeah, Nancy, I'm thinking hard alright. And thanks for the coffee." He stood up and took the mug from her hand. "This will help me think even harder."

She smiled affectionately at him. "I forgot to ask you—did the nurse show up yesterday?"

"Yes, she did. She seems nice. But only time will tell if my mother will like her."

"Describe her to me."

"Well, very efficient. She brought tons of medical supplies and accessories. God only knows what they're all for. I have her lodged up on the second floor."

"You haven't told me what she looks like."

"Aw…she's a looker, Nancy. You didn't need to send me someone that good-looking, you know. She's a bit of a distraction."

Nancy frowned. "I'm a bit jealous, now. I didn't meet her beforehand—the agency just said they would send one of their best." Her frown changed quickly to a sly smile. "I can phone them back and ask them to send you over an ugly girl, if you want."

"No, no. Ugly would be an even worse distraction. I'd have to escape to other rooms in the house and would probably force her to wear a bag over her head whenever she's near me!"

Nancy laughed and headed out the door. "Well, if you change your mind, let me know. And if she seduces you, I don't want to hear about it, okay?"

Dennis laughed back and watched her lovely rear end sashay its way out the door. He knew Nancy had always had a crush on him. He had never encouraged her, but he could just tell by the way she was when she was around him. She had her little ways of letting him know. They had never talked about it, but she also knew him well enough to know that he would never allow himself to get romantically involved with someone who worked for him. She knew that. It was unethical, and for all Dennis' faults, unethical was not one of them.

So, their relationship was what it was: affectionate, protective and professional. Dennis knew that if they had met some other way, some other time, he probably would have dated Nancy. But…it was not to be.

Nancy was single now, divorced from her husband for about six years. He knew she had dated a few times since then, but was always guarded because of what she had gone through with her ex. She was wary of men now…afraid, apprehensive.

Dennis thought back to that day seven years ago, when she was sitting at her desk crying over her morning coffee. Seeing her like that almost made Dennis cry. He called her into his office, sat her down on the couch and put his arm around her slender shoulders. Then she just poured out her heart. Her husband was having an affair. She found the evidence on his computer. He denied it at first, but when she told him how she had found out, he slapped her hard across the face, making it her fault for snooping. Dennis noticed the extra makeup she had been wearing that morning.

He advised her to just leave him, which she did. But after that he came after her. Tracked her down at the women's shelter and knocked out a couple of her front teeth. She switched shelters. Luckily they had never had children, so she only had herself to worry about.

Once the divorce went through she thought things would calm down. He had resisted the divorce, did not want her to leave him, promised he would be a good boy. She wouldn't let his charms change her mind—she was determined to escape. So, the divorce became final and for months she didn't hear from him.

But one terrible night he came back. She was living in her own home by that time, and he knew where. He phoned her from his car but she refused to talk to him. He knocked on the door and she refused to open up. Then he kicked it down.

The hour he spent with her was a blur to sweet Nancy. After he'd had his way, she crawled to the telephone and dialed 911. Then she phoned the only man she really cared about. Dennis was there in fifteen minutes, just in time to meet the paramedics as they were wheeling her out on a stretcher.

She had been raped with a wine bottle, all of her teeth were gone—some swallowed—and her hair was matted in blood from the effects of the same wine bottle being smashed over her head after it had done its sordid work. Dennis cried when he saw her. He held her hand as he asked her, "Who?" She answered, "You know who."

After a month in the hospital and undergoing extensive dental implant surgery—refusing the entire time to identify to anyone who the assailant was—she was back in the office, smiling and laughing as she used to. Dennis pleaded with her to press charges. Nancy laughed mockingly. "Why, so you guys can let him out and he can come back to finish me off?" He knew she was right. "Maybe he has it out of his system now and will just leave me alone. I can't take a chance on enraging him." She was kidding herself.

But then out of the blue, ex-husband Keith just disappeared. Never to be seen again. In five years Nancy had heard nothing of his whereabouts. She figured he had just packed up and moved. Keith was gone.

As he reflected on the tragic story of his lovely secretary, Dennis felt the need for movement—a special kind of movement. He did this daily, at home, in the office—several times a day. It was how he trained. It was the way of *Shaolin*.

He opened the bottom drawer of his desk and withdrew a very special piece of wood. It was four inches thick and about twelve inches long. It was characterized by dents all along its length. Not deep dents, more like indents as if a hammer had been taken to the wood.

Dennis fastened a clamp to the edge of his desk and screwed the vice grip tight to the piece of wood. Then he took a deep breath and began systematically pounding the extended forefinger of his right hand into the wood. Softly at first, then hard, then harder. After about ten minutes he would switch to his left hand. After ten minutes of that hand, his socks would come off and a similar exercise would be performed with the toes of his feet.

It relaxed him. And it helped him focus.

*****

Keith stumbled out of the bar, just another night of charming the ladies who needed to feel beautiful. As usual, he had a slut on his arm, and they would head back to his penthouse apartment where he knew, just like all the other pathetic desperate ones, she would let him do what he wanted. Because it made them feel good to be loved for even just one night by a handsome rogue like him. He knew. They were desperate, and those were the ones he liked. Not at all like his confident ex-wife…the bitch.

He liked his life now. He could do whatever he wanted to whomever he wanted. And these bars always had a vast selection to choose from. He avoided the really beautiful girls though. The ones he picked weren't ugly, mind you; they were just…past their prime. And he knew they were the easier ones. The really beautiful ones were far too confident and generally weren't interested in a dirty little roll in the hay. They ignored him. So he ignored them.

He could quickly determine who the eager ones were within minutes after entering a bar. They dressed a certain way so as to advertise their wares, and they acted a certain way that guaranteed they would be noticed. And he noticed…boy, did he notice. And they weren't the gorgeous ones. So they needed to dress and act the way they did to make up for what they were lacking. And he knew that they did it just for him. He never failed. He never spent a night alone.

As usual, Keith had forgotten the name of the girl whose ass he was squeezing. Yeah, this type of girl didn't even care that he was doing this right out on the sidewalk. He liked it…but also despised it. He couldn't understand the lack of dignity, but he sure as hell was going to take advantage of it. And he might just slap her around a bit too. Teach her a thing or two about dignity. His bitch of an ex-wife would never allow him to squeeze her ass in public. He hated her for that…but strangely, also loved her for that.

They sauntered up the street together. His apartment was a short ten minute walk. They could just squeeze as they walked…this was foreplay at its best.

The blow seemed to come out of nowhere. A sharp thud to the side of his neck that left him zombied on his feet. He heard the slut next to him gasp, was barely aware of a hand pointing down the street ordering the tramp on her way. He couldn't move, but his eyes watched as she ran for her life.

Then he felt a strong hand grab his longish hair dragging him into an alley. The man was tall, Keith could tell, dressed in black and wearing a balaclava. Keith knew he was doomed but he didn't know why he knew. This wasn't just a simple mugging.

The man in black shoved him back against the wall, and stared at him silently for a few seconds. Keith tried to talk but the only thing coming out of his mouth was drool. He heard the man sigh just before his hand moved like a lightning bolt. A sharp thud to his chest this time. He started to sink to the ground.

Sitting on the pavement in the alley, back against the wall, Keith glanced down curiously at his chest, at the spot where the pressure seemed to be coming from. There was a hole in his shirt, which seemed strange, and the hole was quickly beginning to spew blood like a pulsating fountain. The hole was exactly where Keith figured his heart was.

Strangely, there was no real pain—just numbness and an accelerating feeling of fatigue. Keith looked up at his assailant, silently questioning. The man knelt down in front of him. He never said a word. Keith heard him sigh once again, and his left hand suddenly became a blur of movement. Another thud, this time right in the centre of his forehead. It felt to Keith as if he had a hole in his head.

While the blood from the gushing forehead began to fill his eyes, Keith stared at the man kneeling in front of him, hoping for some words, some answer, some reason. But he knew in his heart that there would be no time for that. Time was quickly slipping away...

CHAPTER SIX

She arrived with a flourish, as she usually did. Tossed her straw wide-brimmed sunhat onto the deacon's bench, removed her high heeled shoes reducing her height by at least three inches, and planted a big kiss on Dennis' cheek—leaving a slight trace of pink blush lipstick.

This was Barb Jenkins in the flesh, a powerhouse of a woman even at sixty-five years of age. Charisma beyond description and a confident air about her that would challenge even the most accomplished man.

Dennis couldn't wipe the broad smile off his face—the woman he used to have a crush on still had a magical effect on him. Perhaps it was because she had the same kind of personality that his mother used to have? The same kind of intellect? He shuddered at the thought that he had had a crush on someone who reminded him of his mom. He didn't have a 'mother complex' going on here, did he? Dennis gave his head a furious shake, then just kissed the beautiful Barb Jenkins back, but his kiss was right smack on the lips.

"Well, aren't you the friendly little boy today? Are you happy to see me, or did you just want to try out my lipstick—you don't suit the color though, Denny, I have to tell you!"

"It is good to see you, Barb. And to be honest, I just couldn't resist those lips of yours."

"Well, I'm glad. Let's chat for a minute or two, okay? Before I see Lucy?" She grabbed his hand and led him past the drawing room where Lucy sat rocking. Barb didn't even glance into the room. She went to the kitchen, put her flowers in a vase, filled it with water, then led Dennis into the rear living room. Dennis felt like a little boy—the way she took charge, this seemed more like her house than his. But he didn't mind. He just admired Barb's spunk so much, he was just glad to let her be her.

"Can I get you something, Barb? Beer, wine?"

Barb smiled coyly at him. "What would a woman like me do with a beer, Denny? I'm insulted, I must say. How would I drink it—from the bottle? Or one of those tall macho beer mugs you have? Would either of those really suit my image?"

Denny laughed. "Okay, okay. Yes, a southern belle like you does deserve a glass of wine. I'll never offer you a beer again!"

Dennis poured them each a glass of Merlot. He handed her the glass and they toasted to Lucy. Then Barb's tone turned serious. Dennis was never surprised by this—she could turn on a dime, and cause her adversaries nervous frustration. Sweet and flirtatious one moment, a tigress on the attack in the next.

"So, tell me what's going on. You were excited on the phone yesterday."

Dennis stretched his long legs out on the stool and told her everything that had happened from the moment he had wheeled Lucy out to the sidewalk in front of the nursing home. She listened intently, nodding and asking brief lawyerly questions from time to time. When Dennis had finished his tale, she sighed and smiled.

"That must have been quite the thrill for you—having your mom back ever so briefly. Spooky, but wonderful at the same time."

"Yeah, it was. It was exhilarating. But then, just as suddenly, earth-shattering when it ended."

Barb nodded. "So what do you think this 'package' is? Any guesses?"

"No, none at all. But I know that whatever it is, it caused her serious stress just telling me about it. She really wanted me to get it. And I really don't think that it was in that room. If there is a package at all—it might just be a twisted memory about something. But from what I could tell, aside from what the spooks were removing, there was nothing left in that room."

Barb uncrossed her shapely legs and leaned forward to pour herself another glass of wine. Dennis admired her for a second—she was wearing a red and white polka dot dress—and not too many women could pull that off. But she did. She looked like the perfect southern matron. Dignified, head erect, looking like a lady—but a lady who always seemed to be on a mission, always ready to fix whatever needed fixing.

"So, it sounds like it was the trauma of the purse snatchers that caused her memory to snap awake for a few minutes. The stress of it, the quickness of it, perhaps somehow fired her brain cells? Do you think?"

Dennis took a sip of his wine. "I do think that, yes. And I'm thinking it could easily happen again."

"Would you make it happen again?"

Dennis stood up and walked to the window, taking a few minutes to gaze pensively at his garden. He turned back to Barb. "Yes, I think I might. You know me, I can't let things rest. And you know also that I would never put my mom at risk, but if I can cause some harmless stress to trigger another event, I might give it a try." He paused and stared at her. "Are you ashamed of me for that?"

Barb smiled tenderly at him. "I could never be ashamed of you, Denny. I have to admit though, I'm shocked that you would want to try something like that, but I understand it in a weird sort of way."

"Yeah, it is kinda weird. But I have a strong feeling about this 'package' thing. Especially after discovering those guys snooping in mom's room. It seems to me like she knows something that they want to know. Why else would they have bugged her room?"

"Well, I can pretty much confirm to you that it's bullshit what they told you. I myself had a high security clearance with the Department of Defense, and I've moved houses twice since I retired. I never once, nor did the new owners, encounter anyone checking out the places I lived in. So, they were scrambling for an explanation when they gave that one to you."

"That's what I thought too. Something tells me there's just something fishy going on, and I'm obsessed now with getting to the bottom of it."

Softly, Barb asked, "How can I help, Denny?"

Dennis scratched his chin. "I would hate to drag you into this."

"Crap! You would love it! You know I have connections, and if I didn't just offer this to you, you would have eventually asked me. Right? Don't bullshit me."

Dennis laughed. "You've got me pegged. Yes, I would have."

"So, quit trying to pretend to be considerate—again, how can I help you?"

"Well, two ways. You can help me figure out ways to unlock my mom's memory again. And you could give me the name of someone fairly high up over at the DOD who I can contact on the quiet. Someone you can trust. Someone discreet. Someone who's also a bit brave."

Barb fluffed her marvelous blonde hair and stood up. "Let's go pay your mom a visit, and I promise I'll give some thought to the two things you would like from me. Okay?"

Dennis gave Barb a big hug. "Thank you. I couldn't expect more than that."

She smiled. "Yes, you could." She winked. "But we can talk about that some other time."

Two hours later, Dennis escorted Barb out to the front porch. They sat down in the Adirondack chairs and looked at each other wearily.

"It is exhausting, isn't it?"

Barb nodded. "It is. I don't envy you at all. I'll bet you can hardly wait until another nursing home comes up."

"Sad to say, I'm counting the days—but I fear it's going to be months rather than days. They're all filled to overflowing. I need a few people to die."

The front door opened and out walked a shapely young woman in white. "Mr. Chambers, I've just run the bath for Lucy. Is it okay if I take her to the washroom now?"

"Oh sure, Felicity. By the way, this is my long-time friend, Barb Jenkins. Barb, Felicity's the nurse I hired to live with us while mom is here."

"Hello, Ms. Jenkins. Very nice to meet you."

Barb stood up and took her hand. "My, you're a pretty little thing. Very nice to meet you."

Felicity smiled—hazel eyes twinkling. Dennis couldn't disagree with Barb. The young nurse was very striking to look at.

Barb frowned for just a split second. "You wouldn't happen to be from the Casper Agency, would you?"

Felicity seemed surprised. "Why, yes I am. How did you know that?"

Barb chuckled. "If I told you, I'd have to kill you. We wouldn't want that now, would we?"

Felicity seemed to rock back on her heels until Barb put a friendly hand on her shoulder. "I'm just kidding, dear. That's the way I am. I just come out with things, and shock people. I do it to entertain myself!"

Felicity laughed, politely bowed at the waist, and went back inside the house to deal with the bath—the next thing on her list of tedious geriatric duties.

Barb turned to Dennis. "Hmm. She seems too pretty, Denny."

"Is there such a thing, Barb?"

"Yes, believe it or not, sometimes there is. Watch yourself."

"Oh, you're just jealous."

Barb smiled patiently at him. "We may banter around, you and I, but it's all just in good fun. I do worry about you and when I ask you to be careful, do be careful. You have a lot of money; you're handsome and alone. She's young, attractive—and living here now. Too close for comfort? Sometimes motives aren't pure. Or sometimes there are other motives."

"Yes, Barb. I will be careful. Hey, why did you ask her about the Casper Agency? They're top notch, from what I've heard."

"Yes, they are. I just guessed that that was where she worked, that's all. Nothing meant by it. She's just the style of nurse they tend to employ."

Dennis frowned, puzzled at what she meant by that. He shook it off and gave Barb a big goodbye hug. She walked down the porch steps but stopped at the bottom to turn and face him before going to her car. "I'll get back to you on those two issues, I promise." Then her pretty face twisted into a wince. "Denny, do you ever think about your dad? Are you over that yet?"

Dennis felt his fists begin to clench, and an annoying twitch making its presence known in the corner of his left eye.

Softly, he answered her. "I'll never ever be over that, Barb. Never. Ever."

CHAPTER SEVEN

His eyes were being hypnotized by the rhythmic spinning of the ceiling fan. Lying on his back, eyes wide open but wishing they were shut. Remembering, but trying hard not to remember. Crying, but trying hard not to cry.

He quietly cursed Barb for asking the question about his father. Dennis was pretty good at mind control—controlling his own mind that is. He was able to shut out things that troubled him, resurrecting them only when he needed to for other reasons. But remembering just for remembering's sake was not something he generally allowed himself to indulge in.

His dad was a prince. A lobby consultant who everyone wanted to consult with. A gentleman in the true sense of the word. His formal education was in marketing and public relations, a Princeton graduate. He used that background to develop a specialty in what was an essential skill in Washington, D.C. Lobbying was an industry unto itself in the country's capital city, and smart men and women who knew how to lobby were precious commodities. Dennis' father, Alan, was one of the most precious. Because he was one of the most honest.

He consulted and taught others how to lobby, how to influence, how to manipulate thinking, which buttons to press, when to exert leverage, when to capitulate. He knew his business.

The last night he saw his dad alive was on his sixtieth birthday. Dennis was thirty-five years old and had just ended his marriage. His dad had become his rock once again, just like when he was a kid. He was there for him. And Dennis was there for him. That night was a special birthday dinner. His mother wasn't able to attend and neither was Melissa. Both of them had an important event to attend raising money for disabled children, a charity they volunteered for. So instead, they had an early birthday dinner a couple of days before for Alan. But Dennis wanted to do something with his dad on the very day of his birthday, and this was going to be just their special time together, father and son.

They had dinner at their favorite Italian restaurant, Denny's treat, in downtown Washington. An older seedier area, but one that surprisingly had the best Italian restaurant in town. So, people in the know made their wary way down to Temple Street, to savor the delights of Emilio's. Alan joked beforehand that they really had nothing to worry about because, after all, Dennis was a cop and he had to wear his firearm at all times. So, they figured they were the safest of all of Emilio's patrons. And they probably would have been.

If they hadn't been at the wrong place at the wrong time.

Denny closed his eyes and concentrated on savoring the breeze from the overhead fan. The whirring noise was strangely soothing and he imagined himself laying on a beach somewhere, anywhere, the ocean breeze caressing his face. He sighed and felt himself slipping away…

They were laughing about everything, anything. Denny joked with his dad about being five years younger than mom, and how she had robbed the cradle when she married him. Alan agreed and responded that he had always had a fascination with older women: wiser, experienced, the ability to tame the wild beast. Dennis laughed, happy that he and his dad could joke candidly about things like this. They had always been able to do that—their relationship as father/son had always been special that way.

They raised their wine glasses and toasted to older women. Alan looked at his watch. "We need to head home. Your mother will be worried sick."

Dennis felt his heart sink—the night was over. It was rare these days to get his dad alone, away from his work, away from Lucy. Even though Dennis was a mature thirty-five years old, he still needed his father alone once in a while. His wisdom and sense of humor were things that Dennis always cherished, and that hadn't ended when Dennis had become a man.

Well, there would be other times.

Dennis paid the bill and toasted a Happy Birthday to his wonderful dad one more time. He could tell that Alan had enjoyed this little outing just as much as he had. His only son, spending time with him, man to man. And he was proud of his only son, having made detective at the ripe age of thirty. Dennis had possessed the gold shield now for five years, and at his young age there would be no stopping him. The sky was the limit. He could see Chief of Detectives in his future, then Chief of Police, then Police Commissioner, and then maybe Mayor. Alan had high hopes for his son. And Dennis shared those hopes.

They walked arm in arm out of the restaurant, laughing about the days when Dennis had tried his hand at baseball and failed miserably. Despite his dad's cheering from the sidelines, Dennis had been hopeless at the sport. But, never fail, after every game Alan would tell him that he was proud of him. Proud that he had done his best and tried hard. Then he took him home to their backyard and worked with him on the fundamentals. No matter what Alan tried though, Dennis couldn't grasp the game of baseball. And Dennis gave up on the sport long before his father did. Twenty-eight years later, the memories were fun and provided good fodder for fatherly teasing. Dennis loved it.

Dennis' car was parked about eight blocks away. It was almost midnight and a shortcut through the alleys would shorten the trip to the car by about fifteen minutes. So they took that route. And the route took them.

He felt their presence before he saw them. That eerie feeling of being watched, stalked. He fingered the revolver on his hip reassuring himself that it was still there. But he didn't have a chance.

In the second alley a dark figure jumped out of a doorway, quickly followed by two from behind and two from the front. All from concealed doorways. Coordinated, lurking. Two grabbed Alan, and two grabbed Dennis. The fifth man, the one apparently in charge, sneered at them, spit on their expensive suits. He calmly withdrew the wallets from their jackets and emptied the contents. He salivated over the cash, and got really excited about the credit cards.

Alan looked over at Dennis and said, "Stay calm, son. Just let them have whatever they want." Dennis grimaced—his father had just innocently let them know they were father and son. As a cop, he knew that was always the wrong thing to do.

The leader smiled. "Ain't that cute. Daddy and his little boy." He pinched Dennis' cheek and said, "You do what your daddy say now, got that boy?"

Then the punk's demeanor changed. He found a card in Dennis' wallet that changed everything. "You're a cop!"

Dennis struggled with the two men holding him and just managed to slide his gun out of his hip holster. But not enough time to cock and aim it. The gun was ripped out of his hand before he had time to even think about who he would shoot first.

The leader changed the tempo. He pointed over to a doorway, and the four followers dragged Dennis and Alan through the opening, into a dark and damp warehouse. Abandoned for years. But apparently still useful for some things.

Two chairs were pulled over, facing each other. Dennis was thrust into one, Alan in the other. The leader was animated now, excited, angry. "Last year, you pigs shot my father dead like he were a dog! He weren't no dog. He was my dad. I don't got a father no more because of you pigs."

Dennis didn't say a word. He glanced up at his father—they were now face to face in the old wooden chairs. There was no fear on Alan's face—just calm reassurance.

The leader was playing with Dennis' pistol, spinning it, twirling it. He yanked a large knife out of a sheath at his waist, and without warning, thrust it into Alan's chest. Alan lurched and let out a gasp. Dennis lunged forward only to be clotheslined from behind and yanked back into his chair.

The thug pulled the knife out and admired his handiwork. "See how good I am? I shanked him away from his heart. He be okay."

Dennis glared at the punk. "You've got our money and our credit cards. Just tie us up and you'll have plenty of time to go on a shopping spree before someone finds us. Please—wrap my dad's chest. He's going to bleed to death."

"I don't give a shit, man! You killed my father—maybe I kill yours, huh?"

"Please don't—don't make this worse than it needs to be." Dennis was starting to feel panic. The crazed man was talking serious shit. Probably drug-laced. And he had a serious hate on for cops, understandably if he had indeed lost his father in the way that he said. Even if that shooting was justified, these street punks just wanted to hate and never accepted blame upon themselves or their families. You couldn't reason with them. They just wanted to hate.

"Better yet, maybe I get you to kill your own father—whaddaya think about that, huh?"

Dennis glanced at his dad. He was starting to lose color as the blood drained out over his shirt. He was losing it fast. Tears started to drip from Dennis' eyes—his father managed a smile despite his pain, making the image worse for Dennis. This was his father, who only minutes before he had been laughing and talking trash with. This was his birthday.

"I wanna recreate the Deer Hunter. Remember that movie, copper?" The man spun Dennis' revolver and expertly discarded five of the six bullets. Then he laughed. "This gonna be fun, eh boys?" The other four just laughed along with their leader. He gestured to his partners and two of them pulled pistols out of their waistbands.

The leader shoved Dennis' chair to within a foot of his dad's. Then he put Dennis' gun back into his hand. At the same time he brandished his knife once again, and poised with it over the area of Alan's heart. "I may be a punk, but I true to my word. I give you a possible five chances to save your papa's life. Put that gun up 'gainst his forehead and start pullin the trigger. If you have five blankies, I let you guys go free."

Dennis looked up at the maniac. "You can't do this. It's barbaric. We've done nothing to you. Take our money and go—now, before it's too late!"

"Do it! You see this knife, bud? If you don't start pullin that fuckin trigger, I gonna

plunge this into daddy's heart. You got no choice here. You have to start pullin the trigger. He surely die if you don't. And don't even think bout shootin me with that thing. My boys will shred you and your daddy to pieces."

Dennis retched. His entire dinner came up in one choke. The punks laughed.

He wiped his mouth and looked up at his dad. His own eyes were teary, but he could see that Alan's were worse. Not only teary, but weary. Alan nodded at him, and mouthed, "Do it, son. It's okay."

Dennis brought his gun-hand up to his dear father's forehead and placed the cold steel against his furrowed brow. He thought for a second how bizarre this was, that it must be a dream, that he couldn't possibly be holding a gun to his father's head.

The maniac with the knife was getting excited. He started laughing and breathing hard, pumping his knife hand up and down simulating the stab that would surely come if Dennis didn't pull the trigger.

Dennis pulled it. Click. A deep breath. He pulled it again. Click again. Three more clicks and they'd be free.

Dennis took a deep breath and pulled the trigger again. He had fired his gun many times in the past, but the sound he remembered was nothing like the roar that he heard at that moment. In slow motion, he saw his dad's kindly eyes forgiving him as his head burst open into a sickeningly unreal chasm.

As Dennis retched again, he heard the cackle of laughter from the animals who had devised this horror. This was the highlight of their night—and the end of Dennis' world.

Dennis lurched up in bed, sweating, panting, crying. Uncontrollably. The horror was too much to bear. He had shot his own father dead. Sure, it was the only option he had, but it was still his finger that pulled the trigger. And the memory of that was too much to bear.

He stumbled into the bathroom and splashed water on his face. He glanced into the mirror and his eyes moved to his forehead. The image of his wonderful father came back to him. Alan's wise eyes, at once forgiving, then lifeless, at the very moment his head was being blasted wide open by the index finger of Dennis' right hand.

CHAPTER EIGHT

Dennis sat on the couch watching his mother rock. Incessant, annoying, non-stop rocking. He wished he'd thrown the damn chair out after all.

Felicity came into the drawing room with a steaming cup of coffee and handed it to Dennis, along with the flash of her sweet smile. Dennis smiled back. She turned her back to him and went over to Lucy. "Well, Mrs. Chambers, it's time once again for me to take your blood pressure. I'm just going to inflate this little balloon here, okay?"

Lucy looked up at her and scowled as Felicity wrapped the rubber band around her forearm and began to pump. "That thing looks dangerous to me—what is it for again?"

"Blood pressure, Mrs. Chambers. I just need to check to make sure that strong old heart of yours is beating properly." She studied the gauge. "And sure enough it is! You're as good as gold."

Lucy scowled again. "I don't have any more gold. My children stole it from me!"

Felicity patted her shoulder. "I'm sure that's not true, ma'am. Your children love you, I know that. Do you remember their names, Lucy?" The nurse turned her head and winked back at Dennis, who was taking the entire scene in with a grim smile on his face.

"No, I don't remember them—they don't remember me, so why should I remember them?"

Felicity knelt down to be at eye level with her. "You have a son and a daughter. And you have two grandsons. Your son's name is Dennis and your daughter is Melissa."

Lucy shook her head in disgust. "All you nurses do is lie, just to keep us old folks calm and under control."

Felicity stood up again, and then bent over to adjust the blanket around Lucy's chest and shoulders. Dennis couldn't help but notice the shape of

Felicity's bottom—nice, round and tight. She was shapely, no doubt—not an ounce of unwanted weight anywhere on her body—from what he could tell. For a brief moment he remembered the warning words from Barb Jenkins, and in that same moment he pondered that Felicity did seem to be dragging out the bending over exercise a little longer than necessary. Was she doing it for him? He shook his head—*need a clear mind--and she's too young.*

Felicity turned back to face him. "Is there anything I can get you, Mr. Chambers?"

"No, Felicity—I'm just fine, thanks." *Coffee, tea, or me?* "I have to go out later, by the way. Are you planning to be in all day today?"

"Yes, no problem. I'll be here. You go do what you have to do."

"Okay, great. I'm working from home today, but I may have to drop into the office for a little bit. I'll let you know when I'm leaving."

She smiled her wonderful smile, and winked her wonderful wink. "I'll take good care of her, don't you worry. By the way, have you noticed that Lucy seems to react well to music? Every time I put the stereo on, she seems to rock herself slightly and she actually hums occasionally—just a little bit, but it's kind of nice to see."

"Yes, I have noticed that. She always loved music. Always used to sing around the house."

Felicity sat down on the chair across from Dennis. "I've also noticed that she seems to like the 'oldies,' you know, songs from the 50s and 60s."

"Makes sense. That was her era—she was young and vital then."

"Mr. Chambers, deep down inside, your mom is still vital—you know that."

Dennis grimaced. "I know. Forgive me, I must sound heartless sometimes. I'm not. I'm just cynical and this disease just sucks the life out of everyone, not just the person who has it. It's an insidious thing and I hate it."

Felicity got up slowly and walked over to him. She knelt down on her knees again and made eye contact with him. She raised her hand and rubbed his shoulder. "I don't think you're heartless at all. I think you're a kind man who cares about his mother. That's why this is so upsetting for you at times. If you didn't care, you wouldn't be upset."

Dennis squirmed. "Thanks, Felicity." He avoided eye contact with her, but she stayed on her knees and continued to rub his shoulder.

"This disease does affect everyone, you're right. And one of the benefits of having a nurse living in to look after the patient, is that the family members can be taken care of too. Don't hesitate to ask me for any care that you might need from time to time, Mr. Chambers. Sleeping pills, tea, hot water bottle— anything at all that might calm your nerves." She paused. Pregnant silence. Dennis gulped. "I know this is hard on you, and those of us who work at the Casper Agency are taught to treat the entire family, not just the patient." He was still avoiding her eyes. She moved her face over in front of his, and cocked her head. "Okay?" A big smile.

Dennis rose from his chair and she rose with him. "Okay, Felicity. I understand. And thanks for caring."

He was leaving the room when she called after him. "Mr. Chambers, do you mind if I put the music on in here for Lucy again?"

Dennis mumbled under his breath. "No...no...that's fine. She'll enjoy it." He moved at warp speed down the hall toward the kitchen. He needed a cold drink of water, fast.

*****

Case files were always boring—because they had to be read over and over again, in the faint hope that something would pop out. And that 'something' usually did. But for that to happen detectives had to read the files again and again and again...with the full knowledge that the human brain never absorbs everything the first time around. Clues abound, but only dogged perseverance unlocked them.

In Dennis' position, he wasn't obligated to review case files anymore. He had dozens of detectives who did that for him. All he needed for his job were the executive summaries. However, the bigger, more controversial cases, needed his personal attention. The potentially explosive ones. He had to be on top of those and give day-to-day direction to the lead detectives. Any case that had the chance of blowing up needed his highly paid experienced brain.

He was embroiled right now in a real mysterious one. It hadn't been announced to the city yet, but it appeared as if a serial killer was on the loose. There had been six murders in the last five years plus one man who had simply disappeared. There was no evidence to necessarily tie that one in, but there were similarities to the others—all of the victims, including the one who had just simply gone missing, were the scum of the earth.

The man who had gone missing was his own secretary's ex-husband.

Dennis was having difficulty with the premise of this missing person being labeled as the work of a serial killer. He'd had numerous debates with his detectives as well as a few of his superiors on that. There was a tidal wave of support from many in the department to lump them all in together. In one respect Dennis was a bit relieved—it took attention away from Nancy as being a possible suspect in her ex's disappearance. On the other hand, he didn't like the connection to a member of his staff. He wanted the man's disappearance to just be forgotten.

Serial killers were always true to a certain modus operandi, a signature. The actual murder victims were left to be discovered, not hidden, with specific wounds that made them differentiated from 'run of the mill' murders. The missing man was simply…missing. The only thing they all had in common was that they had criminal records, were bad dudes, and had been on the loose in the big city—most likely ready to offend again. Someone may have wanted to rectify that. A vigilante. For that reason, he had been reluctant to release anything to the public, despite pressure from above. Vigilantes were romantic figures, heroes who were cheered and revered. They always led to copycats as well, and he didn't want his city infested with copycat heroes who were incapable of carrying it off safely. Innocent people would no doubt die.

Dennis rubbed his tired eyes and laid the files on the coffee table. He'd tackle the cases again later, maybe after dinner. He laid his head back and closed his eyes to the sound of the radio announcer on the stereo in the drawing room. He was doing the lead-in to yet another oldie but goldie. The next song was by a one-hit wonder named Jonathan King. A song from 1965, titled "Everyone's Gone to the Moon." Dennis loved this old song—an eerily romantic tune. Dreamy. But eerie. And right now he felt like dreaming. And he had always been a student of the moon.

Streets full of people, all alone,
Roads full of houses, never home,
Church full of singing, out of tune,
Everyone's gone to the moon.

Dennis opened his eyes and listened more closely. There was a pronounced creaking sound coming from the drawing room. Felicity, who was in the kitchen, heard it too. She called out, "Mr. Chambers, what's that noise?'

They both walked up the hall toward the drawing room, and stopped dead in their tracks in the doorway. Lucy was rocking in rapid motion in her chair, head in her hands. Felicity put her hand on Dennis' arm to stop him from going to her. They watched, and listened.

Eyes full of sorrow, never wet,
Hands full of money, all in debt,
Sun coming out in the middle of June,
Everyone's gone to the moon.

Lucy was groaning now, and her tiny feet were pushing furiously at the floor, rocking the chair beyond what it was designed for. Yet Dennis couldn't move. He just watched. Felicity was beside him with her hand still on his arm, gently restraining him. Neither of them wanted to disturb what they were witnessing.

Long time ago, life had begun,
Everyone went to the sun.

Lucy removed her hands, and raised her eyes to the ceiling. Then she joined Jonathan King in her own karaoke version of the last verse of the song.

Hearts full of motors, painted green,
Mouths full of chocolate-covered cream,
Arms that can only lift a spoon,
Everyone's gone to the moon.
Everyone's gone to the moon.
Everyone's gone to the moon.

Lucy lowered her head and covered her eyes once again with her hands. Then she started to cry. Her frail little body was trembling.

Dennis ran over to her and knelt down beside the rocking chair. He put his arms around her slender shoulders and squeezed her gently. "It's okay, mom. That song just brought back some memories of your younger years, didn't it?"

She raised her head, and looked right into Dennis' eyes. "Denny, I'm not that sentimental. You know that. That song is just so sad. Because it's so true."

Dennis wasn't prepared to be shocked again so soon after the last episode. She was back. He needed to talk fast—she could be gone again in a matter of seconds.

"It's just a song, mom. What's true about it?"

"Apollo 19."

Dennis could barely contain his astonishment. "What?"

"You don't know. Very few know. I know."

Dennis could feel the blood surging through his veins. "What do you know, mom?"

She looked away, through the window at nothing in particular. "It's snowing outside. You're going to have to shovel soon."

It was a bright, warm, spring day.

Dennis sighed, rose to his feet, and walked back to Felicity who was standing quietly in the doorway.

"What was that all about?"

Dennis glanced back at his mother again. "I don't know, Felicity. Except that it doesn't make any sense."

"Well, she seemed to make sense. She was talking about the moon missions, wasn't she? That song seemed to remind her of them."

Dennis folded his arms over his chest. "On the face of it, yes, she was talking about the Apollo moon missions." He paused and took a deep breath.

"Okay, so why do you look so concerned?"

Dennis exhaled slowly, deliberately. "Felicity, there was no Apollo 19. There wasn't even an Apollo 18. The last mission to the moon was in December, 1972, Apollo 17. We haven't been back to the moon since."

CHAPTER NINE

Brett Horton poured himself a scotch neat, and sucked it back. It stung gloriously all the way down, so much so that he poured himself another. He was sitting at his desk with his laptop on, sipping and surfing.

Researching was something he was good at; lots of practice when he was with the Secret Service. And his friend from the DOD, Bill Charlton, probably knew that it wouldn't take long before Brett dug deep.

Normally Brett didn't bother to dig—it wasn't his job to protect the U.S. Government any longer. Assignments were just assignments now, nothing more. As long as he got paid, he didn't care.

However, a little voice told him this new assignment was different, much different. Because it didn't involve the usual sex scandals, trashy cover-ups, or assassinations for posture. He could kill with impunity, and he was usually perceptive enough to understand why he was given an assignment to kill. Brett knew the political maneuvering that took place in the world, he understood the game—it was simply a real-life version of the board game, 'Risk.' Killing, for him, was impersonal. However, he knew that if he were ever asked to kill someone he knew or cared about, it would be a different story. This comforted him slightly. It meant he still had some kind of conscience, some empathy.

But this assignment just seemed to have something about it that tweaked his curiosity and his intelligence. He thought back to Bill's words: *"One of the hiding places is the demented mind of an eighty-five year old woman."* Wow—this was what movies were made from. Brett chuckled—maybe he'd write a screenplay depending on how this story unfolded.

He didn't know much. Bill wasn't too forthcoming on the details, and he never was. He couldn't be. It was 'need to know.' So, Brett knew he would have to do some digging on his own to find out more. He thought to himself how out of character this was for him. But, there was just something…

He knew this much: his target was Lucille Chambers, a former powerhouse lawyer with the Department of Defense. She had been a senior counsel there for many years, then took over as Acting Chief Counsel after the suicide of her boss, James Layton. However, it was curious that she only performed that job for one year, proceeded to remove her name from the list of candidates for permanent replacement of James, and then just retired with a full pension at the tender age of fifty. These were the scant details that Bill had shared with him—not much, but not too little either for a brain as sharp as Brett's.

Brett had asked Bill a question that he knew he wouldn't get an answer to. But he tried anyway, didn't hurt to try. He asked, *"What is it that you want me to find?"*

Bill just smiled at that, and answered, *"All I can tell you is that it has to do with the Apollo moon missions. That's all I can say, and that's all you really need to know."*

Outer space! That's all Brett needed to hear to get the juices flowing in his central nervous system. Now, this was an assignment he could get excited about. Who wasn't intrigued by outer space, and in particular those heady days when every country that mattered talked about the moon, circled the moon…or went to the moon. He was only five years old when history was made: Neil Armstrong became the first man to walk on the moon, after having descended in the lunar module 'Eagle' from the command module, 'Columbia,' in the most famous space mission of all time, Apollo 11. "The Eagle has landed," words that always stirred Brett's soul. It was July 20th, 1969. A date that Brett had always wished in his childhood soul that he could have been a part of.

And he still looked at the moon with longing. If Brett had one Achilles Heel, it was this.

He had been at it for a few hours now, scanning information on the Internet about the various moon landings. Most of it was mundane, stuff he knew already. But once he got around to surfing the very last moon mission, Apollo 17, he realized that he didn't know very much about that one. Perhaps it was because by that time, moon landings had become so routine that he, along with everyone else in the world, just stopped paying attention. Well, he was going to pay attention now.

Apollo 17 landed Eugene Cernan and his crew onto the surface of the moon on December 11th, 1972. They remained there until December 14th, at which time they lifted off in the lunar module, 'Challenger,' and docked with the command module, 'America.' The next day the lunar module, since it was just excess baggage and couldn't be transported back to earth anyway, was jettisoned back down to the moon. Its impact was recorded and analyzed by scientific instruments left on the surface, and Brett discovered that this process was conducted for every lunar module in all six moon landings. Each impact was recorded by the instruments, and the data relayed back to earth.

But more than just the impact of the lunar modules was recorded, Brett was surprised to read. During missions on the moon, the astronauts used mortar packages to lob and detonate explosives on the moon's surface. *Explosives on the moon?* Geophones were set up on the ground and left in place even after the astronauts left for their return to earth. These geophones were used to gauge the planned explosions, and subsequent moonquakes that occurred naturally from time to time. Again, data was sent automatically back to earth.

But that was only part of the overall elaborate system. Every single landing site that was used in the six moon landings was equipped with what were known as ALSEPs (Apollo Lunar Surface Experiments Packages). These arrays had their own generators, powered by Plutonium-238. Brett made a note to research that nuclear fuel.

So, in effect, due to the power and half-life of plutonium, these systems had the ability to basically function forever. And that seemed to be the intention. They were designed to conduct long-term studies of the lunar environment, not just moonquakes and explosive impacts, but also solar winds, volcanic activity, thermal activity—heat activity from the interior of the moon, asteroid and meteor activity, etc. Brett counted at least ten experiments that the ALSEP arrays were designed to handle and transmit to earth regularly. The sophisticated technology had been devised and perfected by Bendix Aerospace. Brett thought back to an assignment he had been asked to execute one time involving Bendix. He winced.

He continued to read, learning more about the moon with each click of his mouse. There was information about the moon's magnetic field, and how things on the moon weigh only 16.7% of what they would weigh on earth. The moon's magnetic field was very weak, the reason being that its magnetics were generated by crustal effects as opposed to what was known as Dipolar. The earth had a Dipolar magnetic field, which meant basically that it had a large magnetic core, a geodynamo, that generated most of the earth's polarity.

The moon, on the other hand, had a core that was far too small proportionately to generate any kind of magnetic field. So, any magnetic field detected on the moon was crustal, in other words sitting on the surface. Astronauts detected that the moon's magnetic field was strongest near crater zones—areas that had clearly been impacted by asteroids or meteors. So, it was conceivable that the moon's magnetic field was provided for totally by other space objects hitting it and leaving their residue behind.

The moon also had a mini-magnetosphere, which provided only minimal protection from the sun's radioactivity. Whereas, the earth had a maxi-magnetosphere, giving it excellent protection from the sun's dangerous plasma discharges. Earth's magnetosphere was entirely attributable to its geodynamo.

As Brett reflected on what he had learned, he was shocked by several things: Astronauts detonated explosives on the moon. NASA left behind operational experimental stations, which relayed data to earth right from the very first of six moon landings. Astronauts introduced plutonium to the moon and left it behind to power the stations. NASA seemed obsessed with the effects of explosions and seismic activity on the moon, so much so that they recorded the impacts of each of the lunar modules when they were cut loose to fall to the moon's surface. And, they deliberately set off explosions on the moon to record what happened hundreds of feet below the surface. And they left the equipment behind to record and relay data related to regularly occurring moonquakes. Finally, NASA seemed very interested in what levels of heat were being generated from deep within the moon's crust.

Brett scrolled to the final page of the document he had been viewing. He caught his breath as he read. There was a very short note, almost a postscript, stating that all the ALSEP systems were turned off remotely from earth on September 30th, 1977. They all became 'white elephants' on that day—at every single one of the six landing sites. The reason given was "budget cuts."

Brett wiped the sweat off his brow—it was another hot day, and sitting in front of a computer screen simply made it feel hotter.

He pondered this last fact of the decommissioning of the ALSEPs. Budget cuts? Who was kidding who? Back in those days NASA seemed to have an unlimited budget, and it was the beginning of the age of the shuttle program. And how much ongoing expense would there have really been with simply receiving data signals from the moon? The vast majority of the expense would have already been incurred with each moon landing. The arrays were set up, the generators powered up, and...Voila! Done! Any expense after that would have been extremely minor.

Brett leaned back and put his feet up on the desk. He smiled to himself. More government bullshit reasoning, that the public and media always seemed to just swallow—no questions asked.

It wasn't logical to leave such expensive and sophisticated equipment dormant when it was sitting there ready to send data about one of the most important space objects, let alone the fact that it was the closest celestial body to planet earth. And why were they all shut off on the same date? And who was the 'rocket scientist' who dreamt up the idea of taking plutonium to the moon? And who was the idiot who decided to just leave it all up there? Why had man never returned to the moon after the Apollo 17 mission in 1972? Questions, lots of questions.

And what had *really* happened on September 30th, 1977, that caused a complete shutdown of communication from the moon? Brett was convinced that it had nothing whatsoever to do with budget cuts.

But could that date possibly have something to do with the mysterious 'treasure hunt' he had just been assigned by the U.S. Department of Defense?

CHAPTER TEN

Dennis sat on his front porch, soaking up the late afternoon sunshine. And thinking. Thinking about his father.

He had attended many funerals throughout the years, but none were as horrifically sad as that one. His mother was a basket case that day and for weeks afterwards, and his sister, Melissa, was in a wheelchair sedated into oblivion. To this day, she still didn't remember one minute of the funeral. Probably a good thing.

There were at least eight eulogies—Dennis had lost count after a while. He himself gave a eulogy too, but broke down after five minutes and had to be gently escorted from the podium by the kindly priest.

The kicker was, no one knew what really happened that night. He had to agree to a cover-up for safety reasons. Safety for all of the other police officers and their families out there. Dennis bought into it. It was the right thing to do. His superiors were horrified by the tale that Dennis told them from his hospital bed. They immediately swung into damage control with the media and within the department. There was no way that story could be told, as it would cause such an avalanche of publicity and possibly an even worse avalanche of copycats, that their city, and other cities, wouldn't be able to cope. The identity of officers would have to be protected like Fort Knox.

The mere fact that crazed hoodlums were so obsessed with taking out revenge on police officers that they forced one to play Russian Roulette with his own father, was horrifying beyond belief. The Department was convinced that this method would be copied—again and again. They couldn't take that chance.

Dennis couldn't disagree. He signed a confidentiality agreement and the story put out to the media basically said that the killers shot Dennis' father dead in a botched mugging. No mention that a police officer's gun was used either.

Dennis could still picture the dingy old warehouse in his mind's eye, hear the laughter of the five killers as Alan fell over backwards in his chair, and could see himself retching all over his dad's shoes.

It was a nightmare that wouldn't leave him.

After the punks had finished laughing, the leader turned to Dennis and said, "Now it's your turn, pig."

At that point Dennis didn't care. They could do with him what they wanted. Now that his dad was dead, they no longer had leverage over him. Even his own life wasn't worth anything, as far as he was concerned. Part of him just wanted to die in that alley with his dad.

Dennis could hear himself screaming like a banshee as he rose from his chair and scooped it up in one hand. He spun, swinging the chair with him at head-height. First he took out the leader; then in the merry-go-round swoop, two others went down, all from powerful slams to the head from the chair legs.

The remaining two thugs attacked. One grabbed him from the front, the other from behind. They began pummeling him. Dennis clenched his stomach as hard as he could, and focused on the energy and anger within. The power he felt was shocking—he lifted himself in the air using the punk behind him as a fulcrum, and rammed his feet into the face of the guy in front. Then, putting his feet back on the ground, he bent forward and threw the killer behind him over his head and onto the ground. Then he pounced—easily twisting the neck of the guy into a broken distorted mess. He was dead instantly.

Jumping to his feet, he grabbed the other one as he was struggling to his feet. He ran with him full speed ahead, toward a cement wall—pretending the wall wasn't there. And in Dennis' intense stare, the wall truly didn't exist. The sad little man stuck to the wall by the pulp of his crushed and flattened face for just a moment or two, then slid slowly down the wall to the floor.

Dennis spun around. The other three who had been stunned by the chair were now on their feet, two with their own pistols in hand, the leader with Dennis' pistol. He was calmly picking up the five discarded bullets and inserting them back into the cylinder. He smiled, evil personified. A face that Dennis knew he would never forget.

He rushed them. All three fired. Dennis went down.

The leader stood over him, still smiling. Dennis sneered at him. "Kill me, you bastard."

He put the barrel up against Dennis' forehead. "Now, copper, don't lose your head like your papa done." Laughter from all three. Cackles.

"I not gonna kill you. That be too…nice, yes? No, I want you member what you done here. You kill your daddy. Coward! Have a nice life, pig! Catch me if you can!" At that, they left and took their laughter with them.

Dennis was in the hospital for three weeks after that, with bullet wounds to his shoulder, chest, and hip. He had survived—and countless times he wished he hadn't. And only he and his superiors knew what really happened that night. He consoled himself with thinking that his silence had probably prevented an onslaught of police family murders.

He would remain silent about it for the rest of his life; he knew he would. Dennis was always true to his word. But he would never forget. Never forget that evil face. And never forget what was now painfully obvious to him—cruelty like he and his dear father experienced that night could not be reformed, could not be tamed, and could never be forgiven.

*****

He looked out the window to see if Barb's car had pulled up yet. Then he checked his watch. She was always a bit late, or as she referred to it—'fashionably late.'

He still had time to finish his daily routines. Socks off, board mounted, fingers poised. Wide aggressive stance. Forefinger thrusting. Slam. Slam. Slam. Then his toes. Thud. Thud. Thud. He did this continuously, no rest in between impacts. For each forefinger, for each foot, one hundred times each, every day.

He had been doing this for almost twenty years.

Ever since his trek through China.

Dennis was a martial arts expert, but not in the familiar forms made popular in movies. His specialty was different, exceptional in fact, and extremely deadly.

The discipline of Shaolin Gongfu covered seventy-two unique forms of fighting, and originated from the Shaolin Temple in China's Henan Province. The Buddhist monks had perfected the seventy-two techniques long ago and have been passing them down to generations ever since.

Henan Province was known as the birthplace of Chinese civilization, with over 5,000 years of history. It is the third most populous province with numbers exceeding ninety-four million people. Henan is located in central

China, divided—and flooded from time to time—by the Yellow River. There are vast floodplains in the east and mountains in the west. Dennis went west.

He had always wanted to travel to China, ever since a project he had completed brilliantly in high school. His topic had been China and he focused on the country's fascinating history, in particular its cradle of origins from Henan. He became intrigued with Henan: the mystics, the monks, the monasteries—and the mysterious and legendary fighting techniques that focused on calm, deliberate incapacitation.

After Dennis had recovered from the horrible ordeal in the alley, out of the hospital and back at work, he was summoned by the man who had his job back then. The Chief of Detectives sat humbly behind his immense desk, and flashed Dennis a wry smile. A smile that said, "I have no idea what you're going through." He held a piece of paper in his hand and said simply, "Your request for 'leave of absence' is granted. Take the year and get this out of your head in the best way you can. Then, come back to us."

Dennis nodded a 'thanks,' shook the Chief's hand and left for his sabbatical. He knew he needed it desperately, and if left on the job he probably would have become a dangerous man. So, he had no regrets about leaving. And neither did the Chief.

Dennis needed peace—peace of mind. Something powerful, mystical, to focus his mind away from the horror. His life, in a lot of ways, had ended that night in the alley and he felt he needed a way to reach his inner primal self, start over again with a fresh point of view on his life and the world around him. He knew he couldn't talk about his feelings with too many people either—he knew he sounded like an aging hippie. 'Getting in touch with himself' was not something he wanted to share with others. It was too hard to explain.

So, he said his goodbyes to his sad mother, his astonished sister, and even his bewildered ex-wife. He just told them it was a vacation he'd always wanted to take. They bought it.

When he arrived in China, he backpacked through some areas of the country that he remembered studying in high school. And of course, only those areas that the Communist Party officials would allow an American to visit. But he knew where he really wanted to go, so he didn't spend too much time dawdling. He hopped the Longhai Railway system and traveled west—west to the Yuntai Mountain region in Henan Province. Home of the Shaolin Academy of Martial Arts.

He was blown away by the beauty of the region. The greenest of green foothills, rising to majestic snow-covered mountains. Fertile river valleys, primitive people happy with their simple lives. Peace. Heaven. Redemption.

For the equivalent of six American dollars a day, he had his accommodation, three full meals a day, and expert martial arts instruction for seven hours a day, seven days a week. They made it clear when he enrolled that there would be no slacking or he was out. They didn't want his money that badly. And they also made it clear that he would be in extreme pain for the first three months. If he made it that far, he would never feel pain again in the parts of his body that he would be working with. And he would be able to inflict pain and death if he ever needed to, with very little effort.

Dennis discovered, as did the other students, that the instructors weren't lying about the pain. Forefingers, forearms and toes were swollen and torn for at least three months. For him, it was closer to six. For others, it never ended. The dropout rate was seventy percent. Dennis hung in.

His mind gradually came to rest, focused on other things instead. The culture, the rigorous ritual, the mystical discipline that was taught, the mind control—and of course, the constant pain.

Dennis' training at the Academy lasted one full year, after which he was sent home with strict instructions on how to continue the training. The entire regimen of training took three years, but the Academy only provided the first year. After that, students were expected to simply continue the training on their own, following the regimen to the letter.

Dennis did. In three years time, he was an expert in three of the seventy-two Shaolin martial arts. The first one was known in English as 'Diamond Finger', or in Chinese, 'Yi Zhi Jingang.' In this art, the forefinger of both hands was the focal point. Daily training, which consisted of not only the mind control exercises but most importantly the fighting techniques, brought his two fingers to the point of having the strength of a thick tree branch. Along the way, he had had to suffer with torn skin and the swelling of the muscles and sinews—for months. By the end of the three years he was unable to feel pain any longer, and no outward signs on his skin would appear if he rammed his finger into a board, rock or tree trunk. With ease, he could crack a stone into two pieces, put a hole through a board just as if it were drilled, and smash bricks into clumps of cement dust. Just with his finger. It was powerful stuff...and mysterious as hell. He was fascinated by it.

The second martial art he mastered was 'Striking With Foot.' In Chinese it was called 'Zu She Gong.' The training was basically the same as with 'Diamond Finger,' except that it was done with the toes. Toes used singly, or all together. With this powerful skill, the impact against an opponent is delivered at the lower part of the body, and the power of the hit is so severe that the opponent is simply flung through the air. If delivered properly and with the brain focused, the adversary could be thrown up to twenty lateral feet into the air.

The third skill that Dennis learned was known as 'Twin Lock,' or 'Shuang Suo Gong.' This one involved building the strength and resilience of the forearms to the point where they can easily break a person's arm with one hit. And when the forearms are thrust towards each other with an unfortunate victim in between, the effects would be crushed internal organs and shattered bones. The training for this skill involved three years of banging the forearms together constantly. Very painful work—the worst, Dennis thought, of all the three skills. He was told that the forearms would have reached their maximum peak once he no longer felt pain when banging the arms together—and most importantly, when he finally heard a distinctive 'thump' when the arms hit.

After a little more than three years, he heard the 'thump.' The 'thump' he'd been waiting patiently for.

After his year in China, Dennis was welcomed back at work with open arms. He was glad to be back. And he felt much more at peace with himself. The year away and all the rigorous training had done him a world of good.

His career continued to advance over the years, and he knew that that probably wouldn't have been the case if he hadn't given himself that important time away. He was a whole person again.

He was promoted through the ranks to the point that he was now the Chief of Detectives, holding the same position that a very wise man had held twenty years before. A wise man who had seen the troubling signs and encouraged Dennis to go away. Just for a little while.

Dennis came back.

Or, more correctly put, a new and improved version of Dennis came back.

And he had a certain 'thump' about him.

CHAPTER ELEVEN

"Apollo 19?"

Dennis nodded his head soberly, with an almost apologetic look on his face.

"Denny, she's just talking nonsense. Don't fret about it."

They were sitting in Denny's rear living room, while Lucy performed her usual rocking routine up the hall from them in the drawing room. Barb Jenkins was resplendent in a green summer dress accented with a diamond necklace, bracelet and gold high-heeled shoes. She looked fabulous.

"Barb, how the hell can I just forget about it? First, I witness three spooks turning mom's room upside down after she spilled the beans to me about some kind of package. Something that seemed to scare the shit out of her. Then, out of the blue she becomes lucid again and mentions something about a non-existent Apollo 19. And you think I should just forget about it?"

"You just said it. Non-existent. There was no Apollo 19. And no 18 either."

"That's exactly the point, Barb."

She cocked her head and stared at him with a question on her lips. "You mean…"

Dennis rose from his chair and went over to the portable bar. "Another glass of wine, Barb?"

"Make it a scotch, Denny. I think I need it."

He poured them each a scotch, and sat down beside her on the couch. They clinked their glasses. "We should be toasting something, Denny."

"Okay, let's toast to learning the truth." They clinked again.

Denny took a long swallow then looked into Barb's brilliant green eyes. "Do you happen to know something, Barb?"

"No, I don't know anything about the moon missions. After your mom retired, I moved out of her department and into International Affairs."

"Mom was in Intelligence, wasn't she?"

"Yes, but remember, she was the legal arm of Intelligence. She wasn't an Intelligence Officer."

Dennis nodded. "I understand, but she was the head of the legal team for that department, correct?"

"Yes, just like I eventually became head of the legal team for International Affairs. You have to understand, Denny, the Pentagon is huge. The legal team numbers in the hundreds, all sectioned off just like the Pentagon is, assigned to each discipline of the Pentagon."

"So, only a handful of people know everything."

"Correct."

"That's the way the DOD wants it."

"Correct again."

"So, whom did mom report to?"

"Well in her position, she reported in two directions. Her main report was to the Chief Counsel, who in return reported directly to the Secretary of Defense. Lucy's secondary report would have been to the Undersecretary of Defense for Intelligence."

"Who in the DOD would know everything?"

Barb sipped her scotch, and paused. Silence.

"Barb?"

"I heard you, Denny. I'm just thinking." She took another sip. "This would just be my own educated guess, but obviously the Secretary of Defense would know everything about everything. And the Chief Counsel would probably be the only other person in the DOD who would know simply everything, just out of necessity. International law is a tricky thing, and warfare today is fraught with legal landmines. The U.S. may appear on the surface to go to war too easily, but trust me, the legal beagles have done their work with the United Nations expeditiously beforehand.

"And they've used our legal leverage vis a vis ironclad contracts over virtually every nation that wants to remain on good terms with us. No one moves on anything serious in the DOD without the Chief Counsel. The Chief Counsel also prepares whatever bribery is needed over nations to get them to agree to whatever it is we want them to agree to. Contrary to what the average person might believe, international agreements aren't made because of a meeting of the minds. In most cases, they've simply been bribed... or sometimes, threatened. The Chief Counsel for the DOD delivers those threats, or at the very least, prepares them."

"And that was who?"

"Well, that's a bit of a strange story. At that time, his name was James Layton. Lucy reported directly to him—until he committed suicide. That was back in December of 1977."

"And that's when mom took over, right?"

Barb winced. "She did…and she didn't. She was appointed Acting Chief Counsel until a permanent appointment was made. But, several months into the job, she withdrew her name from the candidate list. Then, six months later, she retired. As you know, she was only fifty years old then."

"She got a severance package."

"Yes, she would have. All the lawyers worked on a contract basis, with severance terms spelled out in advance."

Dennis frowned. "Mom never flashed her money around. But she retired a wealthy woman. You know that, don't you?"

"Wealth is a relative term, Denny. Your mother also made a substantial amount of money when she was a corporate attorney, before even joining the Defense Department."

Dennis walked over to the wall unit and fingered an old framed photo of his mom and dad. He ran his fingers around the outline of their images. Talking with his back to Barb, he said, "When she retired, she was paid five million dollars in severance, Barb."

Barb choked on her drink, and broke out into a coughing fit. Denny ran over to her and rubbed her back as she bent over the coffee table. It took a few minutes for her to catch her breath—Denny handed her a bottle of mineral water, and she took a long pull.

"You…must be…mistaken."

"No, I'm not. Melissa and I have that wealth between us now, an amount that has grown exponentially over the decades. It's now worth about twenty-seven million. So I'm quite familiar with my mom's finances. The papers were clear when we took over 'power of attorney.' It was described officially as 'severance.' We had no idea until then that mom even had that kind of money."

"Did you question her?"

Denny laughed. "Barb, come on, get real. We only found out about the money five years ago when she was finally committed to a nursing home. Mom's mind was already pretty much gone by the time the 'power of attorney' kicked in. Sure, we asked a couple of questions, but we mostly got blank stares—not that we really expected anything more.

"She clearly didn't need to tap into that money. As you say, she always made a high income as a lawyer, in both the private and public sectors. She was a woman of privilege, for sure. And my dad also made big money in his field. So, this severance money, or whatever it was, became simply a nest egg for her."

"Denny, there is no way that money was a severance payment. I'll give you my own example, and I would have had the same kind of contract as your mom did and I retired just a few years ago. My contract required me to be paid two years salary if severed or if I just chose to leave—and I made, at my height as head of International, half a million a year. So, when I left, I got a million. That's in today's dollars—your mom got paid five million in 1978 dollars. Geez!"

Dennis chuckled. "Was mom just a better negotiator than you, Barb?"

Barb snorted. "I admired your mom, but I can tell you this—there was no better negotiator than me. So, all joking aside, what she got was not a severance package. It had to have been for something else."

"Like what?"

"That's the five million dollar question now, isn't it?"

Dennis put his feet up on the ottoman, and clasped his hands behind his head. "Tell me, Barb. How did that guy kill himself…what was his name… Layton?"

"Shot himself in the head—in his Pentagon office. It was all hush-hush."

"Yeah, mom never mentioned anything about it. Just that her boss died, and she was now running things temporarily."

"It was a mess. And the media was shut down completely on it. Those of us who knew had to swear out confidentiality."

"Was there a note?"

Barb cleared her throat. "Apparently, yes. But it was never disclosed to anyone."

"Not even to his family?"

"No. I knew his wife, Margaret, quite well. Lovely woman. She confided in me after it happened. She tried to get a court order for the suicide note, and her action was summarily rejected."

"On what basis? She was his wife!"

"National Security."

"What?"

"I know—really makes you wonder, doesn't it?"

Dennis stood up and looked at his watch. "Can I take you to dinner, Barb?"

"Not tonight, handsome. I'll take a rain check—and look at that, it's actually started raining outside!" They both looked out the window. Sheets of rain completely shielded the view of the backyard.

"Okay, I'll hold you to that. There's a lot more that I want to talk about. Including that other matter—did you think about whether or not you could put me in touch with someone in the Pentagon?"

Barb smiled. "I knew you wouldn't forget, you curious devil. Yes, I did think about it and I do have a name for you. In fact, I've talked to her already. She's more than willing to meet with you to chat. I didn't tell her what it was about, just that you had some concerns and questions pertaining to your mom; kind of a family history thing you're doing. She's familiar with Lucy's tenure—Lucy was quite the legend over there."

"What's her name?"

"Fiona. Fiona Perry. A sweet lady, but also tough as nails. She's the Deputy Director of Press and Public Relations at the Pentagon. Well connected. And…not too happy. Very frustrated and worried about being shut out of things she feels she should know in order to do her job. You've probably seen her on TV a few times; she acts as the spokesperson on a lot of Pentagon issues. Trouble is, she has this nagging feeling that most of the time she's lying…but doesn't know she's lying. Just a feeling she has."

"So, she may be ripe to talk—or help?"

"She might. That'll be up to you. I'll have her call you to set up a meet."

"I could just meet her at the Pentagon."

"Good luck with that. Even you, Mr. Chief of Detectives, would have a tough time getting past those doors. No, I think you'd better plan on springing for lunch somewhere, you cheapskate."

Denny laughed. "Hey, I'm not a cheapskate! I just offered to buy you dinner!"

"True, you did. But, I do recall that the last time you 'bought' me dinner I got stuck with the check. Remember that, Prince Charming?"

"Hey, I got paged about a murder. I had no control over that, my dear. Duty called."

"Excuses, excuses."

They walked up the hall together toward the front door, then stopped at the doorway to the drawing room. Lucy was still rocking intently, seemingly with some kind of purpose. Barb went into the room and gave her a hug and kiss. Then she turned and walked back, tears in her eyes.

Dennis held her hands in his and squeezed. She allowed a faint smile.

"Dennis, there's virtually nothing left of that vibrant woman we both knew so well. It must be so heartbreaking for you. It is for me."

He nodded and lowered his eyes. "She's just a skeleton now, Barb. Just a skeleton."

CHAPTER TWELVE

It was lunchtime at the Pentagon. Bustling, hungry, military and civilian employees together as one long parade of human bodies, making their way in and out of the more than twenty fast food operations. No one had to leave the building; in fact the DOD preferred they didn't. There was plenty to choose from right inside the hallowed halls: Subway, McDonald's, Dunkin Donuts, Panda Express, Starbucks, KFC, Pizza Hut, and Taco Bell—just to name a few. No one in the Pentagon would ever go hungry.

Fiona Perry fought her way down to the main lobby area in the southeast corner of the building. It was like this every lunch hour, and she hated it. Crowds of people fighting for a bite to eat during pitifully short lunch breaks.

Many times, like today, she skipped lunch. Instead she spent the time at the Pentagon Athletic Center, a fully equipped health spa with all the required perks. She just finished an abbreviated aerobics session and felt invigorated, ready to take on the rest of the day.

She looked at her watch—still had about fifteen minutes before she was due to begin yet another meeting. She was meeting her guests at the southeast entrance lobby, the only one designated for visitors. But she wouldn't be able to shake their hands until after they had been dutifully screened by the United States Pentagon Police; or as those in the know called them, USPPD.

Fiona was never worried about being late for meetings. Despite the massive size of the Pentagon, its shape and design allowed for anyone to walk from one point in the complex to any other point in no more than seven minutes. Remarkable.

As she got closer to the main lobby, she passed by a group of students— just one more tour of the Pentagon, led by an experienced Pentagonner. No less than one hundred thousand people toured the Pentagon each year. No surprise—it was one of the most impressive structures in the world.

Fiona smiled as she thought back to the tour she was given when she first joined the Pentagon ten years ago. All the facts she knew that this fresh group of students would be hearing for the first time, all crammed into a one-hour tour.

The Pentagon is the home of the U.S. Department of Defense, and a lot of people are surprised to hear that it's not actually located in Washington, D.C. But it's darn close. The Pentagon actually resides in Arlington, Virginia, which is just across the Potomac River from Washington. So, a different state, but close enough to be considered part of the metropolis of Washington.

It's the largest office building in the world with about 6,500,000 square feet of space. A mind-boggling small city of about 30,000 people work here. The building has five sides, five floors above ground, two basement levels and five ring corridors on each floor. Doing the math, there are almost eighteen miles of corridors.

The Pentagon was a mysterious but oddly ignored building until September 11th, 2001. Most people knew little about the structure until that infamous day. The official story was that a hijacked American Airlines 757 jet slammed into the western side of the complex that day, killing 374 people.

Fiona grimaced as she thought of that day. She didn't join the Pentagon staff until a year after that incident, but she and many others still stuck their tongues solidly in their cheeks whenever they heard the official story spouted. She didn't believe for a second that it was a jet—she was convinced it was a missile. And who fired the missile? She didn't want to think about it.

But, she couldn't believe how anyone could think that a massive jet could soar over Washington's perimeter, swoop in over busy thoroughfares and come in as low as just a few feet off the ground to ram a hole in the Pentagon shell. And no one got a photo. That's why she couldn't believe it—this day and age, no one got a photo?

A missile flying at warp speed would be a little harder to photograph—but a jet, flying so close to the ground that it could have been shaving the grass, was not captured on camera? She shook her head in disbelief as she walked—she suspended belief almost every day on this job, she reflected. If it wasn't one thing, it was another.

She remembered a coincidence that was almost too weird to be true—but it was true. Construction on the Pentagon commenced on, of all dates, September 11th, 1941.

The building was erected during WW2, so compromises on materials were made due to steel being needed more in the manufacturing of warships.

Couldn't be wasted on buildings, even a war building. So, concrete was used extensively instead of steel. And the outer walls were made of limestone instead of the usual marble that would typically have been used for a government building of such majestic caliber. President Roosevelt insisted that marble would not be used, as Italy was the major supplier in the world of marble products. Since Italy was one of the three countries the U.S. had declared war against, they couldn't be seen as buying their products while bombing the shit out of them.

Fiona thought back to when she first joined the Pentagon, almost ten years ago now. She had been recruited as a junior staffer, and worked her way up to the position she now held: Deputy Director of Press and Public Relations. Before joining the government she had been an up and coming reporter at The Washington Post. A job she thought she'd enjoy doing forever—a perfect application of her Masters degree in journalism from the University of Southern California.

But Uncle Sam had called, or more appropriately, summoned. They appealed to her sense of duty and patriotism and it had worked. She was forty-two years old now, and perfectly in line for the top job in Public Relations. And the money was good too—much more than she could have ever made at the Post.

She wasn't surprised at the money she was making, knowing what deep pockets the military establishment seemed to have at their disposal. The DOD budget accounted for a whopping 25% of the entire U.S. Federal budget, and 53% of all Federal discretionary spending. The total budget for the Department of Defense was now approaching 1.5 trillion dollars, an amount that made Fiona shake her head in dismay.

And despite the feigned fretting about energy consumption and government efforts to make lowly consumers think of their responsibilities for conserving energy, the Department of Defense was the largest single consumer of energy in the country, a fact that the government certainly didn't ever talk about. The DOD spent almost 2.5 billion on energy each year, enough to power millions of homes. And fuel was another story—the DOD burnt an average of 12.6 million gallons of fuel every single day.

She looked through the glass corridor windows as she walked, and remembered being told on her tour ten years ago that there were a total of seven gleaming acres of glass in the Pentagon. There were also thirteen elevators and 131 stairways. Everything was big and over the top in government, especially the U.S. government where image was everything.

Fiona wondered whether or not anyone on today's tour would ask why the building was basically an occult-symbol pentagram. And whether it was true that the man who commissioned the building construction, Franklin D. Roosevelt, the thirty-second President of the United States, was a Freemason inaugurated into that secret society way back in 1933. And was there any occult significance to the fact that the Pentagon was a five-sided building, with five floors, each floor made up of five concentric pentagrams, separated by five interior courtyards, with a five acre courtyard in the middle. And did the number five and pentagrams not have some significant attachment to Satan?

Fiona chuckled at the thought—she knew it wouldn't be the first time some smart-ass university student who belonged to the Bush-era hate club asked questions that made the tour leaders cringe and squirm.

Finally arriving at the lobby area, she was just in time to see her visitors being screened through the metal detectors. She waved at them and they waved back. Looking at her watch, she realized that time was once again tight today. After this group, she had two more meetings and one press conference before her day was over. She loved it...and hated it at the same time. Well, hate was a strong word—she felt uneasy. For some reason, she felt uneasy—about the words she had to deliver, about the stories she was told to believe. At times they were, well, unbelievable.

Today she was meeting with two representatives from CNN. They wanted updates from her on the Pentagon's plans for outer space. This meeting was triggered by recent reports that she had had to produce for the media relating to yet more satellites that were on their way to terra firma. Two of the beasts had lost their orbit and were on their way down. She had no choice but to admit that they were nuclear-powered and had small amounts of plutonium on board. All indications were that they would crash safely into the Pacific... but who knew for sure? The public was nervous, and CNN loved it. They wanted to milk it. Fiona would keep her cool as she always did, and spout the company line: "These satellites had nothing whatsoever to do with the military. They were put into space for mapping and communication purposes. They were not, I repeat, not spy satellites."

Of course the media wouldn't buy it—and Fiona couldn't blame them. She didn't really buy it either.

Today, CNN didn't just want to talk about the satellites that were ready to return to earth. This meeting also pertained to an ongoing series they were doing on the 'future weaponization of space,' going back to the Reagan years when 'Star Wars' became the topic of the day. Fiona would have to handle that one gingerly, because it was still a taboo topic around the Pentagon. She didn't know what to believe and really didn't know what to say. In her heart of hearts, and being a bit of the cynic that ten years at the Pentagon would make one, she didn't really believe at all that weapons weren't already out there. She shuddered at the thought.

While she was waiting patiently for her visitors to finish being screened by the USPPD, she caught a quick glance of herself in the lobby wall mirror. Fiona adjusted her skirt a bit, which was being plagued by a bit of static today. She smiled contentedly. At forty-two, she knew she didn't look her age, and that made her feel good. She took care of herself. Today she was wearing a very proper beige blouse, with a stylish black skirt. Her hair was down today—sometimes she wore it up, but liked it best when it hung to her shoulders. Auburn hair, hazel eyes that sometimes looked green, and a body that still betrayed the athlete that she had been in her youth. And still was, but to a lesser extent—aging did have its limitations, unfortunately.

She was still attractive and she knew it. But she wasn't obsessed with it. And Fiona hated the leers that she would get from time to time—did those clowns really think that girls were flattered by tongues hanging out in mock horny? Making her feel like a piece of meat?

Her brain was such that she could talk rings around almost any man. Yet, most of them would never take a good-looking woman seriously. She still attracted admiring glances from younger and older men alike, and while flattered to have those glances, she didn't care all that much. She was a confident woman, secure in who she was, and didn't need the flattery of men to make her feel good about herself.

Weary of dating, she'd dropped herself out of the race over the last two years. She had a social life, but it was with her girlfriends or groups of people. She had grown tired of the one-on-one games.

Older men had baggage and were usually two-time losers. Younger men just wanted to have sex right away—bing, bang, boom. And wanted to brag about bagging a cougar. She hated that term. She wasn't a cougar, and she certainly wasn't going to spend an evening listening to some shallow little snot-nose bragging about himself and hoping to impress her enough to take him to bed.

She sighed—where were the real men? Where were the modest guys who showed respect towards a girl, wanted to know her and not just her body? She didn't know if she'd ever meet one again.

She had one, was married to him for twelve years until a drunk driver killed him on his way home from work. That was five years ago now and Fiona knew she still wasn't over it. And the shallow self-centered men she had met since, convinced her even more that she would never be over it. Had Matt been the only one for her? She sniffed and wiped away a tear.

Then she remembered. Tonight she was meeting a man. But it wasn't a date, thank God. Her old friend Barb Jenkins had asked her to meet one of her friends, the son of a legendary DOD lawyer, Lucy Chambers. His name was...Dennis, yes, that was it. She would enjoy this. A night out with no pretensions. A non-threatening evening with a man. No games. Just dinner and a chat.

She saw the CNN predators heading her way. She smiled her biggest Pentagon smile and walked towards them. Fiona Perry would charm them today into thinking that the Pentagon was the equivalent of Winchester Cathedral. They'd be putty in her hands...and then afterwards she would wash her hands thoroughly.

CHAPTER THIRTEEN

While painstakingly adjusting his tie in front of the hallway mirror, a sweet voice called out from the kitchen. "Don't you look handsome tonight!"

Dennis turned his head and smiled at Felicity. "Well, thanks. I guess I can still dress myself up once in a while, eh?"

"Oh, you look handsome even in your shorts and T-shirt."

Dennis blushed. While it was nice to get this kind of attention from a young twenty-something, he felt uncomfortable at the same time.

"So, if you don't mind my asking, do you have a hot date tonight?"

Dennis laughed. "No, no, nothing like that. I'm just meeting a friend of Barb's for dinner—to talk about some of the strange stuff that's been coming out of my mom's mouth."

"Male or female?"

"Well, female—but it's just a dinner meeting. Nothing more."

Felicity smiled her coy little smile. "Hmm…lucky girl."

Dennis blushed again.

"Is she pretty?"

"I don't know. I'll report back to you after I meet her."

"Make sure you do that. Does she have a pretty name?"

Dennis finalized the tightening of the knot on his tie and walked to the kitchen where Felicity was standing in a flirty little pose.

"I guess she does, yes. Fiona Perry. Has a nice ring to it, doesn't it?"

Felicity sighed in frustration. "Dennis, your tie is not right at all!" He noticed that she was no longer calling him 'Mr. Chambers.'

She walked up to him and wrapped her fingers around his collar, sliding them against the skin of his neck. She pulled, twisted, and tightened.

"There, that's better." She stood back and admired her handiwork. Dennis felt drips of sweat forming where her fingers had just been.

"Thanks. I think I'm ready to go. Wish me luck."

Felicity walked with him to the front door. "Don't worry, I'll take good care of your mother while you're gone. And good luck—but what am I wishing you luck about? The girl? Or the information?"

"Felicity, I told you—I just want information."

She put her hands on her hips. "Okay, I believe you. But what makes you think this Fiona girl can help?"

"Well, she works at the Pentagon where my mother used to work. And she's a little unhappy with things over there, so she might be disgruntled enough to help do some digging around for me. The Department of Defense is a pretty secretive organization. I could use someone who cares enough to search out a mystery."

Felicity nodded. "Makes sense. But Lucy's only mentioned two things to you so far: that package thingy, and something about a moon mission that everyone knows never happened. And as you pointed out, not only did an Apollo 19 never happen, but neither did an Apollo 18. How can this girl possibly help out with these things?"

·"I have no idea—I'm just shooting blanks right now. Any place to start would be nice. I have nothing to go on. Except that in addition to those two things my mom mentioned, I know that she left the Pentagon at fifty years of age with a huge severance payment. What that means, I don't know."

Felicity scratched her chin. "Would you like me to try from time to time to get your mother to open up about some of these things? She seems to trust me more now."

Dennis suddenly realized he'd been talking too much. He looked at her hard. "Don't ever suggest something like that again, Felicity. I think I've told you too much already. I don't want anyone prying into my mom's brain without me being here. Understand?"

Felicity pouted, but Dennis noticed that it was more of a flirty pout than a sad pout. "I'm sorry, Dennis. I was just trying to be helpful. As a nurse, I have special training and usually develop a rapport with my patients. You might be able to use me that way." She reached up and began brushing some specks of dust off the shoulder of his suit jacket.

Dennis grabbed her hand and lifted it gently off his shoulder. He spoke in a low soft tone to her. "I think you should go back to calling me 'Mr. Chambers,' okay?"

*****

As soon as he walked into Luigi's Italian Eatery on Constitution Avenue he saw her, and knew it was her. Not because he knew what she looked like, because he didn't. And not because she was the only one sitting alone, because she wasn't. He just knew. There was something instantly familiar about her, and he knew that it was her table that he was supposed to be walking towards. Which he did.

The hostess tried to stop him. "Sir, can I help you find your party?" He ignored her and kept walking as if in a trance.

"Fiona?"

She looked up from her menu and smiled at him. Then she stood and held out her hand.

"How did you know it was me?"

"Didn't Barb tell you? I'm a cop."

She laughed as they shook hands. Dennis slid into a chair across from her and smiled. In fact he couldn't stop smiling—felt like a little schoolboy. She was so pretty. And so strangely familiar.

First order of business was ordering wine. Fiona deferred to Dennis so he ordered his favorite Merlot from the Sonoma Valley. They toasted to new friendships, and began the mandatory small talk.

But the small talk grew to big talk, and Dennis was astounded to discover how much he was opening up to this complete stranger. And she was opening up to him. The time just flew by. By the time dessert was served, they had pretty much shared their entire life stories with each other. And Dennis was still smiling.

"Dennis, I must say I've really enjoyed this dinner with you. But…we haven't yet talked about why we're even having this dinner. So…why are we here?"

Dennis leaned his elbows on the table and gazed into her hazel eyes. "I need your help."

"In what way? I know of course about your mother—sad about the Alzheimer's especially considering how brilliant she was. They still talk about her over at the Pentagon, and how brave she was to just throw it all away at such an early age."

"Can I tell you some things, Fiona? I mean, you barely know me and if you can't help me I understand totally. But I'll need to share some things with you that might make you uncomfortable. So…thought I'd warn you first. If you'd rather not, I won't and we can just say we had a nice dinner together. And maybe do it again sometime."

She cocked her head. "Oh, that's so sweet: warning me and giving me the opt-out option. Let me just say first that I would love to have dinner with you again, regardless of what you might tell me. So…that being out of the way, share whatever you want with me and we'll see if I can make any sense out of it. Remember, I deal with the press all the time, and I handle PR for the largest, most powerful military machine in the world. There's little that can shock me." She smiled warmly at him.

Dennis caught his breath. Not because he was nervous about what he was going to tell her, but because she left him breathless. He had never ever gazed at such an expressive face before. She made little motions with her mouth, little expressions that were hard to describe and impossible to forget. The twinkle in her eyes and the way they opened wide when she talked about something she was happy about.

There seemed to always be something going on in that pretty little head, and she would shake that head in adorable little ways when she was trying to make a point. He could see that she would be a dynamo in meetings—her animated way of expressing herself was both charming and disarming. And one thing he liked that surprised him—she wasn't flirty in the least. Fiona was classy and professional. He could tell she liked him though, and maybe she was indeed flirting with him in her own subtle way. But she wasn't like a lot of the other women he had met—where the flirting was obvious, brazen, and sometimes nauseating. Fiona kept it classy and he found that nicely refreshing.

He thought about why she seemed familiar to him and he remembered Barb telling him that he might have seen her on TV from time to time. But he hadn't—catching political news wasn't something he was into, so tuning in to a Pentagon press conference wouldn't be his style. There had to be another reason she seemed familiar to him, and he knew he would puzzle over it for the next few days—or at least until he saw her again. Was it karma?

"Okay, Fiona. Here goes."

He spent the next hour discussing Lucy's career, the apparent suicide that brought her to the top job and then sudden retirement. He told her about the five million dollar severance payment. Then he detailed Lucy's sudden lucidity after the attempted purse theft and her panicked mention of a package that she wanted him to retrieve. Fiona frowned when he described the DOD staff searching Lucy's room at the nursing home. When he told her about Lucy's most recent lucid incident when she mentioned 'Apollo 19,'

Fiona put her hands over her mouth and gasped.

Dennis could tell she was thinking hard. She didn't say a thing. She didn't have to—those amazing eyes said it all.

"Fiona, penny for your thoughts?"

She pulled her hands down from her mouth and allowed herself a thin smile.

"I don't know what to say. Adding it all up, beginning right back from the so-called severance payment—which seems to me like it was more of a payoff—something isn't right. I think we can go back a little before that severance payment too—the suicide of James Layton. There's a pattern there. Then nothing at all for more than three decades, and now Lucy's brain has come out of its slumber with little spurts of troubling comments. Something is awakening in her that her smothered brain is screaming to tell. And you're getting it—piece by piece."

Dennis poured more coffee into both of their cups from the large coffee pot the waiter had deposited on the table. "Do you think that she might be just speaking nonsense—the ramblings of a dementia patient?"

"I have no idea. But if I was a betting woman—and I'm not—I would bet that your mother was paid off for something, paid to go away and shut up. And now she's beginning to ramble. And the spooks were interested enough to toss her room.

"In her lucid moments, there was a package she was panicked over—remember, in that moment of lucidity she wasn't demented. Maybe a bit forgetful because she couldn't remember what the package was, but not demented. She knew you perfectly well—so you have to assume she was herself and of sound mind for those brief moments. And I shudder to say this—I feel goosebumps down my back right now—but you have to assume the same thing with the Apollo 19 comment. For some reason she thinks there was an Apollo 19—which would mean there was also an Apollo 18. Christ, I can't believe I'm having this discussion." Fiona shook her head. Her face looked troubled.

Dennis wrung his hands together. "What do you think, Fiona? Can you help? Will you help?"

She nodded slowly. "I like you, Dennis. And I love Barb. And your mother left a legacy of honesty behind her, which still permeates through the Pentagon even to this day despite all the dishonesty that exists there. I'll have to be very very careful though. But hell, yes, I'll help. This intrigues me—and kind of angers me, even though I haven't got a clue what it's all about."

Fiona smiled her most charming smile of the evening. "Dennis, I have no doubt that you can relate to my main reason for helping you, though. I'm still a journalist first and foremost, so I just love a mystery and adore a good story. Bring it on!"

*****

Brett Horton was at his desk, phone to his ear, pen in hand. "Okay, repeat that name again for me, will you?"

"Fiona Perry."

"And you're sure she works at the Pentagon?"

"That's what he said."

"Okay, I'll check it out. So, all that's come out of the old woman to this point is the mention of some package, and the Apollo 19 blabbering? Is that correct?"

"Yes."

"Think hard—is there anything else at all that she said? Even something that might have seemed immaterial?"

"Well, she did imply that very few people knew about Apollo 19, and that she was one of them. That's pretty much it. She faded back out again so fast. Oh, and Dennis mentioned that Lucy received a huge severance payment when she retired. He didn't say how much, but I got the impression that it was much larger than a normal severance."

Brett scratched his head. "Interesting indeed. Felicity, keep up the good work and continue to report to me daily. And, just a reminder that you need to pick a safe day for me to get into that house. We'll need a few hours with the old lady, and I'll want you to be at your very best that day."

"I will be."

"I know you will. Your hypnotherapy talents are well respected within our tight little circle."

Brett hung up the phone and began doodling frantically on his pad of paper.

Then he let out a loud whistle and banged his fist on the desk. "Apollo 19! What the fuck have those assholes done?"

CHAPTER FOURTEEN

Barb smiled in her sly, knowing little way. "So, how did it go?"

Dennis smiled right back. "Just fine—and please wipe that silly grin off your face."

They were sitting in the drawing room, each with a coffee in hand. Lucy seemed to be absorbed in thought; no rocking, just staring out the window. Dennis glanced over at her, then back at Barb. "Look at her. She seems pensive today—I'd love to know what she's thinking."

"Probably nothing at all, Denny. I hate to say that, but it's probably true. Here we are sitting in this room today keeping her company, yet she's oblivious."

"Something has to be going on in her head, Barb. Hard to believe even a demented brain isn't thinking about something. Hell, it still controls her movements: eating, drinking, when to go to the bathroom. She hasn't reached the point yet where she has to wear diapers, so she's definitely aware of her needs."

Barb slowly nodded. "Yes, that's true. But remember, after eighty-five years those things are pretty much automatic and hard-wired."

Dennis got up and walked over to his mom. He looked into her eyes—they seemed empty. Didn't look back. Looked right through him. He winced and walked back to his chair.

"Anyway, you deftly changed the subject, Denny. How'd you like Fiona?"

Dennis decided to play coy. "Very professional lady. And I think she's going to help me. She's fascinated by this Apollo 19 comment that mom made, and she seems convinced in her mind that mom's severance payment was a payoff of some sort to shut her up about something."

Barb took a slow sip of her coffee. "C'mon—give me some juice here! How did you like her, handsome? You know what I mean—did she get you excited?"

"Barb! I'm shocked! Such a serious subject and all you're interested in is whether or not I found her to be alluring? I'm ashamed of you."

She stood up and did a little mock dance, put her hand on his shoulder and squeezed. "I can tell—you liked her, didn't you? You little devil!"

"Okay, okay. Yes, I liked her. She's very attractive and actually strangely familiar to me. I can't place her, don't understand why she seems familiar. I was instantly comfortable."

"Well, I told you, remember? You've probably seen her on TV."

"No, no. That's not it. I've never seen her spots on TV. It's... something else."

Barb playfully fluffed Dennis' hair. "I know what it is, you big romantic teddy bear. It's 'love at first sight.' Happened to me once a long, long time ago. Never happened again."

Dennis smoothed out his hair and stood up. "What happened?"

Barb's face showed a rare dark moment. "He died." She turned and walked down the hall toward the kitchen. "I'm getting some more coffee," she called back. "Do you want some?"

"Sure, just black this time. Bring me a fresh cup, will ya?"

He walked over to his mom again. She was still sitting, staring. At nothing in particular. He knelt down in front of her and studied her eyes. Knowing in his mind that the eyes were the gateway to the soul, he was hoping he might see some signs of awareness, some feeling. Nothing. No one seemed to be home.

"Here's your..." *Crash!* Barb tripped on the area carpet and went down hard, both cups flying from her hands and smashing onto the hardwood floor. Lucy lurched in her rocking chair and yelled out something. Dennis ran over to Barb and helped her to her feet, then they both just stared at Lucy. Her arms were flailing and she was screaming one word, over and over.

It sounded like 'Skeleton.'

Dennis grabbed Barb's arm and led her out into the hallway. "The sound of you and the cups smashing to the floor has shocked her into some kind of rant. But it sounds like she's saying 'Skeleton.' Do you think she heard me saying that to you the other day, when I said she was just a skeleton of herself now?"

Barb whispered, "I don't know. I hope not. Would mean that her feelings might have been hurt, and she's expressing it now."

They both peeked their heads around the edge of the doorway and watched. And listened. Lucy was still screaming the word. They listened hard.

Dennis brought both hands up to his forehead and began massaging it with his fingers. "She's not saying 'Skeleton,' Barb. Listen carefully."

Lucy kept screaming.

Barb gasped. "She's saying…'Shackleton.'"

*****

A fat little man with pale pockmarked skin, made his way down H Street, apparently on a mission. He had his backpack slung over his shoulder, which contained his usual tools: candy, teddy bear, duct tape, camera phone, rope, … and a hunting knife. At one time or another, and sometimes at the same time, all these tools came in handy. He never left home without them.

Home now was a halfway house, where he'd spent the last six months vegetating. Listening to all the other ex-cons talking about their pathetic lives, and how they were going to turn things around and go straight. Well, Melvin Steed knew where they'd be going straight to—straight to hell, that was where.

He chuckled as he walked. At least he knew where he was going. His roommates were just kidding themselves. There was no such thing as redemption, and as far as Melvin was concerned he didn't even want redemption. Because he didn't want to change.

Sure, he'd been a good boy at the penitentiary. Said all the right things, took the sexual predator mind-bender courses, and fooled the psychologists royally. They testified on his behalf at his parole hearing. He sat there and listened to the 'victim impact' statements from the pathetic relatives, tolerated their whining—and even faked a few tears. All for effect. And it worked.

Ten years he had spent in that hellhole of a prison—his asshole torn in twenty different directions by the black mamas who wanted a fat white man. He had tolerated that too. Didn't matter to him. He knew he'd be out long before those black murderers.

Melvin didn't consider himself a murderer—he was a 'life absorber.' He snuffed out tiny young lives whose energy and happiness were better off inside him. Their lives hadn't really mattered. He laughed to himself—if only the authorities knew that there had been more than one life absorbed by him. He was only convicted on that one murder—well of course, he had also been convicted of ten rapes but that was before he got smart and started absorbing their lives. They only found the one dead one—the others they'd never find. Too well hidden. If they had found the others, he knew he never would have qualified for early parole from his thirty- year sentence. The public outcry had been ferocious enough just for that one miserable life. Aside from his shrinks, no one wanted him on the street again.

He fingered his backpack. He felt secure having it with him. Of course, he would never be allowed to have these 'tools' back at the halfway house. Every bag was examined; on the way in, and on the way out. He had been smart enough to hide the pack behind a dumpster a block away from the house. So, when he was granted his freedom for a few hours a day, he just picked it up and headed out.

He hadn't decided on a target yet. He was just on a scouting mission right now. But soon. Soon. He had a girl in mind. She was about eight years old, long black hair, lovely little figure. He could imagine what she would look like when she grew up, but that image didn't do much for him. He wanted her to stay eight.

The girl whose life he had gotten caught absorbing had been around eight as well—lovely little lady, screamed like a banshee, struggled like a tiger. But, talented as hell once he'd put the hunting knife to her throat.

Melvin felt a bulge in his pants as he re-lived the episode. He needed it again. Soon.

Okay, he could see a nice bench over near the teeter-totter. He waddled over and sat down. There she was, with her pathetic protective mother. Swinging on the swing, mom pushing ever so gently. Melvin admitted grudgingly that the mother was somewhat good looking too, but she did nothing for him. He wouldn't waste his time on her.

In his practiced subtle manner, he removed his camera phone from the backpack and snapped off a couple.

He made his decision. This was the one he wanted. Today, he would do his last reconnaissance. He would follow mom and daughter home and find out where they lived. He knew they walked here every day, so it wouldn't be too far. Then one night, he would wait until the little girl's bedtime and watch which window lit up. Then he would find a way—no, he would execute a way—to remove her from the house and absorb her. Bliss.

Suddenly Melvin had a feeling. A feeling he'd been tuned into his entire adult life. Someone was watching him. He whirled his head around quickly, glancing in all directions. Nothing. He got up and strained his neck to look down the street—on the alert for any parked cars. Seemed all clear.

Probably nothing—just paranoia. But Melvin knew that occasionally parole officers would follow their stooges when they were out for their few hours of freedom. Could be. He had to be careful. His parole conditions prohibited the things in his backpack, but most importantly they prohibited him from being within 500 yards of a child less than sixteen years of age. So, he knew he was a double-violator at this very moment. He didn't want to go back to prison. He couldn't absorb any more lives if that happened, and his ass still hurt like hell. He couldn't go through that again.

Suddenly feeling scared, Melvin decided to skip his reconnaissance today. He'd do it another day. On a bright sunny day when the birds were singing. And when he didn't have a sick feeling in his stomach.

He looked furtively to his left and right and decided in an instant to avoid the street. He began his cut through the park, which was pretty much deserted at this dinner hour. He could hide as he walked through here—lots of thick tree trunks and bushes. He could make his way back to the dumpster, drop off his backpack and check in at the halfway house just in time for dinner. Tonight was roast beef. Melvin loved red meat.

He was nearing the end of the park and so far the coast seemed clear. He began to relax and at the same time regretting that he didn't follow through with his complete plan for the evening. Oh well, there would be a lot more evenings and that little girl wouldn't be turning nine years of age until a few months went by. He had lots of time.

He felt like he was flying. His feet went out from underneath him at the same instant he felt the impact just below his throbbing ass. He landed in the grass about fifteen away from where he had been. Was he dreaming?

Strong hands lifted him up underneath his arms. For a brief instant Melvin got a look at his assailant. Tall, handsome, piercing angry eyes. He wanted to ask him why he was attacking him, but he never got the chance.

The impact to the sides of his head shut his mouth. Probably because his mouth was now a crushed version of what it was. Incapable of sound other than a gurgling noise that Melvin didn't recognize. His view of his assailant was brief—because his eyeballs were now pushed out of their sockets, hanging onto his cheeks. Before his senses were robbed, Melvin was aware of a blur of movement from each side of his head, as the attacker's forearms thrust inward. For a brief violent instant, Melvin's head was in a vice grip. A vice grip that had crushed his head, shrunk the diameter of his skull by at least three inches. A squeeze that forced snot and wax from his nose and ears, blood from his mouth, and pulp from his eyes.

Melvin couldn't see a damn thing. And he couldn't think of anything other than a little dark-haired eight-year old girl. In his dying breath he was overwhelmed by the stark realization that he would not have the chance now to absorb her life.

CHAPTER FIFTEEN

From what he could discover, Fiona Perry was a pistol. An up-and-comer who bucked the system time and time again. An enquiring mind. Brett Horton loved that in a woman. And someone who didn't just accept the status quo—that was refreshing indeed.

She was pretty too—very pretty. He had pulled up some old clips of her press conferences, and she certainly was a looker. But a classy looker, very professional, someone who looked good but didn't dress for flash. Didn't expose her charms, even though from what Brett could tell, she had many.

He would arrange to meet Fiona Perry very soon, but he would wait a bit to give her time to do some digging for Dennis Chambers. Might as well let her do her work, so she could share it with him too. She might need some convincing though.

Putting his Fiona Perry file aside for awhile, Brett pondered that mysterious date, September 30, 1977—the day that all six communication arrays on the moon were shut down at exactly the same time.

He didn't know why, but a little voice was telling him to pursue that strange event. Why did that happen? And the fact that James Layton, Chief Counsel for the DOD, purportedly committed suicide three months later, on December 30th, 1977, and Lucy Chambers mysteriously retired as his heir apparent on December 31st, 1978. From all accounts, with a very handsome payoff.

The wheels were turning in Brett's curious brain. There were just too many odd things crammed into that short span of time back then.

Not to mention the old lady blurting out something about a non-existent Apollo 19, and his latest report from Felicity telling him about Lucy blurting out something else too: the word 'Shackleton.' Just one more thing that was now added to his research list.

But for now, he needed to learn more about that date and see what pieces might fit together.

Brett plugged the date, September 30, 1977, into the search bar of his browser and waited. His old computer was getting slower and slower by the day it seemed, but Brett was a patient man. He took a sip of his coffee and reclined in his leather executive chair. Feet up on the desk, he stared at the screen.

He scanned down the list of world events on that date. Ringo Starr released his fourth solo album. A meeting of world leaders took place in Montreal, Canada, and an addendum to an old treaty pertaining to civil aviation was signed.

Brett yawned.

Suddenly he perked up. The old Soviet Union had performed an underground nuclear explosive test on the archipelago known as Novaya Zemlya located in the far northern reaches of Russia, in the Arctic Ocean. *Hmm…that was interesting.*

Brett searched 'Novaya Zemlya.' He discovered that it consisted of two major islands and was a sensitive military area during the Cold War years. And it was still used today.

The Soviet Air Force, at that time, maintained a base on the southern part of the archipelago. It provided interceptor aircraft operations, but also supplied logistical support for the nearby nuclear test zone. This was the part that Brett found interesting. And shocking. This was the site of the largest and most powerful nuclear weapon ever detonated—a monstrous fifty-two megaton beast that was tested in 1961, nicknamed Tsar Bomba.

In the history of Novaya Zemlya from the commencement of nuclear tests in 1957 until their conclusion in 1990, the Soviet Union had conducted a mind-boggling 224 nuclear detonations with a cumulative explosive energy of 265 megatons. To put this into perspective, all the explosives used in World War II including the detonations of hydrogen bombs over Japan, amounted to only two megatons.

Brett was fascinated. And dumbfounded. Why didn't he and the rest of the world know about this?

He hit the 'back' button and reviewed again the events from September 30, 1977. Nothing more of any substance jumped out at him.

So, aside from Ringo Starr's record album, the only events of importance that day were the meeting of world leaders in Montreal about a civil aviation treaty; the exploding of a nuclear device in Russia; and the complete shutdown of six arrays of communications equipment on the moon—purportedly due to budget cuts.

Then something odd jumped out at him. It was odd because it had nothing to do with anything, yet it triggered a memory. Brett's brain was quick, and capable of recalling virtually any tiny little detail. Especially words that were said that seemed strange at the time they were said—his brain would recognize that they were out of context and store the memory away for a rainy day.

Today it was raining. And a postscript on the September 30, 1977 page showed a totally unrelated item. Unrelated in that it indeed happened on September 30th.

But in 1955, not 1977.

The death of iconic actor, James Dean.

This on its own wouldn't have caught Brett's attention at all. But his razor sharp brain made a connection. About ten years ago, he'd been having a beer—okay several beers—with an old friend. The friend was John Switzer, a prominent nuclear physicist and aerospace engineer with the Pentagon. John had been involved in almost every aspect of the space program when he'd been seconded from time to time to NASA.

John was much older than Brett, but they had hit it off right away when Brett had been involved in a couple of assignments with the Pentagon. One of them had been to provide protection for John and several of his nuclear colleagues. This wasn't normal practice for the Secret Service, but the White House made an exception due to threats that had been posted against several nuclear scientists. So, Brett was assigned—and he and John had become fast friends.

John was a genius. And a little bit crazy as geniuses tended to be. His most prominent fault, though, was his loose tongue. Especially over a few beers. John loved beer.

About ten years ago, they had been in a bar together, catching up. John had already been retired for five years and was spending far too much of his retirement drinking. His brilliant mind was no longer stimulated, so he turned to booze to try to forget how brilliant he had once been.

Brett was laughing and joking with him over some of the silly governmental things that both of them had witnessed over the years, and in one story he was telling John about a protection detail he had been asked to provide for the Queen of England on one of her visits to the White House.

John sucked back his tenth beer and slurred, *"That's nothing. I worked with The James Dean. Trust me, no story you could tell me could compare to that!"*

Brett simply looked at him and thought that he had truly drunk his limit. He said, *"John, what are you talking about? James Dean died decades ago."*

John poured another beer from the draught jug. *"I'm sure you can live with what you did for the Queen of England. I'm having a tough slog living with what I did for The James Dean."*

"What did you do, John? What on earth are you talking about?"

John just drank his beer and ignored the question. Back then Brett had shrugged it off as just the incoherent ramblings of an old, drunk genius.

But now he thought about it. Was it just coincidence that the date he was researching had a connection with the death of the actor? The same date, different year.

A nuclear blast happened that day in Russia. Communications equipment was shut off on the moon. And a drunk nuclear scientist was hinting that there was something he had done that was related to James Dean. How could all of this be connected? Was he just reaching?

No—Brett was convinced he was not. And that memory from the past had struck him strange at the time, but he had retained the memory because there was something sinister about what John was saying. And John clearly hadn't wanted to say anything more.

He had to be in his mid-eighties now. Brett wondered. Would he say more at this late stage of his life?

He was determined to find out. See if John could be convinced to say more. Maybe at such an old age now, he wouldn't give a shit.

And Brett's computer-like brain had held onto one thing that was the most befuddling. Why had John referred to the incident as 'The James Dean.' He hadn't said 'James Dean.' He'd said 'The James Dean.'

Almost like it was a thing rather than a person.

Brett thought that was a significant anomaly.

Very significant—and he was trained to pay attention to significant things, even if they seemed immaterial in the larger scheme of things.

CHAPTER SIXTEEN

"This isn't working at all. She's totally unresponsive. Not even listening to my voice."

Brett leaned his head in close to Lucy, and passed his hand in front of her eyes. Her pupils didn't move.

"Do you think she's hypnotized and we don't know it? I mean; she does seem to be in kind of a daze."

Felicity shook her head. "No, she's not under. There would be a response to my questions, my voice. I think her mind is just too far gone for me to be able to hypnotize her. I knew our chances were slim—Alzheimer's patients are poor subjects, unless they're in the earliest stages of the disease."

Brett looked at his watch. "What time does super-cop come home?"

"Oh, not for quite a while yet—we still have time, at least a couple of hours."

Brett realized that they had neglected to close one of the window blinds in the drawing room. He got up and pulled the wand.

His movement provoked a reaction from Lucy. She started rocking in her chair, and her eyes darted nervously around the room.

Felicity started talking to her again—real slow, real soft.

"Lucy, can you hear me?"

Lucy nodded.

Encouraged by the tiny reaction Felicity decided to cut to the chase, fearing that this new alertness may not last long.

"Lucy, could you please tell me about Apollo 19?"

Lucy continued to rock, but Felicity could tell that she seemed to understand the question. There was pensiveness in her eyes.

"Can't talk about it. They'll kill my family."

Brett moved back to his seat, captivated by Lucy's answer.

"I understand that, Lucy. But we can protect you. We're good friends of your son, Dennis."

Lucy suddenly smiled—a big broad motherly smile. "Is Dennis home? Call him for me?"

"He's just making coffee for us all in the kitchen. He'll be back in a few minutes. But you have real reason to worry, Lucy. Dennis is in terrible danger. Unless you tell us about Apollo 19, we can't protect him."

Tears began rolling down Lucy's cheeks. Felicity raised a tissue to her face and dried her eyes. "Do you understand, Lucy? Dennis is in danger. He wants you to help us."

Lucy nodded and raised her hand to her forehead. She began rubbing her right temple. "I have a headache. This is all too much for me."

Felicity picked up her personal recorder from the coffee table and placed it on her lap. She didn't want to miss a thing. Lucy was ready to talk.

"Lucy—Apollo 19. When did it fly?"

Lucy winced. "Are you sure Denny's in trouble?"

"Yes, Lucy. We want to save him. Help us, please?"

Lucy squeezed her hands together until the whites of her knuckles showed.

"It flew in 1977."

"And was there an Apollo 18 as well?"

Lucy started to squirm in her seat. "Yes."

"When did it fly?"

"1975."

Felicity looked closely into Lucy's eyes. She was starting to lose her. Her pupils were becoming fixed again. She knew she would probably only have time for one more question.

"What is 'Shackleton,' Lucy?"

Lucy started rocking again, and bobbing her head up and down. Felicity grabbed her arm, squeezed hard, and repeated the question. "What is 'Shackleton,' Lucy?" She asked it louder this time and that seemed to shock Lucy back into submission.

She stopped rocking. "I knew it as 'Rebel's Cause.' They didn't call it 'Shackleton' until 1994."

"Called what, Lucy?" Felicity was yelling now. "Called what—tell me! Save your son, tell me! Now!"

Brett put his hand on Felicity's shoulder. "C'mon, Felicity. She's just an old woman. You're going to scare her to death."

Felicity spun her head around and glared at him. "Hey, you want answers, don't you? And I've been promised a big bonus out of this if we can find out where the package is, so let me do what I'm trained to do."

Brett glared back. "I'm calling the shots, Felicity. We're not going to torture this old lady to get our answers."

"You wimping out, Brett? Cold feet? Big bad killer can't watch an old lady get yelled at?"

Brett slapped her hard. Hard enough that she fell backwards out of her chair.

Lucy screamed.

Felicity stared up at him from the oak hardwood floor, anger seething from her cold eyes.

"You're right, I can't watch an old lady get yelled at, Felicity, but I can sure as hell hit a young one. Wrap this up. We've lost her now, anyway. And I have enough information to dig further. So—wrap it up, understand?" Brett ran his fingers through his thick sandy brown hair. "I'm gonna use the loo. Calm her down while I'm gone."

Felicity pulled herself up off the floor and watched Brett walk down the hall toward the bathroom. "I'll calm her down alright, you arrogant prick," she whispered under her breath.

She reached into her medical bag and brought out a syringe, a cotton ball and a bottle of pure alcohol. She worked fast—poured the alcohol onto the cotton ball, roughly grabbed Lucy's right arm and rubbed the alcohol onto a spot on her forearm. Then she raised the syringe, tapped it twice, and jammed it into Lucy's arm pressing hard on the plunger.

Lucy lurched backwards causing the rocking chair to almost tip over— Felicity caught it just in time. Then she steadied it, watched, and waited.

"What the fuck is that in your hand?" Brett was back. "What did you give her?"

"Settle down—it's just Sodium Pentothal. We use it in hypnosis sometimes. We call it drug-assisted hypnosis."

Brett grabbed Felicity by the hair, yanked her to her feet, and dragged her off to the side out of Lucy's view. Bringing her face within inches of his, he growled, "I know what it is, you little bitch. I've used it before. Truth Serum. And it's dangerous as hell."

She wriggled free. "I'm a nurse and a trained hypnotherapist. I know what I'm doing. The drug doesn't make someone tell the truth; it merely inhibits them from telling a lie. It's very effective. We should have all of our answers within a few minutes."

First they heard heavy breathing, then choking noises. Just before Lucy toppled forward out of her rocking chair, she clutched her chest with both hands and whispered, "Help!"

She fell hard before either of them could react. Face-first onto the hardwood floor. Blood was trickling out of her nose by the time Felicity was down on the floor beside her.

She rolled her over and checked her pulse. Felicity shrieked. "No pulse! Help me, Brett, help me!"

She began CPR and when she'd completed 100 cycles, Brett took over. They took turns for about twenty minutes before finally giving up.

Brett sighed, and wiped the sweat from his brow. "The poor soul is dead. This was totally unnecessary, Felicity. A waste."

He reached down to the floor, picked up Felicity's personal recorder and shoved it into one of the six inside pockets of his Saville Row suit.

"I'm taking this with me. You phone 911, clean up here, and give the best explanation you can as to what happened. Sudden heart attack. You were in the kitchen when it happened, blah, blah. You know the routine."

Brett got up and walked to the front door. Just before turning the handle he heard a car door slam. He peeked out through the tiny window beside the door.

"Shit, he's home! What's the best way for me to get out of here?"

Felicity jumped to her feet. "Don't go out the back door—it's too visible from the neighbor gardening in the yard behind. Take the stairs to the office on the third floor, on this front side of the house. It has a door onto an outside landing, and a fire escape down to the street. It's shrouded in trees, so no one will see you."

Brett took the stairs three at a time. Ran to the office and found the door to the fire escape. As he spun himself onto the spiral metal staircase, he lost his footing and fell head first to the next landing down. Aside from torn pants he was none the worse the wear, and quickly continued his journey down to the relative solace of the side yard.

As he snuck quietly through the bushes he heard a deep voice resonating through the open drawing room window.

"Hi Felicity. How's Mom today?"

CHAPTER SEVENTEEN

Brett was relieved to be home. He cracked open a beer and sank down into the supple Italian leather couch in his living room. He took a sip and sighed. The death of Lucille Chambers had affected him. Brett was a tough guy but he had a soft spot for the vulnerable. His own mother, who was about ten years younger than Lucy, was herself in a nursing home. She too was afflicted with Alzheimer's disease.

When he saw Lucy being tormented, he saw his mother. When he watched Lucy die, he watched his mother.

That little power-mad whore, Felicity, was out of control. He'd have to take care of it. She was a loose cannon, and as the one in charge of this investigation, it was his responsibility to handle it. He hadn't yet decided how he would do it—perhaps put her on a plane with some money and order her to never return if she valued her life. Or, just take her life.

He slipped his hand into one of the inside pockets of his jacket...and felt a surge of panic. He quickly checked out all of the other pockets. It was gone! The personal recorder was gone!

And in a flash, he knew where it was. It was either on the fire escape or lying down in the garden below. When he had fallen it must have come tumbling out. In his haste to get out of there, he hadn't been aware that the weight in his pocket had been lightened.

Shit!

Brett grabbed his cellphone and hit the speed dial for Felicity's mobile. It rang three times, and then went to voice mail. He didn't want to leave a message—too risky in case the police were suspicious about anything at all and confiscated her phone.

He knew he couldn't go back there right now. The paramedics would be at the house, probably the medical examiner too and no doubt the police as well. He would have to patiently wait a day or two and then make a visit under the cover of darkness. It would normally be difficult at nighttime to find a small object like a recorder, but it wouldn't be for Brett. He had a nice pair of night-vision goggles.

All he could do was hope that the recorder would still be there. If not, it was a game-changer. He would just have to deal with it.

But while his voice was on that recorder, he couldn't be identified by just his voice. So he was clear, he rationalized. And his phone was a disposable untraceable one, so they couldn't track him with the history on Felicity's phone.

And while he wanted to get that recorder back, he couldn't take a chance snooping around that house looking for it and then getting caught with it. If that happened they would definitely be able to connect him to the voice.

Other than the voiceprint on the recorder, there was only one person who could identify him as being in that house.

*****

Mai Lee went about her business—the business of cleaning Mr. Chambers' house. It was the day after Mrs. Chambers' death. The burial would be quick, to be held the day after tomorrow. The house had been a hive of activity since her passing, and the reception after the funeral would attract over 100 guests to the house. The place was a mess now and would be an even bigger mess that day.

But this is what she was paid to do, and she loved hard work. Mai had worked for Mr. Chambers for five years, and he was always so generous with her. Gave her much more than her agreed wage. He tipped generously and always complimented her on the splendid job she did. And he trusted her to just tidy up after him, put things away in their place—even if it was a place she alone decided was best, he didn't care. He trusted her. And she looked out for him. In her eyes, he was a prince.

Mai had finished most of the house, and was now concentrating on Mr. Chambers' third floor office. He hadn't spent any time up here over the last twenty-four hours. She knew he'd use it as his refuge for the next little while though. Once his dear mother was at rest.

Mai also had one more room than usual to clean, with Mr. Chambers' sister, Melissa, staying over. But she didn't mind—she liked Melissa.

Mai noticed that the door to the fire escape landing was unlocked. Unusual—perhaps Mr. Chambers had taken up smoking again? She wouldn't be surprised, with the terrible stress he'd been under.

She opened the door and looked out. Quite a few leaves had piled up on the landing—not safe at all if Mr. Chambers had to use the escape. He might slip.

She took her broom outside and began sweeping them down to the lawn. Then she noticed something—an object lying on the next landing down. She carefully negotiated her way down the spiral staircase and picked it up. Mai could tell that it was an electronic gadget of some kind. Mr. Chambers must have dropped it when he was out here smoking.

She went back up the stairs and into the office. There was one shelf on his bookcase where he kept some electronic things: mini stereo, cellphone, Blackberry, coffee maker. She decided to just put the thing there, a logical place where he would see it.

She smiled. Mai loved taking care of Mr. Chambers and putting his things where they should be. Sometimes she even felt as if she was his wife. She smiled again.

*****

Brett's night-vision goggles were working like a charm. But aside from a few worms squirming around in the moisture of the lawn, there was nothing to see. He checked the fire escape and noticed it had been swept clean of the leaves that had caused him to slip. He checked down in the flowerbeds and in the grass—it was gone. He had to assume it was in the hands of Dennis Chambers now. He had to assume the worst.

He cursed his clumsiness—unusual for him to ever slip up. And unusual for him to tolerate a loose cannon like Felicity. Now that the recorder had most likely been played by Chambers, she had become a huge liability. She could identify him. The death of Lucy was, at the very least, manslaughter—and he had been a party to it. The DOD wouldn't protect him, because officially he wasn't even working for them. For them, he didn't really exist. So, Brett had to clean up the mess.

Felicity had to disappear, one way or another.

*****

Dennis sat in his office staring out the window. He felt empty inside. It had been a long few days and putting his mother in the ground, while inevitable, still broke his heart. She had been mentally gone for so long now, only making brief appearances in the last few weeks. He felt guilty because he had used those brief appearances mainly to probe her mind about the mystery. He had used her, and now she was dead.

Melissa moved in the day after Lucy's death and she was still here. He was glad to have his big sister around, but regretted that it took the death of their mother to prompt them to spend time with each other. He had chatted with Mel already about mom's lucid moments, but didn't want to volunteer too much information to her yet. He hadn't told her anything about a supposed 'package,' or Lucy's ramblings about Apollo 19, 18 or Shackleton. He intended to keep that to himself for the time being.

Felicity had been so upset. He felt sorry for the poor girl. Apparently, she had heard the crash from the kitchen and came running in to discover Lucy face down on the floor. He was grateful for her heroic attempts at CPR to bring her back to life. The medical examiner had confirmed that aggressive attempts had been made—three of Lucy's ribs were broken, which was not unusual with aggressive CPR. He knew she'd tried.

The cause of death was confirmed as a massive coronary. Dennis had waived his right to have an autopsy conducted. What was the point? At her age, Dennis knew it had only been a matter of time, and the Alzheimer's only made things worse. There had been no quality of life for her anymore, so in a way it was a blessing. At least that's what Dennis told himself. It made him feel a wee bit better.

He got up and went over to the coffee machine. He needed a serious jolt of java.

Hello? What's this thing?

He picked it up and recognized it right away as a personal recording device. It wasn't his. He had never even owned one of these things. *How did it get into his office?*

He sat down and hit the power button, then 'rewind,' then 'play.'

He listened.

As he did, his stomach tightened into a knot, a knot that he knew only vomiting would cure. The forefingers of both hands instinctively stiffened into rigid shafts, and the toes of his feet curled back in unison.

As the tape progressed it became harder and harder for him to breathe. He tried to generate saliva to soothe his dry throat, but it was impossible.

And during this time that his bodily functions were playing tricks on him, he thought of only one person. A person who just a few days ago he had thanked profusely for trying gallantly to save his mother's life.

*****

Felicity Dobson was tired. Carrying her packages back from the all-night grocery store, she thought about how quickly she had been assimilated into a new assignment already: a lesbian diplomat attached to the Russian Embassy. Olga, or whatever her real name was, had secrets that the DOD needed to learn. And she had a weakness—a weakness for young women who looked like Felicity Dobson.

Felicity didn't fancy women in the least—but she fancied power and money. And she would do anything for either one. It was just a job. And one day she would be the one handing out assignments like this one to other young women. She would have earned her stripes and the others could do the dirty work. She could hardly wait for that day to come.

In the meantime, she would be content to prostitute herself. For the United States of America.

She actually loved her job with the Defense Intelligence Agency. They had recruited her in college, paid for her education and set her up in the nursing service, The Casper Agency. All of the nurses at Casper worked for the DIA. The Casper Agency was simply a division of the DIA, a front for spying activities.

And the work she did was intriguing to say the least. But it required her to work with, and defer to, operatives like Brett Horton from time to time. She could tolerate that—he was an asshole as far as she was concerned, but she could work with assholes. Most people trained by the government were assholes and she included herself in that description. It took one to know one, and she knew what she was.

The most annoying part of Lucy Chambers' death was having to give up her cellphone to the police. Confiscating her phone was the first thing they did once they heard her story. Felicity knew it was just routine, but it meant she now had to go out and get another phone. And she had liked that old phone. She had just become accustomed to all the features. At least she didn't have to worry about anything incriminating on it. Felicity was always careful how she used her cellphone. Whenever she had talked to Brett, she'd used a landline.

She opened the front door of her downtown brownstone with her free hand, and walked down to the kitchen. Ginger, her beloved Siamese cat, was waiting patiently for her. Felicity opened her back door and let Ginger out. She wouldn't be out long. Ginger was a sophisticated house cat, not a wanderer. Within two minutes on the nose, she'd be scratching on the door.

Felicity carefully put her groceries away and then checked her phone messages. Nothing but annoying telemarketers. She thought about Dennis Chambers as she deleted the messages, wondering if she'd hear from him in the next few days. She would love it if there were a message on the machine from him. Even though her assignment with him was over, she'd try to arrange to bump into him again. He seemed to have bought her story hook, line and sinker, and was clearly enamored with her heroic efforts to save the old bag's life. A night out with him, then a night in, might be very pleasant indeed.

She checked her watch. Ginger? She'd been outside for ten minutes now. Very unusual. She opened the door and called her name. No sign of her.

Felicity put her jacket back on and went out into the yard. It was dark, but she knew she could easily see Ginger just by the white of her eyes. She scoured the yard with her eyes.

It felt like her head was being drilled from behind. The impact came at the base of her skull, penetrating her spine. She could feel her body lurching forward, then her head flopping back. In that instant she knew she had a hole—she could feel it. The back of her neck was getting wetter by the millisecond and she could do nothing other than flop helplessly to the ground. Felicity felt the dew of the grass on her cheeks and knew without a doubt that her life was slipping away.

Just before her eyeballs rolled upwards never to be seen again, she glanced up and saw a dark figure kneeling beside her. He sighed. Then his arm moved at lightning speed, and she felt as if her forehead had been jackhammered.

Felicity's tongue shot out of the corner of her mouth and tasted the dew. And she wondered...*where's Ginger?*

CHAPTER EIGHTEEN

John Switzer said, "Brett, if you're buying the beer, I'll be there!" So Brett was buying. They were meeting at a very quiet and classy bar located in the far east end of the city, well away from political and military eyes. But in Washington, you just could never truly be sure, safe, or nonchalant. They were indeed everywhere—who 'they' were could be anybody.

For a man in his mid-eighties, Brett thought that John sounded pretty sharp, especially considering that he'd probably been drinking his life away the last ten years. His wife was long dead, and John had never married again. So he was alone—which for most people was not a good thing. Brett hoped that a few beers and the natural cynicism that usually set in at old age, would allow John's tongue to wag. And wag a lot. And John's tongue had always been loose to begin with.

Brett checked his watch—still a couple of hours before he was to meet John. Time enough to do some more Internet surfing, to help give background and ammunition to the questions he was going to ask John today.

Surfing the word 'Shackleton' brought up two things: one that fell under the 'who cares' category, and the other one…well, it caused Brett's heart to skip a beat.

Ernest Shackleton had been an Anglo-Irish explorer of the South Pole. On earth.

But there was another 'Shackleton.'

On the moon.

A crater on the moon was known as 'Shackleton Crater,' named after the noted explorer, presumably because it was on the moon's South Pole and good old Ernest had staked his claim on the earth's South Pole.

But this wasn't just any old crater. It was immense: twenty-one kilometers in diameter and over four kilometers deep; about as deep as earth's oceans. Due to the orbit of the moon, the interior of the crater lies in perpetual darkness. But…the peaks along the crater's rim are exposed to almost continuous sunlight.

It is suspected that a huge comet caused this impact crater, and since the composition of comets is primarily ice, it is likely that the extreme low temperature interior of 'Shackleton' functioned in such a way as to trap and freeze the remnants of the comet. Measurements taken by orbiting spacecraft indicated higher than normal amounts of hydrogen inside the crater.

Ergo—ice, water.

Brett made himself another coffee, and checked his watch again. Good, still another hour before he had to leave to meet John. He was reading so fast, his eyes were starting to sting. He retrieved some eye drops from the bathroom and applied two to each eye. The soothing cool feeling was a relief. He couldn't stop reading—excitement was surging through his veins, the more he read about 'Shackleton.'

He clicked on a couple of additional articles, some fairly recent. Apparently, there was serious talk about future mining projects at the crater, to capture deposits of hydrogen in water form. Also, there seemed to be plans for a large infrared telescope to be placed on the crater floor. The extreme low temperatures made it ideal for infrared observations. And solar cells placed on the perpetually illuminated rim of the crater could provide eternal power to any new observatory built on the crater floor.

The last important notation that Brett read was NASA's interest in making 'Shackleton' the site for a future lunar outpost—possibly to be up and running by 2020 and staffed by a permanent crew by 2024. It was considered an ideal site due to the continuous sunlight at the rim of the crater and outwards on the surface of the moon's south pole. Solar power would be easy, and the mining potential of the crater was immense.

Brett took a deep breath, and said out loud, "So, this is what 'Shackleton' is."

But he knew this wasn't enough—there was more to this. More than met the eye and more than the Internet was revealing. And Lucy knew about it. And he was 100% certain that John Switzer knew about it—whatever it is.

Then his quick brain retrieved information once again. "Rebel's Cause." That's what Lucy had said 'Shackleton' had been called originally. She said the name was changed in 1994.

Brett's mind began connecting the dots.

During the discussion ten years ago over beers with John Switzer, John had said he'd worked with 'The James Dean.' Lucy said Apollo 19 flew in 1977. The Russians tested a nuclear bomb on September 30th, 1977. The moon's communications equipment was shut down on September 30th, 1977. James Dean died on Sept. 30th, 1955. And Lucy had referred to 'Shackleton' as having been called 'Rebel's Cause.'

The iconic actor's most iconic movie was 'Rebel Without a Cause.'

*****

The black van cruised slowly down Elm Street, passing by a high school, then turned slowly into a mall parking lot. Fraser Benton pulled into a parking spot close by the entrance to a twenty-four hour convenience store. This was where he did some of his business several nights a week. Stupid kids hung out here waiting for him and others like him. He didn't care—it was just a business.

He sold heroin. And he killed young people. Or, at least his product did.

Fraser had been in and out of prison most of his life. Why they kept letting him out, he had no idea.

He was tapped into one of the most lucrative drug trades in Washington, D.C. The business was always waiting for him when he got out. He had stashed at least five million dollars away in safe places over the years, money that the crooked cops could never get their hands on. God knows they'd tried. Tried to make deals with him, cut him loose if he shared. He always refused. He figured the only people in the world more despicable than him, were the ones who pretended to be honest and tried to profit from him.

This mall was just one of many locations in Washington that were his turf at certain times of the day and night. Drug dealers knew each other and for the most part respected each other's right to earn a living. Sometimes there were problems, but for the most part it was civil.

Fraser got out of the van and walked around to the passenger side where the sliding door was. He opened it and took a quick glance inside—he had it filled with tarpaulins, cases of pop, and of course his stock. He sat on the edge and waited. Waited for the throng of kids who knew enough to show up at this time, at this place.

Ha, so predictable. Three waif-like girls were crossing the parking lot heading straight toward him. He'd seen these girls before, they were regular customers—couldn't be more than seventeen. He was still offering them the discount versions of the product.

Heroin was actually cheap on the streets, cheaper now than the prescription drugs which had become so popular lately. Their popularity caused the prices to rise, and heroin's price to drop. But what was necessary was to get the kids hooked, and to do that he had to sell it to them cheap for the first few weeks or months. Then, once they were hooked, his price would rise—dramatically.

He thought it was just like fishing. Tease, tease, tease. Then set the hook—once he was able to complete that fishing process, they were loyal customers for life. Then they would kill, steal, prostitute—anything at all to get their fix. That's when the spin-off revenue would start. He didn't just make his money from selling heroin. He made some by selling kids to pimps, thieves, and killers. The kids became useful once they were hooked. Robots who would do anything to get high, and it was profitable business. Kind of like corporations that did strategic alliances with other corporations.

Fraser was a corporation.

He studied the girls as they got closer. God, they were almost at the point where he could set the hook. He could tell just by their frail, gaunt appearance. They looked a mess.

Fraser had promised himself a long time ago that he would never ever take this shit himself. He would sell it, but he wouldn't take it. He didn't want to get fucked up—he didn't mind fucking up other people, but he wouldn't do it to himself.

He wondered to himself if these girls ever got screwed—like, who would want them? They looked like skinny little sacks of shit.

They stopped in front of him. Didn't say anything. Didn't need to. They knew that he knew why they were there. Fraser took a quick glance around him. Coast was clear—it usually was. The D.C. police were severely understaffed and hopeless at their attempts to stop men like him. He had pretty much a free ride.

Fraser reached back into the van with a big smile on his face. Reached for his bag of tricks.

He watched in shock as a tarpaulin was shed and an arm shot out faster than he could blink. A figure dressed in black from his head to his toes slammed Fraser's forearm with his own. He heard the snap and saw the jagged edges of bones sticking out as his arm broke into two useless pieces, resembling a broken branch after a windstorm.

The girls screamed and ran—Fraser figured in that instant that the man wanted to not only hurt him, but wanted also to scare his clients into perhaps thinking of buying ice cream next time instead of heroin.

Strangely, he felt no pain—just numbness and shock at seeing the abomination that used to be his arm. He looked up at the figure in the van. He was wearing a balaclava.

Fraser said calmly, "Okay, you've made your point. Now, drive me to a hospital quickly." Blood was pouring all over the floor of his van, and Fraser now began to feel the numbness beginning to subside. The pain was starting and he knew it was going to be ferocious in just a few seconds.

He didn't have a few seconds, and the balaclava didn't even acknowledge that Fraser had spoken.

Both of the man's hands worked in unison now. Fast, a blur, and just fingers. One stabbed him in the chest, and the other slammed into his forehead. Bam, bam! The impacts threw Fraser out of the van, crashing him onto the pavement.

As darkness overtook his brain, Fraser heard the familiar sound of his beloved Suburban's engine start up and was only slightly horrified as it backed up out of the parking spot, rolling its twenty inch tires over his flailing legs.

CHAPTER NINETEEN

"It was sitting on the cabinet in my office."

Barb pushed 'stop' on the recorder, and looked up. "Do you think she was snooping around in your office, and just forgot to take this with her?"

Dennis frowned. "No, I don't think Felicity would be that stupid. This is incriminating as hell. She killed my mother. And who the fuck was that man on the tape?"

"Well, at least he seemed to have some sense of decency about him."

"Yeah, I'll give him that. He seemed to be the one in charge, didn't he?"

Barb got up and poured herself another coffee. "Yes, he did. He was the controller."

Dennis glanced up, puzzled. "Controller? That sounds like kind of an official term, Barb. What's the deal?"

Barb looked away. "No deal, Denny. Just that he sounds like the boss."

"Don't look away. I can see right through you. What's going on, Barb? Tell me."

Barb sat down again and faced Dennis. "I warned you about Felicity, remember?"

"Sure, I remember—but you weren't specific. You said something about her being too pretty, and that the Casper Agency hired nurses who looked like her. That wasn't much of a warning."

"I had a top security clearance, Denny. Some warnings I give out have to be vague. Protecting secrets is an obligation that continues even after retirement."

"Bullshit! Your best friend has just been killed. If you could have just warned me enough to make me fire this girl, mom might still be alive. What didn't you tell me?"

Barb crossed her legs and shifted herself back in her chair. Dennis could tell she looked uncharacteristically nervous. "Oh, Denny, what have you got yourself into?"

"Answer me, Barb! Tell me now so I can at least choose to prevent myself from getting killed. You tell me what I've gotten myself into here."

"It's something they want." Barb swallowed hard. "The Casper Agency is a front for the Defense Intelligence Agency. So, Felicity was a domestic spy. The nurses at the agency are all trained spies. Their job is to obtain information. The agency gets all the lucrative health care provider assignments in the city—for politicians and foreign embassy staff. The nurses then do double-duty."

Dennis stood up. "Shit!" He threw his coffee cup into the fireplace, smashing it against the brick hearth surround. "You couldn't have told me at least that much?"

Barb clasped her hands together and looked up at him, pleading. "Denny, I didn't think they'd hurt her. I figured they just wanted to be close to her to get some clues as to where that package is. If I thought for a second that Lucy would be in danger I would have brought a halt to it."

"Too late now, Barb. You missed your chance. You showed allegiance to the wrong people. Get out!"

Barb stood. "Denny…don't do this. Forgive me…please, Denny."

"Maybe later. But right now, I need you to leave. I don't want to see your lying face."

*****

The food at Luigi's was as good as ever. Dennis and Fiona were just finishing up their seafood linguini, and he for one was thinking seriously about ordering dessert. This was their fourth dinner together. Each time he'd learned a little bit more, but mainly things about Fiona, not about the mystery.

She hadn't discovered too much yet about any secrets at the Pentagon, except that everyone she talked to was tight-lipped about the Apollo missions. The standard answer she got from people in the know was, "Don't ask."

He'd learned one important thing though—he was immensely attracted to her, and he was getting similar vibes from her side of the table. Dennis made a vow to himself that the next time they got together, they wouldn't be talking about the Pentagon, secret packages, Apollo 19, or 'Shackleton.' They would have a real date.

"Dennis, it's sad that your mom died the way she did. I know she was not in her right mind most of the time, but it hurts me to think that she suffered a heart attack and no one was in the room to help her."

Dennis had decided before tonight's dinner that he would tell Fiona about the recorder. He had to trust her. So he did. And she listened.

When he finished his story, she shook her head slowly, sadly. "God, Denny, that's horrible. That's murder, or at the very least manslaughter."

"Yes, and I would love to get my hands on the man whose voice was on that tape."

"But it sounds like he tried to keep it civil at least."

"He did, but he was still there, and he was the one in charge."

"Denny, are you going to take that recorder to the police?"

"I am the police, Fiona. And no, I'm not going to. It'll just get buried. It was made very clear to me that the Washington Police Department will not investigate anything to do with the Pentagon. Outside their jurisdiction, and too hot a political potato to handle. So, I'd be wasting my time—and I'd get into trouble."

"That's a heavy burden for you to carry around."

"I'm tough. I can handle it."

Fiona sipped her wine. "So, it's clear on the tape that Apollo 19 went into space in 1977, and Apollo 18 was there in 1975. If your mother can be believed. If those missions did take place, they were kept totally from the public. I remember that Apollo 18 had been scheduled, then a public announcement cancelled it."

She took another sip, a longer one this time. "Do you remember that movie that came out a year or so ago? It was called 'Apollo 18.' Based on the premise that the mission indeed took place under the cover of darkness, and control of the mission was taken out of NASA's hands and put under the control of the Pentagon. So, in essence, it became a military mission."

"Yes, I saw it. A dead cosmonaut was found on the moon and living organisms infected the American astronauts—they never returned to earth."

Fiona pushed the fringe of her hair away from her eyes. "Perhaps that movie only scratched the surface?"

"Yeah, perhaps. And this 'Shackleton' thing. I did some checking on the Internet—Ernest Shackleton was a South Pole explorer and there is a crater on the South Pole of the moon named after him. Quite a huge crater, and it's thought to contain ice from comet impacts."

"You said your mom referred to it as 'Rebel's Cause'?"

"Yep—don't have a clue what that means. The name of the crater was changed to 'Shackleton' in 1994. So despite the state of mom's mind, she was bang-on correct with that date. I checked online. However, I couldn't find any reference to the original 'Rebel's Cause' name."

Fiona pushed her plate toward the middle of the table, and rested her elbows on the edge. "This is what I find intriguing. Her mind was in an almost catatonic state most of the time—okay, that's an exaggeration, but you know what I mean. Yet, when she was lucid, she was able to give that date convincingly, and she was correct. We have to give some credence to those other two dates: 1977 and 1975."

"Yes, we do."

Fiona shifted uncomfortably in her chair. "Barb called me."

Dennis grimaced. "Okay."

"I know you don't want to talk to her right now. She told me you haven't returned any of her phone calls."

"No, I haven't."

"She's really upset, Denny. And she's very sorry. She told me about the Casper Agency thing. I wasn't aware of that, and I know that Barb is violating confidences by even telling me that, let alone telling you that. But she wanted me to understand what made you upset."

Dennis began cracking his knuckles. "Okay, so you understand. What does that do for me?"

"Nothing—except that I think you should forgive her. You have to understand what a difficult position she was in. The conflict. The confidentiality. But she's thrown that out the window now with what she confirmed to you. She desperately wants to help you still."

Dennis winced, and looked down at the table.

Fiona cocked her head trying to make eye contact. "Denny, she's told me something else. Kind of an olive branch to show you that she's sincere. She wanted to tell you herself, but you won't call her back."

Dennis looked up, interested now. "What did she tell you?"

Fiona lowered her voice. "Lucy's boss, James Layton, the former Chief Counsel for the DOD?"

"Yes, the one who committed suicide?"

Fiona whispered. "He didn't commit suicide. He was murdered."

*****

Fiona got out of the cab in front of her handsome row house on P Street NW, having just given the driver an extra big tip. She felt especially buoyant tonight, and when she felt that way she tipped anyone generously even if their service sucked.

She knew she was falling in love with Dennis Chambers.

Tonight was only their fourth time together, but she felt drawn to him. The chemistry, just talking together, was amazingly electric. She found it difficult to take her eyes off his handsome face, and when he looked into her eyes it was like he was peering into her soul. He seemed so intelligent, and passionate about things he believed in. And his curious brain lit a fire in her journalist's mind—he was fascinating to talk to.

And tonight they agreed upon a real date. Next week they would see a movie together—the latest 'end of the world' disaster flick. She discovered that he loved the same types of movies that she did—shockers, thrillers, science fiction, mysteries.

She never thought she would ever meet a man like Dennis Chambers. He made her want to be in a relationship again.

Fiona unlocked her front door, and skipped happily inside. She did a little pirouette in the hallway just before she was grabbed around the neck from behind, and thrown to the floor.

His face was shielded by some kind of black mask, and the rest of his outfit was black too. She could feel his moist breath through the wool of the mask, and when he began to speak his voice was muffled.

He sat on top of her with both hands at her throat—not squeezing, just threatening. Fiona swung her fist towards his face, but he deftly dodged the blow. He grabbed both of her arms and forced them down to her side.

He was kneeling now, with both knees pinning her arms. His ass was parked on her stomach. And the hands went back to her throat.

"Just relax, little lady. I'm not going to hurt you unless I have to."

Fiona was terrified. She feared the worst; a worry of most single women who braved living in Washington's violent city core. She was going to be raped.

The dark figure shifted his weight, and released his hands from her throat. His muffled voice continued. "You had dinner tonight with Dennis Chambers. Yes, I know what you do, and when you do it. So let's get that out of the way so you know how capable I am, okay?"

Fiona was frozen.

"I want you to at least nod your understanding."

Fiona nodded.

"Good. We have a connection. Now, what information did you pass on to him tonight and the other three nights you met with him?"

Fiona swallowed hard. She shook her head.

The dark figure sighed and raised his hand high above his head. Then he brought it down towards her face, shifting at the very last second and slamming it into one of her cherry hardwood floorboards. She heard a distinctive crack.

The man grabbed her head, lifted it up and swiveled it sideways so she could see the floor. What she saw was a crack that resembled the San Andreas Fault extending all the way along one of her precious boards. She was shocked that a mere hand could do such damage.

He rested her head gently down on the floor again. "Now that you've seen what I can do to hardwood, just imagine what I could do to your skull."

Fiona nodded furiously.

"Good. Talk to me, Fiona Perry."

Fiona swallowed hard again with what little saliva she was able to generate. Her mouth felt like sandpaper. "I...haven't told him...much. I found out that...a man named James Layton, former Chief Counsel at the Pentagon... didn't commit suicide...back in 1977."

"So he was murdered?"

Fiona nodded.

"What led to the murder?"

Fiona was fighting the urge to cry. "He...was despondent apparently... and becoming hard...to control. He...went downhill in his last few months... on the job. Became abusive...to his superiors...and threatened to go to...the Press."

"Go to the Press about what?"

"I...don't know. Something caused him to...go over the edge."

"Would you say that his downhill slide started after September 30th, 1977?"

Fiona thought that the man's questions sounded like they were coming from a lawyer. "Yes...around that time. I was told it was in the Fall of 1977... that it became a crisis with him."

The dark figure shifted his weight again. "Tell me, did your source tell you whether or not Lucy Chambers knew that it was murder?"

"Yes...my source confided in her...after she took the interim position. My source wanted to...warn her."

"Is that why Lucy retired early?"

"Yes."

The man leaned his masked face down close to Fiona's. She could feel his breath coming through the mask again. It was intimidating.

"Tell me this. I'm guessing to myself who your source is. I won't ask you to confirm that though. But—if I'm right, she would have been a young woman back in 1977, certainly not high enough up in the Pentagon to know these things. So, how did she know?"

Fiona started choking. Her mouth and throat were so dry; it felt like they were closing off her oxygen supply.

The man lifted her up and breathed into her open mouth through his moist-laden woolen mask. He seemed to know instantly what the problem was.

Disgusted as she was to have his wool in her mouth, the rush of moisture from his breath was glorious. She relaxed as he lifted his face from hers. Strangely, she felt all of a sudden that this man was not a threat to her.

"Better now?"

"Yes. Thanks." *Why was she thanking him? Stockholm Syndrome?*

"Okay, answer that last question. And I promise you—that will be my last question for now."

Fiona relaxed. "My...source...said she had an...affair...with James Layton. She was...in love with him."

CHAPTER TWENTY

Brett Horton was sitting alone in his favorite Italian restaurant. He felt comfortable here—it was only a few blocks from his house and they knew him. They made him feel like family. As a guy who lived alone, and one who was naturally social, he needed a special place like this. Whenever he needed comfort, this was the venue.

The waitresses knew that he was a good tipper too, so he never kidded himself into thinking that they flirted with him because he was irresistible. It didn't matter anyway—if a good tip made him feel good for an evening, so be it.

Why he was still alone at this late stage of his life, he had no idea. He figured that after he left the Secret Service, his life might settle down a bit. More time to meet someone special, someone to care about.

Not too late to have kids either. He knew he would be a good father. At least his kids would grow up protected. No better protection that an ex Secret Service agent as a father! But they'd also know how to defend themselves. He'd make sure of that.

Brett had dated a lot of ladies, but just never seemed to make a connection that he wanted to hang onto. Nothing special, no effervescence. He wouldn't be capable of falling in love with just anyone—it would have to be someone very special.

He was confident enough in himself that he knew he could have his pick of ladies. That was never a problem. The problem for him was *wanting* to have his pick. Most of the time he just didn't care. Was it because he had always been a lone wolf? A loner who didn't need people around him as a crutch to make him feel good? Or was it the extreme discipline taught by the Secret Service: being self-sufficient, able to handle things himself, not depending on others, and knowing no fear?

He didn't know. It gave him a headache trying to analyze himself. All he could do was hope that the right girl would come along one day for him, and in the meantime just be content to enjoy the looking-around part.

He did envy Dennis Chambers though. That Fiona Perry seemed like a very special lady. He felt a little guilty thinking that way about her after he had just about scared her half to death the other night.

He knew however that he would never have hurt her—she was innocent of everything. There was no margin in someone like her getting hurt. She wasn't his assignment.

Assignments handed to him to hurt or kill were generally sleazy political figures or crooked high-powered executives who deserved it. He could justify those in his mind. Hurting or killing them was somehow justice to him. And getting paid for it made it even better.

But sweet Fiona was just a pawn. A pawn who had some information that he needed. He had hoped that she would have had more that he could use. He guessed that the doors of power were slamming solidly in her face back at the Pentagon. Those folks knew how to circle the wagons. Brett knew that from first-hand experience.

So, the dynamic Barb Jenkins had had an illicit affair with James Layton. Interesting. She must have been privy to whatever stress he'd been under and when she told Fiona that James had been murdered, Barb either guessed that from what she knew James had been going through or she'd heard some rumblings after the fact.

Either way, Brett put faith in what Fiona told him. Barb Jenkins was a genius, and had never been saddled with a reputation for making quick uneducated judgments. Not like some of the other clowns at the Pentagon.

Brett ordered a second bottle of wine from his cute flirty waitress—she'd get a good tip tonight just for being so flirty. And she knew she would.

She brought the bottle, let him sample a glass, then asked if she could sit down and join him. The restaurant management was very casual and actually encouraged their attractive waitresses to hang out with the customers if it wasn't too busy.

And it wasn't busy tonight because it was late—only one couple in the restaurant other than him. Brett smiled and said no. But he told her he'd wait for her to finish and walk her home. She smiled knowingly. Brett squinted at her nametag: Olivia. Nice name. One he thought he could get used to saying for the rest of the night. But just for the night. She wasn't special.

While he drank his wine and waited for Olivia to cash out, Brett reflected on his barhopping with John Switzer two nights ago. The old guy had a great time, and could still hold his liquor. They started with beer at the first bar, and ended with brandy at the fourth. Brett then stuffed John into a taxi, gave the driver John's address and paid him what amounted to at least triple what the fare would be. But the driver had to promise to get John safely into his house and onto the downstairs couch. He promised. Brett glared at him and said he'd find him if he didn't do what he'd promised. Brett's glare always got results.

John's lips had been loose, as usual, but much looser than ten years ago. Brett was right—the man just didn't give a shit anymore. What did a man eighty-five years of age have to worry about anymore? Could they really threaten him with his life? Not bloody likely. So, he caught John at the right moment.

Brett remembered the troubling conversation that took place at bar number three:

"Another beer, John?"

"Don't mind if I do, Brett!"

"Hey old man—ten years ago when we last did this, you teased me about a royal protection junket that I had to do. You said that nothing could come close to what you did for 'The James Dean.' You never did tell me what that was."

"Are you sure you want to know? Just like in that Jack Nicholson movie, 'You can't handle the truth!' Ha, ha. Well, maybe you can. If you keep your mouth shut I'll tell you. You might be impressed."

"John, everything you've done in your life has impressed me. But, let's face it, most of it was pretty ho hum. For a genius like you, it's almost like you were wasted."

"That's only because you weren't in the inner circle, Brett. What I could tell you might make your toes curl!"

"I doubt that. But, try me. What was 'The James Dean?' Let's see what ya got."

"It was a command module, Brett. For the moon mission that no one, outside of just a few of us, knew even happened. It flew September 1977. The mission was Apollo 19."

"Are you shitting me?"

"Told you you'd be impressed. No, I'm not shitting you. And there was another secret mission before that one—Apollo 18, in 1975."

"Why did NASA keep these missions secret?"

"Had nothing to do with NASA. The Pentagon took over after the last official moon landing in 1972."

"Why?"

"A crater was discovered. The 'Shackleton Crater' on the moon's south pole. The military boys got real excited. It was deep, probably held massive quantities of ice and most likely precious metals. But Apollo 18 found that it contained other stuff too. They brought back samples of things that were literally crawling around the rim of the crater."

"What the fuck?"

"Yeah, living organisms, bacteria, creepy crawlers—you name it, they found it."

"So, I'm afraid to ask. After Apollo 18, what happened?"

"They did tests and realized these combinations of primitive living creatures could be combined into unbelievable weapons of mass destruction. Except that they wouldn't necessarily have to destroy anything—other than life."

"And after the tests?"

"Well, this is the part that will really impress you about me. Get ready. I was assigned to design a weapon, one that could be jettisoned within the moon's limited gravity, directly into the center of the crater. A nuclear weapon. One that would open up the crater and, at the same time, test the viability of nuclear weapons in space."

"There's a Nuclear Test Ban Treaty in place, John! It forbids any nuclear weapon detonation in outer space! Christ, it's been in effect since 1963! Did anyone consider that? That's a clear violation of international law! For fuck's sake!"

"Ask me if I give a shit. I just do as I'm told, and put my brain to work when it's needed. And I was needed."

"Wasn't the detonation detected?"

"No, and this is the genius part. We timed the detonation at exactly the same time as the Russians conducted an underground nuclear weapons test, on September 30th, 1977, at the exact hour, minute, and second. They had announced their test well in advance, so all we had to do was time it. Any sensors detecting a nuclear signature in the atmosphere were just confused, and the geeks reading the results were even more confused. It was written off as just the effects of the Russian explosion. Clever, huh?"

"What happened after that?"

"Well, 'The James Dean' circled the moon for several days—to let the dust settle so to speak—and we then landed the lunar module, 'Rebel,' onto the surface of the moon a few hundred yards from the crater. This module was larger than any previous ones that landed, and was as high-tech as they come. I was involved in designing that too. It was a flying warehouse. Our astronauts collected massive quantities of organisms from the vicinity of the crater, bundled them up safely and after four days of work flew off the moon and connected back with 'The James Dean.' The prize was then brought home."

"The prize? You call it a prize? Where is this shit now?"

"I don't know. Not my problem."

"Weren't you worried that the nuclear explosion would cause some havoc on the moon other than just opening up the crater?"

"It was only ten megatons—doubtful that it would do any permanent harm."

"That's a sizeable bomb, John!"

"Yeah, it is. But it's within allowable limits."

"Maybe on earth, and underground. But this was shoved into an open crater, on a celestial object a lot smaller than earth."

"Nothing to worry about. Let's have another beer."

"If I remember correctly, that crater wasn't named 'Shackleton' until 1994. I remember reading something about the potential of water ice in that crater. What was it called before?"

"When we knew what we were going to do with it, we called it 'Rebel's Cause.' The Pentagon loves symbolism, as you know, with all their little adventures. The whole James Dean thing—September 30th being the anniversary of his death and all that."

"I read recently that they still intend to colonize the crater area sometime in the next decade or so."

"Ha, ha. That's just a smokescreen. It's uninhabitable—and dangerous. Those little organisms have probably mutated terribly by now from the radiation, and the blast opened up the crater to reveal a whole new world above ground to those little buggers. Who knows how big they are now, and how contagious. No, we got what we wanted. We won't be going back."

"Jesus, John! These little fuckers are on earth now! Doesn't that scare you? Where the hell are they?"

"Brett, I'm eighty-five years old. Nothing scares me. I have to admit I had a case of the guilts for a few years, but I'm over that. I've reconciled it in my mind. It'll be someone else's problem now, not mine. But, I'm sure the military have things well under control and the little buggers are probably being tested in a very safe environment, just like Ebola, Smallpox and other contagions. The plan was to play around with these things for a few decades before actually using them in a war environment. So, I guess they must be close— it's been over three decades now. Maybe the next war won't last too long, eh? Ha, ha."

"None of this is funny, John. Not at all."

Brett finished off the last of his second bottle of wine. He normally didn't drink so much in one sitting, but tonight he just felt like it. The wine went down like water.

He thought about that pathetic egotistical nuclear scientist who was near the end of his life, and didn't give a shit about the younger generations. Brett pondered how ironic it was—we breed and educate geniuses and make them feel like gods.

Flatter them and pamper them and then just use their genius for whatever evil we want to unleash upon the world. All for dominance. All for looking for an edge over the others, our so-called enemies. And proceed to sign Nuclear Test Ban treaties with our fingers crossed behind our backs. *Just kidding—didn't mean to sign that stupid treaty. Yeah, we broke international law. Tell someone who cares.*

Brett was feeling the wine now. Probably because he felt so despondent to begin with. *Who's side was he on? Who's side should he be on?* For the first time in a long, long time Brett was reminded that he had a conscience. And it was nagging him mercilessly at the moment.

Maybe it was just the wine.

He jerked his head around at feeling a gentle tap on his shoulder. Olivia was standing behind him, her coat on and a bling purse hanging from her shoulder.

"Are you ready, Brett?"

He nodded and stood up warily.

Then he thought to himself, *'Are any of us really ready? And do we have any idea what it is we have to be ready for?'*

CHAPTER TWENTY ONE

Dennis couldn't remember the last time he had this many people sitting with him in his formal dining room, let alone having dinner with three women.

He couldn't be bothered cooking, so he ordered Chinese food from a fantastic place a few blocks away. Together, they polished off a feast of ginger beef, chicken fried rice, chop suey, sweet and sour shrimp, and fresh hand-rolled dumplings. Delicious.

He'd just served coffee and liqueurs. They were about as relaxed as was humanly possible after discussing Fiona's ordeal of two nights ago.

That night Dennis had just crawled into bed when he got the frantic call from Fiona. He was still on 'cloud nine' after his dinner with her, knowing they'd now set up an actual movie and dinner date—their first real date. He was just dreamily falling off to sleep when the phone rang. At first her voice was hard to recognize, she was breathing so hard in between words.

He rushed over to her house and spent the next two hours consoling her. He saw the damage her assailant had done to the floor, and while he wasn't surprised that a man's hand could do that kind of damage—he knew he could easily do it too—he was alarmed that the man had gone to such great lengths to extract information out of Fiona.

Once she'd calmed down, Dennis bundled her up and took her back to his house. She'd been staying with him ever since—in one of the guest bedrooms on the second floor.

She was almost ready to return to her place now, reconciling in her mind that the man had just wanted information and hadn't planned to hurt her. In fact, towards the end of her ordeal she had already come to that realization after he had taken care to breath moisture into her throat. He had done it so gently, even though she was more than aware that he was capable of incredible violence.

And she told Dennis that there had been something in his muffled voice that had put her mind somewhat at ease even at the same time as she was feeling panic. It was a strange combination of emotions that the stranger had evoked in her.

Tonight was the night Dennis had decided he would make nice again with Barb Jenkins. So Barb joined them for dinner, and he'd also invited his sister Melissa.

Mel had moved back to her house a few days after the funeral, but she agreed to come over tonight only if Dennis told her the entire story. She knew he'd been troubled about their mother's death, but all he had told her so far was that she'd had some moments of lucidity before she died. She knew there was more, and demanded to know what he had been so evasive about.

Tonight was a brainstorming session with the three people Dennis cared about the most in his life. He was proud to now include Fiona in that exclusive club.

Barb came over to the house first. Dennis gave her a big hug and told her he was sorry for reacting as strong as he had. He told her he understood. They had a good chat about Barb's disclosure regarding James Layton, and Fiona's terrifying ordeal. They cleared the air between them, and were once again the best of friends.

Melissa arrived just before dinner. She seemed to be warm enough toward Fiona, but Dennis could tell there was a little bit of big sister jealousy going on. He wasn't surprised.

He and Mel had always been close growing up—she'd even asked him to take her to her senior prom after her boyfriend broke up with her. Even though Dennis was three years younger, he'd always looked older than Mel. So, he cut a handsome figure on the dance floor with her, and part of him knew that she'd asked him to go with her just to make her ex jealous. The games. He never minded playing them for his lovely sister.

Melissa was a brunette, with a slender athletic figure that belied her age. Still very attractive at fifty-eight, looking more like forty-two. She was a serious sort, very detailed and intense. Perhaps typical for an accountant—and a very successful one at that. She'd handled audits for numerous Fortune 500 companies. Mel was also a talented artist, a hobby she indulged in daily now that she was retired from the rat race.

The way she dressed screamed 'artist.' Funky, casual, unpretentious—

Dennis loved Mel's laid-back style, which in itself was in stark contrast to what her occupation had been.

Sipping his liqueur, a nice Grand Marnier on ice, Dennis opened up the conversation about what he really wanted to talk about. Up until now, the conversation over dinner had been fun, relaxed and more of 'get to know each other' stuff between Mel and Fiona, with he and Barb jumping in from time to time.

But now he was getting impatient.

"Ladies, I'm into something pretty serious here. And now Fiona's involved, and Barb, whether you like it or not, you are too. I think the time for 'protection of secrets' is over, do you agree?"

He looked straight at Barb. She looked back, and simply nodded.

"Okay, I'm glad we agree. I want to summarize what we know so far, and some of this will be new to Mel. But it's important she know the whole story now."

Dennis then summarized everything as concisely as he could: Lucy's revelation that there was a secret package of some sort. The DOD staff tossing her room at the nursing home. Lucy's reaction to the song about the moon, and then revealing that there had been an Apollo 19 mission.

Then her mentioning of 'Shackleton,' and Dennis' research that told him it was a crater on the moon. The truth about The Casper Agency being a domestic front spying operation for the DOD caused Fiona and Mel to gasp in shock.

And last but not least, Lucy's sudden retirement from the Pentagon at fifty years of age, with what appeared to have been a handsome payoff. What was the payoff for?

He took a deep breath before detailing what was on the personal recorder, knowing that Mel was hearing this for the first time. Hearing for the first time that her mother had been killed.

After telling that part of the story, Dennis could see tears rolling down Mel's cheeks. She excused herself and went to the bathroom. Fifteen minutes later, Barb went in and joined her.

When the two of them came back out, arm in arm, Mel said, "I'm okay now, Denny. Who could have known this hard-nosed lawyer here could be such a consoler?"

Barb chuckled. "Sweetie, it's always been easy for me to 'mother' you. You bring that instinct out in me, an instinct that I've never had the chance to use in my own life. So—let me 'mother' you any time you need it, okay?"

Mel gave her a kiss on the cheek and they hugged each other.

"Okay, okay—if you two are finished with this little love fest, I'd like to continue."

Fiona playfully punched him on the shoulder.

Barb and Mel sat down and Dennis continued. "The tape discloses so much—the fact that there was not only an Apollo 19 but also an Apollo 18. These missions were kept totally secret from the public. The big question is 'why?' Also, mom mentions on the tape that 'Shackleton' at one time was called 'Rebel's Cause.' What does that mean, and what is the significance of this crater?"

Dennis took another sip of his Grand Marnier and glanced around the table. They were each staring at him, with puzzled looks on their faces. He continued. "Mom said that Apollo 19 went up in 1977 and Apollo 18, in 1975. We have to assume these were both moon missions—all the Apollo-named missions were. So, what in God's name were they doing up there in those two years, that had to be kept so secret?

"Now we get to a more sensitive part of the story. Are you ready to discuss this, Barb? About you and James Layton?"

Barb winced. "Yes."

Dennis nodded. "Okay. Fiona had the living daylights scared out of her the other night. I'm betting that the man who attacked her is the same one who is on the personal recorder. I played it for Fiona, but because his voice was so muffled through his mask she can't say for certain that it was the same man. But, let's just assume that it was.

"Fiona disclosed to him what Barb had already told her. That Barb and James Layton had an affair. The official story is that James committed suicide by gunshot to the head in his own office. The Pentagon refused to release the suicide note, even to the family. They claimed 'national security' as the reason, and a judge allowed that privilege.

"That was in December of 1977, the same year that this Apollo 19 purportedly flew. Then mom took over as interim Chief Counsel for the Pentagon, and presumably would have been made privy to all of the high security stuff that James would have been privy to. She did the job for a year, then retired at the end of 1978 with a full pension and a hefty payoff in the amount of five million dollars."

Denny looked over at Barb, and made a flourish with his hand. "That's as much as I know—so the floor is now yours, Barb. Fill in the blanks for us if you could please?"

Barb sipped her brandy and sighed. "You'll remember when we were talking a few weeks ago, Denny, that I confessed to you that I had experienced 'love at first sight' only once in my life. You asked me what happened, and I told you that 'he died.' That was James. Yes, he was married and all that, but I couldn't stop myself. Our affair lasted two years; right up until the day he died. My heart was broken, completely."

She took another sip—a longer one this time. "James was a loyal soldier to the Pentagon. But something horrible happened in September of 1977. He flipped out. He told me only that it involved the moon. He never mentioned Apollo 19 or 18. He just said that what the United States of America had done was irreversible and a tragedy waiting to befall all of us. He said we'd violated international law and had taken a reckless action. He wouldn't tell me any more than that. He was obviously better at keeping secrets than me."

Dennis jumped in. "What did he do about it?"

"He told me that he had confronted the Secretary of Defense and the President himself. They wouldn't listen to him."

"He must have become a very frustrated man."

Barb wiped away a tear. "Oh, the dear man was a wreck. He had a conscience—I know that sounds funny knowing that he was having an affair with me, but it's true. And he did always feel guilty about the affair, by the way. But for him, like me, what happened between us was so powerful, he couldn't turn away from it.

"Anyway, he started seeing a psychiatrist and went on anti-depressants. None of that helped. He couldn't sleep at night, started behaving erratically. He told me he'd pretty much had it and was going to go to the Press."

Dennis was jotting down notes. He looked up. "So, Barb, did he go to the Press?"

"I don't know. But my gut feel tells me he did. And within only days of him telling me that he was going to go to the Press, he was dead."

"You said that it wasn't suicide. How do you know that? Did someone tell you that?"

"I'm the one who found his body. He died late at night. The halls and offices were empty. We were scheduled to meet at his office that night and grab a late meal together. I had a key to his office; I know, I shouldn't have, but I did. I worked one floor down from James."

Dennis was writing furiously. "Geez, Barb. That must have been horrible!"

"It was. I was stunned. I felt for a pulse, and then ran. I didn't report it. I waited for someone else to find him and do that. Denny, there was no suicide note that I could see."

"That doesn't mean there wasn't one."

"No, it doesn't. But it wasn't suicide."

"Barb, maybe you just didn't want to believe it was suicide."

"Denny, the entry wound was on the right side of his skull. James was left-handed."

*****

Cliff Tonkin was a happy man. He had the world by the tail. He couldn't believe how lucky he was, and he was so glad that he'd hired that lawyer. Although, if truth were known, the Washington Police were so incompetent even an untrained chimpanzee could have gotten him off. But, he had to give credit to his lawyer for at least pouncing on the stupidity the way he had.

No warrant to search his apartment, no service of his Miranda Rights. Ha! Idiots! He had to endure a trial anyway, despite all that. But the trial was based solely on an eyewitness identification of him running away from the house. The judge wouldn't allow the jury to hear of the stolen goods found in his apartment. The goods that came from that family: the TV, stereo, iPad, iPhone, iPod, Blackberry. The jury couldn't hear about any of that.

Now he was a free man. The case against him, after all that stuff was excluded, was a joke. They couldn't even include the DNA evidence because that was taken illegally from his apartment. And he hadn't been read his Miranda. Idiots!

He thought back to that night. Knocking on their door, the father opening up. Cliff kicking him in the balls before he had a chance to say, 'Can I help you?' Then forcing the father at knifepoint to tie up his two teenage boys. Then forcing the sobbing mother to tie up her husband. Then gagging all three.

Cliff was getting excited thinking about it.

But he left the mother free as a bird. He made her usher him around the house, filling his sack with all the electronic toys and whatever money was sitting around.

Then Cliff got the sudden urge to make love.

She wasn't particularly good looking, but he didn't care. He pulled the duct tape out of his back pocket again, and wrapped her mouth tightly. Dragging her into the living room where the rest of the family was, he threw her onto the couch. He wanted the entire family to watch.

And they did. And they cried. And Cliff laughed, right up until he slit her throat from ear to ear. He did the same to the other three. First the boys, so dad could watch. Then, finally dad.

Yes, Cliff was a happy man tonight. And a free one.

He opened the door to his apartment while humming 'For Once in My Life,' Stevie Wonder's hit song. He locked the door behind him, and hit the light switch.

He knew the man was there. He just knew it.

He whirled around and saw him, lounging on the couch with one of Cliff's favorite beers in his hand. He was struck by how nonchalant the guy was—really, sitting in his apartment drinking one of his beers, how could he be so calm?

The man didn't say anything.

In the instant before Cliff yanked the knife out of his back waistband, he marveled at the movie star handsomeness of the guy. Strong jaw, piercing eyes, broad shoulders.

He lunged at the stranger.

His eyes felt like they had blurred over. Movement was surreal. He felt his knife hand being hit square on by a bullet-fast beer bottle, liquid spilling over his arm and chest. Then the man's body moved as if being levitated. It seemed to rise from the couch with no effort at all, into the air feet first.

Cliff felt the impact against his throat and he fell to the floor, choking.

The man stood over him with absolutely no expression at all on his face. No anger, no regret, no sorrow. Just passive, the same kind of look that Cliff saw every day at the gas station where he worked—people just filling their tanks, faces blank.

The stranger knelt...and sighed. Then Cliff watched as he rammed his forefinger into his abdomen. So deep that Cliff felt as if it would come out through his back. Finger withdrawing now, blood and other stuff morosely dripping from the tip.

He simply wiped his finger along Cliff's shirt. Twice—to make sure it was clean.

Then he got to his feet and started walking toward the door.

Cliff panicked. "Hey, man! Don't...leave me like this! This is a gut wound— the worst kind. I'm gonna...die real slow if you...leave me. Take me...somewhere, anywhere! A hospital, a drugstore—I don't care! Somewhere I can get help!" The pain was horrible, an ache that shot from his ass to his throat. He felt his life ebbing away, and in fact watched it ebbing away onto his cheap shag carpet.

He looked on as the man yanked the phone out of the wall and smashed it with one swipe of his hand.

He was walking back toward him now. Cliff was encouraged.

But all he did was unclip the cellphone from Cliff's waist, toss it into the air and explode it into pieces with a lightning stab of his forefinger. Cliff shivered.

He glanced down at his stomach and was shocked at how much blood and other disgusting material was pouring out of the wound. It was pouring out real fast now. Blood he recognized, but he didn't want to know what that other stuff was.

Cliff glanced up at his attacker and could feel the confusion in his own eyes.

The man still hadn't said one word. He turned around and left the apartment without a backward glance.

And Cliff was left wondering why on earth anyone would want to kill him.

CHAPTER TWENTY TWO

Brett picked up the phone and dialed John Switzer. It had been a couple of nights since their long drink-fest, and he wanted to pretend that he cared about how John was feeling.

In reality, he wanted—no, he needed—more information and hoped he could possibly squeeze it out of the egotistical old bugger. He'd have to stroke his ego a bit.

He knew he could probably get all he needed by just hurting the old guy, but Brett didn't have the heart to do that to an eighty-five year old man. God, he was getting soft.

"John?"

"Yes. Is that you, Brett?"

"It's me, alright—your drinking buddy! I wanted to ask how you've been feeling the last couple of days. Recovered okay?"

"Yeah, I'm fine for an old guy. I can still drink you under the table."

"Well, if I recall correctly, I was the one who rolled you into a cab in an almost comatose state! So, I think I won that drinking contest, old man!"

Brett could hear John chuckling. "Okay, I'll give you that one. But next time will be different."

"Hey, John—gotta tell you, I was blown away by all that stuff you shared. And trust me, it's just between you and me. As you know, I've always been impressed by your gray cells, but geez, what you did with that moon mission was pretty 'over the top' brain-wise."

John was chuckling again. "Us scientists are usually flying under the radar—no one really gets to hear about the brilliant stuff we do. The Suits and the Generals take all the credit, and we get the gold watches."

"Yeah, not quite fair, is it? We should honor our brightest lights more than we do."

"At least I know what I did for them. That's what really matters to me."

Brett carefully chose his next few words. "John, it must have been real hard for you to have been involved as deeply as you were, only to be completely cut out of the picture once the…um…material was brought back from the moon. Hard to believe they wouldn't still tap into that brain of yours as the project moved forward."

"Well, they did to a certain extent, Brett. They had to still consult with me on some of the aspects. But, my role was largely finished—I'm a nuclear and aerospace engineer, not a microbiologist. The next set of brains had to take over—although I think they had the easy part."

"Sounds like they would have. Were they afraid to keep you in the loop after awhile? Kind of a 'need to know' thing?"

"I'm the one who chose not to know any more after they brought the things back. I'm sure they would have kept me informed if I'd asked to be."

"I'll bet they went ahead and gave the next stage a funny name just like the 'Rebel's Cause' they used for your side of the project. I'm sure if they'd asked you, you could have given them a good name to use, eh?"

"Well, it just so happens that I did name it for them. The microbiology stage was called, 'Creepy Crawlers.' Isn't that a good one? Thought of it myself."

Brett faked a good belly laugh. "Ha, that's a good one, John. Very appropriate! Did they take you to the site they used for the experiments—you know—to kind of christen it for them?"

"No, I wouldn't want to go, to tell you the truth. I trust plutonium and uranium much more than that microbiology stuff. Scares the shit out of me!"

"Have to agree with you there. I wonder where they took the stuff."

"Don't know. Don't want to know. What I do know though is 'Creepy Crawlers' became a joint project of the Pentagon and the Centers for Disease Control. I believe the CDC chose the location and staffed it with their best scientists. The Pentagon probably does inspections from time to time, handles security and directs the experiments."

"Makes sense. Well, let's hope they're doing it right otherwise we're all going to suffer for it."

"Well, maybe you will—not me. I'm too old to give a shit."

"I guess you're right on that, John. Hey, we'll grab another beer real soon. Take care, John." Brett hung up and immediately chastised himself for not going over there and just torturing the old asshole to death.

*****

The four of them were meeting for lunch at a downtown restaurant. Fiona was dressed in a classy beige business suit, Mel was wearing something that resembled a smock and Barb was once again the shining star, adorned in a green sleeveless dress contrasting nicely with her silver high heels. Dennis was wearing a boring business suit, having snuck out of the office for this extended lunch.

Seafood salads around, they started recapping once again the things they had discussed a couple of nights before.

Mel stated the obvious. "If James Layton was murdered, it was to silence him. They must have seen him developing into a loose cannon, somebody they couldn't control any longer."

Dennis washed the last bite of his salad down with the remnants of a vintage Merlot. "And mom took over the job, after which you warned her, Barb." He looked across at Barb Jenkins.

"Yes, I did. But I waited until after Lucy was announced as the interim Chief Counsel. I knew then that she would very soon be made privy to all of the secrets she needed to know to do that job. Including what drove James to question everything."

"So how did mom react? What did she do?"

"She believed me. She didn't tell me why, but she said she believed me. I think she already knew a few things by the time I told her. Her face went ashen, and all she said was, 'What have I gotten myself into?'"

Mel leaned forward with her elbows firmly on the table, smock crunched up to her chin. "Barb, do you think she blackmailed them to save her life and also walk away with a big payday?"

"Yes, I do. But she couldn't do it the way James tried. They would have just killed her too. She couldn't have just threatened to go to the Press. She was too smart for that, knowing how James met his end. She must have had something—something she got out of the Pentagon, something that she could threaten them with if anything ever happened to her."

"The package."

"Yes, the package."

Dennis rapped his knuckles on the table. "Well, something has happened to her now, hasn't it? If something was to be released upon her death, guess what, it's going to happen soon."

Barb gasped. "Holy shit! You're right, Denny! It could be in the process of happening as we speak!"

Fiona was listening carefully to the exchange. She finally spoke. "Whatever it is, it's serious enough to have caused the murder of a high level Pentagon official more than three decades ago. And to have tried to extract the information from an old Alzheimer's patient. They were then—and still are now—desperate to keep this quiet, whatever it is."

Dennis scratched his chin. "Desperate is right—even scaring the life out of you. But let's think about this for a second. Mom might have been naïve to think the Press would even do anything about it. They're pretty much controlled by government, told what to say, not to say. I think that's pretty obvious with the pathetic reporting that takes place, and the real issues and questions that are never addressed."

Fiona grimaced. "Unless, Dennis, she had arranged with a lawyer to have the package sent to foreign Press outlets. Certain countries wouldn't hesitate to embarrass the U.S."

"True. But you know what—I'm so cynical about world powers, that I don't think they would do anything with it other than extract better loan and import/export tariffs with the U.S. Just a higher level of blackmail—they're all prostitutes. They don't represent the people, they represent themselves."

Barb laughed. "Denny, dear, you are in a mood today, aren't you? And don't forget, you work for a branch of government yourself. What does that say about you?"

Dennis chuckled. "I guess I'm a hooker too. Wait until you get my bill for your share of lunch. I'll add on a 'special services' fee!"

"Promises, promises. Always teasing me but never delivering. What 'special services' are you going to give me, Denny?"

Mel scoffed. "Why don't you two just go get a room?"

They all laughed as the coffee and dessert wagon came rolling by their table. Each went for the coffee but no one wanted to indulge in the rich looking pastries.

There was a moment of silence around the table as they began sipping their coffees. Melissa was just putting an extra spoonful of sugar in her cappuccino when her hand began to shake. The spoon gave her away by clinking against the side of the cup.

Dennis noticed that her face had turned white as a sheet. "Mel, are you okay? What's wrong?"

She put the spoon down and clasped her hands together. "Denny, the old cabin on Chesapeake Bay!"

CHAPTER TWENTY THREE

"What about the cabin, Mel?"

"That's where she's hidden it!"

They all leaned forward to listen to Mel. Barb rubbed her shoulder. "What makes you think that, dear?"

"Mom has owned that cabin for decades. Denny and I used to go there as kids with mom and dad. In fact, dad was the one who bought it. He loved the place. After he died, mom refused to sell it even though none of us wanted to bother going up there anymore."

"Yeah, I haven't seen the old cabin for at least twenty years now. I don't think mom's been up there since dad died."

"If she did, Denny, she went without us knowing. Do you remember that after she retired, she told us she would never sell it while she was alive? She even transferred the ownership out of her name and into a blind trust."

"I remember that—don't know why she did that. Maybe for tax reasons?"

"There's no tax advantage to her in doing that, Denny. She was still the sole owner of the Trust. It simply shifted the ownership out of her name and off the records if her assets were searched."

"Jesus, I think I'm starting to follow you."

"You'll also remember that I agreed to be the executor of mom's estate."

"Yes, being an accountant, you were the obvious choice over me."

Melissa continued. Her hands were no longer shaking. She was getting quite animated the more she spoke. "Well, here's the kicker. Mom's will stipulated that the Trust be liquidated upon her death. She knew we didn't want to be burdened with the place, but said that in dad's memory she didn't have the heart to sell it while she was still alive. So, we'll get the proceeds of the sale."

Denny scoffed. "The place is probably worthless. Rat infested, crumbling—it will probably cost us to liquidate. We'll have to tear it down and just sell the land, which might not even cover our costs. Also, if I remember correctly, there was asbestos insulation in that place. We could face huge environmental costs just demolishing it."

Mel gave Dennis a disapproving 'big sister' look. "Denny, you're getting off track. Just listen to me for a few minutes and stop interrupting."

Dennis nodded at his clever sister, and smiled. She'd done this to him his whole life—and he loved it.

"Mom's lawyer, Sydney Fox, phoned me a couple of days after the funeral. I didn't think much of it until we all started talking more today about this package thing. And it was just expected that he would get in touch with me. I'm the executor and whatever is left of mom's estate that you and I haven't already taken possession of has to be dealt with. The will has to go into probate."

"I understand, yes." Dennis glanced over at Barb and then Fiona. He could see that their eyes were transfixed on Mel. She had everyone's attention.

"He wants me to go with him to Maryland to see the property and decide how best to sell it. The will requires that it be sold as soon as possible after mom's death. And get this—I never really paid much attention to this clause until now, but the will requires that Sydney Fox as the trustee of the property, be allowed to inspect it alone. There's some legal gobbledygook about this keeping the inspection objective and without conflict of interest. Sounds convincing anyway."

"So, you're telling me that you have to sit out in the car while he inspects our property?"

"Yes."

Denny jumped to his feet. "Jesus Christ, Mel! Sydney's the one who was given the instructions to release the package upon mom's death! He's going up there to retrieve it! He knows where it's hidden!"

"Exactly."

*****

Salvatore Badali stood across the street from the pawnshop, watching. Good, only one attendant on after 9:00 p.m. Perfect. He knew the hero would be armed, but Sal wouldn't give him the chance to use it. He always went in guns blazing. Kill first, no questions later.

Sal loved pawnshops—they were the best places to rob. Virtually all cash. And the owners were slime-balls, buying cheap and selling high. He remembered when his mom had to sell all her jewelry when Sal was just a little boy. His dad had run out on them, leaving them with nothing. His poor mom had to sell everything she owned, even her grandmother's wedding ring—just so they could eat.

He hated pawnshop dealers. And he loved killing them.

Tomorrow night he would hit this place. He concentrated on looking at the dealer through the window. Knowing that tomorrow night he would no longer be standing, breathing, dealing, cheating. Scumbag. It was surreal watching someone who only he knew was enjoying his last full night on earth.

This would be the fifth pawnshop he'd robbed, and the fifth dealer he'd killed. No one could catch him. Sal was a night stalker. He had only been arrested on suspicion once, when the security camera caught a little more of his profile than he'd planned. Someone had recognized him. He didn't know who it was, but he wished he did. That person would no longer be breathing the polluted Washington air.

Anyway, he got off. The image wasn't strong enough to convince a grand jury to indict him. Now he was more careful. He wore a full balaclava now. No chance of being recognized. And his modus operandi was based on being quick. Quick in and out.

It always followed the same pattern. As soon as he entered the shop, he would shoot the dealer through the head, or the heart—didn't matter. Depended on how much he'd had to drink. His Marine training made him a marksman, but even a marksman found it hard to shoot someone through the forehead after eight beers.

So, with the easy part over, he would blast his way into the cash drawers and take only the available cash. He didn't waste his time with the safe—didn't want to coerce the dealer into opening it for him. That took too long. He just wanted what he could grab and run. He was always out and back into his car within two minutes. Worked like a charm.

Sal smiled. He was getting a rush just thinking about tomorrow night.

He walked around the block and back to his car—a black '69 Camaro. Hot. Dark tinted windows. He was surprised the cops hadn't stopped him yet and ticketed him for blackout glass. Well, maybe not so surprised. They were incompetent at the best of times, and also badly short of manpower. And firepower.

Sal opened the driver's door and hopped in. Turned on the engine and leaned his head back against the headrest. Just for a minute. Just to hear the growl of his 350 horsepower monster.

Suddenly he was aware of a shadow, movement, or something above his head.

Then impact. Something hit the top of his head and it felt as if it had caved in. It had caved in. His ears seemed to be flopping sideways and outwards. Sal was barely able to glance to his right just in time to see a man's forearm being pulled back to its owner in the rear seat.

Salvatore Badali's chin bounced up and down on his chest. His head couldn't stop bobbing. It seemed to weigh a hell of a lot more right now than just a few precious minutes ago.

*****

Brett Horton was on the phone. He realized with chagrin that most of his work time now was spent either on the phone or the Internet. How times had changed from when he had first started out with the Secret Service. But—it was a necessary evil.

"So, are you keeping busy these days, Randy?"

"Very. Everyone in the world right now is worried about Internet security. I don't blame them. It's a scary world out there, and unfortunately, everybody's world is online now."

"Isn't that the truth? How dependent we've become on this Internet shit, eh?"

"Yeah. But let me guess—you've got something for me, right? You're dependent on me too."

Brett laughed. Randy McEwen was sharp. He had been one of the top cyber-agents with the FBI, until retiring to go into private practice four years ago. He had been an FBI agent, sure, but in reality he was a hacker. One of the best in the world. He was just one of a team of specialists who Brett used from time to time as needed. They had a privileged relationship. They respected each other, not to mention that Brett paid Randy handsomely.

"I do have something for you. It's very tricky. Very confidential. And very risky."

"Big deal. No one can catch me. You know I'm far too good for that to happen. So, sock it to me."

"Randy, I need you to hack into the Pentagon and the CDC. I need to know anything and everything to do with a project nicknamed in typical tacky Pentagon style as, 'Creepy Crawlers.' It has to do with microbiology experiments, dating back as far as 1977."

"Wow—you weren't kidding. This *will* be risky. Okay, shouldn't be a problem, however I'll have to take this one to the 'stable.' I'll need to relay it around the world. Where would you like it to end up this time? Iran or Israel?"

"Randy, I would shit my pants thinking that the Pentagon and White House clowns traced the hack back to their good loyal friends in Israel. That will keep them busy with shuttle diplomacy for a while! Go with Israel, if for no other reason than just my amusement!"

"Done. Shalom."

133

CHAPTER TWENTY FOUR

Brett was patiently awaiting a call back from Randy. The hacker extraordinaire had indeed discovered something pertaining to 'Operation Creepy Crawlers,' but wanted to get back into the Pentagon site once again to do a bit more fact checking.

So, Brett strummed his fingers on the beautiful mahogany wood of his executive desk while straining his eyes at his computer monitor. He knew he was going to need glasses soon—his eyes had started going downhill at age forty but he'd resisted taking the big leap. Male vanity, he guessed. He knew also that society was now seeing an earlier deterioration of eyesight since the advent of computers. The premature strain was evident in virtually everyone, even young people. Prosperous times for opticians.

Today he was reading about the 'Partial Nuclear Test Ban Treaty.' It was a treaty signed and ratified by the governments of the old Soviet Union, the United Kingdom, and the United States of America way back in 1963.

It prohibited all test detonation of nuclear weapons in any mode other than underground. No more nukes in the ocean, none above ground, and most definitely none to be allowed in outer space. The treaty's intention was to slow down the nuclear arms race and put a halt to the release of nuclear fallout into earth's atmosphere.

The agreement almost didn't get signed due to a clause that was in the original draft that banned all nuclear testing including underground tests. There was general disagreement over this until concessions were made by the Soviets to ban only testing above ground, in the sea, and in outer space. Underground testing would still be allowed.

This seemed to make sense to all parties, because it would have been difficult anyway for any of the signatory countries to police and enforce an underground test ban. When those suckers exploded underground, the seismic effects closely resembled earthquakes—and indeed on several occasions had actually triggered earthquakes.

Brett shook his head in disgust. Treaties apparently meant nothing to these clowns. The U.S. had clearly violated a decades-old treaty by dropping a ten-megaton nuclear monster into the moon's 'Shackleton' crater. No wonder they needed to desperately protect that secret. The resultant worldwide chaos if that fact became known would be immense and insurmountable on the diplomatic stage. All bets would be off, all similar treaties nullified, and the arms race would escalate beyond anyone's imagination. All that, plus international condemnation and charges against the U.S. filed in the World Court.

In short, a disaster.

But all that didn't even consider possibly the worst part of this whole mess. If they did indeed bring living organisms back from the moon, what did that mean? Where were they? How secure were they? What were they doing with them?

He placed his elbows on the desk and rested his face in the palms of his hands. Then he started gently rubbing his forehead. What had started out as a curious adventure was now turning into something that was causing him more stress than he could have ever imagined.

Normally things didn't bother him—his prior assignments had all been serious and usually dangerous and he had caused real harm or death to many, all of whom had probably deserved it. But this…this was different. His instincts told him that this far surpassed anything he had ever been involved in before, and made even the most severe action he had ever executed seem miniscule in comparison.

And he couldn't stop now. He was in too far.

Brett's official assignment from the Pentagon was to retrieve the 'package,' whatever and wherever it was. But Brett was starting to feel betrayed. They gave him the assignment not only because he was the best at what he did, but also most likely because he had shown a total lack of conscience throughout his career. He felt a little insulted all of a sudden. Did they really think that he could overlook an abject violation of an international treaty, and overlook the introduction to Planet Earth of alien organisms?

They assumed too much. They had gone too far. And he was now determined to follow whatever semblance of conscience he still had left. Retrieving the package and handing it over to these power-mad wing nuts was fast becoming the last thing on his list.

He was jarred from his deep thoughts by the phone ringing. In an instant he had it up to his ear.

"Talk to me, Randy."

"Holy shit, Brett! What the fuck are you into here?"

"It sounds like you found something?"

"Yeah, I did! Are you ready for it?"

"Yes, do you mind if I record this?"

"No, but promise me that once you take your notes, you'll destroy the recording?"

Brett clicked on his recorder. "I promise. Now, give it to me, laddy."

"Okay, 'Operation Creepy Crawlers' does indeed exist as a project under the supreme supervision of the Pentagon. The CDC are subordinate, but they're the ones firmly in charge of the experimentation."

"Experiments?"

"It all seems to be about weaponization, Brett."

"What kind of weaponization?"

"You name it—there are references to bodily injections for soldiers to make them super-soldiers, contamination to populated areas, and bio-tipped warheads. And a bunch of references to 'dumbing' of populations, sterilization, population eradication in unfriendly countries—you name it, they talk about it. I even saw notations about bio-induced insanity, bio-induced aggression, and bio-induced fearlessness."

"Dr. Strangelove?"

"Good analogy."

"I'm catching my breath here, Randy."

"Hopefully you're breathing clean, fresh air. Because from what I've been reading, I feel like I should be wearing a mask."

"What documents have you been reading?"

"Well, I managed to hack right into the Pentagon site. 'Operation Creepy Crawlers' exists in a file all its own, with a link to the Centers for Disease Control. There's some correspondence back and forth between the Pentagon and the CDC. They're very careful in one respect—no names or signatures on the correspondence. Just reports of test results, questions and answers, statements of intention."

"Have their tests been successful so far?"

"Doesn't look like it—seems to be a lot of dissatisfaction from the Pentagon, threats of more frequent audits at the laboratory site, and it looks like a couple of scientists at the CDC were fired. But it doesn't look like they're giving up—they seem to be actually *kicking* it up."

"Geez."

"All of the testing seems to revolve around animals—primarily monkeys. They refer to one species of monkey as "Greenies." And the other species is clearly the Chimpanzee."

"Christ!"

"Yeah, the most violent species of ape in existence. But—get this. They've already tested some of these chimps in populated areas. I saw reference to the necessity to observe at these early stages how the modified chimps would behave in urban areas, and other areas where humans are predominant. They wanted to gauge the fear level of the animals and the degree of unprovoked aggressiveness, strength, and anger."

"So they transported these animals to cities?"

"Yep, saw observation notes in the files. Two chimps were on the loose in Las Vegas recently. They went 'ape,' pun intended. Ran down the streets scaring the shit out of anyone who saw them. Came across a police car, jumped up and down on the roof caving it in. The officer started the car up and drove—the chimps hung on for a while then leapt onto the hood of an oncoming car, smashing the guy's windshield. One chimp reached in and grabbed the man around the throat and began choking him while the car was still moving. At that point one of the officers stationed along the sidewalk took a shot and killed the thing. Great shot—the driver was just shaken up, managed to stop the car with the dead chimp lying on top of him."

"They should autopsy the beast."

"Can't—report states that the body was removed securely."

"What happened to the other ape?"

"Ended up in the backyard of a house, threw the father under a rider mower and actually figured out how to turn it on. The guy lost his leg."

"For God's sake!"

"They tranquilized the thing, and it too was taken away to parts unknown."

"I read about that Vegas incident, but these details were not mentioned at all. It just said the chimps went on a rampage and that they were in fact pets that escaped."

"Obviously sanitized media."

"Were there other experiments in urban areas?"

"There sure were. A chimpanzee sanctuary in South Africa, which allowed tourists and university students to tour the facility, had an incident that was also sanitized. A tour guide was yanked under the fence of the enclosure by two chimps, dragged by his feet for more than a mile. They were described in the report—very clinically I might add—as being in an extremely frenzied state. It was almost as if someone was standing around taking notes! Anyway, there wasn't much left of the guy when they found him. He'd been cannibalized."

"Chimpanzees are unpredictable...and very strong."

"Yes, they sure are. The report says their normal strength is six times that of a human being."

"Jesus! Any other tests?"

"Several more chimps on the loose—one report in Canada, one in Wales, and another in Germany. No violence in these incidents—but again, clinical reports on what they did, where they went, how they behaved. Then, they were tranquilized and removed."

"You mentioned other animals?"

"Yes, cats. The experiments with cats seem to have been geared to making them robotic and compliant. Whatever they did seemed to strip the cats of their natural independent loner tendencies, and make them basically sublime. Interesting—with apes the tests tried to achieve the exact opposite of what they were trying to achieve with the cats."

"Different strains? Different objectives? Different weapons?"

"Perhaps."

"Okay, where is this fucking lab, Randy?"

"I wish to God I could tell you. The reports are very cryptic about the location. They keep referring to it as 'Snow Lady.' I haven't had time to research that, so I'll have to leave it to you. If anyone can figure it out, you can, Brett."

"Snow Lady? That's it?"

"Yeah—sorry."

"Okay. You've done great as usual. I'll probably be back to you on this again, but in the meantime the check's in the mail."

"Thanks, Brett. Good luck—and be careful. This is pretty serious stuff."

*****

Jim Morton watched as she walked down the street—no, she wasn't really walking, she was dancing. Dancing just for him. She was blonde—his favorite color—and a body that was made for sex. Her ass wiggled as she moved, her arms and shoulders swung like she was ready to take on the world—or take on any cock that came her way. Yes, that's what she really wanted, Jim was convinced of that. He knew it. She'd seen him already and she wanted him. He was powerful and she knew it.

He'd been lurking at a new corner tonight. He couldn't use the same corner all the time, even though he had his favorites. But this corner seemed to be productive. It was near five pick-up bars and he'd seen her come out of one of them. He was surprised she was leaving alone. With the way she displayed her ample chest, he figured guys would have been all over her.

But then, he hadn't been in that bar. If he had, she would most likely have made a move on him. He was convinced that all of his targets had wanted him, and when they fought him, they were just playing hard to get, just like the teasing bitches they were.

She was his tonight. He hadn't had sex in a week now, and the pressure was building, building badly. She was most definitely his tonight.

Jim waited about a minute and then began his pursuit. Close enough to watch that wiggling ass, but not close enough to alarm her.

He had to be careful. There were four rape convictions against him, a total of twenty years in prison, and no less than eight other attempts to convict him that failed in the justice system due to lack of evidence. His next conviction would probably send him to prison for life. He figured he'd been stupid before—he sincerely believed the girls had enjoyed their experiences with him. So he had no reason to kill them. They told him they enjoyed it. They wouldn't say that if they didn't believe it, would they? No, of course they wouldn't.

Some busybody friends must have convinced them to file charges. Friends who had miserable frigid lives, and were jealous of the joy his targets had experienced with him. He should have just found out who their friends were and killed them. A pre-emptive strike.

Well, he would definitely have to change his modus operandi. He couldn't take a chance on going back to prison. And he sure wasn't going to change who he was. Why should he?

Jim picked up his pace a bit. They were getting real close to an alley that he had scouted out beforehand. She was about thirty yards away from it. The street was deserted. Just the way he liked it. He'd have her naked ass up against a wall in just a matter of minutes.

He was five feet behind her now. He saw her glance to her side, hearing his footsteps he guessed. He reached out and grabbed her blonde locks from behind, yanking her sideways into the alley. She started to scream but he put a stop to that real fast with his other hand. He was strong. She wasn't. In a few seconds she would experience how really strong he was.

Jim rammed her up against the wall and relished the terror in her eyes. He liked to see them scared, but then loved it when they softened up and enjoyed him. He knew they enjoyed it. They wouldn't be able to fake something like that.

He reached under her dress and ripped her panties into shreds, the pieces hanging at her knees. Jim's penis was out through the open zipper of his Levis, and he wielded it in his hand like a weapon. He rammed it forward and up.

Then he heard a scream—but it was his own mouth that was doing the screaming. The zipper seemed to zip up all by itself, catching his erect penis in its teeth. He'd never felt a pain so severe and so instant as this before—and he had been shot twice in his life. Those bullets didn't even come close to inflicting the kind of agony he was feeling right now.

He let go of the blonde and started dancing and hopping, trying desperately to unzip it from his skin. He couldn't. It was impaled on his skin and when he tried to pull it down it only made the pain worse.

As he hopped around he could see a dark figure, with the only sign of light being from cold eyes peering through the holes in a ski mask. The figure wrapped his arm around the blonde, gently ushering her back to the street—and pointed. She ran in the direction of his point. She was gone. Jim's plan for the night was in ruins.

The man moved toward him now. Jim had one hand on his bleeding penis, and the other hand was up now in a 'stop sign' position. "Hey, man! She's gone! She's okay! You can leave me alone!"

The man reached down and gave one more yank on the zipper. Jim screamed in agony, but only briefly. The sound from his mouth was silenced instantly by a forefinger that jabbed right through his throat. Right through his 'Adam's Apple.'

Jim gasped. That was the only sound that was possible. And it sounded to him more like a rasp. His throat was soaked with blood and he knew he was in trouble. He raised his hands in defense but it was a pathetically hopeless gesture.

The man in black stood in front of him now, feet wide apart, arms poised. Both of his hands now moved quickly in unison, pounding Jim in the head and the chest at least five times in a matter of seconds.

He flew back against the wall and promptly sunk to the ground. Each of the impact areas felt like bullet holes.

Jim knew what bullet holes felt like.

He looked up and saw his attacker walking calmly back out to the street.

Jim knew his power was waning. He'd never love again. He just knew it.

CHAPTER TWENTY FIVE

Dennis was on the phone. First with Melissa, during which she confirmed that she and Sydney Fox were heading to Maryland to inspect the cabin next Thursday. He then phoned Fiona and asked her to take that day off work. Fiona would ride with him in his car. The plan was that they would be there before Mel and the lawyer, waiting inside.

Then he phoned Barb. She was more than anxious to accompany him. "Denny, a day in the country with you would be wonderful, only made more wonderful by this mystery!" Dennis chuckled—he loved her style.

Barb decided she would drive up separately as she had some other business to attend to early that morning. They agreed they would meet at the cabin at 5:00 p.m. next Thursday. Mel and Sydney were due to arrive no earlier than 6:00 p.m.

When they arrived, they would stash their cars around the block in front of some other cottages on Chesapeake Bay. Then make the walk to the cabin, which would only be about 200 feet away from where they would park. He gave Barb a complete description of the cabin, landmarks like the old oak tree in front of the property that had a trunk shaped like a scythe. Unmistakable. She'd have no problem identifying the cabin based on just that alone. And, as Dennis pointed out, it would probably be the most rundown cabin on the cliff.

It was actually a large building, with four bedrooms upstairs, three bathrooms, large dining room, country kitchen, and a monstrous living room. So, while he and Mel referred to it as a cabin, it was in reality a house. Just a poorly maintained house.

There would be a lot of places in the house for them to hide when Sydney started his inspection. Dennis guessed that the main floor would have more secretive places for something like a package, so he, Fiona and Barb would hide on the second floor and get ready to sneak down the stairs when Sydney made his appearance. Sydney probably knew exactly where the package was, so they wouldn't waste time when he arrived. They would head down the stairs once they heard the rummaging.

In about ten days' time Dennis hoped and prayed that they would finally have some answers to what this package thing was all about. His mother's wish would come true, albeit too late to save her life.

*****

"Bill, you'll have to be patient. I know some things, but not enough yet to finish the job properly."

Brett's friend, Bill Charlton, from the Department of Defense was on the phone, looking for an update. Brett knew he just had to buy time, and he wasn't about to disclose any of what he knew so far. He knew that wouldn't be safe—for him or the others.

"Well, Brett, old buddy—maybe I can help you out a bit. We've received word that your boy, Dennis Chambers, is on his way up to Chesapeake Bay, Maryland, next Thursday. I don't know who else is going with him. Apparently, Lucy Chambers owned a cabin up there, and it's been held in a blind trust for years. We couldn't spot it with a standard asset search—because the records just show that it was sold about thirty-five years ago, around the time she retired from the Pentagon. It was sold all right, right into a blind trust that Lucy owned 100% of. Sneaky old broad, eh?"

"Yes, she was. How do you know about this visit to Maryland, Bill? You been holding out on me?"

"Brett, Brett—you know full well we can never rely on just one person for any assignment. Even for assassinations, there's always a backup."

"Okay, so you have a snoop."

"Hey, with technology these days we really don't need a human being anymore for most of what we learn, you know that."

"True enough."

"I'll email you the specifics: where the cabin is, the time Chambers is supposed to be there. You be there too."

"I will."

There was silence at the other end. Brett waited—he knew something else was coming.

"Brett, have you been sticking your nose in where it doesn't belong?"

Brett felt his throat go dry. "What do you mean, Bill? As an investigator, my nose is always where it doesn't belong."

"You know what I mean."

"No, I don't. And I resent the inference. I never accept boundaries when I take on an assignment, and you didn't specify any to me when you gave me this job. If you had, I would have refused."

"Okay, okay. Settle down—just asking."

Brett sighed. "Bill, don't ever ask me a question like that again. I don't have the patience for being doubted."

*****

Brett was toiling away on the computer once again. He knew Bill was on to him now. He wouldn't have asked that question if he didn't have some suspicions. Except that all Bill could possibly know was that Brett had been browsing the Internet for information. And Bill knew Brett well enough that it shouldn't have come as a surprise to know that he had been digging.

He didn't think Bill could have clued in yet about Randy hacking into the Pentagon or CDC databases. That would be impossible to trace back to him or Randy. It would instead lead right to Tel Aviv, and when the Israelis denied as they always did about everything, the Pentagon would still think it was the Israelis.

So, Brett figured they must have a trace on his own computer at home. They must have seen the surfing he had done pertaining to 'Shackleton' and the moon missions. But, if that's all they knew, it was harmless. He was puzzled however by Bill's volunteering the comment, *"don't know who else is going with him."* Why would Bill have said that? It's almost as if he did know who Dennis was going with and was going out of his way to convince Brett that he didn't know.

Today, Brett was sitting in an Internet café. He wasn't going to take any chances at getting caught surfing for information surrounding what Randy had given him. That would betray the Israeli cover they had set up.

What bothered Brett the most was how Bill had been able to find out about Dennis' upcoming trip to Maryland. Brett was well aware there were 'doubles' with every major assignment. But he hadn't given much thought to that with this assignment—until just recently. At first it had seemed pretty simple—he and Felicity would work together to get the information. It didn't seem that difficult or all that serious.

But in light of what he had found out since embarking on this assignment, it did occur to him in the last few days that there probably was a 'double.' It was that serious. But who was it? He had to be on his guard more than ever now. Or, it was indeed possible that Bill found out about Dennis' planned trip to the cabin just from monitoring phones or the Internet. It was impossible to know, so Brett had to err on the side of caution.

The Internet café computer was a lot slower than his IBM at home, but at least it was safe. He strummed his fingers on the desk waiting for the machine to display the browser. It seemed to be taking forever.

Ahh...finally. Brett wanted desperately to find out where this microbiology lab was located. All he knew from what Randy had told him was that it was referred to as 'Snow Lady.' He entered those words into the search bar. Up popped all sorts of articles pertaining to strippers, hookers, and models.

He switched it around, entering 'Lady Snow.' This time nothing but articles about royalty.

Brett downed the rest of his cold coffee and wandered over to the machine for a refill. Returning to his desk, he took a nice long sip. He could feel the caffeine having an instant effect on him.

Time to try again—he had all day if he needed it. He typed: "Lady of Snow.' Reams of articles popped up, but his scanning eyes stopped on one. The item referenced 'Our Lady of the Snows.' He clicked on it.

The Island of Nevis in the Caribbean.

Brett felt his heart begin to pound as he read. Nevis was the sister island of St. Kitts, located in the Leeward Islands of the West Indies. Located close to the U.S. owned island of Puerto Rico, Nevis was separated from its sister island by only a two-mile channel known as "The Narrows." The island was famous for being a getaway for the rich and famous, including the late Princess Diana.

The name 'Nevis' was derived from the Spanish phrase, 'Nuestra Senora de las Nieves,' which, translated, meant 'Our Lady of the Snows.' Even though the residents of Nevis, past and present, had never seen snow, it was named this by the Spanish in the 16th Century. Apparently the constant appearance of a cloud over the mountain known as Nevis Peak in the center of the island reminded someone of a miracle snowfall that was recorded to have occurred on Esquiline Hill in Rome back in the 4th Century. This was heralded as just one more of countless Catholic miracles and was astounding for the mere fact that the warm Italian climate could not support snowfall. Seeing the cloud over Nevis was reminiscent of the miracle snow in a climate where it didn't belong.

Brett continued to search for more information about Nevis. He was excited now.

He got even more excited by what he read next.

He remembered Randy's reference to monkeys being tested at the lab in addition to chimpanzees. Those other monkeys were nicknamed 'Greenies.' Nevis and St. Kitts both had very high and out-of-control populations of African Green Monkeys, otherwise known as Vervet Monkeys. There were tens of thousands of these little green monkeys, vastly outnumbering the human populations of both islands.

Brett cracked his knuckles and took another long sip of his strong coffee. He could feel the adrenaline rushing through his veins. So far, he had found the 'Snow Lady' connection and it connected to Nevis. And so did the 'Greenies' reference. He kept surfing.

He read about how the government of St. Kitts and Nevis had been struggling for years to control the Vervet Monkey population, which were plaguing farmers. Crop destruction had been widespread and for a country that had been trying desperately to be self-sufficient, these little monkeys had become a dangerous threat to the fragile economy.

The country even had a 'Monkey Task Force,' charged with finding ways to eliminate the little buggers, humanely or otherwise. Their motto was: 'The only good monkey is a dead monkey.' The government even offered its citizens twenty dollars a head as a monkey bounty, and some of these unfortunate murder victims ended up in the kitchens of some of the finest restaurants on the island.

Spaying and neutering programs as alternatives to killing them outright had been undertaken on the islands as well. There were even attempts to export them to whichever countries would take them for purposes of scientific research or zoo display. There hadn't been too many takers, due to the concern of introducing a non-indigenous animal to foreign environments. All zoos ran that risk of course, but the animals in most zoos had been born in those countries, and most animals also didn't have the disturbing reputation of anti-social behavior like the Vervets did.

One of the most prominent complaints showing up in the articles came from affluent homeowners and condominium investors. There were so many monkeys on Nevis that new developments inevitably encroached upon the habitats of the green little beasts. Cute at first, but inevitably very dangerous. Brett saw a reference to one development in particular, and he made a note to check on that one later—a place called 'Paradise Villas.'

Hello? What's this?

An American-run laboratory was located on Nevis!

And it was a monkey lab!

Known as the 'Behavioral Modification Foundation,' it was situated in the lush jungles inland from the beaches and about halfway towards Nevis Peak in the center of the island. The article reported that this lab had been operated by U.S. interests on Nevis for several decades.

That timeline fit nicely.

The existence of this lab on Nevis had created a whole new industry: Monkey Trapping. The lab paid trappers to bring them monkeys, after which they were reportedly either exported or experimented with.

The experiments were apparently done for pharmaceutical and biotech corporations. Some experiments were referred to in the article: pumping them full of PCP, alcohol, and chemicals to observe the creation of Parkinson's disease; drilling into their brains to implant human tissue and stem cells; cutting off limbs to practice microsurgery; and the deliberate sacrificing of their little lives to cure a vast array of human disorders.

Without a doubt, this was the island that Randy had detected in his hacking. This was 'Snow Lady.' This was the island that had 'Greenies,' Chimpanzees, and a laboratory run by the United States of America. This was where the microbiology experiments were being performed with the organisms and creepy crawlers collected from the moon. Brett had no doubts now.

He went back to his notes. 'Paradise Villas.' He searched this—hundreds of articles popped up pertaining to condominium and hotel complexes from every corner of the globe.

But there was only one article he was interested in. It just jumped out and seemed to scream at him.

Brett read:

"Nevis Luxury Condo Development a White Elephant

There were great expectations when international developer 'Paradise Luxury Living Corp.' came to the island of Nevis with a proposal. A proposal that would set a new standard of luxury on the idyllic island.

A complex situated on one of Nevis' prettiest

stretches of beaches, with every high-end luxury imaginable including private pools for each of the forty-six villas, became a reality within two years of breaking ground.

The average selling price for the villas was 1.2 million dollars, with most of the buyers being from the United States and Great Britain. But elation of home ownership quickly turned to horror, when a 'troop' of Vervet Monkeys rampaged the complex two months ago. Information is now slowly leaking to the media from owners who abandoned their units, vowing never to return to Nevis.

It was a celebration night. The developer was hosting a party for the new owners in a central area of the complex. Music was playing, drinks and food were flowing, when suddenly a 'troop' of monkeys descended on the festivities.

Monkeys are frequent pests on the island but rarely are they violent. That night they were.

Twelve owners were killed—literally ripped apart, with their remains dragged into the jungle. As this was happening, the remainder of the 'troop' began pelting the partygoers with rocks, chasing them back to the safety of their villas.

Several former owners were interviewed by this reporter. One common refrain seemed to come from all—the attack appeared organized and almost seemed military in precision.

And, a surprising observation came out in the interviews: the killer monkeys seemed much larger than the others; they resembled Chimpanzees. The smaller Vervet Monkeys seemed to be running interference for the larger ones; they were the first wave. Then the big ones attacked.

It is to be expected that the horror of what these unfortunate people witnessed could cause their memories to be somewhat distorted. But what is indeed fact and can't be disputed, is that twelve people lost their lives that horrible night.

And a beautiful development is now a white elephant, a ghost town, probably never to be occupied again.

For purposes of clarity in this article, it should be noted that Chimpanzees are not native to Nevis, and Horatio Gibbons, Minister of the Interior was quoted as follows: "Chimpanzees have never been allowed entry to the country for zoological, scientific or any other purpose. The government sympathizes with the victims of this horrible animal attack, and although rare, there is always an inherent risk where wildlife is concerned. The Vervet Monkeys are the only animal primates that inhabit St. Kitts/Nevis, and as with all animals, they should be treated with caution and respect. New developments do encroach on their natural habitat. This is a fact that must be understood."

CHAPTER TWENTY SIX

It was date night.

The popcorn had been delicious. And 'The Amazing Spiderman' was the best version of that movie series Dennis had seen yet.

Fiona had looked stunning.

First, they had spent two wonderful hours at an exclusive French cuisine restaurant, where they dined on escargots, foie gras, and roast duck a l'orange. After that they walked down to the movie theatre to watch Spidey climb walls and save the world. Dennis thought 'Spiderman' was probably the most endearing of all the cartoon vigilantes.

Now they were sitting on the couch in Fiona's living room.

And Fiona looked even more stunning.

She had just poured them each a glass of Zinfandel and they continued the discussion they'd started over dinner.

"Denny, the things I told you about Matt—I hope I didn't go on too much about him. I mean, it's been five years now since he died and I'm probably not completely over it, but I want you to know that I'm not one to live in the past." She cocked her head. "You do believe me, don't you?"

Dennis reached over and gently squeezed her bare shoulder. "I don't know if I believe you—and I don't know if it's even all that important if I do or not. You had a great marriage, something I didn't have. You loved him. I didn't really love Cathy. You lost Matt to a drunk driver—your dreams shattered. How can you not live in the past sometimes?"

"But I don't want to."

"It doesn't matter if you want to or not. It may be something you have no control over. You may just need more time—but time itself may not even make a difference. And maybe that's not such a bad thing."

Fiona reached her hand over and rubbed Dennis' knee. "Does it bother you if he's still on my mind from time to time?"

Dennis shook his head. "No, it doesn't. Probably because I know that I'm such a mesmerizingly handsome and charming dude, that eventually you won't even remember your own name, let alone anyone else's!"

Fiona laughed and curled up close to him, laying her head on his shoulder. "You know what, Mr. Mesmerizingly Handsome and Charming Dude? You are all that. I like you. I like you a lot."

"I like you too, Fiona. In fact, I think it's getting past the 'like' stage. I love spending time with you, whether we're discussing this mystery we've stumbled upon, or discussing our lives. I just love it."

She turned her head toward his. "You're so easy to talk to. Why is that? I've found most men to be so shallow and self-centered. You make me feel so comfortable."

Dennis smiled tenderly at her. "I have a confession to make. You were instantly familiar to me when I first saw you. I felt as if I knew you already; talking with you just seemed so natural to me. Like I'd known you, and cared about you my whole life."

She smiled, cute little crinkles forming around the corners of her eyes. "It is weird, isn't it? Is this what they call 'chemistry?'"

Dennis kissed her on the tip of her nose. "I don't care what they call it. But to be honest, I think it's just my mesmerizingly handsome and charming nature."

Fiona sighed and swung her legs up over his and wiggled her ass up onto his lap. She put her bare arm around his neck and curled her hand around the side of his face. Fiona kissed him on the lips and allowed it to linger, sliding her own lips from side to side. Then she used her tongue to pry the door open. Dennis met the gesture with his own eager tongue.

He felt an incredible rush of passion just from the kiss. He pressed hard, she pressed back. Dennis wrapped one arm under her legs, the other under her arms, and stood up, lifting her gently. He carried her with ease over to the double chaise, their lips and tongues still probing while he walked.

He laid her down on the chaise and reached under her hiked skirt. In one swift move her panties were on the floor, while Fiona was quickly pulling her dress up over her head. She worked on the buttons of his shirt while he struggled with the clasp of her bra. She was quicker. Fiona giggled and pushed his hands away, and simply pulled the bra up over her head. She whispered, "Why do you guys always have trouble with bra clasps?"

Dennis grinned. "They're far too dainty for us. We think big."

Fiona giggled again and reached for his belt. "Well, let's just see how big you think."

She slid his pants down to his ankles and began rubbing the bulge in his underwear. "Ooh, I believe you do think big!"

Their lips connected again, frantically this time. Dennis felt his breath coming in gulps as he moved his hands across her smooth skin, exploring as quickly as he could every aspect of her beautiful body. Her skin was like velvet and her breasts felt so warm and comforting pressed up against his chest. He wrapped his fingers around the back of her neck and pulled her face tight to his. She sighed and slid her fingernails down his back.

He teased her. Entering for a few seconds, then out again. Dennis did this for several minutes until Fiona finally had enough and placed both her hands on his buttocks, digging her nails into his flesh. She held him firm and wouldn't let him withdraw. He knew she was ready.

Dennis moved rhythmically inside the beautiful woman underneath him. He could feel the heat from her skin and savored her labored breath inside his mouth. She was getting wetter and wetter, then suddenly tighter and tighter—in a pulse. The pulse was unmistakable, a contraction that seemed to shudder all the way up to her mouth. Fiona said, "Hold on," then grabbed his hair and yanked his head to the side, away from her mouth.

She gasped and then giggled—to herself, not to him. And the pulse through her body made Dennis gasp himself as he felt the explosion. He lost control and he prayed to God in that instant that he had held on long enough for her.

They lay together breathing hard for several minutes. Her left hand still had a firm hold on his hair. Dennis turned his face sideways and found her staring at him. The dreamy smile on her face told him that he had indeed held on long enough for her.

And that dreamy smile convinced him in that instant that he had fallen hopelessly in love with this girl.

*****

Lloyd Foster had his shopping cart full of the usual bachelor stuff—TV dinners, red meat, chocolate bars, cookies, and pop. Sustenance. He moved slowly through the aisles, double-checking to make sure he hadn't forgotten anything tasty that he would have a sudden urge for in the middle of the night.

He was starting to get good at shopping. It was his wife, Janet, who had always done this. Lloyd had had to force himself to do this domestic stuff now, because...well...he had no choice.

Janet was dead.

And so were Trevor, Hayley, and Bobby.

Lloyd wasn't responsible. That's what the jury said. And that's what the court-appointed psychiatrist had said. Hey, Lloyd was a doctor himself—he knew the score and he knew how to play the game. He spent months planning it, faking it, creating a pattern of bizarre behavior that he knew would have to be presented in court.

He was deemed legally insane.

Five years in a mental institution and he was deemed cured.

Just as he'd planned it. And the insurance policies had no choice but to pay up.

He still lived in his old house—it had waited patiently for him. Seeing the rooms where he'd given his family fifty whacks with a hatchet didn't even bother him. Lloyd was desensitized.

But naturally the court had seen tears and remorse, and total confusion as to how he couldn't believe he had done such a thing, couldn't remember one single moment of that horrifying night. And the mental home saw the same things. He played them all like useless fiddles.

He made his way up to the checkout counter. The looks he got—well, what could he expect? He still lived in the same neighborhood as he did five years ago and people remembered him, or at least recognized him from his photos in the newspaper. It had indeed been a high-profile case, ripe with outrage and hatred. He hated it when people hated.

He was free as a bird now. No more screaming, whining, ungrateful kids. Sure, they had all been under twelve years of age, but he didn't really think they'd get any better over time. And Janet had become a bore. The kids were everything to her, and he felt like he didn't matter anymore. And the expenses—the big house, the mortgage, car payments, saving for university. It all became too much. His gambling debts hadn't helped of course, but he needed some kind of release and that was it.

He could no longer practice as an orthopedic surgeon; his license having been revoked shortly after the trial. But that didn't matter now—the insurance proceeds had been more than enough to pay off all the debts and leave him with enough money in the bank that he didn't really have to do anything anymore. And he didn't want to do anything anymore, except have fun and enjoy his freedom.

The checkout lady frowned at him as he piled his groceries up onto the conveyor. He recognized her. She'd worked at this store for at least ten years, and by the look on her face he could tell she recognized him. A familiar look of disgust and horror.

He smiled at her. "How are you today, dear?"

She glared back at him. "Did you find everything you were looking for?"

Lloyd figured he'd have some fun with this busybody. "Well, there was one thing I was hunting for and couldn't find. Maybe you can help me?"

She put her hands on her hips, and mumbled, "What is it?"

Lloyd smiled. "A hatchet."

She put her hand up to her mouth and started gagging. Lloyd laughed. The checkout lady made a mad beeline down the exit aisle toward the washroom. Lloyd laughed again.

A new girl came over and finished the job, packing all his goods into two bags and handing them to him with a smile. "Have a nice day, sir."

"Oh, I intend to."

It was dark outside now. Lloyd loved these twenty-four-hour supermarkets. Whenever he got the urge to shop, he could just shop.

He walked to the back of the parking lot where his BMW X6 was parked. Another little present from himself to himself in celebration of his new freedom. He placed his parcels in the trunk and before he had the chance to close the hatch, he found himself being spun around from behind.

He was a handsome sort, tall, piercing eyes, dimples. The man smiled at him, and reached into the trunk. He took out one of the just-purchased cans of pop and began spinning it around in his hand, then tossing it into the air and catching it.

"Hey, what are you doing? Put that back!" Lloyd was annoyed. Probably just another angry neighbor wanting to give him a hard time.

Suddenly the man moved his left arm—jabbed his index finger forward into his stomach. Lloyd screamed and looked down. Blood was pouring out of his shirt from an almost perfect circular hole. He looked up and the very instant he did, he could see the blur of a red pop can ramming toward his shocked open mouth.

The tinkling sound of smashed teeth was sickening. But the ram didn't stop at his teeth. The can continued making its way part way down his throat, widening his face and neck in the process. He raised his hands in defense, but the other man's hands were faster, breaking his wrists with what seemed like no effort at all.

Lloyd was choking to death.

He could see the round edge of the bottom of the can peeking out of his mouth. He instinctively tried to push the can out with what was left of his tongue, and struggled to contract his broken jawbones. Nothing was working. As a doctor, he knew he had little time left.

His handsome assailant grabbed him by the shirt collar now and threw him backwards into the trunk. Then he slid him down so that Lloyd was facing upwards at the edge of the hatch lid. The man smiled again, reached his hand up and slammed the lid downward.

Lloyd could see it coming. And his neck was clearly in the way of the locking mechanism.

He would see his family again now. He hoped they'd understand.

CHAPTER TWENTY SEVEN

Brett was drinking coffee and surfing the net once again in his favorite Internet café. He felt safe here, and it was usually almost empty.

He started wondering about how safe he would be after the 'package' was retrieved. He knew how ruthless the government could be—first hand knowledge. He was well aware of how many people he had had to silence over the years. Even though he never knew all the details, he presumed the predominant reasons for losing their lives was that they knew too much. Or couldn't be controlled. Or they were just plain evil.

Even poor James Layton lost his life for two of those reasons. This Barb Jenkins had told Fiona that he was threatening to go to the Press. Shortly thereafter, he was shot in the head. According to Barb, on the wrong side of the head. If anyone had dug deeper on that point, the suicide theory would have been discounted quick.

And now here he was, being suspected by his good friend, Bill Charlton, of sticking his nose in where it didn't belong. It was true, of course. Bill wasn't accustomed to discovering that Brett had researched deep background on an assignment. Usually Brett just did the job, gave Bill what he needed, and pocketed the cash.

But Bill had told him that the 'package' had to do with the Apollo moon missions. If he hadn't told him that, Brett would have happily gone ahead with the job as he usually did—with brutal efficiency.

But how was Bill to know that outer space, and the moon, were absolute obsessions of Brett's? He had never shared that with him when they'd had beers together. It was one of those nerdy interests that had developed when he was just a kid. And Brett was far from being a nerd, even back when he was a kid. But growing up was tough, and friends could be cruel. If a boy had a hobby like science, astronomy, animals, music, he kept it quiet. Enjoyed it on the sly. No one needed to know. Because if they did know, all hell could break loose on the precious image.

And to a kid, image was everything. Just to survive.

As an adult, Brett figured he had just gotten used to keeping his interests to himself, even when he was together with friends like Bill. They just didn't need to know.

So, Bill had innocently let something slip; something more stimulating than he could have possibly realized when he told Brett that the 'package' had something to do with the moon missions. He had no idea what kind of 'Pandora's box' he'd opened in Brett's brain when he said that.

A little voice was now whispering away inside Brett's brain—a voice that he had listened to numerous times during his career. A voice that had never failed to warn him of imminent danger.

He had no idea how much Bill knew he knew—that was what bothered him. For his friend to actually ask him the question that he did was telling enough. Was he trying to warn him off? Was he basically hinting that as long as he didn't discover anything else, he'd be okay? Did he really not know who was going with Dennis up to the cabin? Was he keeping that secret from Brett rather than betray who his contact double was?

Or was it like what the Mafia liked to do—a kiss on the cheek told you the end was nigh.

Brett decided that Bill's question was either the equivalent of a kiss on the cheek, or a horse's head under the sheets.

And he knew that friendship meant nothing in the business he was in. It was a cold, brutal world, and a bullet could find you in the middle of the night if you weren't alert enough to know it was coming. Bill could easily order Brett's death, and probably wouldn't lose one night's sleep over it. Brett knew that for a fact—he wasn't naïve. Friendship was low on the totem pole of power.

At this point, Brett didn't know how he would handle the trip to the cabin on Chesapeake Bay next week. There was a good chance the 'package' was there. Would he open it and read it? Would he turn it over to Bill?

If indeed Brett was now in danger due to his snooping, it would be ironic if this 'package' which presumably had kept Lucy Chambers alive the last three decades, would now be needed by Brett to keep himself alive. Could he risk turning it over? And what was he going to do about everything he'd discovered? He doubted that the 'package' would tell him anything more than he already knew. But, it would be a valuable object of blackmail.

He now knew the horror of what had happened on September 30th, 1977. He knew that a nuke had been exploded on the surface of our precious moon. He knew that international law had been broken. And he knew that alien life had been brought back to earth—to be weaponized in a variety of ways.

And our closest relatives, Chimpanzees, were being used to discover how man could be manipulated, made stronger, more violent, more docile, smarter, weaker—every which way from natural.

Today Brett was reading all about Chimpanzees.

Chimps live in West and Central Africa, and are members of the Hominidae primate family. In that family are Chimpanzees, Gorillas, Orangutans...and Human Beings. The Hominids are otherwise referred to as the "Great Apes." Brett chuckled—*we think we're so superior, but look at the company we keep. And we're just considered one of the "Great Apes."*

Full-grown chimps can weigh up to 155 pounds and stand up to four feet tall. They rarely live past the age of forty in the wild, but have been known to survive to sixty in captivity.

They're omnivorous, which means, like humans, they eat food that comes from animals or plants. And they hunt—in troops, led by an alpha male.

Chimpanzees are considered to be the closest living evolutionary relatives to humans, sharing a common ancestor with us going back five million years. Chimps and humans have ninety-eight percent of their DNA in common. While the similarities are uncanny, the differences are also striking. Chimps rarely have heart attacks, are resistant to malaria, and never go through menopause. Most cancers common to humans are never found in chimps.

Males compete amongst themselves for status, and the dominant males mate promiscuously with the females. The child rearing is handled entirely by the females and those children actually become independent of their mothers within the very first year of their lives.

Chimp males don't hesitate to kill the children of their male rivals. And when a former alpha male leader is replaced by another alpha male, it's not uncommon to see the retiring male killed or maimed. Brett thought that this was an odd practice, and probably one of the biggest differences between chimps and humans. Retiring human leaders are revered and honored. He figured that chimps must consider their mere presence to continue to be a threat even after handing over the reins of power.

He read how Chimpanzees are now largely considered to be savage killers and ruthless cannibals—quite the contrast to how the world believed them to be before massive studies were undertaken in the last couple of decades.

Brett was surprised to read that chimps have their own primitive form of language, which gets passed down to new generations. And…they make and use tools; a trait that scientists had always insisted was one that humans owned exclusively.

Brett found it fascinating to read that, out of 4,000 other mammal species and ten million other non-mammal species, chimps and humans are the only species that are known to hunt and kill members of their own kind. Chimps do tend to take it one step further though—they'll cannibalize their own kind as well. Humans tend to do that only under extreme 'last chance to survive' scenarios, and only if the other human is already dead. Chimps will just make them dead.

A study at Harvard, by Richard Wrangham, proposed the 'demonic male hypothesis' to explain violent behavior seen in both male chimps and male humans. It suggests that since this trait is obviously inherent in both, that this tendency toward male violence in both primates was garnered from that common ancestor five million years ago. Both offspring primates held onto that trait, as they went off in different directions to evolve into chimps and humans.

Brett turned off the computer and walked over to the lounge area of the café. He helped himself to a glass of juice from the bar.

Looking out the window, watching normal everyday people walking down the street, he wondered which ones were the killers. He figured with chimps it was much easier—when they looked at each other they knew they were all killers. But humans had evolved in such a way as to stifle or hide that tendency, and in the vast majority of humans it was non-existent. Or at least, never provoked or stimulated in such a manner as to erupt. So, with humans, one just didn't know who the killers were. But it seemed likely that we all had the capacity to kill, under the right circumstances.

Brett knew he was a killer. But when he killed it always had a purpose. It wasn't for sport, it wasn't to eat. It was a job. And his victims always deserved it in one way or another—well, he hoped that was the case. He wasn't always privy to the details so he did a lot of assuming. Brett winced— he knew he was trying to justify himself. Was he no better than a chimp? Was he a perfect example of the evolution from that one common ancestor?

He was struck by the similarities between chimps and humans, and he got the shivers remembering that these beasts were six times stronger than humans.

And they were being stimulated even further now. Evolution was possibly taking another turn like it had five million years ago. This time with alien life from the moon. He wondered about the one chimp that had the honor of being the next 'Ancestor X'—the one who would mimic what our common ancestor had done five million years ago. Create offspring that would evolve into two new species.

Two alien species.

This time not on the African continent, but on an island nicknamed 'Snow Lady.'

CHAPTER TWENTY EIGHT

At first, he didn't see her. Where did she go?

Dennis was a bit groggy. A bit too much wine last night. He rolled off the side of the bed and onto the floor. Then he saw the unmistakable shape of a woman's body completely encased in the sheets, head hidden under the pillow.

He walked around to her side of the bed and shook her gently. Fiona moaned and lifted her head out from under the pillow.

"I can't move. What have you done to me? Help, please?"

Dennis started unwrapping her. Somehow Fiona had rolled herself up in her sheets, arms pinned to her side. She looked like she'd been mummified. And somehow without using her hands, she had buried her head under the pillow.

Amazing.

He couldn't help but laugh. "Do you do this often, Fiona?"

"Stop laughing. And no, this has never happened before. I think you did it to me!"

"Now why would I do that? You didn't exactly resist me last night."

Fiona ran her fingers through her hair. "No, but maybe your kinky side came out after we fell asleep." She paused, with her hand stuck in a lock of hair.

"Oh my God, look at my hair! Yikes! It's all curly and frizzy! Out of my way—I'm off to the shower!"

With that she was gone.

Dennis chuckled as he pulled on his underpants and jeans. He figured he might as well make them some coffee while she was in the shower. He knew he really should get a move on, and visit the office. He hadn't seen it in three or four days. Preoccupation with everything else that was going on. Well, maybe later—hanging around with Fiona for a few hours today appealed to him more. She had the day off and he figured maybe he should just take part of the day off too.

Dennis made the coffee strong—he hoped she'd like it that way. After last night's wine, he figured they could both use a good strong jolt.

She was out of the shower when he brought the coffees upstairs, a towel wrapped around her head, another one around her body.

"Well, so far this morning, the only way I've seen you is wrapped up in various forms of cotton. How about a couple of good strong arms now?"

Fiona smiled with that captivating little twinkle in her eyes that she seemed to be able to produce on demand.

She dropped the towel.

*****

An hour later they were drinking cold coffee in bed. And talking.

"So, what do you think we're going to find at your mother's cabin next week?"

"I really believe we're going to find the damn thing—the damn package. And God knows what it's going to contain. And God knows what I'm going to do with it."

Fiona leaned on her elbow, chin resting in her hand. "It absolutely has to have something to do with Apollo 18 and 19, and this 'Shackleton' crater. The moon is what was causing your mom all that anguish—and those are the things she blurted out."

"Yep, I'm bracing myself."

Fiona grimaced as she took another cold sip of coffee. "Why do you think the moon has always been such a fascination to…well…virtually everyone?"

"There are a lot of scientific aspects that are beyond my level of understanding. So, some people a lot smarter than me have designs on it, I'm sure. But also, maybe we're all so interested in it because it's there. And it's romantic. And it's comforting. Maybe all of those things keep us almost hypnotized."

"And because it's so close. It's the only celestial body we can see clearly with the naked eye."

"You're right, Fiona. And did you know that it used to be a lot closer?"

"Tell me a story, Denny." She smiled and laid her head on his chest.

"Well, okay. Are you sure I won't bore you?"

"It doesn't matter. I just love the sound of your voice—it soothes me.

Say anything."

"Well, once upon a time about 4.5 billion years ago, the earth which was at that time even more of a watery planet than it is now, collided with a smaller planet called Orpheus. This blew half of earth's water out into space. Orpheus bounced off the earth, then the earth's gravity grabbed it and sucked it back in again for one more hit. A big chunk left over from that second impact bounced away again and began orbiting the earth. That's how our moon was formed."

Fiona kissed him on the cheek. "I didn't know that. Keep talking, moon man."

"This is what I meant when I said it was a lot closer at one time. After that impact, it was orbiting at a distance of only 14,000 miles away from us."

Fiona stroked his chest. "How far away is it now?"

"It's 234,000 miles away from us now. But, get this—back when it was a lot closer, it was also a lot larger. Fifteen times larger than it is now. At that size, it had a 4,000 times greater pull on earth's landmasses and seas. Can you imagine how high the tides might have been back then, and the massive earthquakes we probably had? Unfathomable."

Fiona shook her head and pursed her lips. "Unfathomable, Denny." She giggled.

He kissed her gorgeous lips and held her close for a few seconds. "Are you sure you want to hear all this? You're mocking me."

"Oh, I just love it when you get all serious. Carry on, Einstein."

"Okay. Well, back when the moon was that large, our days on earth were only four hours long. So, size does matter, Fiona.

"However, now that the moon is a lot smaller and farther away from us, our days are a pretty much constant twenty-four hours, the moon's gravity pull keeps the earth's tilt at a constant 23 degrees and our seasons are fairly stable—although lately I'm starting to wonder about that a bit."

"What do you mean?"

"Well, you have to be worried about the weather extremes we've been seeing. Floods in Europe and Asia, monster hurricanes, tornado swarms out of season, massive earthquakes that shifted the earth's poles, and incredible heat waves that last longer and visit us earlier. Makes you wonder if everything is okay with the moon, doesn't it? Or it could be something else that's causing these things. I don't know, but I don't think what we're seeing is normal, and it seems to be getting worse every year."

"That's a scary thought."

"Yes, it is. Do you know that if we didn't have our moon, the earth would wobble like a spinning top, continuously? Snow would fall in Egypt, polar ice caps would boil, and entire islands would disappear. And let's say we still had the moon but it was in a different orbit half the distance from the earth than it is right now—our ocean tides would be eight times higher. That would only be one part of the chaos we'd have on earth."

"How big is the moon. It looks so large, doesn't it?"

"Yes, but it's only twenty-five percent of the size of earth. It takes about twenty-seven days to revolve around the earth. Fiona, the moon is moving farther away from the earth because its orbit is expanding as it slows down its speed. It's moving away at the rate of one and a half inches per year. Which means that a long, long time from now if it keeps moving away, our earth will look a lot different, our days will be much longer, and our climate will be unrecognizable."

Fiona shivered, pulled the sheets up over them and closed her eyes.

"Suddenly, the moon doesn't sound so romantic, Denny."

Dennis laughed. "It's just one of many things that we take for granted, I guess. Most people wouldn't even think that it serves any real purpose other than to cause tides, or give us something nice to look at at night. I've been fascinated by the moon since I was a kid, and most people I've talked to about it just yawns and change the subject to something else. Our lives would sure be different if it wasn't there, or if it wasn't the size it is, or if it wasn't in the orbit that it is. Any one of those things would cause a multitude of cataclysms. And despite that, most people just nod off."

"Fiona?"

CHAPTER TWENTY NINE

"Catch me if you can!"

Five words that still resonated in Dennis' mind twenty years later. And five words that were issued as a challenge—one that Dennis took very seriously.

He had spent a year in China trying to forget, trying to work out his anger and desperation. Not just about his dad's death, but about society in general. How sick the underbelly was. How he got to see so many innocent victims die horrible deaths only to have the sick killers walk.

China, in so many ways, had helped him deal with his demons. But they never really went away. And he knew they never would. He began to look at everything sideways after the death of his father, how unfair it all seemed to be, why so many good ones had to die and so many bad ones got off scot-free. It made him furious. It made him want to do something about it.

Dennis had to admit that the system just didn't work. The stupid gun freedoms in the U.S.—idiotic. Just because it was entrenched in the Constitution—the beloved sacred cow Constitution—gave every sick freak the right to walk around with a gun. The Bill of Rights was repeatedly used as a patriotic pathetic excuse to be barbaric.

The so-called 'Right to Bear Arms.' Dennis thought that maybe the idiots who drafted the Constitution just couldn't spell right. Maybe they were just trying to patronize women and really meant to say, 'Right to Bare Arms.' Maybe a mere spelling mistake had led to this madness.

And the justice system itself? The countless number of rapists and murderers who Dennis and his men locked up who gleefully walked due to silly technicalities, even though everyone knew they were guilty as sin, made him sick. Made him feel useless. And impotent.

He didn't have to work anymore, but for some reason he still did. Despite his frustrations he still felt he could make a difference. Being on the job rather than out of the job gave him the ability to make a difference. And Dennis, despite his cynicism, still had hope.

China had given him discipline and order. Focus and intensity. And the deadliest martial arts skills available to man.

Dennis Chambers could still make a difference.

"Catch me if you can!"

Dennis had already caught the beast. The asshole just didn't know it yet.

He had him sixteen years ago. He just chose not to keep him.

It had been almost four years to the day of his dad's death when Dennis got the call. A man who had been arrested on drug and attempted murder charges was sitting in a jail cell awaiting trial. He had bragged to a cellmate that he had once forced a policeman to kill his own father in a game of Russian Roulette. The cellmate excitedly told the jail guards hoping to strike a better deal for himself.

Dennis was summoned to the precinct where the man was being held, to view him in a lineup to see if he could identify him. Dennis remembered racing down to the station with his siren on and lights flashing. He wanted it to be the right man so badly he could literally taste it. Bile was rising from the boiling mess that had become his stomach, ever since he heard the words: *"Denny, you won't believe this—we think we have him!"*

Standing behind the one-way glass, Dennis was seething. He didn't think he would be able to stop himself from going into his Shaolin stance and breaking the thick bulletproof glass with his mere forefinger. He just wanted to kill him.

In marched five men—Dennis recognized three of them as undercover officers. They all did what they were told and stepped up onto the little stage set up just for them.

Dennis didn't have to look at him for very long. Even though four years had gone by, it was a face he would never forget. He stood about six feet tall, broad shoulders, stubble on his chin, cold squinting eyes. He had a scar snaking down the side of one cheek, and his hair hung in greasy strands down to his shoulders.

The beast hadn't changed much in four years, except perhaps a tiny bit uglier. The man was fidgeting with his hands until yelled at by the police guard to 'stand still.' He sneered back at the officer and allowed the sneer to linger—Dennis thought he looked very much like a taller stockier version of Charles Manson.

A face of pure evil.

The Assistant District Attorney excitedly asked Dennis, "Well, what do you think?"

Dennis was careful not to portray any emotion whatsoever on his face when he replied, "Nope, it's not him. Wrong guy."

The prosecutor stared back at him with her mouth agape. Several seconds went by until she said in a whisper, "Denny, take another look. We're sure he's the guy."

Dennis patronized her by looking through the glass one more time. He shook his head, "No Jessica, that's not the guy. I would know his face anywhere."

"But Denny, he basically confessed!"

Dennis shoved his hands into his pockets and walked to the door. "There's no one who wanted it to be him more than me. You know that. He's probably just some creep who heard the story from someone else or from the real killer, and has adopted it as his own story. He's trying to be a big man. We'll keep looking—we'll find him one of these days."

That was the end of it. The creep was convicted of the dual crimes of dealing cocaine, and the attempted murder of another drug dealer. He got a sentence of ten years, and was released six years ago.

And now Dennis had him in his sights.

He was sitting in his Mercedes on Q Street, watching Travis Wilkinson walking home from work. Dennis was parked near the man's house, a modest brownstone in a fairly nice neighborhood.

He watched as Travis walked up the steps; the door opened before he got to the top. A pretty brunette greeted him with a smile and a hug, and a toddler came toddling out the door into his waiting arms. He swung her around and kissed her on the cheek. Travis had a family. He was a husband now…and a dad.

Dennis had used his connections to keep track of Travis while he was in prison. By all accounts, he had been a model prisoner, taking courses in accounting and finally achieving a Bachelor of Math degree. He had also 'found religion' in prison and developed a talent for public speaking. Once a month, Travis gave lectures to fellow prisoners in the mess hall, on topics that would help them adjust to life on the outside.

He had developed into quite the motivational speaker, giving rousing speeches on leaving the past behind and embracing the future as 'better people.' He worked on his diction, handing over the money he earned in prison to hire a speech therapist. The therapist came to see him once a week for two years. Apparently, Travis' command of the English language was now superb.

Dennis observed the happy family scene on the doorstep and was taken by how different Travis looked from when he had seen him in the lineup sixteen years ago. He was now clean-shaven, short styled hair, elegant black suit. He knew he worked as an assistant actuary at a local life insurance company. The man was a junior executive now—able to afford all the things his little family deserved. And he seemed to adore them.

Dennis wanted to put a hole in his head.

He could have identified him in the lineup sixteen years ago, but that would have meant a trial, which if convicted, might have added another twenty-five years to his ten-year sentence. That wouldn't have been good. Not good enough.

Dennis wanted him out, wanted him free as a bird.

He could have contacted Travis when he first left prison six years ago. But China had taught him to be patient, be disciplined. Focus and wait for when it would mean more than just vengeance.

Dennis wanted Travis to have a life—to fall in love, have a child or two, get a great job. Things that added value to a life. Things a person wouldn't want to lose.

It would have been too easy and less impactful earlier. There would have been no fear of loss, no fear of leaving behind people who loved him and depended on him. The pain would have only been partial—Dennis wanted him to have total pain. Pain that tore at his gut. The kind of pain Dennis had been feeling for the last twenty years. The pain his mom had felt before she lost her mind. And the pain that Melissa had felt so strongly that day of the funeral—so strongly that she had to be drugged into an almost comatose state.

Dennis wanted all of that for Travis.

So, he had waited.

And it was almost time.

He had been doing surveillance on Travis for six years now. He had been a very good boy and most definitely had turned his life around. He was probably the ex-con's poster child. Proof that evil can turn into good, or at least be suppressed so that good could prevail.

As a police officer, this is exactly what Dennis wanted to see happen with ex-cons.

Except for the one who had killed his father.

He enjoyed seeing it happen with Travis only so that he could see the fear in the whites of his eyes when it suddenly dawned on him that he could lose it all. And that the ones he loved could lose him.

Soon. Very soon.

Dennis and Travis had one final match to play.

One more game of Russian Roulette.

CHAPTER THIRTY

"Denny, I'm so sorry. They called me in and asked me a bunch of questions, and I couldn't lie. You know me. I hope what I told them doesn't mean anything."

Dennis got up from behind his desk and came around to hug his secretary. She was sobbing and he handed her a tissue. "Calm down, Nancy. Who are 'they' and what did you tell them?"

"Oh, Denny, I know they're digging for something. Be careful. They asked about your martial arts training. I don't know how they knew, but they did. They asked about your workouts, times away from the office, things like that."

Dennis gently rubbed her back. "Again, who were they?"

"Well, you know Grant Folsom of course, Chief of Police; your friend Bart Davis, Chief of Internal Affairs; and someone named Bill Charlton with the Pentagon."

"The Pentagon?"

"I don't know what he was doing there. He didn't say a word—just took notes. A rather cold fish, to be honest."

"Nancy, you did the right thing by telling them the truth. I have nothing to hide. So, don't worry about it, okay?"

Nancy Willis stretched up on her tiptoes and kissed Dennis on the cheek. "You're everything to me, you know that. Be careful. And...they want to see you in half an hour—in the Capitol Board Room."

Dennis shrugged. "I'll see what they have to say. Don't worry about me, Nancy, okay?"

"Dennis, if they fire you, I'm quitting."

He smiled tenderly at her. "That's sweet, but it's a bit premature for that."

*****

The Capitol Board Room was the most officious of all the meeting rooms. It had dark lighting and a monstrous board table. There were windows but Dennis had never seen the blinds open. It seated twenty people. Seated at the head of one end of the table was his boss, Grant Folsom, Chief of Police. To his right was Dennis' buddy, Bart Davis, Chief of Internal Affairs—the one who had refused to help him and actually warned him about snooping around the Department of Defense. To Grant's left was the Pentagon guy, Bill Charlton.

Dennis was told to sit at the other end of the table, which he thought was weird. From that alone, he knew this wasn't going to be a friendly chat. It was going to be a formal inquisition, and he'd either conducted or sat in on dozens of them during his career.

Grant started it off. "Dennis, you've had a storied career with the Department. There is no one who could question that. In fact, you've been one of the top candidates to succeed me in my job."

He paused.

"But we have a serious situation here that we need to discuss. There's a serial killer on the loose and we received indications from one of the major media outlets a few days ago that they're going to break the story if we don't release something ourselves first. You've been in charge of this investigation—and there have been no results whatsoever."

Dennis stared right back at Grant without blinking. "This is not an easy case. Whoever the killer is, he or she is a pro. Let's say for now it's a 'he.' The extent of the injuries and the apparent strength of the killer lead us to believe it's a man. But that's where it ends. We have no leads, no witnesses, and our customary informants have picked up nothing on the street. I can't just manufacture a suspect from thin air."

"I know that, Dennis. But the three of us are very concerned."

Dennis pointed at Bill Charlton. "You say 'the three of us.' Who on earth is this guy, and what is he doing here? This is a police matter, not at all a matter of interest to the Department of Defense. Please give me the courtesy of an explanation."

"Mr. Charlton is here because one of the victims was a Defense Department employee."

"Which one?"

Charlton finally spoke. "I'm not at liberty to say. It's not important."

Dennis scoffed. "Well, it might be important to the investigation, you don't know that. You people want us to share everything with you, but you don't feel it works both ways, do you?"

"No, we don't, for obvious reasons."

Dennis scoffed again. "So, I'm wasting my time addressing you, aren't I? I won't bother. If you have a question of me you can submit it to my secretary, you arrogant prick."

"Now, now, Dennis. Calm down. There's no need for that." Bart Davis finally opened his mouth.

"Fuck off, Bart. And what are you doing here? Am I under investigation?"

Grant could tell he was losing control of the meeting. "Okay, emotions are high here and you're obviously frustrated Dennis, about the investigation. Let's just cool our jets. What we want you to do is simply walk us through each of the murders attributed to the serial killer. Give us a brief synopsis."

Dennis took a deep breath. He was angry and he seemed to be on the carpet due to the actions of an ingenious killer. He reached over to the water jug and poured himself a long cool one.

"I figured that was what this meeting was about. So, I came prepared. I'll briefly talk about the six murders that we definitely attribute to the serial killer. They've all occurred within the last five years, and with definite similarities in the fatal wounds.

"However, we have had a lot of debate between you and I, Grant, and many other members of the department about a missing person. I disagree that it's the work of the serial killer. You feel it is. Do you want me to address that one too?"

"Yes, I do. And there's one more missing person we want you to add to the list. We'll discuss that one after."

"Who?"

"We'll discuss it after."

Dennis frowned and opened his binder. "Okay, then, if you want the missing person included, then the first work of the serial killer was the husband of my own secretary, Nancy Willis. His name is Keith. Keith Willis. They were divorced about six years ago and he simply disappeared a year later. No one has heard from him, and we can't find any trace of him anywhere. We assume he's deceased. He was a philanderer and an abusive husband. He assaulted her once at a women's shelter. Nancy refused to press charges. Several months after the divorce we presume it was he who assaulted her once again. A terrible ordeal, it put Nancy in the hospital for a month. Once again, she refused to press charges. She was afraid for her life. Then he just disappeared. That was five years ago."

Dennis looked around the table. "Any questions?" Slow deliberate shakes of all three heads.

"Okay, I'll continue then. The second victim of the serial killer…er, let me clarify…in my opinion, the first victim of the serial killer, was a man by the name of Melvin Steed. He was a convicted child murderer and a known pedophile, having been convicted of ten rapes before the one murder pinned on him. We suspected there were more killings, but he wasn't talking. Anyway, for some reason the parole board felt he deserved early parole from his thirty-year sentence. He went to a halfway house, and we suspect he used that as a base for more attacks on children—or at least planning more attacks. At the scene of the murder—in a park—we found his backpack, which contained a number of items that a parolee shouldn't have had. Anyway, the fatal injuries to Melvin consisted of a severely crushed skull—crushed from the sides. Equal force on each side of his head. In short, his head shrunk inward, causing severe bleeding. His brain basically exploded within a few seconds of impact. We'd never seen an injury like this before—almost as if a vice grip had been applied to his head."

Dennis raised his head. "Any questions from the floor?" Silence. All three were writing notes.

"Well, the next murder was six months later. A man by the name of Fraser Benton, a notorious heroin dealer. Spent half his life in prison, and never showed an inclination toward reforming himself. In fact, despite his admission of this to the parole board each time he came up, they kept letting him out. He was suspected of having stashed millions in drug money somewhere in the city. Some lucky gangbanger will no doubt find it one of these days. Fraser's specialty was selling drugs to kids—teenagers. He'd get them hooked, then jack up the prices and eventually sell the kids into prostitution. A real charmer. His body was found in a parking lot, one of his forearms smashed into two pieces hanging together by a shred of skin, and both legs had been crushed by the wheels of a large vehicle. But oddly, he had injuries to his chest and forehead that resembled bullet holes at first glance. But the diameter was too wide. Both holes had penetrated about three inches deep and they were almost perfect circles. Possibly a blunt object, however forensics turned up nothing."

Dennis took a sip of water and could feel sweat forming under his arms and inside the collar of his shirt. The silence was unnerving. "Chief, you seemed anxious to hear about these killings, but none of you are showing any interest whatsoever. Am I not addressing certain aspects that you want to hear about?"

Grant looked up from the table. "No, Dennis, please continue. You're doing fine and you have our full attention."

"Alright then. The third murder—and please note that when I give numbers to the murders, I'm talking about actual known murders. I'm not including the disappearance of Keith Willis in my count. So, the third one was a man named Cliff Tonkin, killed about a year after Fraser Benton. This guy was charged with the home invasion slaughter of an entire family, including the rape of the mother. However, we screwed up—didn't get a search warrant for his apartment and didn't read him his Miranda. Needless to say, he got off. Cliff was killed in his own apartment—no signs of forced entry. Either he let the killer in, or he was waiting for him. Injuries to this victim consisted of trauma to the throat region consistent with a hard kick or punch, and a deep puncture wound through his abdomen right through both the front and back walls of his stomach. Again, possibly a blunt object. A stab of some kind, although the wound again was more circular in nature, not at all consistent with a knife. Death would have been slow for this victim.

"I'll move on to the fourth murder. This was a mere month after Cliff Tonkin. The victim's name was Salvatore Badali, an ex-marine who was suspected of being the infamous pawnshop killer. He was arrested on suspicion once and had been under surveillance for a time, but he was a slippery character. Nothing we could pin on him, and never any witnesses. There were four pawnshop killings that matched the same modus operandi: the robber would kill the proprietor as soon as he entered the store and then take all the cash from the drawers. In and out quick, no messing around. Anyway, he was found dead in his car, just around the block from another pawnshop. We suspect he was casing it. Salvatore died from a crushed skull that resulted in severe bleeding of the brain. The interesting fact of this death was that the skull was crushed from the top, as if a heavy object had been smashed directly downwards onto his head. At first, we thought the murder had been committed elsewhere and his body was placed in the car afterwards. But, no, the blood spatter evidence pointed to the murder being committed in the car. A strange murder, this one. The car was a Camaro, a low ceiling vehicle. Hard to believe anything would be able to hit him from above with that much force as to actually crush his skull when there wasn't much ceiling room."

Dennis looked up again. "I'm getting tired of asking this, but are there any questions? Anything at all?"

Heads shaking.

"The fifth murder was almost a year to the day after Sal Badali's death. Jim Morton was his name, and he was a four-time loser. A rapist who had raped more times than he'd been convicted of. We tried to lock him up eight other times but the evidence wasn't strong enough. He'd spent a total of twenty years in prison, but once again, we kept letting him out on parole. We found his body in an alley; horrific injuries. He'd been attempting to rape a young lady, and someone stepped in and prevented the attack. His penis was impaled onto the zipper of his jeans, and he had a hole through his throat, three in his forehead and three in his chest. This time we had a witness. A young lady came forward to report the attack, and the only description we have of the killer is that he was tall, dressed in black, and wearing some kind of ski mask. She was traumatized and that was the most we could get out of her. She said the man was gentle with her, and guided her out of the alley away from the rapist. She didn't even know what had happened to her assailant until after she reported the attack to us. We then told her he'd been killed.

"Okay, the sixth and final murder happened just four months ago. The victim was high profile: Lloyd Foster, an accomplished surgeon, who was charged with slaughtering his family with an axe—well, actually a hatchet. An axe would have been better—there wouldn't have been as much painful trauma to the victims. He went to trial and was declared legally insane at the time of the murders, thus totally exonerated. He went to an asylum for five years after which he was considered safe to return to the community. The murder of Lloyd Foster was particularly gruesome. He also had a deep hole in his stomach and...a pop can was rammed into his mouth so deep it broke his jawbones and ended up partway down his throat. His face and throat were completely distorted—the can would have to have been shoved into his mouth with incredible force for it to lodge as deep as it did. But that wasn't the end of Lloyd's ordeal. His torso was found in the trunk of his BMW, with his head on the ground behind the trunk lid. The lid had been slammed shut on his neck, decapitating him."

Dennis folded his binder shut, and looked down the table at his rapt audience. "You must have some questions now…or comments? Anything?"

Grant cleared his throat. "Dennis, it seems clear to me that we have a vigilante at work here."

"Yes, I would tend to agree. But I implore you—we can't even hint at that to the Press. The citizens will be behind this guy, whoever he is, and we could have a rash of copycats. No one is going to sympathize with the deaths of these characters; perhaps some will feel sick at the manner in which they died, but for most people there will simply be applause."

Bart jumped in. "Denny, while these six murders bear the signature of one person, probably a vigilante, and probably someone on the police force, we need to include the disappearance of Keith Willis in this string of crimes too. I know you disagree, but we feel strongly that it's the same perpetrator."

Dennis just nodded.

Finally, Bill Charlton spoke up. "There is one other disappearance we need to include as well. A nurse who attended to your mother—Felicity Dobson—disappeared shortly after the death of your mom. There is no trace of her whatsoever."

Dennis glared at him. "Is that the Defense Department employee who was referred to earlier? Are you in the habit of employing nurses for private care, courtesy of the Pentagon?"

"I told you before; I'm not at liberty to discuss who our employee was."

Dennis was starting to lose control. He hated the 'holier than thou' demeanor of this prick.

"You may think the rest of the world is stupid, Mr. Charlton, but it's a simple process of elimination here. I doubt if your employee was an abusive husband, a pedophile, a drug dealer, a home invader, a rapist, a pawnshop killer, or a family killer. So that leaves the nurse—geez, am I on the right track?"

Dennis wasn't prepared yet to admit what he knew about the Casper Agency being a front for the Defense Intelligence Agency. It was better that this spook didn't know what he knew.

"I'd rather not comment."

Grant cleared his throat again—Dennis noticed he was doing that a lot.

"Dennis, what concerns us is that both of the missing persons had a connection to you. Your secretary's husband, who was clearly abusive. And the nurse, who was entrusted with the care of your mother when she passed away. You had motive in both of those murders."

Dennis stood up and leaned forward with his fists resting on the table. "Correction—they are disappearances, they aren't murders. We do not have any evidence that those two people were killed. And what is this—am I a suspect?"

"We consider you a 'person of interest.' The coincidence of two missing persons being connected to you is too much for us to ignore."

Dennis was at a loss for words. He just stared into Grant's eyes. Grant gulped back a long sip of water. Dennis could tell he was extremely uncomfortable.

Bart waded back in to fill in the gaps for Grant. "We're also concerned that you might be connected with the six known murders too, Denny. We have learned that you acquired very dangerous martial arts skills while you were in China twenty years ago. You never disclosed that to us. You're not required to, but it would have been the right thing to do."

"Bart, everyone on the force knows some form of Karate or Kungfu. We were taught that at the Academy."

"Yes, Denny. But those rudimentary skills pale in comparison to the Shaolin skills that you acquired. I've done some research—some of the wounds recorded for the victims are consistent with one particular Shaolin art, known as 'Diamond Finger.' Would you deny that?"

"No, I wouldn't deny that. And it already occurred to me a long time ago that someone might be using skills similar to what I have in these killings. But we have no forensic proof to lead us in that direction."

Bill Charlton leaned forward on the board table and gestured his finger in Dennis' direction. "You are the perfect candidate for vigilantism, Mr. Chambers. Your father was brutally slain. You killed two of the bad guys that horrible night, but the other three culprits were never caught. You exiled yourself to China to learn secretive and deadly skills. And you had opportunity and inside knowledge with all of these killings and disappearances, being a highly trained police officer. I would suggest you get a lawyer."

Dennis ignored the prick. He turned his head to Grant. "Chief, am I under arrest?"

Grant glared at Bill Charlton, then turned his kindly face toward Dennis. "No, and Mr. Charlton had no cause to speak to you that way. But I would like you to take some time off, Dennis. Paid leave. Indefinite. You're not under suspension, please don't think that. But I have to tell you, we will have an independent team of investigators take over this case and report directly to me. I need an objective view on this. You have to admit that it doesn't look good at all right now."

Dennis picked up his binder and walked to the door. Then he abruptly turned on his heel and came back, grabbed Bill Charlton by the necktie and yanked him out of his chair just as easily as if he were a sack of potatoes.

He softly whispered in his ear so that the other two couldn't hear, "How many friendly ghosts do you have working at the Casper Agency, Bill?"

CHAPTER THIRTY ONE

The sun was shining brightly as they headed east towards Chesapeake Bay. Dennis was driving, and Fiona was lazing in the reclined passenger seat enjoying the rays pouring in through the sunroof of the Mercedes.

She gushed, "What a beautiful day for a drive in the country!"

Dennis looked over at her. Her long-tanned legs were stretched out as far as they could go, and her hands were clasped behind her head. Fiona had her eyes closed and her face was glowing. He couldn't resist—he reached over and stroked her forehead. She grabbed onto his hand and kissed it.

"I almost hope that we find nothing at the cabin, Fiona. Then you and I can just stay there overnight and enjoy the place—although it may be a bit dusty!"

"Oh, I don't care about a little dust. It would still be more civilized than camping. And…I know that you'd be a gentleman and clean the place for me if I asked you to. Right?"

Dennis laughed. "Oh, for sure. You can tell that I'm the real domestic type, eh?"

She grinned. "You keep that talent hidden, I'm sure—just like a lot of other hidden talents that I know you must have."

He had just turned off the Suitland Parkway onto MD-337 E. It had only taken them ten minutes to reach the outskirts of DC and enter the state of Maryland. Now the rest of the drive would only take about forty minutes. Dennis figured they should be at the cabin by 4:30 p.m. Barb was due to arrive around the same time in her own car, and Mel would be there by 6:00 with Sydney Fox.

"Okay, Fiona. Time to tell me what you found out. You've been teasing me by saying, 'later, later,' every time I ask. So, spit it out."

She pushed the power button and raised her chair. "I don't know what it means and I've been thinking about it a lot. There seems to definitely be a connection to what we're looking into. It's just so weird—it jumped out at me."

"I'm listening. And don't worry about it sounding 'weird.' Everything about this so far is weird."

"Well, as you know, I have a security clearance but not a high one. My boss, Frank Suskind is cleared at a fairly high level though. Anyway, I had my weekly meeting with the CNN representatives yesterday, and they threw me a curve ball. Something they said they intended to report unless I could give them a good explanation."

Fiona leaned forward, pulled her can of Coke out of the cup-holder and took a long refreshing sip.

"Hey, we don't allow drink breaks here, girl! Keep talking!"

Fiona gave Dennis a playful punch on the shoulder. "Okay, slave driver. I asked them to fill me in. They said that they had information in their hands from someone on the inside, to the effect that Pentagon officials have been making frequent trips to the islands of St. Kitts and Nevis. In fact, six in the last three months alone."

Dennis shrugged. "I guess it wouldn't be the first-time government employees took pretend business trips on taxpayer money. I would think that's probably been going on for quite some time."

"True. But why not Puerto Rico, or the U.S. Virgin Islands—both of which are only about half an hour from St. Kitts? And they're American territories. And they're much easier to get to. Flights to St. Kitts aren't that frequent from the U.S., and from there you have to take a ferry ride over to Nevis. Seems inconvenient, an odd choice of places to go. They're two beautiful islands to be sure, but more quiet and laid back.

"You would think that if government folks were going to take a chance on getting caught wasting taxpayers' money, they would at least make it worthwhile by going to where the action is. The action isn't on St. Kitts or Nevis—at least not that I know of. And six trips in three months? Seems rather excessive."

Dennis started tapping his fingers on the steering wheel. "Good points. I see what you mean. A bit of a red flag."

"That's what I thought. Anyway, let me tell you what I found. Frank, my boss, occasionally asks me to work on some of his documents. He starts them, gets stumped, and I finish them. He's always afraid to let them off his computer, so he won't email the drafts to me. I have to work on them on his computer and then save them to his hard drive. He looks at them the next day, and either approves or asks me to do them again."

Dennis interrupted. "You mean, you do his work for him and he gets all the credit?"

"Yes, basically. But remember the old adage, 'to make yourself look good, first make your boss look good.' So, that's what I do—I make him look good."

Dennis slowed down and took the turn onto MD-260 E, a pretty route that would take them directly to Chesapeake Bay. "So, when do you do this work for him?"

"Always after hours. He rings me and tells me he's left a document open on his computer, so I run up and he briefs me. Then I take it from there, finish the draft, save it on his hard drive, then log off—but of course I'm logging off as Frank Suskind."

"He sure must trust you."

"He does. He probably shouldn't, especially after what I did last night. But Frank's lazy, and he'd rather trust someone than actually do the work himself."

Dennis turned his head from the road and stared at his pretty traveling companion. Pronouncing his words slowly, he asked, "What did you do last night?"

"Well, after my meeting with the CNN folks, I immediately went up to Frank's office and asked him about it. He said they had the wrong information, that no one from the Pentagon is visiting those islands on taxpayers' money. If they're going there, it's for vacation."

Dennis nodded. "He may be right—but Fiona, cut to the chase. I can't see the relevance here."

"Dennis, don't let that quick impatient brain jump ahead so much. Some of us normal people have to work our way through these things."

He smiled. "Ah, now you're patronizing me. I know what it means when you do that—you're basically telling me to shut the hell up and listen. And my dear lady, you are far from normal. I mean that in a good way."

She smiled back at him and rubbed his arm. "I know you do. And yes, shut the hell up, okay?"

Fiona took another sip of her Coke and continued. "Last night, when I was working on one of his documents, I noticed that Frank was still signed in to several high security Pentagon sites; sites I don't have access to. He had them minimized in his menu bar, and he was in such a rush to go home he forgot to log off.

"I couldn't resist. I checked them all. There was no risk to me, because they were already open under his password, whatever it is. I figured I'd never get another opportunity like this, so I took it."

Dennis grinned at her. "I'm getting kinda turned on here—my sexy little spy!"

"Wipe that grin off your face—this is where it gets serious. One of the sites was for Pentagon travel for their top officials. Frank must have been doing some of his own checking after I asked him that question. Anyway, contingents of officials: political, military and scientific, most definitely visited the island of Nevis not just six times in the last three months but a total of forty times over the past ten years. Sometimes by military jets, sometimes by commercial jets. Forty times, Dennis!"

Dennis could feel his stomach flip. "Fiona, what the hell?"

"I know. Something is drawing them to Nevis."

CHAPTER THIRTY TWO

Brett printed off the email from Bill Charlton. Okay, the three stooges were going to be there around 5:00 p.m., followed by Dennis' sister accompanied by the nerdy lawyer no later than 6:00.

He looked over the directions—easy. He'd been to Chesapeake Bay numerous times and in fact had used the spot before to dispose of certain... things. And with some of the high cliffs in that area, it was also a perfect spot to make murders look like suicides. He'd orchestrated those before too. Brett had pretty much done every despicable thing that a human brain could imagine.

He walked over to his desk, opened the top drawer, and took out his holster and pistol. He snapped the holster onto his belt and checked his trusty Smith and Wesson 357 Magnum. Brett snapped open the cylinder. Yep, eight shiny bullets...big bullets.

He grabbed a handful of extras from inside the same drawer and stuffed them into one of the six inside pockets of his cream-colored Saville Row suit jacket.

Next, he went to the closet and pulled out a leather case. He didn't use the contents of the case too often, but today he figured he'd need it. He took out the equipment and inserted two fresh AAA batteries into the compartment. These little batteries would give him 100 hours of listening fun...but he certainly wouldn't need that much time today. A couple of hours at the most, he figured. This wouldn't be that complicated, or that lengthy a field trip.

He admired his tool—a sophisticated long-range listening device. It came with a recording device too, but he wouldn't need that today. He would bring along the headphones, amplifier, laser transmitter and laser receiver. That would do it.

This slick little machine shot an invisible laser infrared beam at any window of a target building. The long-range laser beam—invisible—could detect vibrations on the window glass, sift through regular static and other noise, and translate the voice vibrations back to the laser receiver. Then the vibrations converted to voices, then amplified—and Voila! Right into Brett's headphones.

And he could listen to lovely conversations from about 1,500 feet away.

He pulled another case out of the closet and opened it up. He wanted to make sure all the pieces were there for him to assemble when he was out at the cabin. This particular little darling was a parabolic microphone—a dish—about twenty inches in diameter, complete with tripod. He would use this once his targets exited the house. The laser unit was only effective for listening to what was going on inside buildings. He needed the dish for when they were outside.

Brett glanced at his watch. Time to roll. He wanted to be in place long before anyone showed up.

He wondered if today was the day he would come home with the package in his hands.

But most of all, he wondered if today was the day he would start keeping things for himself.

*****

Chesapeake Bay is the largest estuary in the United States. Lying off the Atlantic Ocean, its beauty is hugged by the states of Maryland and Virginia. Its drainage basin covers a massive 64,000 square miles and a mind-boggling 150 rivers and streams drain into the bay.

The bay itself is about 200 miles long, from the Susquehanna River in the north to the Atlantic Ocean in the south. It's actually a drowned valley— an area that the river used to flow to when the sea level was much lower than it is today.

The bay was formed by a bolide impact, otherwise known as a meteorite hit, some 35 million years ago. The entire Chesapeake Bay is simply an impact crater. Parts of the bay are framed by cliffs, particularly in an area known as Calvert County, and these cliffs are famous for fossils, particularly ancient shark teeth.

This is an area of the country that is renowned for its tourist attractions— the beauty of the bay itself, the majesty of the cliffs, and the beaches that have formed down near the Plum Point area of the bay. Oyster harvesting has always been a huge industry here, but in the last few years, either due to over-harvesting or environmental reasons—the debates rage on as to who is to blame—the oysters seem to be disappearing.

Dennis remembered shucking oysters with his sister Melissa—and crabbing too which was even more fun—when they were just kids. They also found their share of sharks' teeth. He still had some of them in a glass case back in his office.

He thought to himself how sad it was that he hadn't been back here in so long. The memories he had of this place as a kid were precious to him. But maybe that's why he hadn't come back. With his father dead, and his mother who had lost all memories of this place when she was alive, it just wouldn't have been the same. In fact, it was just plain sad to remember sometimes.

The cabin was located in the Calvert County area of the bay, right on the edge of one of the massive cliffs. The views were spectacular.

He remembered sitting on the bay-facing porch with his parents and sister, each bundled up and bracing themselves against the ferocious winds that sometimes fought their way up from the ocean. His mother would make hot chocolate and his dad would always be struggling to keep his pipe lit.

Eagles and hawks soared effortlessly with the wind currents, barely moving their wings. The water down at the base of the cliffs licked the rocky shoreline and sent their watery songs up to the porch, seemingly just for their private enjoyment.

The smell of the salt air was something Dennis always loved—it wasn't as strong as he remembered from being at ocean resorts with his parents, mainly due to the fact that as an estuary the bay water was a rare combination of both salt and fresh water. So, the smell was somewhat muted—but more pleasant than the strong ocean salt smell.

He turned onto Bayside Rd and headed south in the direction of Plum Point. The cabin was only about ten minutes away now, and he was starting to feel a knot in his stomach. He didn't know whether that knot was there out of anticipation of what they might find, or out of nostalgia.

Dennis reached over and rubbed Fiona's shoulder. "Continue your story, Fiona, dear. I know you're not finished yet."

"You're starting to know me too well, I think."

"Yeah, I'm getting used to your little methods of telling me things. You work up to things, don't you? And I always just cut to the chase."

"I guess so. And yes, there is more. The travel itineraries I saw online had little notations beside each trip. Kind of like noting what the trips were for—just words or expressions, no detail."

"Okay. You have my complete attention."

"On countless itineraries, I saw references to 'Behavioral Modification Foundation,' apparently a facility on Nevis. And I saw the word 'Chimps,' usually notated beside the names of the scientists. And…I saw something very curious that was noted over and over again— 'Operation Creepy Crawlers.' This was generally seen beside the names of the military personnel."

Dennis looked over at her and stared, almost forgetting to put his eyes back on the road.

Fiona continued. "The other sites that Frank had left open on his computer had nothing to do with any of these words. But I checked his search history—it looked as if he had done some surfing within the Pentagon database, trying to access files associated with those words. He didn't succeed. The 'source' pages showed that he tried to log in but failed. So, his security clearance obviously didn't allow him to get that far."

The cabin was now just a few hundred feet away and Dennis' stomach was doing cartwheels. Most of the homes looked the same as he remembered, and they were all immaculately maintained. Then he saw his cabin and he felt ashamed.

It was in horrible shape. The roof shingles were all curled and the paint was flaking off the spruce siding. It looked like the house that was owned by the 'Adams Family,' a show he used to watch as a kid and always thought to himself that their ramshackle house was one he could never ever live in. Now he had one of his own.

The old oak tree shaped like a scythe was a lot bigger than he remembered. He drove past the house, glancing at an old pickup truck with dark tinted windows parked along the side of the road. He thought to himself, 'that truck and my house go together well.'

He parked his Mercedes about 250 feet away. He and Fiona got out and walked, both absorbed in their own thoughts.

Fiona held onto Dennis' arm. "Are you okay?"

"Yeah. A little sad and a lot ashamed—but I'll get over it."

Dennis suddenly stopped walking and wrapped his arms around Fiona, hugging her hard. Then he pulled his head back and kissed her. He smiled at her. "You're doing it to me again. You haven't told me everything yet."

Fiona lowered her eyes. "Denny, I don't know what to make of this part. There was one person who popped up in the itineraries as having made two trips to Nevis—the first one ten years ago, and the other one five years ago. The notation beside this person's name on the first trip said, 'Execution of Shackleton contract.' The second trip showed 'Renewal of Shackleton contract.' The person's name was 'B. Jenkins.'"

Dennis caught his breath and felt the knot in his stomach getting tighter. "It must be someone else. Someone on the Pentagon staff."

Fiona shook her head. "I did an exhaustive search through the tens of thousands of Pentagon employees. The 'Barb' we know is retired now. But other than her there are, and were, no other 'B. Jenkins' working at the Pentagon; in fact, not even anyone with the last name 'Jenkins.'"

Dennis grabbed hold of Fiona's hand and squeezed it, then pulled her gently in the direction of the cabin. They still had 100 feet to go. He said softly, "We'll just have to ask her. There has to be a logical explanation."

The two lovers walked in silence the rest of the way to the neglected cabin on the cliff.

Neither of them could have known that every word they said had been listened to by a handsome, well-dressed man sitting in run-down pickup truck 1,000 feet away.

CHAPTER THIRTY THREE

Dennis took a deep breath, pulled the old skeleton key out of his pocket and unlocked the front door. It creaked as he expected it would—in fact, it had always creaked. A childhood memory. One that calmed him.

He led the way inside, with Fiona holding on tight to his belt from behind. The furniture was in the same spots as he remembered—now all covered with white sheets. The old upright piano was the only furniture not covered—Dennis wondered why.

As they walked through the living room, their faces were bombarded with spiders and their webs. Fiona was making some disgusting noises as Dennis swatted away in front, trying to clear a path.

He stopped at the entrance to the dining room. Fiona rubbed his shoulder.

"What's wrong, Denny?"

He wiped away a tear from his eye. "Nothing's wrong. And everything's wrong. I can hear voices, see the smiles, I can see myself laughing along with everyone else. We used to have so many wonderful meals in this room—Christmas time, Easter time, any time. It was just wonderful."

Fiona hugged him from behind and nestled her cheek in between his shoulder blades. "Memories are sad sometimes. But they were obviously nice ones. Worth holding onto and shedding a tear for."

Dennis nodded and forced himself to turn away from the ghosts of the formal dining room. The ghosts seemed so real to him—the energy in that room had been palpable.

Suddenly, the front door opened again and in bounced Barb. She smiled her million-dollar smile as she gazed around the room. "Well, I guess I don't have to take my shoes off in here, eh?"

"No, I think we'll let you off the hook this time." Dennis walked over and gave her a hug. Fiona followed suit, but her hug wasn't quite as affectionate.

Barb gave her a strange look as Fiona turned away.

"I get the feeling I interrupted something. Did I walk in on a deep conversation between you two."

Dennis winced. "No, but there is something I need to ask you about once this business is over with today. No big deal—I'm sure you'll have a logical answer for me."

"Well, now I'm intrigued. Are you really going to keep me waiting? You know I don't like to be teased, Denny."

Dennis put his arm around Fiona's shoulder as they both stared at Barb. He knew that they were both having a tough time keeping the look of suspicion off their faces. "We'll wait. More important things for us to do here right now. I suggest we head upstairs to make sure we're out of sight by the time Mel and the lawyer get here. He's insisted that Mel wait in the car, but he doesn't know we're here. We'll surprise him at the right moment."

Dennis led the way to the second floor and to the front bedroom, which used to be his. Its window looked out to the street, so they could easily see when Mel and Sydney arrived.

Dennis couldn't resist—his old bed was still in the room. He plunked down on the edge and then stretched his seventy-four-inch frame out along the length of the mattress. As a boy, he remembered thinking that this bed was huge, but now his feet hung well out over the end. However, the feeling of comfort that he used to get as a child was still embedded in the old mattress. He could feel the indent that his body had left as a permanent souvenir of his presence. It was a strange sensation he was feeling at that very moment.

"They're here!" Fiona was peering through the blinds. "But it looks like they each brought their own cars. Sydney probably wants to just do his duty and get back to the city. No time for watching Mel walk down memory lane."

Dennis walked over and peeked through the blinds too. He watched Mel and Sydney walk up the front steps together. Sydney Fox looked very lawyerly—expensive slacks, designer golf shirt. He was a skinny guy, but he walked like someone who was still athletic. A certain confidence about him. Dennis figured he was in his late seventies now, but he still resembled the man he had met a long time ago.

Dennis whispered, "Mel has to use her key to let Sydney in. Did you remember to lock the door behind you when you came in, Barb?"

She whispered back. "Yes, Denny. Don't worry."

They heard the key in the lock, and then Dennis watched Melissa walking back down the steps to her car. She was obeying the instructions of the will to the letter.

Footsteps sounded on the hardwood floor in the living room, and they could tell the steps were moving from the front door to the far north wall of the living room. Right beneath where they were standing.

Silence.

Now a scratching noise. Followed by a creaking sound. Dennis knew what this was. A screwdriver was being used on stubborn screws that hadn't been turned in an awful long time.

He motioned with his index finger to the two ladies and tiptoed out into the hallway. Barb and Fiona were close behind. Dennis held onto the railing and slowly led the way down the grand staircase. It wasn't so grand anymore, but at one time it had been downright regal.

Reaching the foot of the stairs, he held his finger up in front of his mouth and pointed to the living room doorway. Slowly, carefully, step by cautious step, the three of them made their way into the huge lounge.

Dennis motioned with his hand behind his back and they all stopped in their tracks. Each of them watched the old lawyer kneeling on the floor with a single hardwood panel in his hand.

Dennis broke the silence. "Mr. Fox, what are you doing?"

Sydney whirled around, clearly shocked by the sound of a voice in the gloomy old house. He laid the wood panel onto the floor and struggled to his feet.

"Oh, it's you, Dennis. You gave me a start." Sydney shoved his eyeglasses further up his nose.

"Yes, it's me. Why are you ripping up our floorboards?"

Sydney got to his feet. "I'm sure Mel has told you the conditions of the will and the instructions your mother had pertaining to this house. Between your mom and me, there was something she wanted me to recover from the house after she died. I knew where to find it. She didn't want either of you to know about it until she died. She thought it was safer that you didn't know. So only I knew where this was."

"Where what was?"

"Go and get your sister, Dennis. It's okay for her to come in now. I've done my job."

Dennis opened the front door and motioned for Mel to come in. She didn't hesitate for a second. As she came swooping in the front door, Denny swung his sister around and gave her a big hug, just like he used to do when they were kids.

Sydney smiled as he watched them. "You both know that I'll arrange to have the house put on the market, and I'll leave it to the two of you to figure out what your mom wanted you to know.

"By the way, she also had a separate document of instructions to me, an envelope that has been sealed for thirty-four years that was not to be opened unless both of you were deceased at the time of me recovering this from the house. It's safely tucked away in my office safe. The rule on that envelope from Lucy says that if either one of you is still alive, it must be destroyed without being opened, exactly two weeks after I've recovered this thing from the house and passed it over to you. Unless—and this is important—unless you or Melissa advise me to open it and follow the instructions inside.

"So, the clock has started—you have two weeks to decide what you want me to do. Your mom hid this here back in 1978 before she retired, and at the same time gave me the envelope with the separate instructions. So, she obviously went to great pains to protect it."

Dennis frowned. "So, what is it?"

Sydney hooked his index finger and turned back to the gaping opening in the floor. The four of them walked over and looked down.

Barb scoffed. "It's just a hole."

"No, look at the floorboard I removed—not the opening."

Dennis picked up the board and stared at it. "Jesus!"

Mel grabbed his arm. "What! What do you see?"

Dennis took the board over to the window and opened the blinds. "It's easy to see now. Black ink. A message written on the underside of the board in mom's perfect handwriting. Without direct light, no one would ever notice the writing. Mom was smart—if someone ripped up the floor looking for this, they probably wouldn't think to look at the wood itself. They'd be obsessed with looking down into the dark airspace."

Fiona wrung her hands together. "Dennis, you're driving us crazy! What does it say?"

Dennis looked up and smiled. "I'll read it to you."

Sydney Fox raised his hand. "Don't read it aloud in my presence, Dennis. I'm going to leave you all to this now. I've done my job. I was supposed to do three things: protect the secret; not burden you and Mel with it for the last three decades; and then recover it. I don't know what it is and I didn't read it. All you have to do now is watch the clock—in two weeks' time her other envelope will be destroyed if I don't hear from either of you. Okay? Understand?"

Mel and Dennis both nodded, then Sydney bid his goodbyes.

Dennis adjusted the window blinds and turned his attention back to the floorboard.

"Okay, I'll read it aloud now."

Dear Denny and Mel: If you're reading this, then I have passed away. I hope you're both doing well, and I'm glad that Sydney was able to attract you back to this lovely summer home. Your dad and I just loved this place, as you know, and we remember so many lovely times here with you kids. We did have fun, didn't we?

There are so many memories that it's impossible to list them all. All I can hope for is that the two of you treasure those memories. Memories are the most important things we own. We create them, cherish them, and remind ourselves of them. Memories are life itself.

I'm sitting here writing this note to you, and you can appreciate that it's not easy at all writing on hardwood but I'm doing my best. I hope you can read this clearly. As I sit here I have the urge to just encapsulate all our memories on this piece of wood, but the wood isn't long enough and neither is my life! There are far too many.

All I ask of you—and do this for your mother—is if you take anything at all from this house, please take those times we had. Cherish them like I did. This was and still is a very special place.

All my love,

Your mom.

CHAPTER THIRTY FOUR

"That tells us nothing at all. Is that all this is supposed to be? A love letter from your mom?"

Dennis looked up from the piece of wood and glared at Barb. "If this is all there is, then I'm okay with that, Barb. This is our mother talking and it's precious to us."

"But there has to be more! All that we've gone through, all that business Lucy was spouting about a package. The other things she was blurting out. We know all of that has to mean something!"

Mel turned to Barb and pointed at her. "Shut up, Barb. We can't think properly with you shouting. And remember, this note is to Denny and me—not you. This whole subject is ours, not yours or Fiona's. You're both just here because you're friends. That's the only reason you're here."

Barb's expression instantly changed. "I'm sorry. You're right. I guess my impatience with this whole ordeal is showing."

Denny walked over to Barb and gave her a hug. "It's okay. We're all a bit on edge. And admittedly, we all had higher expectations. And you're right, Barb. It's hard to believe that this is all there is."

Barb hugged him back. "Okay, now that we're all friends again, I suggest we chill and get something to eat—and maybe a drink or two? We can talk about this mystery some more there. There's a great restaurant about twenty minutes up the road, at the Chesapeake Beach Inn. It's 7:30 now, so it shouldn't be too busy by the time we get there. My treat."

They all nodded agreement. Fiona opened her purse and took out a legal pad and pen. "Denny, before we go I'm going to copy down that note from your mom—I'll do it exactly as she wrote it, spacing, everything."

*****

Brett waited in his pickup truck until all three cars had made their way a few miles north before he pulled out to follow. He loved this old truck—the windows had such a dark tint he was virtually invisible from the outside. Which was a good thing—not too many men who were dressed in Saville Row suits drove trucks like this one.

It had a huge storage bed with a roll cover that was extremely useful when he had to throw things...or bodies...in for a haul. This truck had seen a lot of action over the years. He saved his Audi S5 for the classy James Bondy type assignments, and he had a few of those from time to time. The Audi always blended in quite nicely at embassy dinners, movie premieres, and business conventions.

He'd listened to the entire conversation—right back to Sydney Fox. So far, Brett knew at least everything they did and of course he also knew a lot more than that from all the investigative work he'd already done on his own—and of course with handy Randy's help.

Brett followed behind at a safe distance. Dennis and Fiona were in the Mercedes, Melissa was driving a nice conservative Toyota Camry, and Barb... Barb was driving a Ford Lexington motorhome with blackened windows.

Brett was already convinced that Barb was his 'double,' he had no doubts about that. The information that Fiona had been able to pull up on her boss' computer convinced him of that. Brett had been listening to Dennis and Fiona discussing that as they walked toward the cabin. He heard it all as clear as day. And Barb's reaction to the letter was the icing on the cake. She was too anxious, too eager, too frustrated.

And he wondered...why did she need that big motorhome?

*****

They each ordered sandwiches, salads and soup...and a bottle of wine to share between them. The place was empty, so they were able to get a nice table by the window overlooking the parking lot—and beyond, one of Chesapeake's famous cliffs.

Dennis glanced out the window. That darn pickup truck was here at the restaurant now. At least it looked like the same one—blackened windows, beat up chassis. He wondered...

Fiona stole his attention away from the window by reading aloud the note from Lucy once again, slowly, deliberately. She emphasized each word that seemed as if it might mean something, seemed out of place perhaps.

Dennis looked over at Mel. She shook her head. They were both drawing blanks.

Barb spoke up—carefully choosing her words it seemed. Dennis thought that she was no doubt worried about another outburst from Mel.

"I know someone who could take a look at this for us. He used to be a decoding expert with the FBI. If you give me that note, I'll be glad to talk to him for us."

Mel put her elbows on the table and leaned in Barb's direction. "Let's get this straight, Barb. There is no 'us' where you're concerned. The only 'us' at this table is Denny and I. Got that?"

Denny used this as his opening. "It's okay, Mel. Calm down—she was just offering to help us out and it may be a resource we can use."

He then turned his head to Barb. "Barb, changing the subject for a bit to a more pleasant topic, I know you've traveled a lot. Fiona and I want to go on a little getaway. We've done some research and I thought that maybe you've been to this island before. Ever traveled to Nevis down in the Caribbean?"

For just a millisecond Dennis thought he saw a flash of fear in Barb's eyes. But maybe he was just looking for that. Whatever, it didn't last long and if she did show something, she recovered quickly.

She smiled warmly and said, "Oh, that's so sweet. And you're in luck—yes, I have been there. Twice. The first time was about…ten years ago. I went down there to take care of some contract work between our government, some bio-med companies and the St. Kitts/Nevis government. And I went back again just before I retired to take care of the renewal of that contract. It's beautiful there. You both would love it. Princess Di used to hang out there."

Fiona shifted in her chair. Denny looked at her sharply, hushing her silently. He could tell she wanted to probe more on this.

Mel suddenly spoke up. "We're going to finish our meal and go back to that house! I'm not leaving today until I've checked every nook and cranny. Every tree trunk and every bush."

Denny grinned. "That's my big sis. You never give up. I agree. Let's go back there and finish this."

Barb suddenly reached into her purse and pulled out her cellphone. She read the screen. "I'm so sorry, folks. I have to go. A bit of an emergency with a friend of mine—she's going through a divorce and it just took a turn for the worse. Forgive me?"

Mel looked up at Barb as she stood. "I'll reserve judgment on that 'forgiving' thing, if you don't mind."

Barb placed her fists on the table and glared at Mel. "I've had just about enough of your attitude today, Melissa. Your mother would be ashamed of you." With that, Barb whirled around with an angry flourish and left the restaurant.

Dennis took Mel's hand in his. "Sis, you have to calm down. Barb's been a friend of the family for a long, long time. Don't overreact."

"Denny, something has changed with that woman. Maybe it's a 'woman's intuition' kind of thing, but I sense something is wrong."

Fiona jumped in. "I agree with her, Denny. You're so close to Barb that I don't think you can see it."

"Fiona, she answered my question with complete candor. She didn't try to hide the fact that she'd been on the island of Nevis."

"She's quick on her feet, Denny. She's a lawyer. And you're a cop. She's sharp enough to know that cops and lawyers don't generally ask questions that they don't already know the answers to. She sensed a trap."

"I don't know."

"You should have let me ask her why the contract work she did was nicknamed 'Shackleton.' I saw the look you gave me and I shut up. But I was dying to put her on the spot about that. All along she's pretended not to know what the word 'Shackleton' meant, and yet here she was working on a contract that had that as a code-name."

Dennis nodded. "You're right. I should have let you probe her on that. Okay, we'll do that as soon as we get back to the city."

*****

Brett had been listening to everything from his spot in the parking lot. He'd had his laser device aimed right at the window where they were sitting. He knew the three of them were going back to the cabin, and that Barb was leaving them in a huff.

He watched Barb rush out of the restaurant, put the motorhome in gear and race out of the parking lot.

Hello? Where's she going?

Brett saw the Ford turn left instead of right. She wasn't going back to the city like she said. She was heading back in the direction of the cabin.

In that instant Brett decided he had to follow her. He wouldn't hear the rest of the conversation in the restaurant, but at least he knew that the three of them would be heading back to the cabin in a while. It was better that he be there before them, and essential that he follow Barb.

Barb Jenkins was his most important target at the moment. His instinct told him something was going to happen.

*****

Mel was reading Lucy's note over for about the third time. Dennis watched her face—that serious expression of intensity that he adored so much.

Suddenly her expression began to change. Her eyes widened and her pretty mouth opened wide.

"Denny! I've got it! I know what she's telling us!"

Denny and Fiona both leaned forward over the table. "What, Mel?"

Her hands began to shake and the paper crackled in her hand. "Mom used the word 'take.' She wants us to take something. And she used the word 'memory' or 'memories' five times. She used the word 'times' twice."

Denny nodded politely. "Okay, I follow you. But where are you going with this?"

Mel took a deep breath. "Denny, she also used the word 'encapsulate.' Sure, mom was articulate, but even she wouldn't use a word like that in writing a note or in speaking.

She grabbed his arm and squeezed hard. "Denny, Denny—she's talking about the Time Capsule we buried!"

*****

Brett was following at a safe distance behind—close enough to see where the Ford motorhome was going, but not close enough to be suspected of anything nefarious.

He could see the Ford turning into a driveway now. At a house, down the street a bit from the cabin. He kept driving. Right past the house, glancing at it as he passed.

She'd pulled around behind the house—her motorhome wouldn't be seen from the cabin. Brett noticed the windows boarded up on all sides of the house. He knew why she'd picked this place—she could hide her vehicle, which would have been recognized by the other three when they came back if she left it out on the street. And she knew this house was unoccupied, so it was a safe pick.

Interesting.

Brett continued down the street about a mile, then did a u-turn and parked his truck. He reached into the glove compartment and pulled out a pair of high-powered binoculars. He trained them on the house.

Out along the side of the house she came—but she had company now.

196

Two men wearing long trench coats walked with her through a thick grove of trees on the side of the street where the cabin was.

A minute later, Barb emerged from the trees and walked to the back of the cabin. The two men were still in the trees and Brett knew exactly why they were there. He knew what was under those trench coats. And now he knew why Barb needed that big motorhome. Occasionally she had company with her.

Barb Jenkins was his 'double.'

Brett opened his car door and started working his way through the trees toward the cabin. The forest was thick and there were no houses along this stretch. He could easily pick his way to where he knew the two assassins were waiting.

Brett Horton had to take care of this. He had to work fast. And he had to work quietly.

*****

Harry Bolton lit a cigarette and grinned at his partner. "We'll get a good payday for this one."

Greg Newton grinned back. "Yeah, should be a snap. Easier than shooting Iraqis, eh? This will just be a shooting gallery."

"Yeah, but don't get too excited. She said we can only shoot if she beeps us. She's hoping to resolve it without anyone dying."

"Well, we get paid the same whether we shoot or not. So, I could care less either way. Except that…well…shooting is more fun!"

The two killers enjoyed a good chuckle.

Harry checked the rifle underneath his jacket. Scope was in place, a full magazine—locked and loaded. "So, do you know anything about this broad? She sounds like someone well connected."

Greg shook his head. "No idea. I'm guessing she's CIA, or even the Mob. Her money is as good as anyone else's. I don't care—that's what I love about this mercenary business we're in. Everyone is our customer!"

They laughed harder this time—so hard they didn't hear the footsteps.

He spoke in a whisper. "Gentlemen, I'm here to relieve you of your duties."

Greg was the first to spin around, reaching under his coat for his rifle. Then he stopped himself. He didn't know why. Something in the utter arrogance and confidence in the unarmed man standing behind them. He was a dude—dressed in an expensive cream suit, yellow shirt. Standing with his feet apart. Ready. Confident. Unafraid.

Harry was less mesmerized. "Who the fuck are you, man? Get the hell out of here if you value your life."

The man didn't answer.

Harry lunged at him. The guy wasn't holding a gun and Harry sure wasn't going to blow this assignment by warning off the targets with a gunshot. Harry was a specialist in hand-to-hand combat. He'd used his skills many times when he was in the Seals.

But none of that training prepared him for this. The dude waited until he could almost see his nose hair, then brought both forearms up in a furious blur to either side of his head. Harry could hear the crack of his own skull, could feel his brain turning to mush. His eyes began to blur, but he was just able to make out the shape of a finger racing towards his forehead. A finger!

It seemed to go right through him. Harry fell to the ground knowing that he'd never get up again.

Greg watched in horror as his partner's head was butchered in a matter of seconds. He started to run. His feet were moving as if running but they weren't touching terra firma. He was flying.

When he finally landed, which seemed an eternity, he turned his face upward to the sky. Blocking the light was the dude in the cream suit. He smiled at him. Then Greg saw both man's hands rear back and slam downward. He watched the mirage of two fingers crossing his line of vision. Then the impact to his head which he knew was inevitable. The pressure he felt at that instant was unlike anything he had ever felt in his life.

He got the sudden urge to fight back but he couldn't move.

Then he couldn't breathe.

What was left of his hearing picked up the sound of a weary sigh. And his dying eyes watched the well-dressed man brush himself off and disappear into the forest.

CHAPTER THIRTY FIVE

Dennis stared back at his beautiful sister. Sweet memories were swirling in his head of the two of them together with their parents on a hot July night way back in 1970.

The Time Capsule.

It was July 20th, 1970 to be exact—the one-year anniversary of the Apollo 11 mission, the first ever landing of a man on the moon. Neil Armstrong had become an instant hero to Dennis. He researched everything he could about the mission, about the moon, about future planned missions. He could recite Neil Armstrong's life story by heart. He drove his sister crazy.

Of course, she was sixteen years old by the time the one-year anniversary rolled around, and Dennis was only a thirteen-year-old teenybopper. There was a huge chasm between them. Her interests lay in being 'cool' and hanging out with boys. Dennis was only concerned with fast cars and spaceships. The moon mission fascinated him beyond the understanding of most people.

But his mom and dad understood. That's why they made sure that they were all at the cabin for the one-year anniversary, because it meant so much to Dennis. Melissa went along reluctantly.

They went to the cabin on Saturday, the 18th, which was the night of a beautiful full moon. The timing for remembering the infamous landing couldn't have been more perfect. A full moon for the weekend.

By Monday the 20th, the actual date of the landing the year before, the moon was still bright—and while a bit oblong, still almost full. Dad lit a bonfire near the oak tree that had a trunk shaped like a scythe, and they all sat around in camp chairs. The night was warm and still and the moon was bright. Dennis remembered looking up at it thinking that exactly a year ago men were walking on that mysterious ball. It was surreal. He looked around the campfire and could tell that for once it wasn't just him who was mesmerized by the moon. His entire family was caught up in the occasion.

Suddenly he didn't feel so alone. Mom smiled at him and reached behind her chair and lifted a large box wrapped in sparkly paper. Dennis thought it looked like a starscape.

He could hear her voice in his mind as clear as if she was still with him…

"This is for you, Denny. Open it."

Dennis ran over to her, grabbed the box and tore the paper off. He was so excited. He loved presents, and it wasn't even his birthday! He opened the lid and pulled out the object inside.

It was a replica of the space capsule that brought the astronauts safely back to earth. Dennis lifted it up and admired it. He'd wanted one of these ever since the moon landing. They had been flying off the shelves in stores and he'd pretty much decided that he would never be lucky enough to have one.

He looked around the campfire and smiled at his family. Then he ran over to his mom and dad and hugged them. Melissa got up and joined them—a group hug.

Dennis examined his capsule. It was about three feet high and looked exactly like the real thing. It had a nice big hatch on the side, just like he remembered seeing the astronauts crawl out through.

He thought back to that time—with the help of parachutes, the capsule splashed down in the Pacific Ocean on July 24th, 1969, four days after Armstrong and Aldrin walked on the moon. The capsule was an integral part of the Saturn V Rocket—the only part that was designed to survive re-entry into the earth's atmosphere—and it had sat on the nose of the rocket as it hurtled up into space. When it came down, it was all alone—a tiny leftover of the giant that had left earth eight days before.

Now Dennis had one of his own. But he knew he couldn't keep it.

Melissa and Dennis had been told a month ago that the family was going to bury a Time Capsule on the anniversary of the moon landing. Dennis had no idea in advance that it would be a real capsule they'd be using, but he appreciated the symbolism. He thought it was great. He didn't mind burying this gift—it was serving a mightier purpose than sitting in his room, which was already adorned with too many things as it was.

Dad dug a deep hole a few feet away from the oak tree. Mom thought that not only was it symbolic that they use a replica Saturn space capsule for their family's Time Capsule, but since the scythe-like trunk of the oak tree resembled a half-moon it was doubly symbolic if they buried it near that tree. Dennis thought that his mother was so smart.

Each of them had backpacks with little treasures inside—not too many, just a few little things that someone twenty, forty, eighty years from now would find fascinating.

They took turns stuffing the items inside the capsule, and then Dad placed it carefully in the earthen tomb. All four of them helped cover it with dirt. Then they lay down on the grass and gazed up at the moon.

It was one of the most magical nights of Dennis' childhood.

Melissa squeezed his hand, shaking him out of his daydream.

She smiled warmly at him. "You were remembering, weren't you?"

Dennis nodded. Melissa got up and came around behind his chair. She hugged him and nestled her lips into his ear and whispered, "I love you, little brother."

*****

Brett worked his way through the thick forest until he was on the fringe facing the cabin. He chose an extra-large trunk to hide behind. He sat down with his back to the trunk, and pulled his laser listening equipment out of the inside pockets of his jacket. Brett put the headphones on and adjusted the sizing. Then he checked his 357 Magnum to make sure the safety was off. All set.

He leaned his head back against the bark and waited.

*****

Dennis and Fiona pulled into the driveway of the cabin, with Mel's Toyota turning in right behind them.

Fiona and Mel walked quickly over to the old oak tree, while Dennis went to fetch a spade out of the shed. This was the moment of truth. Digging up a Time Capsule that was never intended to be dug up by the original diggers. It had been hidden from the world for forty-two years.

Dennis and Mel walked around the old tree and then stood back—both picturing where they were sitting forty-two years ago. Picturing their father digging the hole. Trying desperately to remember the exact spot.

Dennis stamped his feet. "It's right here, Mel. It's so vivid to me. I can recall it exactly—it was such an exciting night for me."

"Okay, Denny. Dig."

"No, sis, you dig."

Mel smiled at her little brother. "Denny, pretty please? Will you dig for me?"

"Well, that's more like it. If you ask me like that, I'll do anything for you, Mel!"

Dennis rammed the spade into the ground and began to remove the dirt. The ground was soft due to the recent rains, so the going was easy.

It wasn't long before his spade hit something hard. He got down on his hands and knees and began to feel around the object. It was cylindrical and metal.

"I've got it!" He began to dig furiously now, all around the circumference of the object until he could clearly make out the shape. After six more spadefuls, he had it uncovered. He reached down and lifted it out of the hole.

Mel and Fiona moved in close as Dennis placed it on level ground and brushed off the dirt.

"Are we ready?"

Mel gushed. "Darn ready."

Dennis opened the hatch and began pulling out the contents. He smiled as he saw photos of the Beatles, his miniature models of 1970s cars, a Barbie doll, newspaper articles that his parents had stuffed in. The front page of the New York Times dated November 22nd, 1963 announcing the assassination of President Kennedy, several newspaper articles featuring the 1970 moon landing, a photo of Neil Armstrong. It went on.

Dennis looked at Mel and he could see she was crying. Fiona walked up to her and hugged her hard. Mel sobbed louder.

The capsule was almost empty except for one more item that Dennis didn't recognize. It was an envelope with the Pentagon emblem printed on the front. *Mom had dug this capsule up herself a long time ago, and put something extra inside.* Mel and Fiona leaned in closer as Dennis broke the seal.

He pulled out the contents. Microfilm.

"Jesus Christ—this is it!"

A voice behind them said, "Yes, that does indeed look like the package."

Dennis whirled around. Barb Jenkins was standing thirty yards behind them.

Her steady hand held a pistol pointed at Fiona's head.

"Give it to me, Dennis, or your lover will be no more."

CHAPTER THIRTY SIX

"Barb, what is this? What's going on?"

"Denny, sorry to disappoint you, but I'm not the person you thought I was. I guess that's life, huh?"

Mel took a step forward.

"Melissa, don't tempt me. While I want the first bullet to be in Fiona's head, I'll make an exception for you, trust me."

Dennis raised his hands. "Barb, take it easy. No one needs to get hurt here. Just tell me what you want."

"I just want that envelope, Denny. Your mother got rich off keeping that secret hidden. Now it's my turn."

Denny took a tiny step forward. "Barb, who are you?"

"I work for Defense Intelligence; the DIA. Have for decades. I never retired. That envelope contains information that is crucial to national security. It can't become public."

Dennis couldn't believe what he was hearing. This long-time friend was a fraud. "You loved my mother! You've been a friend of the family for years!"

Barb scowled. "I hated your mother. So honorable and self-righteous. Idealistic. I was a convenient friend. I make friends easy, Denny, you know that. Even you wanted to fuck me. Sorry, Fiona, but it's the truth.

"I fucked my way up the ladder. Until I didn't need to do it anymore. Now I'm one of the top operatives, and this assignment is going to bonus me beyond my wildest dreams. I still have dreams, even at my age."

Dennis was sure his confusion was written all over his face. "But you warned my mom after James Layton was murdered! You tried to help her!"

"I never warned her about anything. She found out all by herself, the clever bitch. And I'm the one who killed James Layton. I told you a bunch of lies to earn your confidence.

"James was my assignment. Sure, I did fall in love with him—but the money was just too tempting. He was out of control and he endangered everything America believed in with his threats. So, you see, it won't be difficult for me to put a bullet in Fiona's head. Hand me the package and we can all go our separate ways."

Out of the corner of his eye, Dennis saw Melissa make her move. He should have known that she wouldn't be able to control her temper. She took off like a sprinter and rushed Barb like a linebacker.

She yelled as she ran. "You murderous bitch!"

Barb calmly turned the gun from Fiona and fired. Mel went down. Blood immediately started gushing out of her right thigh.

Dennis ran over to her and ripped off his shirt. He motioned to Fiona to help.

"Hold her leg up, Fiona, above her chest level." Dennis wrapped his shirt around the bullet wound, and tied it tightly. Mel's face was ashen and she was moaning in pain. He leaned over and kissed her lips. "Hold on, hon. Please, hold on."

Dennis turned his attention to Barb and snarled, "I'm going to kill you."

Barb laughed. "Denny, if I wanted to kill you guys, I could have done it already. I just want the package. I'll make you a deal —you let me live and I'll let you live. Just give me what I want."

Dennis' eyes caught a sudden movement in the direction of the forest. He turned his head and saw the strangest sight. A man in an immaculately tailored suit was strolling out of the woods. A vision so out of place that it surpassed the surreal experience he was already going through.

Barb noticed it too. She turned her gun in the man's direction. "Stop where you are! I'm a Federal Agent! Identify yourself!"

The man kept coming. No fear, no hesitation. He raised his hands and held them high as he walked. When he got within about twenty feet of Barb, he stopped.

"Hello, Barb. My name's Brett Horton. I'm your silent partner. I'm sure you've heard of me before."

"Ah, I knew I had a double. And yes, I've heard of you. So, what is this? You pop out of the forest after I've done all the work? I'm not splitting any of my bonus with you, asshole!"

Dennis took in the scene. Could this get more bizarre? A long-time friend turns out to be a killer. And out of the woods walks James Bond? He stuffed the envelope into his back pocket. Dennis wasn't going to give it up without a fight.

Barb walked closer to them and lowered her gun towards Mel's head. Then she lowered her left hand to her waist and pressed a button on a beeper clipped to her belt. "I'm sorry, Brett, but I'm in control of this. You're on the outs."

Brett laughed. "Are you waiting for sniper shots, Barb? If so, you'll be waiting an awful long time. In fact, eternity. I've relieved your incompetent little assassins of their duties. They're already in hell."

Barb looked towards the woods. She frantically pressed the button again. And again. She glanced over at Brett just in time to see his hand whip a gun out of his holster with lightning speed.

Her head exploded. Pieces of her skull and brain matter splashed over Mel's anguished face. Then Barb's lifeless body fell to the ground, twitching as it lay.

He's going to kill us all—just over this stupid package. Dennis rushed him. Keeping low to the ground, he lunged at warp speed. While still in the air, his left hand flung outwards and knocked the gun out of Brett's hand with a vicious swipe.

They were on the ground now with Dennis on top. He brought his right hand up and rammed it downward, forefinger extended—aimed at Brett's forehead. With the same speed, Brett's left hand came up and deflected it, then continued upward without missing a beat. His hand caught Dennis in the throat, then his right hand slammed into the side of Dennis' head. Fiona screamed.

Dennis rolled off him and sprang to his feet. Brett was already up. They both went into their stances and began circling, eyeing each other warily.

Dennis made the first move and dove feet first into the air and swept Brett's legs out from under him. Then he was on him again. Before he could deliver a fatal blow, Brett's forearms came up and smashed into the sides of Dennis' head.

Dennis flipped to the side and saw Brett move to get on top of him. He swung his feet upwards in a violent move that sent Brett flying back several feet.

They were both on their feet again, up close and personal. Dennis rammed his right palm into Brett's face and could feel and hear the sickening crack of the bones in his nose. Then his left hand rammed into Brett's throat, slightly blocked by a hand that flew up at the last second.

Brett went down, and as Dennis pounced the man's feet came flying out of nowhere. Dennis felt himself airborne and before he had a chance to recover, Brett was on top this time. His right hand poised, index finger extended and ready to ram down into his forehead for the killing blow.

But it didn't come.

Brett seemed to be slightly out of breath, but he managed to say, "I'm going to let you up, Dennis. And I want you to walk over there into the woods and take a good look at the wounds of the two assassins who were ready to shoot you on Barb's command. Judging by what I've seen of your skills, I know you'll recognize the work. After that, come back here and we'll talk."

CHAPTER THIRTY SEVEN

Brett watched as the shirtless Dennis jogged back from the edge of the forest. The man didn't look shocked at what he'd just seen—more like he'd just returned from an invigorating hike.

He ran past Brett straight to his sister who was still lying on the ground, right leg held high by Fiona. Dennis' shirt, tied around her leg, was now soaked in blood—it was helping to stem the flow but she would need medical help soon.

And it was definitely on its way.

Dennis pulled his cellphone out of his side pocket and began to dial.

"Put that away, Dennis."

Dennis glared at him. "I'm calling 911. Melissa needs an ambulance, badly."

"I've already called one. It should be here in about fifteen minutes."

Dennis shoved his phone back in his pocket. "I'll ride with her to the hospital."

Brett shook his head. "She's not going to a hospital."

"What?"

"Trust me on this. She's going to a much better place—a private clinic. No waiting, first class medical care."

"Why not a hospital?"

"Dennis, think about it. She has a gunshot wound. A hospital would have to report it to the authorities. Do you want to explain this mess here? All that happened?"

Dennis walked up to Brett until they were almost nose-to-nose. "We didn't kill these three people—you did."

"True. But you're involved in this up to your neck. You have an envelope in your back pocket that could get you killed. And if you think I'm going to confess to these killings, you have another think coming. I'm very good at disappearing—and I can do that right now if you want. I'll call off my people and I'll be gone."

Brett could tell that he had Dennis' attention. The facts spoke for themselves.

Dennis nodded. "Okay, you're right. But will Mel get the kind of care she needs?"

"Better than what she needs. This private clinic deals just with people like me. They're staffed with highly paid physicians and surgeons. And they work 'above the law.' The public has no idea places like this exist. But they do. And they are very discreet. Mel will be as good as new, I promise. I'll pay the fees."

"Where is this clinic?"

"In the country, on the outskirts of D.C. I can't give you the exact location, and unfortunately Melissa will have to be blindfolded on the way in and on the way out again. We'll make sure her family is contacted and she should be home in a couple of days."

"Christ! You know I'm a cop, don't you?"

"Of course, I do. But this is bigger than you, Dennis. You're very familiar with the 'underworld' in your job. Well, what I'm talking about is the 'overworld.' A world you'll never see. And trust me, you don't want to see it."

Dennis swatted at a bee that was buzzing around his head. "Okay, let's say I buy all this. What about these dead bodies? We can't just leave them here. The cops will be here in droves and I'm connected to Barb. They'll be all over me."

"Already taken care of. That was the second phone call I made. I have a 'cleanup' crew on the way. They'll be here around the same time as the ambulance."

Dennis shook his head. "Who the fuck are you, anyway?"

Brett held out his hand. "Let me formally introduce myself. Brett Horton, former Secret Service Agent, now self-employed. And whether you like it or not, I'm your new best friend."

Dennis hesitated for a second and then gave Brett's hand a firm shake. "We'll see about that."

Brett let his keen eyes wander around the area. "We are very lucky that this is a weekend getaway kind of place. It's deserted right now. We would have some serious problems on our hands if there were people living here."

Dennis nodded soberly. "Yeah, even on weekends it's kind of empty here. A lot of older people own these homes and they can't make the trip from the city anymore. And their kids are grown and don't care to come. Kids like me and Mel."

Brett reached out and squeezed Dennis's shoulder. "Don't worry about your sister. I've seen wounds like that before and I'm sure you have too. She'll be fine. When you were in the woods, I looked at the wound. The bullet hit her on an angle so it's not in too deep."

"I'll still worry until I know she's finally home safe and sound."

"She will be before you know it. In the meantime, me, you and your friend Fiona have to disappear for a while and have a chat. A serious chat. And we have to take a look at that microfilm."

Dennis frowned at him. "I'm puzzled. Whose side are you on? You told Barb you were her 'silent partner.' I'm supposed to trust you?"

"Yes. I don't think you have much of a choice."

Suddenly Dennis' expression changed. He was looking past Brett now, through the trees to the main road.

"Shit! Look!"

Brett whirled around and saw them.

A frail old couple, holding onto each other for dear life, were shuffling along the side of the road clearly enjoying a nice evening walk. Brett figured they had to be in their mid-eighties at the very least.

His quick brain arrived at the only solution that was possible. Crazy, but possible. It might just work.

"Dennis, this is what we're going to do. We're filming a scene for a movie. We can't show any signs of trying to hide anything. I'll talk to them. And the ambulance and cleanup crew will be here any minute. They'll fit right into the movie scene perfectly."

Dennis laughed. "With what? Where's the camera?"

Brett whipped the laser transmitter gun out of his pocket. "Right here. These old folks won't have a clue about the latest technology. They'll be convinced this is the newest miniaturized version of a video camera. I'll just point and pretend."

Dennis winced.

"Look, it's all I have. Do you have a better idea? It might buy us time to get cleanly out of here. They may report it later after they've talked to a neighbor or relative, but at least we'll be long gone by then."

Dennis nodded. "Okay, you're right. It's all we've got. What do you want us to do?"

"Get over there beside Fiona and wait for the ambulance. Tell her and Mel what we're doing. Then just follow my lead and my instructions." Brett smiled. "I'm not only the cameraman, I'm also the director. You don't want to fuck with me."

With that, Brett began a calm stroll over to the old couple, who by now had stopped by the edge of the road. He could tell they were considering walking across to the clearing to see what all the action was. Brett had his laser transmitter in hand, walking purposefully toward them, like a man on a mission.

"Hello, folks. Lovely evening for a walk, isn't it?"

The old man looked at him suspiciously. "We heard what sounded like gunshots, so thought we'd check er out. Who are you?"

Brett held out his hand and the old man shook it.

"My name's Manny Tomlinson, from Universal Pictures. We're filming a couple of scenes for an upcoming movie."

The old lady gushed. "Oh, my gosh. I think I've heard of you. Didn't you make that movie about snakes on a plane?"

"Yep, that was me. Did you like that one?"

"I loved it! I love all the scary, gory movies. Will this movie be gory?"

"Oh, yes, I can guarantee that for you!"

Brett could hear the sirens in the distance—the ambulance was getting close.

The old man seemed to be catching some of his wife's enthusiasm. "What'll this movie be called?"

"Forest Primeval."

The old lady put her hand up to her mouth. "Oooh, I love that. Sounds scary."

"Watch for it. Should be out by Christmas. May even be an Oscar contender."

"I'm so excited!"

Brett pointed up the road. "Well, I have to get busy." He waved his laser gun. "This little devil is the latest in video cameras. Compact, but the cinematography is fabulous. I'll have to ask you to just stay right here where you're standing. We have a pretend ambulance pulling up to take away a pretend injured woman. And then we have a large van coming which will haul away three pretend dead bodies—one from the clearing there, and two more from the forest over there."

The old lady started to tremble. Brett could have sworn she was having an orgasm. "Oh, my God. We can watch?"

"Oh, absolutely. I'd love for you to watch. Just stay where you are though. The script doesn't call for a beautiful woman like you being in the scene."

She smiled coyly, then her face turned a crimson red as she flashed Brett a wink. The old man frowned.

Brett walked off toward the ambulance and directed them to where Dennis was waiting with Fiona and Mel. Then he held the laser gun up and pointed it at the vehicle as it drove across the grass to the clearing.

He heard another engine coming down the road. The panel van was here. He directed it over to the woods first and followed it, holding the laser gun aloft. After they finished loading the bodies of Barb's hired assassins into the van, he directed them over to Barb's body. He held the laser gun in the air again, pointing it at the van and the scene that awaited them.

Within minutes the ambulance and van disappeared off down the road, and Brett walked over to the old couple again. "Did you enjoy that?"

The old man spoke this time, apparently trying to assert his manhood. "I held her back. She wanted to run over to where that body was in the field. I know you folks don't need distractions when you film these scenes. I used to be in the entertainment business myself."

"Oh, what did you do?"

"I was a puppeteer. Very popular in my day, if I do say so myself."

"I'm sure you were, sir. I'm sure you were."

CHAPTER THIRTY EIGHT

"You can't go home—you both know that, don't you?"

Fiona leaned against the fender of Dennis' Mercedes, clearly weary from the events of the day. "Where on earth are we going to go, Brett? This is out of control!" Dennis wrapped his arm around Fiona and jangled his keys in his hand. "It's okay, Fiona. He's right. But I have the same question, Brett. What do we do now?"

Brett strode confidently around to the driver's side of the car and threw Dennis a shirt. "Here, put this on. I always keep extra clothes in my truck. You just never know…"

Dennis buttoned up the shirt and repeated his question. "Again, what do we do now?"

"Well, that's the main reason I wanted you to put the shirt on. That bare chest of yours will drive the women crazy down in Norfolk."

"Norfolk, Virginia? Why are we going there?"

Brett smiled. "Because I have a house there. A 'safe house'—you know what those are. You probably have at least a dozen or so that the Washington Police Department uses. It's well equipped. We can hide out there and discuss things. I have a couple of old microfiche readers as well as a bank of computers. We can do anything from there.

"I keep the microfiche readers around even though they're ancient. A lot of the work I do involves recovering information from the past, before data went on CDs and flash drives. What you've just recovered is a perfect example of sensitive information from the past that's stored on an old medium. We'll look at that data together."

Dennis studied the handsome man—he was clearly the most confident and charming person he had ever met in his life. Brett was a hard person to hate, despite the fact that he had just killed three people as easily as sipping a milkshake—and fought Dennis almost to the death.

He found himself warming to the killer, and couldn't help but be impressed with how he had handled the old couple. For a few minutes, he was worried that Brett would just kill them for being an inconvenience. But he had handled them with charm and brilliance. The man was clearly capable. Probably of anything.

Brett reached into one of his inside pockets and pulled out a card. "This is the address in Norfolk. It's in a neighborhood called 'Ghent.' Old and established. The house sits on a large lot, so plenty of privacy.

"The garage is beneath the house, and you'll see a sloping driveway down to it. It's a large garage—holds six full-size cars. The opener is programmed to respond to honks from any car horn. Hold the horn down for two three-second blasts, and three one-second blasts. Then— 'Open Sesame!' Pull in and we'll toast our survival with a glass of wine."

Fiona smiled. "I don't know who you really are, Brett Horton, but I'm sure glad we met you today. You were our knight in shining armor."

Dennis slapped him on the back. "Fiona's right. You waltzed out of those woods at just the right time. And you gave me a good workout, that's for sure!"

Brett smiled back. "I like your style, Dennis. We're gonna get along just fine. And I do like the way you fight too. It's vaguely familiar." He chuckled.

Dennis rubbed his chin. "Did you spend some time in China?"

Brett grinned. "Yes. How did you know?"

*****

The GPS in the Mercedes was faithfully guiding the way to 702 Brambleton Avenue in the Ghent district of Norfolk, Virginia. Dennis had just taken the 28A exit and was merging onto I-64 E, which would take them right to Norfolk. They had already been on the road for three hours and had about two hours to go.

Dennis knew Norfolk fairly well. It was the second largest city in Virginia with a population of just under 300,000, and was most famous for having a huge military strategic importance. The largest Naval Base in the world was located here, and Norfolk was also the defense headquarters of the world's most important military alliance, NATO. Needless to say, despite all the historic charms that the city possessed, the military presence drove the economy.

Fiona had been quiet most of the trip down the coast. The day's events had clearly troubled her, and she wasn't used to violence. The day had troubled Dennis too, but he at least had the sad luxury of being desensitized to violence with the type of occupation he had.

She suddenly reached over and rubbed his arm. "I want to make love to you."

"Right now?"

"Yes, pull over. Your windows are tinted. I can't wait—I won't wait. Now!"

*****

"She's dead. How do you feel about that, Denny?"

He had just turned onto Brambleton Avenue, which, judging by the GPS meant that they were about fifteen minutes away from Brett's house.

"I don't know how I feel yet. Not completely, anyway. It breaks my heart that a long-time friend is dead, but now that I know she was a fraud, a killer, and who knows what else, I'm just kind of numb to it. Know what I mean? Does that make any sense?"

"I think so. The shock of it is just starting to sink in. I didn't know her as well as you, but I'm astonished at what an actress she was. How was Barb able to pull off that deception for so many decades, with every single person who loved her? And she killed her own lover for Christ's sake, for money and power?"

"Barb was a monster, Fiona. I'll shed no tears for a monster. What bothers me the most is that because she was a fraud, a big part of my life has been a fraud. Because I cared for her. And my mother loved her dearly."

"But Denny, did your mom really love her? Really trust her? She never shared this secret, whatever it is, with her at all. She didn't tell her anything. Barb had to go to these great lengths decades later to try to recover it through us. I think that in a lot of ways your mom was as big a fraud as Barb—but in a good way."

Denny squeezed Fiona's hand. "That's an astute observation. Almost as clever as the way you instinctively picked out a great parking spot for us about 100 miles ago."

Fiona hit Dennis on the shoulder with her tiny fist. "Don't you dare tell anyone about that! Especially Melissa!"

"Melissa—oh, I hope she's going to be okay."

"She will be. I believe Brett. I think I believe in Brett. Isn't that strange? We just met him, and he just killed three people. But I trust him."

"I do too, Fiona. I don't know what it is, but after he and I almost killed each other, I felt this instant affinity with him. Like I knew him. Kind of like I felt about you the first time I met you—in a different way of course, but you know what I mean."

"I do know what you mean. He seems so efficient and organized. Brett leaves you with the feeling that he has everything under control. And I know he's a killer, but I have a sense that he's also a decent honorable man. I don't understand this feeling I have, because it's such a paradox. But I think we can trust him, that we have to trust him."

Dennis nodded. "As he said, we probably have no choice. And if he had wanted to kill us, he could have easily done it when he had the opportunity."

Fiona was silent for a few minutes. Then she blurted out what she was thinking so hard about. "What was with that fighting you two were doing? I have never ever seen anything like that before in my life. It was thrilling to watch, but also damn scary. Where on earth did you learn to fight like that?"

"China."

"Why?"

"Why not?"

"Have you ever had to use it before?"

"Yes."

"Ever killed anyone with it?"

Dennis pulled into Brett's downward driveway at 702 Brambleton Avenue, and answered Fiona's question with two three-second blasts and three one-second blasts on the horn of his Mercedes Benz.

CHAPTER THIRTY NINE

"Get out of the car, both of you, and keep your hands very, very high."

Dennis and Fiona exited on either side of the Mercedes, and did what they were told with their hands. One of the burly men spun Dennis around and shoved him down onto the hood of the car. He frisked him from top to bottom, opened Dennis' wallet and checked his identification. He then withdrew the pistol from Dennis' hip holster.

"You won't be needing this for the time being."

The man walked around to the other side of the car and spun the bewildered Fiona in the same manner—but frisked her with a bit more respect. He opened her purse and examined her driver's license.

The guard stood erect and looked over at his partner who was seated at a desk against the wall of the garage. "They're clean."

Dennis examined the two men carefully. With their broad shoulders, short hair, and brusque manners, they screamed 'military.'

As he was driving into the garage, the first thing he'd noticed was the enormity of it—as Brett had told them, it was large enough to hold at least six cars. There were four already parked—an Audi, Brett's pickup truck, and two BMWs.

Dennis' roaming eyes had next landed on the officious-looking men seated at desks next to the back wall. Both held sub-machine guns in their hands, trained on Dennis' windshield. He heard the air escape from Fiona's open mouth and the sound of a whimper. His first thought was—this is a trap.

He calmed himself. Brett didn't need to summon them here to trap them. He could have had them back in Chesapeake Bay. He reconciled in his mind that this was just one more facet in the complex life of the fascinating man named Brett Horton. And they were being frisked because a man like Brett had to be cautious.

The man seated at the desk put down his Uzi and walked over to Dennis and Fiona. He held out his hand. "Avery Duncan, Marine Colonel—retired. My associate is George Rickett, Army Ranger—retired as well."

Dennis shook Avery's hand and then George's as well. A clearly relieved Fiona followed suit. "Pleased to meet you, I think. What's with all this?"

Avery nodded. "We know who you are of course: Dennis and Fiona. Brett told us to wait for you, but you can appreciate that we can't be too careful. This is a very secure 'safe house,' and I'm the house manager."

"So, you're here all the time?"

"Only some of the time. Brett has other things for me to do from time to time as well. But supervising this facility is one of my responsibilities. Between George and I, one of us is always here."

Fiona jumped in. "But it's just an empty house most of the time, isn't it?"

"Hardly, ma'am. Right now, in addition to you two, there are six other people staying here indefinitely. Which brings me to a few simple rules that I have to ask you to observe while you're here.

"Feel free to chat with the other guests, but use first names only— do not disclose your identities, what you do for a living, why you're here. No personal information at all. This is for your own safety, and the other guests of course have been given the same instructions. So, don't ask them any personal questions. Confine your conversations with each other to the weather, the Washington Redskins, movies, etc.—light stuff only."

Fiona folded her arms across her chest. "Jesus, who are these other people?"

Avery looked at her sternly. "Have you listened to a word I've said?"

Fiona stammered, as if a teacher had just disciplined her. "I'm…sorry. Just…more of an…exclamation…than…a question."

Avery nodded. "I'll continue. No cellphone usage—George will be taking those off you. No leaving the building without our permission. There's a large backyard, but you can't go out there. We do allow you to use a small courtyard in the back that has ten-foot walls, if you need a smoke or a breath of fresh air. All your meals will be taken in the main dining room with the other guests. However, discussions about your…uh…situation, will be conducted with Brett only and perhaps myself and George as well from time to time. These discussions will take place in a separate wing of the house with its own dedicated computers and other electronic equipment.

The other guests will be confined to their own similar wings."

Dennis cracked his knuckles. "Okay, I think we understand. Anything else?"

"Yes, one more thing. While you're here, you will do as we say. If you do anything to compromise the safety of our other guests...or us...we will kill you."

*****

"Sorry about the screening—almost as bad as trying to take a flight these days, huh? At least we didn't body-scan you guys!"

Fiona shuffled her feet under the table. "Brett, I feel like we've just entered the twilight zone. What is all this?"

Brett grimaced. "Just a necessary tool of the trade. I won't bore you or scare you with details, but trust me when I say that this is all sadly essential."

They were seated at one end of a long dining table—the six other guests were busy devouring their steaks closer to the other end. The dining room was huge and could easily accommodate twenty people. Dennis and Fiona met the other folks when they had first entered the room, but it was clear that no one wanted to talk about anything. The stress on their faces was obvious—there were four men and two women. One man and a woman appeared to be a couple, but the other four seemed to be strangers to each other. Nothing distinguished any of them from normal everyday people. No remarkable features. If Dennis saw them on the street he wouldn't think that they were in any kind of trouble. But they obviously were, or they wouldn't be here.

Dennis had placed the envelope with the microfilm on the table in front of his plate. He tapped his finger on it. "When are we going to take a look at this? You said you had the equipment?"

"Right after dinner. We'll go to one of our private conference rooms—there's a fiche reader in there that we can use. Brace yourselves. I'm pretty sure I know what you're going to see. When you do see it, you'll understand why I had to hide you here until we sort this out."

Fiona took a sip of her water. "We can't stay here forever. I hope we're going to talk about a way out of this mess."

Brett strummed his fingers on the table. "Death is a way out, Fiona. Do you like that option?"

She stared back at him, speechless.

"I didn't think so—that's why you're here." Brett waved his hand toward the three men on his side at the other end of the table. "It's been three months for him, a year for the one next to him, and two years for the one at the end. They didn't want to die either."

Dennis shook his head. "We have to review the package fast."

"Yes, right after dinner as I said. And luckily, in your case, I think we have a solution that will work much faster than what was available to these guys." Brett waved his hand again. "It will be dangerous, but I'll throw it out to you and you can decide."

Fiona looked up from her absent staring at the radish salad. "You're a private operator now. I presume these people here are paying you for your services. Why are we here? We haven't agreed to pay you anything. What's in it for you?"

Brett nodded. "Sometimes there's more at stake than money. I never thought I'd hear myself say that, but I'm an angry and confused man right now. My sense of loyalty has been compromised...confused. This 'package' of Dennis' mom is the most serious thing I've ever tackled—you'll see what I mean when you browse through it.

"This whole thing has become personal for me—so no, you don't have to pay me anything. I'm doing this more for me...and all the rest of us naïve people out there. Trust me, I'm not being a hero for you two. You'll understand when you read what's on the microfilm. As I said, I already have a pretty good idea about what you're going to see. I think you'll share my outrage."

Dennis leaned back in his chair and crossed his legs. "How do you know what's on there?"

Brett smiled. "If I told you, I'd have to kill you."

Dennis smiled back. "Barb once said the same thing to that little nursey spy, Felicity. That girl was yours, wasn't she? You were the other voice on the tape, weren't you?"

Brett nodded. "Yes, I was. That was sad about your mom. And Felicity seems to have disappeared into thin air. Are you aware of that, Denny?"

"Yes, why do you ask?"

"No reason. Just curious."

The other six people had long since left the table for other wings in the house, so the three of them were alone now.

Dennis leaned his elbows on the table. "I think you know more than you're admitting. Be honest with me."

Brett sighed. "I know that you've been relieved of your duties temporarily until they get to the bottom of the serial killer case. I know that you're a suspect because you had a motive in the two disappearances that they're trying to tie in to the serial killer. I know that the serial killer is some kind of vigilante and that he kills with very unique weapons. Or…he knows how to kill like you and I do."

"How do you know all this?"

"Denny, you'll have to just accept that there are aspects of the 'overworld' that I'm not going to tell you. It would serve no purpose."

"You seem to know a lot—like what's on the microfilm. I would at least like an answer to that question."

Brett nodded his head. "I can tell you that I was hired to retrieve the package. And I did some of my own research. I have contacts with special talents who I pay when needed. They were needed."

Fiona leaned towards Brett. "You were the one wearing the mask who attacked me in my home that night—the one who I told what I knew about James Layton."

Brett lowered his head and nodded again. "Sorry about that."

Fiona ran her fingers through her hair, then rubbed her tired eyes. "This 'overworld' you live in is one strange and brutal place, Mr. Brett Horton."

"You don't know the half of it…or even a tenth of it."

CHAPTER FORTY

Dennis got up from his chair and started pacing the room. He went over to a sink at the wet bar, turned on the cold water tap and splashed the refreshing liquid all over his face, around his perspiring neck, and through his thick hair. He was exhausted but could feel the adrenaline coursing through his veins.

He felt like he had been reading the script to a horror movie.

Fiona was still sitting in front of the microfiche reader, head in her hands, sobbing uncontrollably.

Brett was smoking a cigarette. It was his house—he could do what he wanted.

Dennis forced himself back to the conference table, and settled down in his chair in front of the fiche reader. He put his arm around Fiona's shoulders and squeezed. She nestled her head into his chest and covered her eyes with her hands. Her shaking head betrayed the tears she was trying desperately to hide.

Dennis raised her head up by her chin and kissed her lips. She kissed back, but weakly, uninspired—her mind elsewhere.

He turned his head toward Brett as he was stubbing out his cigarette. "Is this all pretty much what you found out on your own?"

"Pretty much. This microfilm gives us official documents, orders, authorizations, names, dates, places. What I found out was more general. This is dynamite—in the right hands."

"Brett, I can't believe they would be so reckless as to explode a nuclear bomb on the surface of our moon."

"Yeah, not only a clear violation of the treaty they signed, but we have to ask ourselves—what damage has it done? Do they know? Do they care? If there's damage, is it reversible? It's hard for me to believe that a nuke of that size hasn't done something permanent. Ten megatons is not a small bomb."

Fiona pulled her hands away from her face and turned toward Brett. "They're creating monsters here on earth! Right under our noses!"

Brett got up and started pacing the room. "It's even worse than that. Did you read that stuff about choosing cities in the Middle East—in Iran and Syria—and droning the hell out of them with genetically modified versions of the moon creatures? They've been testing prototypes of these things—death is invisible, silent, and quick. And capable of killing over a wider airborne area than any other contagion known to man. They've created a brand-new contagion—and its alien."

Dennis was wringing his hands. "It's barbaric. Everything I read is barbaric. I can't believe this is my own country that has done this. I mean, they're modifying these creatures in so many different ways, to fight whatever war they want to fight. If it's an economic war they want to fight against Japan or China, they now have the capability by what I read, of "dumbing their populations." A modified version of these organisms can simply be dropped into their water supplies or sprayed into the air, and millions of people will, within mere months, have their intelligence quotients decimated. No longer capable of creating or innovating, having no choice but to buy our products and giving us world supply dominance.

"And they're talking about using commercial passenger jets to spray the shit right out from their jet engines and undercarriage nozzles. A different kind of chemtrail than the world has ever seen before. And everyone's so used to seeing those damn chemtrails that no one up until now seems to be prepared to tell us the purpose of anyway, people won't think anything of it. It'll just be more of the same—chemtrails blotting the blue sky around the world."

Brett lit another cigarette. "It's horrific—all of it. The tests they're doing on chimpanzees are particularly scary. Removing all sense of fear, while at the same time boosting their strength threefold. And it seems to be working. My research tells me they're close to being able to create super-soldiers. Let's remember, everything we're reading in this microfilm dates back to 1978 when your mom buried it. I shudder to think about how advanced all of these theories and intentions are now.

"Their theory with these test chimps was that they could eventually inject young recruits with these organisms and transform them quickly from scared young men and women into gung-ho fearless killers, with the capacity to wage war with no natural desire for self-preservation. These kids will be recruited by Uncle Sam, their naïve patriotic parents urging them on, only to have them genetically modified forever.

"There's one document that refers to the side effect of a reduced life span—cut in half—for each of these super-soldiers, so the need to bring them back to America after one or two tours of duty and get them married and breeding before they die. Since they'll be genetically modified by these alien organisms, their offspring will inherit the same super-soldier qualities. Freaks—and, aliens, all of them."

Fiona poured herself a cup of coffee. Dennis noticed that she seemed to have regained her composure. She walked over to Brett. "Having worked in the Pentagon for an awful long time now, I've come to feel that I couldn't believe anything I was telling the Press. Call it sixth sense, but my brain was warning me that nothing was what it seemed to be—that nothing was the truth. War is an obsession for these people, and gaining an edge over our enemies—enemies that in most cases they've created themselves by their own belligerence—seems to be all that matters. I hate to admit it, but while all this shocks and horrifies me, none of it really surprises me at all. That's the sad part in all of this for me. That's what makes me cry."

Dennis sat on the edge of the conference table. "My mom knew all of this, and she chose to just literally bury it. And take a payoff to shut up about it."

Brett grimaced. "Denny, I think it's more complicated than that. Her boss was killed, and while we know now that Barb hadn't warned her about anything and that Barb killed Layton herself, I think Lucy knew in her heart that Layton hadn't killed himself. Lucy rushed to get the information protected so she could protect herself and her family. Then she quit. She was being a pragmatist. She decided to care only about the practicalities and not the logic. She decided she couldn't save the world but she could save herself and her family. Forgive her."

Dennis wrapped his arms around Fiona and gave her a gentle hug. "Are you okay?"

"No, I'm not. I don't know what it is I'm feeling right now. It's as if the world is about to come to an end and I feel powerless. The world is out of control and we're all just standing around watching it happen. And as Brett says, how far has this gone? We're only reading here about the *beginning* of Operation Creepy Crawlers. They had barely begun back when these documents were buried—Christ, that was over thirty years ago!"

Brett turned off the fiche reader, popped the microfilm back into its envelope and walked over to a wall safe. "We'll continue to protect this in the meantime." He spun the dial, opened the heavy door and stuffed the envelope inside. "The combination is 21-207-21. In case something happens to me, you come back here and get it. Avery and George will allow you access. I've instructed them already."

Dennis walked over to Brett. "You sound worried. What are you planning?"

"Well, with or without you two, I'm going to try to be Captain America and save the world. All it will take is some video—these documents alone are not enough. I'm going to get onto the island of Nevis and find a way to gain access to that laboratory."

Dennis looked over at Fiona. She hesitated for a second, then nodded.

"It looks like we're both with you, Brett. Way back when I heard my mom muttering what I thought was the word 'Skeleton' and then realized she was actually saying 'Shackleton,' at that very moment I had the eerie feeling that my life was going to change. I can't explain it—I just know now that I want to have some say in how it's going to change. And it looks like Fiona feels the same way."

*****

"Randy, I have another little job for you."

"I figured you'd be back to me. The same thing, right?"

"Yeah, the same thing—I'm not finished with it yet."

"Okay, Brett. Israel again?"

"Most definitely Israel. Let them take the hacking hit. Deflects nicely away from America's imagined enemies. Little do they know, Israel's their real enemy anyway."

"Done. What do you need?"

"I need you to go back into the Pentagon and CDC sites, 'Operation Creepy Crawlers,' and tell me what trips are planned down to Nevis within the next two weeks. And who exactly is going."

"Shouldn't be a problem. Anything else?"

"Once you have that info, I'm going to be asking you for a rush job on fake identifications and passports. There will be at least three of us, and possibly more, depending on how many people in the Pentagon and CDC contingent are making the trip."

"Again, no problem. Why don't you give me something really challenging sometime? I'm getting bored."

"I pay you well—so get over the boredom."

"True. I'll try. Shalom."

*****

"I know what happened twenty years ago, Dennis."

Dennis and Brett were sitting in the lounge of the 'safe house' smoking cigars and sipping brandy. Fiona had turned in hours ago. They had been talking about their careers and various little adventures over the years. Dennis had led an exciting life, but it paled against the stories that Brett shared with him. They were now on their second bottle of brandy, which Dennis figured might have contributed to the conversation suddenly turning more personal.

"What are you talking about?"

"Your dad. I know the real story."

Dennis took a gulp of his brandy. The burning ecstasy was leaving him light-headed.

"No one is supposed to know about that. It was sealed."

Brett shrugged.

Dennis leaned forward in his chair, cigar in hand. "Why are you telling me this?"

"Don't do it. You're better than that."

"Don't do what?"

"Travis Wilkinson."

Dennis gulped and involuntarily flicked the ash from his cigar tip onto the carpet. "You're out of line, Brett."

"Don't throw your life away, Denny. You did Keith and Felicity—I know you did and I don't blame you in the least. But don't add another one. They'll surely trace it back to you. There's documentation in the Washington Police Department about Mr. Wilkinson, and how they suspect you deliberately refused to identify him. If you do him, you'll make their case stronger. You have motive and they know it.

"You'll then have had motive in three disappearances—because I know you won't leave him lying around. You'll make him disappear just like the other two. They'll simply make you the guy for the six vigilante killings too. One more killing will do you in, Denny. Trust me on this."

"I don't know what you're talking about."

"Yes, you do."

225

CHAPTER FORTY ONE

"Okay, we have a plan. And don't panic when you hear it—remember, we do have experience with things like this. Avery and I will make sure we're as safe as we can possibly be, trust me."

They were back in the conference room: Dennis, Fiona, Brett, and this time Avery Duncan as well. Dennis looked over at Avery, then at Brett, and raised his eyebrows in a question.

"Ah, don't worry. Avery is right up to date on all of this—and he's probably my closest friend and confidant. We've known each other for over twenty years—in fact I was Best Man at his wedding and the Godfather to two of his children. Feel better?"

Dennis nodded. "Okay, continue."

"We're flying to St. Kitts in four days—so Friday morning. Avery's rented a speedboat for us, so we can avoid having to depend on the ferry service between St. Kitts and Nevis. Avery will also decide where the best landing spot is for us—one of the beaches that will bring us closest to the access point for the laboratory. It's located inland through the jungle, halfway between the shore and Nevis Peak. The channel between St. Kitts and Nevis is only two miles wide, so a short journey…going in will be easy, but coming back may be more perilous. We'll be glad the channel is short. But we won't cross it directly going in—we'll take the longer route down the St. Kitts coast to avoid attention, and then come in at a 180-degree angle to the Nevis shoreline."

Fiona raised her hand. "Sorry to cut you off, but who are 'we?' What roles will we each play?"

Brett smiled. "Typical journalist. You're getting ahead of me and, just like a reporter at a White House briefing, you even respectfully raise your hand! Next time, just shout it out—no need for formality here."

Fiona nodded. "Sorry, I'll be patient."

"Good. I'll continue. My technology expert, Randy McEwen, has come back with some key information. There's a contingent from the Pentagon and the CDC heading down to Nevis on Thursday. An Air Force Colonel named Howard Wentworth, along with two personnel from the CDC: Doctor Gene Sikorsky and his assistant Doctor Angela Huntington. Both of these doctors are microbiologists.

"We've done some photo scanning and decided that Avery here will be the best one to impersonate the Colonel, and since Avery was a Colonel himself he's well familiar with the jargon and aura that a Colonel emits. A makeup expert will join us here on Thursday and convert Avery to look as much as possible like Wentworth. I've used this lady many times before and she's a wizard. It won't take her too long or too much effort to pull off the transformation. She's already looked at the photos of Wentworth and Avery and feels it'll be a snap."

Dennis' organized mind was trying hard to sift through the plan and look for loopholes. "What about the other two?"

"They're the easy ones. Randy says that from what he's been able to tell, it's pretty normal for the lead envoy to cancel these missions at the last minute without any questions being raised. It's happened dozens of times over the past year alone. So, since Wentworth is the lead envoy, Randy will hack into the Pentagon email system and send messages to both Sikorsky and Huntington on Thursday afternoon postponing the trip. He'll send the messages under Wentworth's name."

"What about Wentworth? He'll think the trip is still on."

"I'll handle him."

Dennis and Fiona both raised their eyebrows.

"Folks, there are just some things you don't need to know, okay?"

Dennis and Fiona each reluctantly nodded.

Brett turned to his friend. "Avery, do you have anything to add at this point?"

"Yes. Just the mention that Randy is arranging official passports and identifications for us—me as Wentworth, Brett as Sikorsky, and Fiona as Huntington."

Dennis frowned. "What about me?"

"You'll be manning the boat, awaiting our return to the beach. You're far too tall to impersonate Sikorsky, and luckily for us Brett looks a lot like him without any real change aside from adding glasses. And Fiona is an easy pass for Huntington—our makeup girl just has to dye Fiona's hair blonde and insert contact lenses changing her eyes from hazel to blue. Then she'll be a dead ringer."

"Okay. However, I can't leave the country without being flagged."

"Randy has a new ID for you, too. You're a lawyer named Frank Cotterhill. All the identifications and passports should be here by tomorrow."

Fiona jumped in. "So, once Dennis lands us on the beach, how far a hike will it be through the jungle?"

Brett got up and poured himself some coffee. "We won't hike too far. Avery will research a spot with road access. There are lots of homes along the beach. We'll steal a car and take the road right to the lab's front door."

"Will they give us access to all of the sections of the lab?"

"With our credentials, shouldn't be a problem. But I do need a magnetic access card, which Wentworth has possession of. Randy won't be able to replicate that. So, I'll get it when I pay Colonel Wentworth a visit."

Fiona winced.

"No, Fiona. He's not going to die. He'll just be out of action for a while. Trust me, okay?"

Fiona nodded slowly. "Okay."

Dennis took a long gulp from his water glass. His throat was dry, and all this espionage talk was making it worse. "How are we going to get video? You can't exactly waltz in there with your iPhone held up in front of you. You won't look too authentic."

Brett laughed. "No, we wouldn't, would we? The official purpose of the visit, according to what Randy could ascertain, is just a routine inspection of the facilities. So, they won't be expecting us to take video. And we have to each be careful not to look shocked or surprised by anything we see. We're supposed to be well familiar with what's going on there. So, Fiona, let Avery and I do the talking. We're used to bluffing and bullshitting our way through situations."

"Don't worry, I'll be too frozen with fear to say anything."

"As for the video itself, this is the only purpose for our visit. We need video. I'll be wearing glasses to look like Sikorsky, and these glasses will actually be a high-tech video camera known as Video Optical. They look like normal glasses but contain a powerful video and audio recorder that's tiny and basically invisible. It's a color unit, high resolution and wireless—will transmit directly to a palm size portable DVR which I'll keep in my pocket.

This thing has its own screen and a 40 GB hard drive. It will transfer data to any computer with a USB connector, and it's also completely waterproof in case we end up in the sea."

Fiona shivered.

"Don't worry, the water's very warm this time of the year, Fiona. Sharks would be a worry though." Brett chuckled.

"So, how are we flying?"

"We have a Gulfsteam long-haul jet at our disposal. A G350—hangared at the Norfolk airport. We'll fly from there. The pilots work for me and two other associates of mine—so between us, we keep them busy. They'll simply wait down there for us until our mission is complete, and then fly us back to Norfolk."

"Weapons?"

"We obviously can't take any into the country with us, but we have a contact in Puerto Rico who's already smuggled four Glocks into St. Kitts for us. They'll be waiting for us on the boat we've chartered."

"Jesus, you think of everything, don't you?"

"Yes, I do. I have to in my line of work. But give yourself some credit Dennis—so do you, or you wouldn't have asked the questions you did."

Fiona ran her fingers through her long auburn hair. "Brett, how dangerous will this be?"

Brett paused, and strummed his fingers on the conference table. "I won't kid you. Anything could go wrong, and I think you know by now that they are desperate to keep this travesty a secret. So, there is danger—but I think we've mitigated it considerably. We won't be there long either, which is the key to a successful operation. The longer we're there, the greater the chance of something going wrong."

Fiona sighed. "I'm really concerned about how far this thing has gone since 1977. It's scary to think that they've had thirty-plus years to tinker. While I'm scared, to me it seems worth the danger to expose it."

"And we will expose it. Dennis mentioned something the other day when we were looking at the microfilm, and I can't get it out of my head. Those damn chemtrails that we see all the time, not just in the U.S. but virtually everywhere. I always just kind of accepted, as I think everyone did, the occasional feeble explanation that these trails contain aluminum oxide to help deflect the radiating effects of the sun.

"We all know that the magnetosphere has become weaker over the last few decades, from either man-made creations or natural ones, so most of us just take for granted that this bolstering is needed. But after learning about all this creepy crawler experimentation and their initial plans to use jets to spray contagions into the atmosphere to 'dumb down' populations, I wonder...have they been doing that already? To other countries? And a strain just for us here in the United States of America that makes us compliant and less inquisitive, more accepting? Have they, do you think?"

Dennis was cracking his knuckles. "Christ, who knows? If they can nuke the moon, bring alien life forms back to earth and keep all that secret for over three decades, anything's possible I guess. I don't think we can afford to be naïve about anything anymore."

Fiona walked over to the side table and helped herself to a cookie. "It would indeed be naïve of us to think that they've spent thirty years experimenting only—we already know that they've tested chimps in urban areas, not to mention that horrific slaughter of residents on Nevis by the militarized chimps and vervets. There's probably a lot more going on that only a select few know about."

Brett brought his fist down hard on the table. "We'll do our damndest to expose this mess! It's a fortunate thing that this mystery landed in our laps.

Dennis stood up. "So, are we done for now?"

"Yes. Dinner should be on the table in the dining room in about half an hour. See you all then."

Dennis walked over and put his hand on Brett's shoulder. "Brett, if I need to leave the house for a little while, I need your permission, right?"

Brett eyed him warily. "Yes...me, Avery, or George. And we need to know where you're going and for how long."

"Okay, if I decide I need to go, I'll let one of you know."

CHAPTER FORTY TWO

Colonel Howard Wentworth dragged his well-worn garment bag out from under the stairs and carried it up the stairs to the bedroom. He was glad he was only going to be down in Nevis for one night this time. It was a boring island. Well, it wouldn't be too bad if he were there on vacation, enjoying the beaches and the wonderful food. But hanging around a lab surrounded by the nasal-numbing antiseptic smells, not to mention the chattering and howling of those fucking monkeys and chimps, wasn't his idea of a good time.

But he had to be there. They were getting close to being able to test their latest weaponized vapor on a city in the Middle East. And not just any city either, but THE city in THE country that just happened to be the most despised enemy of his United States of America. He was excited. Years of work coming to fruition. And he was proud to have been a part of this project for so many years. Along with many others, he felt as if Operation Creepy Crawlers was his baby. And for a man who had never been married and had no children, the creep project was a suitable substitute.

So many new faces down at the Nevis facility—he had personally fired about a dozen last year alone. The new people were coming along nicely though, quite a few of whom he hadn't even met yet. He hadn't been down there since last year—luckily there were so many Pentagon officials involved in the project, no single person had to be involved all the time. Those who visited were obliged to give everyone a debriefing upon their return. This ensured that everyone was always up to date, just as if they had been there themselves.

He threw his suitcase onto the bed, and then promptly felt his feet being pulled out from underneath him. Howard hit the floor hard, right smack on his rear end. He feared that he'd broken his tailbone.

He watched as a figure dressed in black crawled out from underneath his bed, a balaclava covering his face.

Howard panicked. "What...the fuck...do you want? Who...are you?"
He tried to struggle to his feet, but the man leaped on top of him and
rammed a finger into his throat. Howard choked, but managed to muster up
enough strength to hit the man back with a hard fist to the side of the head.
It barely registered.

The dark figure grabbed his hand and snapped his wrist back in a
direction it was never intended to go. Howard heard the crack of his wrist-
bones and the pain shot right up to his eyeballs. He screamed, until a fist
slammed into his mouth sending at least two teeth flying.

The figure finally spoke. "Tell me, Colonel, when you saw me crawl out
from underneath the bed, did it remind you of some other creepy crawlers?"

Howard just stared back at the sinister figure, choosing to say nothing.
It was best to say nothing.

The figure spoke again. "I want your magnetic access pass for the lab
on Nevis."

Howard had been trained by the CIA—trained to resist interrogation.
But he hadn't had the opportunity to put his training to the test yet, never
having served even one single day on a battlefield despite his ripe age of fifty.
Now was the time to see if he had what it took. He remained silent as he had
been taught to do.

When he saw an extended index finger racing toward his forehead he
decided in that instant that his assailant had perhaps taken the same training
course as he had. He clearly had no patience.

The impact felt like someone had just hit him lightly with a hammer. But
he felt the finger pull back at the last second, lessening the power of the hit.
It pounded him but it felt to Howard that with the initial speed and power of
the finger it could have gone right through his brain if the man had wanted
it to. Howard wanted to scream again but decided that he might lose more
than just his teeth this time.

He remained silent.

With the speed of lightning the man grabbed his arm with the broken
wrist and snapped the elbow backwards as easily as breaking a matchstick.
This time Howard couldn't control himself. He started to cry, the pain was
so intense. And he felt a puddle forming in the crotch of his pants as his
bladder protested on its own.

"Colonel, I have all night. Unless you want me to turn you into a creepy crawler, I suggest you give me the access card. You'll be flopping like an octopus on dry land within just a few minutes. Your call, hero."

Howard gave up. There was no point to this, and he knew he was no match for this man. He sputtered, "It's in...the wall safe...over there. Combination...digital...9/30/77."

Although he couldn't see his face, he could tell by his voice that the man was smiling. "Now, isn't that cute? You guys are priceless. That combination is the exact date when your predecessors decided to turn off the communication arrays on the surface of the moon. Wow—so cute. Hey, those things were turned off so that there would be no signals to earth indicating that you nuked our moon. Right, Howard?"

Howard decided once again to shut up. Until he saw the forearms slamming inward towards the sides of his head. He flinched. The arms stopped an inch from his skull. The figure waited.

"Yes...that's right! You're right, you're right! Leave me alone!"

Howard watched as the man withdrew the card from the safe. Then he walked with a confident swagger back to Howard's prone figure and pulled packing tape out of his back pocket. He expertly wrapped him up like a cocoon, including his face, leaving only his nostrils free.

The phones were then pulled out of the wall, flung in the air and smashed with the thrust of an index finger. A finger then went through his computer monitor, and a fist smashed his keyboard and CPU to pieces. As a final act of personal invasion, the man pocketed Howard's cellphone. Howard's life was on that cellphone.

Then the stranger was gone.

*****

Travis Wilkinson strolled along lazily, briefcase in hand. Another tiring day at the office, but with his brilliant mathematical mind he knew he made it all look easy. He knew they all envied him, and he loved seeing the surprised looks on their faces when he told them about his old life, his years in prison. Everyone loved a success story, a rags to riches story, and his was one for the record books.

He loved this walk every day. Coming home to his lovely wife, Cynthia, and his darling little two-year old, Mikela. It made working for a living worthwhile, made life worthwhile. Travis loved his life now.

Only two blocks to go and he would get the hugs and kisses he deserved. It warmed his heart and he almost choked up just thinking about it.

Suddenly, he choked up for real. An arm was around his neck, yanking him off his feet and backwards into an alley. The strong assailant dragged him towards a doorway, then kicked it open with a black shoe attached to black trousers.

He felt himself being shoved into the room, and then a powerful impact to his lower extremities sent him flying into the air, landing him hard on his face. Travis heard the door slam shut behind him, then a dim light above him was flicked on. He saw his treasured briefcase lying a few feet away and for one strange moment he caught himself thinking about all the work he'd brought home with him.

The man was tall, but not too tall, dressed all in black with a balaclava covering his face. Travis knew all about balaclavas. He had worn them many times during his previous life.

The man moved fast now, yanking Travis up from the floor by his armpits and flinging him into a single wooden chair. It almost tipped over but Travis stopped it with his foot. He could see that another chair was set up directly across from his. The assailant sat down and faced him.

"Does this all look kinda familiar, Travis? Do you remember that night twenty years ago?"

Travis nodded.

"Sorry I couldn't use the same alley as you used. Progress, eh? It's all condominiums now. That precious alley and warehouse are gone now. Such a shame because I would have loved to have had you walk down that exact memory lane. Oh, well—this will have to do."

Travis watched the man pull a monstrous pistol out of his pocket, spin the cylinder, and ram the barrel up against his head.

"This pistol's cylinder can hold eight bullets, Travis. Eight very big bullets. This is a magnum. I think you know what a magnum can do to a head, eh? You've heard, I'm sure."

Travis was in shock.

"Say something, asshole!"

"Yes…yes…I know what…it can do!"

"Good—signs of life. I want you alive for a little while, Travis. We have a little game to play. You remember this game, don't you? Russian Roulette? You're pretty good at playing this game with other people, but maybe not so good at playing it yourself. We'll find out together, you and I."

Travis saw his life flash in front of his eyes—both his old life and his new life. He wanted to cry. "Man, I'm so sorry. I've changed. I have a family now. They need me."

"Tell someone who cares, Travis. Here's how this game is going to go. I'm going to start pulling the trigger. You're gonna hear the clicks if you're lucky. If you're unlucky, you won't hear anything. There are eight chambers, but there's only one bullet in this magnum. If you hear seven clicks, you get to live. Okay? You clear on the rules, Travis?"

Travis found that his head was bobbing furiously, and his legs were numb.

He wiggled his toes in his shoes but couldn't feel them against the leather.

It was like there was sand in his throat and marbles in his mouth.

"Hold your head still, Travis. I'm gonna start pulling the trigger. Ready?"

First click. Travis bit his lip.

Second click. Travis felt his knee fly up in the air.

Third click. Travis peed in his pants.

Fourth click. Travis shit in his drawers.

Fifth click. Travis felt his left foot bounce on the floor.

Sixth click. Travis felt his hair stand on end.

Seventh click. Travis sighed with relief. He saw in his mind's eye Cynthia and Mikela walking toward him.

"Well, how do you like that? You get to live, you lucky bastard."

Travis watched as the man pulled the gun away from his head. He sighed again. "Thanks, man."

"Oh, you're welcome, Travis. I'm true to my word. But I have one favor to ask of you before I leave."

"Sure, anything man."

The man in black pulled both sleeves of his sweater up to his elbows. "I want you to scratch me hard with both hands. I want you to scratch with each finger of each hand, dig deep, draw blood."

Travis looked at the masked face. "Are you a sicko, man?"

"Yes, I am, Travis. Scratch me now or I'll change my mind about that bullet in the chamber."

Travis shrugged, leaned forward and scratched. Scratched so hard that the blood was flowing down the man's powerful wrists, dripping onto the floor.

"Are you happy now, dude?"

"Yeah, I'm happy now, Travis. But there's one more thing I want you to do, but only if you think it's the decent thing to do. The right thing to do. Penance for all the terrible things you've done, the lives you've ruined that you've never been held accountable for. And I'm going to trust you. Because I think you're now a reformed man."

"I am, I am. But what the hell is it you want me to do?"

The man put the magnum into Travis' hand. "There's one bullet left. I want you to make the right decision. Put the gun up against your head and pull the trigger. You owe it to your victims, Travis. You owe it to your God."

Travis couldn't believe what he was hearing. He now had the gun in his hand with one bullet left, blood and skin from the man's forearms all over his fingers, and the idiot expected him to now just pull the trigger and kill himself? How more bizarre could this night get? The guy was crazy, no doubt. And Travis knew that the best thing to do with crazy people was to play along.

"Sure, man. I'll do it. I need redemption." Travis had to fight hard to keep the snicker rising deep down in his throat from giving him away.

The man in black nodded, rose from his seat, and started for the door. Travis raised the heavy gun, pointed it at the man's back and pulled the trigger.

Click. Travis bit his lip again.

The man in black stopped in his tracks and turned slowly to face him. "I heard that click, Travis. But the gun is pointed at me. Why is that?"

Travis peed in his pants again. How could there be any pee left?

The man in black strode toward him. Travis shit in his pants again.

The man's hands were in the air now, poised, index fingers like daggers pointed at Travis' eyes.

Just before the man in black made Travis' world go black, he heard him say, "This is for Alan Chambers."

CHAPTER FORTY THREE

"Jesus, I can't believe our luck! We have DNA this time!"

Grant Folsom marched into Bart Davis' office, waving a file. Bill Charlton, who had been sitting in the guest chair sipping coffee, jumped up and reached out his hand.

"Let me see that, Grant."

Folsom handed him the folder and walked over to the coffee machine. He felt the adrenaline rushing through his veins with the realization that this long ordeal may finally be almost over. The Press was just about ready to release the story about a purported serial killer haunting the streets of Washington. And Grant knew that if he could answer that story with an announcement of his own—the identification and arrest of a suspect—he might just be able to save his job as Chief of Police.

Bart walked around the desk and peered over Bill's shoulder, then immediately recoiled in horror. The photos of the victim were a shocking sight to see, Grant knew, and he found it slightly amusing watching the stunned look on the face of his colleague.

Bill frowned as he scanned the pages of the file. "Is it possible that our perp has finally made a mistake?"

Grant couldn't wipe the smile off his face. "Nobody's perfect, apparently not even our killer. It appears as if there was quite the struggle—skin and blood all over the victim's fingers and hands. In fact, he scratched the perp so deeply that there's quite a bit of skin under the fingernails. We have perfect DNA samples."

Bill's gaze lingered on one page in particular. He scratched his forehead as he stared. "Grant, I'm reading that the victim has been identified as a Travis Wilkinson. Isn't he the guy who was suspected of being the leader of the gang who killed Chambers' father? I recall reading that name in Dennis' file."

"Yep, that's the guy alright. And Chambers didn't identify him in the police lineup sixteen years ago. We always suspected that he knew we had the right guy, but for some reason he didn't come clean. I never talked to Dennis about that, but I was always puzzled about it."

Bill chuckled. "You're so naïve, Grant. I'm not puzzled at all. If Dennis is indeed our vigilante serial killer, he obviously would have wanted Wilkinson free as a bird so he could exact his own revenge on him."

Bart jumped in to the conversation. "Knock it off, Bill. You're getting way ahead of yourself once again. We have no hard evidence linking Dennis as the killer—and he's a good friend of mine, so I kinda resent you tarring him with that brush until we have something concrete."

"You're being defensive, Bart. Look at these photos, for Christ's sake!" Bill waved them in Bart's face. "You've seen the research on Shaolin martial arts, and you've seen the photos of the other six victims who were found. The wounds are all similar, and consistent with what a Shaolin expert would be able to inflict. And Chambers is, without a doubt, a Shaolin expert."

"That doesn't make him a killer."

Bill glared at Bart. "No, but it puts him right at the top of the list of possible suspects. Unfortunately, there isn't a central registry of people who are experts at the art of Shaolin, but there should be. In the absence of a registry, however, we have a skilled expert right in our midst who has motive in not only the Wilkinson killing, but also in the disappearance of his secretary's ex-husband—plus, the nurse who was caring for Denny's mother. I mean, for the love of God, Bart, it's as obvious as the nose on your face." Bill chuckled sarcastically. "And your nose is pretty obvious, to be brutally honest with you."

Grant took the file out of Bill's hand and opened it to the description of the wounds. "Bart, I tend to agree with Bill. The description of the wounds puts this victim as the work of the vigilante, without a doubt. And Dennis had an overwhelming reason to kill him, with this Wilkinson character having forced him to shoot his own dad. God, I can't imagine the pain of having to live with that for the last twenty years. I would have wanted to kill the guy too, to be perfectly honest. But look at this—it says here that the guy's eyeballs were basically disintegrated with blunt force through the eyes right into the brain. Then, to top it off, there was a finger-width hole right through the prick's forehead—a clean hole through the skull, again smashing through the brain. The result of these three penetrations? The brain turned to mush—so similar to the other six killings, it's uncanny."

Bart shuffled his feet and looked down at the floor. "I know you guys think I'm just in denial because Dennis is an old friend, but it's not like that, really. I accept that this latest slaughter is the work of the vigilante, and I accept that Dennis had motive. But, let's face it; there are probably dozens of people who had motive to kill that scum. Sure, he may have turned his life around, but with the life he lived before prison, he must have left behind enemies galore. And I accept that Dennis had motive to kill his secretary's ex and his mom's nurse as well. But, to this day, those are still listed as disappearances, not murders."

Bart continued, pacing back and forth in his office. "But there are no obvious motives for Dennis to have killed any of those six actual murder victims. And if we believe wholeheartedly in the concept of 'modus operandi,' for the three others that he did have motive in why would he have made two of the bodies disappear and then leave this last one, Wilkinson, right out there for us to find? And with DNA all over him? Makes no sense at all—not consistent and not logical."

Grant made a face. "Well, serial killers have been known to be inconsistent from time to time, even though I would agree that it's rare. And when they do it, it's usually to confuse the authorities and throw them off the trail."

Bart scoffed. "This guy had no reason to do that—we've been confused right from the beginning on this case, and we were never really on his trail at all. We didn't have a clue. He had very little to worry about from us, I'm embarrassed to admit."

Grant put his big arm around Bart's shoulders. "Well, if we do bring Dennis in, he will have a lot to worry about. And since he's a cop, you'll be in the thick of it—Internal Affairs will have to do the damage control with the media and convince them that we're giving this case fair and objective treatment. Our Chief of Detectives being a suspect in a vigilante serial killer case will be big news indeed, national news."

"Have you already tried to arrest him?"

"Not yet—we'll wait for the DNA testing. Should have the results later today. But we did try to contact him—by phone and in person. He doesn't seem to be around. Might have gone away for the weekend, or something. We'll nab him Monday if the tests prove us right, and if we can find a judge over the next two days who'll sign our warrant."

Grant noticed that Bill seemed to avert his eyes at the mention of

Dennis being absent from home. "Do you or your Pentagon cronies know something, Bill? Is there a reason why we can't find Dennis right now? Anything you care to share?"

Bill Charlton shook his head. "Beats me—he's your guy. If I knew something, I'd tell you."

Bart scowled. "Bullshit! I don't think you spooks would tell us anything. You guys have your own agendas. I have a gut feeling that you know every single move that Denny has made ever since our meeting here with him. You recall that meeting, don't you, Bill? The one that Denny ended by yanking you up by your tie and whispering a 'sweet nothing' in your ear?"

If looks could truly kill, Bill's cold stare into Bart's eyes was a weapon with no equal.

CHAPTER FORTY FOUR

"So, Mr. Cotterhill, are you visiting St. Kitts for business or pleasure?"

Dennis leaned against the counter, his yellow and green tropical shirt flapping in the breeze that was blowing through the airport. "Strictly pleasure—I intend to enjoy your beautiful beaches, ride your Scenic Train, and maybe charter a catamaran. Can't wait."

"We don't get many Americans down on these islands. You folks usually go to Puerto Rico or the Virgins. Why did you choose St. Kitts/Nevis?"

"Puerto Rico's too noisy, and the Virgins are over-developed. I wanted something more peaceful."

The Immigration agent nodded appreciatively. "Your occupation, please?"

"I'm a lawyer."

"What kind of lawyer?"

"Tax law." Dennis figured that was boring enough to pass scrutiny.

"I see that you live in Washington, D.C. Are you an American citizen?"

"Yes."

"Anything to declare?"

"No, except for a few packs of cigarettes."

She leafed through his documents. "I see here that you arrived by private aircraft—a Gulfstream?"

"Yes."

"Is it your airplane?"

"I can only dream! No, it was chartered by someone else."

"Are you traveling as a group?"

"No, I responded to a query asking for another traveler to share the costs. I didn't know the other three people, although after a couple of drinks on the flight down here, I have to admit that we're much better acquainted now," Dennis chuckled.

The attractive Customs and Immigration officer managed to crack a slight smile and handed Dennis his passport. "Have a nice vacation, Mr. Cotterhill."

Dennis picked up his carry-on bag and headed towards the exit. He stopped at a kiosk, bought a local newspaper and pretended to read it while awaiting Fiona, Brett, and Avery.

He watched out of the corner of his eye as they too were questioned at the Customs counter. He had to be careful to make sure that no one saw that they were together. He was simply a lawyer on vacation, and the other three were supposed to be here on official American government business. Their interrogation would no doubt last longer than his.

And it did. It took half an hour for all three to make it through. He watched as Brett, aka Doctor Gene Sikorsky moved confidently through the turnstile, wearing a conservative black suit and his newly donned pair of fake glasses—in reality a high-tech video camera.

Next came Avery Duncan, known for today as Colonel Howard Wentworth—his hair now a shock of white, his cheek jowls puffed out with some putty-like substance that the makeup artist promised had a life of twenty-four hours, and his body now resplendent in the uniform and cap of a United States Air Force Colonel. Avery cut a handsome and convincing figure indeed. Dennis barely recognized him.

Fiona followed with a flourish. She strode with an aggressive gait just like Brett had coached her, through the turnstile and into the concourse. Dennis had to admit that Fiona did look convincing as Doctor Angela Huntington of the Centers for Disease Control. Her hair was now blonde, and her eyes were a striking blue color that jumped out even from a distance.

She swung her carry-on bag over her right shoulder and caught up to Avery and Brett. They chatted together for a second or two, and Dennis watched as they went out to the front promenade of the airport to hail a taxi.

Dennis continued for a few more minutes pretending to read the boring local news, and then did the same as his colleagues—hailed a cab that would take him to Pier # 9 at the marina located in the harbor of the capital city of Basseterie. From there they would all cruise together to the sister island of Nevis.

It was only 12:00 noon. While each of them carried overnight bags, those were only for appearances. There was no intention to stay overnight. They would be in and out of Nevis, race by boat back to St. Kitts and then fly back to Washington that same night. Their Gulfstream would be fueled and ready to go on a moment's notice.

Time was of the essence.

Dennis agreed with Brett that the more time they spent on the islands, the more likely it was that they might never return.

*****

The short cab ride from the airport to the marina gave Dennis his first good look at the island of St. Kitts. It was both beautiful and bleak; a paradox. Barren in some spots, lushly tropical in others. It was easy to see the abandonment by the government of St. Kitts/Nevis of the industry that had fueled the economy of the islands for the last couple of centuries. Sugar cane—the government had decided they could no longer compete with world markets, and with subsidies being dropped by the U.K. they had no choice but to find another economic engine. Dennis could see the overgrown fields of sugar cane; the neglected crops just withering in the tropical sun. Large dark patches of soil bore evidence of the fields that had been burned deliberately, either to clear the way to plant other crops, or, perhaps more importantly, to keep the incessant Vervet monkeys at bay.

Tourism was the big thing now—these islands were late into the game but they were surging ahead desperately, trying to find themselves, define themselves. Every island in the Caribbean was pretty much the same, but some had managed to differentiate themselves more than others—such as the glitz of Sint Maarten, the history and sleaze of Puerto Rico, the gambling of Aruba, and the mountainous spice-fragranced splendor of Grenada. What would St. Kitts/Nevis become? The quiet laid-back islands?

Dennis thought cynically—*maybe the islands of alien creepy crawlers?*

The Federation of St. Kitts/Nevis is the smallest sovereign state in the West Indies and the two islands are separated by a two-mile channel known as 'The Narrows.' To the north lies the French/Dutch democracy of St. Martin/Sint Maarten, to the east the island of Antigua, and to the south the volcano-ravaged island of Montserrat. St. Kitts had been the home of the very first English/French colonies in the Caribbean, thus became known as the 'Mother Colony of the West Indies.'

The name 'Nevis' came from the original Spanish designation, 'Nuestra de las Nieves,' meaning 'Our Lady of the Snows.'

Christopher Columbus, back in 1498, named the island of Saba twenty miles to the northwest 'San Cristobal' in typical Christopher Columbus style—after himself. But a mapping error transferred that name to St. Kitts, which was then dubbed 'St. Christopher's Island.' It has been shortened since then to the nickname 'St. Kitts.'

The infamous Vervet monkeys, otherwise known as 'Greenies,' were introduced to the islands by pirates. The creatures ravaged, multiplied, pestered, and now were quite simply out of control.

Of the two islands, Nevis has had more experience with tourism—and resents its big sister St. Kitts for neglecting its unique needs. As a long-time destination for the rich and famous—including such notables as Princess Diana and Mick Jagger—Nevis feels it's owed some special consideration. And it doesn't feel it gets it.

Nevis is small and beautiful—only thirty-six square miles, its centerpiece being Nevis Peak rising 3200 feet into the clouds.

And right smack in between the pristine beaches and the towering peak is a laboratory known as the 'Behavioral Modification Foundation.' Nevis was apparently in the midst of building its own destiny now, with or without the help of its sister island.

But there seemed to be no doubt whatsoever that it was receiving rather eager help from the good old United States of America.

CHAPTER FORTY FIVE

"Avery—you and I'll snap these onto our belts under our jackets. Denny, since you'll be on the boat, you won't have to worry about hiding yours. And Fiona, just shove your gun into your purse."

Fiona fingered the heavy Glock pistol. "Do you really think we're going to need these?"

"I hope not—but better to be safe than sorry, don't you think?"

She nodded slowly.

"Having some second thoughts?"

Fiona shook her head. "No, it's just rather ominous now that we're here, on the boat, ready to go."

"Do you know how to use a pistol?"

"Yes, I've had firearms training. All of us at the Pentagon have to know how to use a gun."

"And Denny, I don't think I need to worry about you."

Dennis snapped the holster onto his belt and slid the gun into place. "Unfortunately, no. Sad to admit that I've had to use mine a few times in my life."

"But you're alive and they're not—that's the good part."

Avery was pacing back and forth on the bridge, not one for small talk. "Brett, we'd better get a move on. Preferable if we're back before dark."

Brett walked over to an inclined table, pulled a map out of his pocket and spread it out. "Okay, gather 'round. This is where we're going." He smacked his finger down on a spot on the map.

"This is the northwest coast of Nevis, and there's a development here called 'The Hamilton.' This entire estate area is known as 'Nelson's Spring.' Lots of condos, villas, and all that jazz. Wealthy high-end residents from mainly Canada and Great Britain. However, either the recession…or perhaps fear of another monkey attack," Brett chuckled, "have kept sales at a low ebb.

"So, the occupancy rate is only about thirty percent right now, which is perfect for what we want to do. We need a place to embark from that's not too isolated because we need to steal a car, but we don't want an area that's too busy either. There should be lots of high-end cars for us to choose from here. When we pull up to the gates of the laboratory we can't be seen driving a Camry. With our military and CDC status, we have to be in a car with some prestige. The villas at 'The Hamilton' sell from half a mill to well over two mill. So, the quality of cars they own will track with that."

Fiona tapped Brett on the shoulder. "But this is the middle of the day— won't we be noticed stealing a car?"

"We'll try our best to avoid that, but yes, we might. We'll just have to deal with that if it happens. We need to arrive at the lab during the day, because that's when the official inspection was scheduled. We can't vary from that itinerary otherwise we'll attract suspicion."

Fiona frowned. "How will we react if we're caught boosting a car?"

"Don't you worry yourself about those kinds of logistics. Avery and I will handle things like that."

"I don't think I like the sound of that."

Brett turned around to face her head-on. "Fiona, this isn't going to be a walk in the park, or some little investigative journalistic adventure such as you used to do with the Washington Post. This is the real thing—people have died in the quest to keep this thing secret. We're venturing into something here that without a doubt is explosive. And we're doing it because we want to blow it wide open and hopefully prevent a disaster. They won't hesitate to kill us, and we may need to kill first in order to survive.

"This is the most serious thing that I've ever encountered, and we're probably dreaming in Technicolor even just thinking that we can expose it and stay alive in the process. So, maybe you should think about that before you come with us. I can't afford to have any one of us squeamish. There may have to be some collateral damage. Get me?"

Fiona looked over at Dennis, who merely nodded. She turned back to Brett and pursed her lips in that cute, serious little way that Dennis adored so much. "I get you, Brett. Don't worry, I know how serious this is—the fact that we're on the precipice of doing this is just freaking me out a bit, I guess. And I don't want to think of anyone dying."

Dennis kissed Fiona on the cheek. "Remember, hon, that the one big thing we do have in our favor is the element of surprise. They're not expecting us—and we're pretending to be the people who they are expecting. We have a huge advantage. All we're going to do is let Brett's fancy glasses take some videos and then we're out of there."

Avery suddenly pointed down the dock—a man carrying a metal container was coming towards them. "Hey, Brett, looks like our delivery is here."

"Ah, good. Right on time."

Dennis watched the stranger struggle to keep his footing as he carried the apparently heavy object on board. He was black, tall, and heavy-set, dressed in trendy khaki pants and a floral tropical shirt. His face was unsmiling, not typical of the usually buoyant Kittitians.

The man spoke. "Do you want me to connect this right away, Brett, or are you going to do it yourself?"

"How long will it take?"

"Shouldn't be more than ten minutes max, then you'll be good to go."

Dennis noticed that the man didn't have the typical Caribbean accent—more like he was from Boston.

"Go ahead and connect it then."

"Okee-dokey. Will do. And you're familiar with this device, so you know how to activate it when you need it, right?"

"Yeah, that won't be a problem."

With that, the man disappeared into the plush cabin below. Denny heard him open the hatch and drag the box down into the engine compartment.

"Brett, what was that all about?"

Brett smiled. "Ah, just our little ace in the hole. This motor launch is an Ocean 62 Super-Sport. Aggressive as hell, with a 1500 HP engine. It cruises at thirty-one knots, with a top speed of thirty-seven."

"What's that in miles per hour?"

"About forty-three."

"Hard to believe a boat this large can go that fast."

"Yeah, it's sixty-two feet in length, and has a diesel fuel tank with a capacity of 1,450 gallons. So, it's not only swift but it can go a fair distance as well."

"So, what's this ace in the hole that you're installing?"

"Well, as fast as it is, it might not be fast enough. My research discovered that the lab has a fleet of 'Sea Rays' wharfed not far from the pier that we'll be docking at. If we're being chased, we're going to need a boost. Those little boats can hit about fifty-five miles per hour. The little gizmo Desmond is installing for us will give the engine a turbo-charge on command. It will thrust us up to sixty in a matter of seconds. All I have to do is manually activate it if we need it. But it only has a life of about fifteen minutes, so I can't take a chance on triggering it ahead of time. Desmond will have it ready to go—all I have to do is crawl down there and hit the switch."

"Who is this Desmond character?"

"Just an associate of mine. Former CIA—he works out of Puerto Rico now. A good man. He's the one who smuggled the guns in for us. He can get anything past anybody."

"Okay, continue telling us the plan. You were talking about the 'Nelson's Spring' area."

"Right. We're going to cruise to a long pier that 'The Hamilton' complex has for the use of their residents and guests. We'll dock there and then Avery, Fiona and I will head off. We'll steal a car somewhere in the complex parking lot, then drive to the lab." Brett pounded his finger onto a spot on the map. "Here's the road that leads to the lab—goes inland about five miles.

"Denny, you'll simply tie up at the pier and wait for us. Give us three hours. If we're not back by then, you'll have to assume that something went wrong. And you'll have to suck that up and just leave. I know that will be difficult for you—leaving Fiona behind—but you'll have to. Get back to the States; get to the safe house in Norfolk—George has been instructed to allow you entry to get the microfilm. Remember, it's in my vault: combination 21-207-21. Get those documents reproduced and send them out to every god damned media outlet in the world. It won't be as good as having the video as the ultimate proof, but it'll be better than nothing and will probably save your life."

Dennis just nodded in response.

Fiona bit her lip.

Avery donned his air force colonel's cap, and Brett cranked up the Ocean 62's engine.

Desmond emerged from the engine compartment, jumped out onto the dock and cast off their lines.

As they pulled away and started their journey south, Dennis noticed Desmond raising his right hand in a crisp salute. Brett and Avery returned the gesture.

Dennis had always been comforted by the fact that his many years on the police force had allowed a certain level of desensitization to develop, which served to insulate him nicely from fear, worry, and pain.

But suddenly that protective envelope seemed to disappear as he was driven to grab Fiona and hold her tightly to his chest. He squeezed her hard while feeling an unfamiliar shiver of dread and anticipation shoot up his spine.

For just the briefest instant he felt the paralyzing panic of wondering if he'd ever see her again.

CHAPTER FORTY SIX

Doctor Angela Huntington of the Centers for Disease Control wandered aimlessly around her apartment. It was Friday, and her weekend plans had been cancelled.

A weekend on the island of Nevis. It would have been her first trip to the island, having just been brought aboard the Operation Creepy Crawlers project within the last month. Her boss, Doctor Gene Sikorsky, didn't care—he'd been there many times before and he was beginning to show signs of boredom. He seemed glad to have been let off the hook this time, giving him a rare weekend that he could spend with his family.

But Angela cared—this would have been a romantic weekend for her, after the obligatory two hours she would have had to spend at the laboratory. She was going to spend one night with her lover after which he'd be flying back to Washington. Then she would have spent the next day lazing around on the beaches, daydreaming about her lover.

And Colonel Howard Wentworth was a wonderful lover.

Now she'd have to spend the weekend with her boring husband, a man whose idea of a thrill was cracking open a can of beer and watching the Redskins.

No, she couldn't do it. She was psyched up for a weekend with Howard and that's the way it would still be. She had to see him—just had to.

When she read his email yesterday it had seemed colder than usual. She knew he had to be careful to keep it official and all that crap, but he could have at least added a nice little smiley face or something. And he hadn't even phoned. She'd expected him to at least suggest they get together for a drink since their trip was now cancelled. Didn't he miss her? Long for her?

They had been seeing each other for over a year now and she knew Howard had pulled some strings to get her onto the Creep project. Her boss, Gene, wasn't one of her biggest supporters so she knew it hadn't been his idea. Howard had talked to her many times in the past about how fascinating this project was, and how if he had the chance he'd get her assigned to it. The Pentagon had tremendous pull at the CDC—whatever they wanted generally got done. So, she was sure that Howard had done something, but he'd played it coy with her nonetheless.

She didn't care about being on the project for the fascination of it—she wanted the travel, the excuses to be away from her husband, the trips away with Howard. That's what she wanted. She couldn't care less about a bunch of alien organisms. As long as they were contained, and she was in a Hazmat suit, they could crawl around all they wanted. And she already had more than her share of challenging assignments—with lots of potentially scary outcomes. She didn't need one more.

No, she needed romance and she needed to get laid.

Howard didn't have a family so that left lots of freedom for the two of them to plan their trysts. Angela's husband didn't really care where she was—in fact he seemed to prefer that she be elsewhere. When she was home, she cramped his style. She never suspected for a second that he was having an affair on her—he was too much of a slob. No woman would give him a second glance. He hadn't always been a slob. In fact, at one time a long time ago, he'd been quite the hunk.

But over the last few years he'd become lazy.

And over the last few years Angela had found her mojo.

On impulse, she picked up the phone and dialed Howard's mobile number. Shithead was in the living room asleep on the couch—he wouldn't hear a thing. And it was reaching the point where she didn't really care if he heard anyway.

No answer. Strange. Howard was usually at home on Fridays. And more likely today than ever, since their trip had been cancelled. He wouldn't have had time to make other plans. And no matter what, he always answered his mobile.

She tried his home number—no answer on that phone either. Well then, she would just have to go over there in person. She had her own key, so if he wasn't there she would wait for him. What a nice surprise for him to come home and find her waiting in his bed, wearing that sexy negligee that he loved so much. Or maybe wearing nothing at all? Angela liked her options.

She tiptoed through the living room past her snoring slob of a husband who was lying half on, half off the couch. Three empty beer cans lay on the floor beside him. Slob.

When Angela emerged from her bedroom, she was wearing a sleeveless vest, no bra, tight jeans, and no panties. She was ready to enjoy the weekend that was stolen from her. Yes indeedy—Howard would be surprised. And lucky her—she would get laid tonight after all.

*****

True to Brett's instructions, Dennis made a wide 180-degree arc on his approach to the northwest coast of Nevis. He marveled at the beauty of the island—palm-fringed shoreline, spectacular white beaches, majestic homes and villas as far as the eye could see.

This truly resembled paradise in his mind, and he thought how bizarre it was that this beautiful part of the world housed possibly the most dangerous creatures imaginable.

It was an interesting parallel—how pirates had introduced the non-indigenous Vervet monkeys to Nevis centuries ago, with how it had now happened to the island once again. Chimpanzees were now here and alien organisms also called this place home. It was rudely coincidental that they were possibly being mated with those last unwelcome invaders.

But the sheer outward splendor of Nevis kept these horrors hidden from the public eye. Who could possibly imagine what was transpiring five miles inland, and what this place and the rest of the world would look like if the things escaped uncontrolled?

Dennis pulled back on the throttle to slow his approach to the pier, and then shoved it into reverse as he slid in for a perfect docking on the starboard side of the launch. There were several other boats already tied up but other than that, virtually no signs of human activity. The place seemed deserted.

Dennis looked up towards the luxurious villas set back from the beach—Adirondack chairs and barbecues adorned the balconies but there were no people enjoying them. He wondered if the world would ever recover from this crippling recession. Would the concept of 'leisure' ever be the same again?

Brett leaped deftly onto the dock, followed by Avery. "Okay, Denny, this is great. I think you can safely linger here until we get back. I'll tie your lines and then we'll be off."

Fiona hesitated before leaving the launch. She looked back at Dennis and smiled. She blew him a kiss. Dennis blew one back.

Then she was gone.

He watched as his newly blonded lover with the freshly minted blue eyes followed Brett and Avery along the dock to the edge of the beach. He loved the way she walked: the subtle sway of her hips, the confident swing of her arms, and the gentle lilt of her head.

Dennis prayed to God that she'd be okay.

CHAPTER FORTY SEVEN

Fiona was confident that the three of them looked sufficiently official; they were dressed the part and they walked the part. But she sure hoped they could find a car, because a five-mile hike in the tropical heat would kill them.

They strolled through the visitor parking lot of 'The Hamilton' villa complex, and she watched as Brett's eyes shifted from side to side. He was looking for something specific but she didn't have a clue as to what that was. His trained eyes clearly knew what they wanted and she was fairly certain that what that was did not exist in this particular parking lot.

Brett led them along the sides of the villas, where the residents would park either beside or in front of their units. They passed numerous cars that would have been suitable, Fiona thought, but apparently not to Brett. She and Avery followed without saying a word.

Fiona noticed that most of the parking spots were empty—only about one out of three had cars parked, and the complex seemed like a ghost town to her. The pool and tennis courts were empty, no one was swimming in the ocean, and not a soul was sitting on the beach. The area was beautiful and deserved to be buzzing, she thought, but there were no signs of life that she could see except for the occasional luxury car.

Suddenly Brett stopped. And Fiona knew why. They were standing behind a late model Lexus LS 600H, a vehicle that would retail in the United States for about 140,000 dollars. The parking spot indicated it was attached to Unit # 21, which was a beautiful pink and white villa, located directly in front of the car. But this unit was different than most—it was on a corner and almost completely shrouded in palm trees and other tropical foliage. Brett looked at Avery with a question mark in his eyes. Avery nodded.

Fiona watched as they silently went to work. Avery walked over to the next car down, removed a tool from his pocket and quickly removed the license plates. Then he did a switch with the plates on the Lexus while Brett stood watch.

When that was done Avery stood on the sidewalk, alert and seemingly at attention in his slick military uniform. Brett tapped Fiona on the shoulder and whispered, "Follow me."

He led the way up the paved patio steps to the front door of Unit # 21. Fiona noticed it was a combination lock. Brett didn't knock—he pulled a tiny little remote transmitter from his pocket and aimed it at the electronic lock. He pushed a button and it began to sing—soft notes that indicated it was searching for the combination. When it found a number, it beeped, and then quickly resumed its singsong. After three beeps, the lock clicked and Brett calmly turned the handle of the carved mahogany door.

He walked in and Fiona quietly followed. They both saw it at the same time—hanging on the foyer wall was a key wrangler shaped like an elephant. Three sets of keys hung like bulky earrings, and two of them bore the Lexus logo. Brett quietly slipped one of the sets off the hanger and passed it back to Fiona. Then he put a finger to his lips and motioned for her to follow.

He led her through the living room and into the master bedroom. An elderly man was lying on the bed, snoring the afternoon away. Brett slipped his hand into his pocket and withdrew what looked like a tiny pistol; more like a derringer. Fiona gasped—she couldn't help herself. That gasp was all it took to stir the man from his slumber.

He lurched up into a sitting position. "What the…"

Brett fired.

The old man choked, reached his hand up to his neck, and then collapsed back into the exact same position he had been in before Fiona gave away their presence.

Brett moved quickly to the side of the bed, put one hand in front of the old man's nose, and the other hand on his wrist. "He's fine—just going to have a longer sleep than he planned today."

Brett then put his thumb and forefinger along the side of the man's neck and pulled. He waved an object in front of Fiona. "Just a dart, Fiona. Not to worry. A sedative—it should buy us four hours."

Fiona placed her hand across her heart. "Oh, thank God."

Brett moved to within two inches of her face and glared into her eyes. "Don't do that again. Next time you could get us killed."

He didn't wait for her response. Brett led the way out the front door and down the steps to a waiting Avery, who was still standing like a statue in front of the Lexus.

"Okay, we're off." Before crawling into the driver's side, Brett removed a sticker from his pocket, peeled off the backing and stuck it onto the lower left corner of the driver's side window. It bore the 'Hertz' logo. "We might as well complete the image, huh? We would obviously have had to rent a car while here; little things someone might notice if we didn't pay attention to them."

Fiona shook her head in disbelief. The efficiency of this man and his attention to detail—she was flabbergasted, while at the same time relieved. She was 100% certain that this mysterious man named Brett Horton would keep them alive.

Avery slipped into the front passenger seat and Fiona sat in the rear. Avery pulled the map out of his pocket, studied it for a second and pointed ahead through the front windshield. "Drive down about 500 yards and hang a left onto Longboat Cay Road. That should take us right to the front door of the lab."

As they cruised along, Fiona watched the world of Nevis slip by. Children on bikes and walking in groups, on their way home from school. Cute little plaid skirts, white blouses with matching plaid scarves for the girls; black trousers and white shirts for the boys. They all looked so prim and proper, a stark contrast to the ramshackle homes they were scampering home to.

Little shops dotted the road, peppered with shacks advertising themselves as bars. No doors, no glass windows, young men sitting at patio tables sipping beers seemingly without a care in the world. Fiona thought, *if only they knew what was going on just mere miles away.*

The road came to a 'T' junction, and Avery motioned for Brett to turn right. Just ahead Fiona could see the barbed wire fences and electronic gate signifying an installation that was intended to be undisturbed. Then she saw the sign: 'Behavioral Modification Foundation.' And beneath that sign was a smaller one, but one that was no less noticeable: 'Trespassers Will be Shot on Sight.'

Brett pulled up to a speaker box in front of the gate and pressed the intercom button. A female voice came through the box asking for identification. Brett answered, "Colonel Howard Wentworth, Pentagon; Doctor Gene Sikorsky, CDC; and Doctor Angela Huntington, CDC."

There was a moment of silence, then a voice. "Please proceed to the Visitor Parking area. Leave the keys in the vehicle and the doors unlocked.

Then advance through the front doors to the Reception area, where the Director will meet you."

Fiona's stomach flipped.

*****

Angela Huntington slipped her key into the lock and crept inside, careful to make sure that no snoopy neighbors saw her. Even though Howard wasn't married, he was still the cautious type. He didn't like his neighbors knowing his business.

She called out his name. In reply, she heard a thump. It came from upstairs. She called out again…another thump…then another. She ran down the hall, then took the stairs two at a time. Angela could feel her heart struggling to keep pace with the speed of her ascent up the steep narrow stairs of the old brownstone.

Out of breath, she burst into the master bedroom and stopped dead in her tracks. Angela stared in disbelief at an almost unrecognizable human figure wrapped from his head to his toes in plastic packing tape. Howard Wentworth looked like a mummy.

She rushed to his side and pulled the tape back from his mouth.

Howard took a moment to exhale with relief. Then he shouted, "Get the scissors—top dresser drawer—cut this shit off me! Watch out for my right arm—the wrist is broken and so is the elbow.

"And Angela, dial the Pentagon on your mobile—quickly! We don't have a moment to spare!"

CHAPTER FORTY EIGHT

The corridors were antiseptic. White ceramic-tiled floors and walls, with shiny metal-clad ceilings. There was a pervasive smell that Fiona pegged as formaldehyde and it made her want to puke.

The Director was tall and nerdy—glasses, slicked-back greasy hair, black trousers and a white lab coat. His sneakers squeaked as he led them down the long bright hallway that seemed to be endless. He introduced himself as Doctor Clyde Shannon. His voice was high-pitched and his manner was brusque. Fiona guessed that the man resented having his facility inspected—a typical scientist. Obsessed with his work and intolerant of any outsiders who felt they had some kind of vested interest. To him the work was probably everything and having to account to anyone for that work was a pain in the ass.

However, Colonel Avery Duncan, aka Colonel Howard Wentworth, played his part perfectly. He did all the talking as the de facto head of their little entourage and dominated the arrogant scientist with his military demeanor. Avery made it abundantly clear that he was having none of this "I haven't got time for you folks" shit.

Doctor Shannon started off by saying, "I only have thirty minutes to spare." Avery responded by saying, "You'll give us all the time we need, sir, and I'll be the one to decide when we're finished."

As they walked, Fiona noticed Brett being careful to aim his face in the direction of the spaces that he wanted to film, but he did it in a way that was subtle—no one would notice that he was anyone other than a man with poor eyesight, when in fact he was a walking talking video camera.

"So, what do you want to see? You folks have been here so many times, I can't even count that high."

Avery answered in his monotone military voice. "We want to see the labs, assess the current status of experiments, and satisfy ourselves that our own deadlines will be met."

"Deadlines—we're doing important work here and it can't be rushed. We have deadlines too, but we make sure that they're responsible and realistic. All you Pentagon types want to do is use things before they're ready. You've already had a couple of disastrous outcomes, and if you'd waited like I begged you to, those wouldn't have happened."

Doctor Shannon, keep in mind that this lab exists because of us 'Pentagon types.' You wouldn't have the luxury of doing your important work if we weren't funding it for you. Please remember that."

Shannon grunted and kept walking.

They rounded a corner and Shannon stopped in front of a steel door with a magnetic pad, which was also equipped with a push-button combination console.

"Colonel, would you please produce your entry card?"

Avery reached into his pocket and pulled out the card that Brett had stolen from the real Colonel Wentworth the day before. He held it up to the reader and it beeped. Then Shannon pushed a button and a shield popped out, hiding from view the numbers that he proceeded to punch in to the combination console. The door clicked open and Fiona quietly sighed with relief. The card hadn't been deactivated yet—which meant that Wentworth was still out of action and undiscovered. They had passed their first big test.

"Colonel Wentworth, you've been here before. And so, have you, Doctor Sikorsky. Do you really need me to explain everything all over again?" The good doctor was clearly frustrated with their imposition and his impatience was showing.

Brett spoke for the first time. "I'll answer that. Yes, we do need you to explain everything all over again. My associate here, Doctor Angela Huntington, will be a new key player on the project. This is her first time at the facility, as you know, and we need her to hear about what's going on right from the horse's mouth. And that horse is you, Doctor Shannon."

Shannon sighed, exasperation seething from his lungs.

"Alright. I'll give brief explanations as we do the tour. I won't go into too much detail, because that may be too much for you to grasp."

Fiona couldn't resist. "Doctor Shannon, I'm a microbiologist and a vascular surgeon. I also have a Master's degree in chemistry and a PHD in zoology. I think I might be able to understand at least half of what you explain to us."

Shannon scrutinized her critically, sizing her up. Fiona guessed that the man's chauvinistic condescending brain was having a tough time reconciling that someone so pretty could be so well educated.

He grunted in his now familiar fashion, and motioned with his finger for them to follow. As the scientist turned his back to them, Fiona felt the nudge of Brett's elbow. She was encouraged to see him wearing an approving grin, along with his thumb and forefinger formed into a circle, which silently said, "You go, girl!"

They arrived at a wall of glass that seemed to be equipped at one end with a sliding glass door panel and a similar entry pad and button console to what the metal hallway door had.

"We won't go inside—you can observe from this vantage point. There are no live organisms, as these Vervet monkeys were injected months ago. But human intervention can disturb them. This is one-way glass, so we can see them but they can't see us. Please do not tap on the glass and make sure to keep your voices low."

Inside the compound were about two dozen little green monkeys, some sitting up with their backs against the wall, others scattered about the floor no closer together than at least three feet.

"These are the Vervet monkeys, which have lived on this island for several hundred years. They've multiplied dramatically to the point that they now outnumber humans. So, no one really cares if we kill a few.

"What you're seeing here is de-socialization. We genetically modified one of the moon organisms to achieve this. Vervet monkeys are normally very sociable creatures—they need each other very much just like wolves and many other members of the canine family. They mate for life and they just love touching each other, cleaning each other, etc. You can easily see that these modified creatures here exhibit none of those inherent characteristics. At this point, they can't stand each other and have no desire at all for closeness of any kind. Also, as a positive offshoot, they have absolutely no motivation to mate."

Brett had his eyes peeled straight ahead of him, video camera glasses catching the entire scene, while the tiny integral microphone picked up every word uttered.

"Why is that a positive offshoot?"

"That's kind of a stupid question, don't you think?"

Brett glared at him. "There's no such thing as a stupid question,

Doctor—only stupid answers."

Fiona noticed a twitch in Shannon's left eye. He clearly didn't like being challenged.

"Well, as you very well know, my role here is as a 'war scientist.' My mission is to weaponize these aliens in a variety of ways. War doesn't necessarily have to be violent—it can be strategic and insidious, depending on what our needs are.

"If we want to preserve a country's infrastructure and resources so we can absorb them, it's in our best interests not to cause destruction. So, in that case we would want to disturb and eventually annihilate its inhabitants. This particular strain of the organism used on these little guys will cause a society to no longer socialize, causing a complete breakdown of family structure as well as business and industrial teamwork. And—they will have no interest in propagating, so, over time, the indigenous population of people will simply cease to exist, making room for whatever population of people we wish to introduce."

"Is the application practical? I mean, you can't go around injecting an entire population of citizens."

Shannon chuckled condescendingly. "No, of course we can't. Every lab environment you will see here has been accomplished through injections, and that is mainly for the safety of our scientists. We can't afford to have anything airborne in this complex. But trust me, we've already accomplished the development of airborne versions of every genetically modified strain that we use here. And we've tested the airborne varieties in jungles on unpopulated islands. We know that they work exceedingly well, just like the injected varieties."

Avery pressed his nose up against the glass.

"Don't do that Colonel. They may look docile but they're actually extremely alert."

"Well, so what? It looks like all that would do is disturb their sleep."

"It would do more than that. They could get quite violent."

"That's hard to believe, Doctor."

"Okay, I'll show you what happens if their little existence gets disturbed."

Shannon punched a number into his cellphone and whispered a couple of words. The next thing they saw was a door in the compound opening and a lab technician appearing with a little green monkey in his arms. He tossed the monkey into the pen and quickly closed the door behind him.

"This Vervet is a normal one. No genetic modifications at all. Watch what happens when it immediately tries to socialize—which it will."

The monkey ran over to one of the GMs that was lying in the center of the room, chattering and wiggling its little bum. The little fellow jumped on top of the sleeping monkey and began stroking its fur. The GM monkey immediately rolled onto its back and sank its teeth into the neck of the friendly little guy. It shrieked in horror and tried desperately to pull away, only making matters worse. Its neck tore open into a grotesquely gaping wound, and it was instantly surrounded by a horde. They had all awakened.

Fiona thrust her hands up to her mouth to stifle a scream—it was like watching a horror movie. The helpless little monkey struggled but didn't stand a chance. Two of the GMs grabbed it by the arms from each side and played tug of war, yanking until the arms popped right out of their sockets. Then they started chewing on the severed limbs, pausing every few seconds to spit out the hair.

The rest of the angry beasts clawed, tore and chewed what was left of him to pieces within minutes. It was like a piranha attack, a ferocious frenzy, and Fiona couldn't watch any more of it. She turned her back to the glass window and threw up.

Shannon looked down at her with disgust, and then made another whispered call with his cellphone. Within minutes an attendant appeared in the hallway with a mop and pail.

"Control yourself, young lady. We haven't got time today to clean up after you."

Fiona looked up at him. "That little display was cruel and disgusting."

Shannon laughed. "And you're supposed to be a zoologist? Grow up, girl. Welcome to my world."

CHAPTER FORTY NINE

"I demand to speak to General Metcalf, right now!"

"Colonel, I already told you—he's in a meeting and left strict instructions not to be disturbed."

Colonel Howard Wentworth bit through his lower lip in frustration and blood was already starting to drip down over his chin. However, the pain in his lip barely competed with the agony shooting through his shoulder from what was left of his useless right arm.

"Goddamn it, girl! This is an emergency—in fact it's a matter of national security! Get him on the phone—now!"

The lieutenant on the other end of the phone was clearly in a quandary, Howard could tell. He had to give her something. "Okay, you run in and tell him we have a 'Code Red at Snow Lady.' Just do that for me, will you? And I promise you, if he doesn't run to a phone within seconds, I'll submit a recommendation for your promotion to Captain."

"Oh, Colonel, I do believe you are serious. All right, I'll disturb him. Hold on."

Howard waited. Angela was kneeling at his side, still cutting some of the packing tape off his legs. He massaged her neck with his good hand. "Angela, the man was a pro. He was cold and capable, and clearly on a mission. I swear, he's on that island right now."

Some muffled voices sounded at the other end of the phone. Howard tapped his finger impatiently against the side of Angela's mobile. Then a booming voice came on.

"Colonel—what's the meaning of this? I was in a tense meeting on the Iran issue, and I don't appreciate being drawn away from that."

"Forget Iran, General. We have something far more serious to deal with. I told the Lieutenant to tell you we have a 'Code Red at Snow Lady.' I'm serious. Last night I was assaulted here in my house, restrained, until a friend came to check on me. I'm now free, but the assailant stole my access card to Snow Lady. And two of my associates who were supposed to accompany me to the island today, received emails from me yesterday saying the trip had been cancelled. Well, guess what? I didn't send those emails. The trip was not cancelled. Some pros are at work here."

"You're being impersonated?"

"I would bet my life on it. I'm betting that a team of three people are there right now impersonating me and the two doctors who were supposed to accompany me. If I'm right, we have a serious breach going on right at this very moment."

"What assets do we have down there?"

"A team of half a dozen marines moderately armed."

"If the impersonators are there, they would have to be with our Director, Clyde Shannon. He would be the only one able to grant them access to the sensitive areas."

"Call him, General. You have the clout to get straight through to him. With all due respect, sir, do it right now!"

*****

The next lab was around the corner and about eighty feet down the hallway. Fiona braced herself for what she might see. She noticed that this compound had the same kind of entry system as the last one—a thick heavy glass panel mounted onto a track, with a magnetic entry pad and push button console.

Shannon seemed to be in all his glory, especially after seeing Fiona fall apart at the last lab. He was starting to enjoy the tour now. Fiona was determined that she would not allow herself to show another sign of weakness, regardless of what she might see.

"Okay, prepare yourselves for a spectacular sight." He pushed a button on a remote clipped to his hip, and steel blinds slid across on the inside of the glass, exposing the interior of the compound.

Brett kept his head aimed straight ahead into the pen while Avery hung back. Fiona moved along beside Shannon and fought to keep her hands from shaking.

She was staring at the most intense beastly creatures she had ever seen in her life—and they were staring right back at her.

She recognized them right away as Chimpanzees, but these weren't normal Chimpanzees. Not at all. They were huge. And they stood straight and tall on their hind legs with their long arms hanging by their sides. Not stooped and loping like chimps normally did—these ones stood almost at attention along the length of the window, glaring intently at their visitors. They didn't seem excited, agitated, or fearful. They were…calm…and confident.

"These are third generation genetically modified Chimpanzees," Shannon explained in almost a whisper. "You will note some significant variances from a normal chimp, especially you Ms. Huntington with your zoology background. These guys are much taller—standing close to seven feet. A normal chimp is only about four feet in height and weighs about 160 pounds at the most. Our friends here are 250 pounds at least. We can only guess about that though, because no one dares try to weigh them." Shannon laughed at his little joke, rather proud of himself.

"You'll notice that while their bodies are covered in hair just like a normal chimp, these guys have a much thinner coat and have virtually no hair on their faces or heads. This gives them an almost human look, but, much closer to what we envision Neanderthal man to have looked like. We've mated human DNA with the alien organisms to produce a concoction that is simply stunning. Well, you can see for yourselves what I mean."

Brett turned his head slowly towards Shannon. "Doctor, are you saying that these creatures are part human?"

"Yes, I guess I am. But remember, Chimpanzees are our closest relatives anyway. No less than ninety-eight percent of their DNA is identical to ours. So, we've just played with that. By fusing human DNA with the alien organisms, what you see now are creatures that have mixed DNA—ninety-eight percent is the common DNA of humans and chimps mixed with alien, and two percent is Chimpanzee. So, the answer to your question is both yes, and no. When we inject the concoction into human soldiers, their offspring will have the same combination for the ninety-eight percent, but the two percent remaining will be human, thus giving them more of a human look than a chimp look. Does this all make sense?"

Brett nodded.

Fiona felt her stomach starting to roll again. She fought off the urge to retch, and asked a question to try to take her mind off it. "Are these… completed experiments, so to speak?"

"I would be happy to put these guys out into the field, yes. But more importantly, we know from these lab specimens that we can do the same thing to a human now. The appearance would be the reverse of course—they would look more human with just some chimp characteristics. But they would have the height, weight, speed and strength of these guys. These beasts have five times the speed of a man, and ten times his strength. They've also been modified with the moon organisms to produce creatures that have absolutely no fear whatsoever.

"That's the one thing that surprised us in our initial studies thirty years ago, and a component that we knew we could put to good use. The creepy crawler organisms that we brought back from the moon just attacked—they never defended. We tested them six ways to Sunday, and they always attacked. We were very impressed—they had no sense of self-preservation. They possessed only the instinct to win, attack, and annihilate."

Brett turned towards Shannon. "So, you could put these guys out onto the battlefield right now and they would just charge tanks, machine guns, mortar launchers?"

"Yes."

"And the eventual human versions would as well?"

"Yes."

"But how would you command them? Do they obey? What's to keep them from slaughtering their own commanders?"

Shannon frowned. "We're not quite there yet. We think some form of hypnosis combined with a microchip would be the way we will need to go. We're just about to commence testing on the command and control aspects. So, you've asked a very timely question."

"You're trying to create a Superman here."

"I guess, kind of. More like a fearless warrior. As the Colonel here well knows, one of our biggest challenges in war is forcing our young recruits to put their necks on the line. The training curve is very high, and long. We lose precious time and ground in every war just due to mere cowardice. I'm talking boots on the ground, on ships and in jets. The public has no idea about how fear has caused us to fight wars much longer than we should have to—even with our high-tech weapons, we still need real soldiers, sailors and pilots to finish the job."

Avery spoke. "What would happen if this glass wasn't separating us right now from these monsters, Doctor?"

"We'd be overrun. And torn to pieces."

*****

Bill Charlton was pacing the floor in his plush Pentagon office when the phone rang. He saw by the call display that it was his buddy, Grant Folsom, Chief of the Washington Police. He crossed his fingers hoping that the DNA results gave them what they needed on Dennis Chambers. He had to shut that man down fast.

"Hello Grant. What have you got for me?"

"Dennis isn't the killer."

"What the fuck are you talking about? Of course, it's him."

"I know you want it to be him, Bill, but quite frankly, I'm relieved."

"So, who is it then?"

"The DNA tests tell us it's someone named Brett Horton."

Bill felt like he'd been kicked in the gut. A pain began in his lower extremities and moved its way up to his throat. He gasped, and prayed that Grant hadn't heard.

"Bill, did you hear me?"

Bill quickly composed himself. "Yeah, I heard you. Who is this guy?"

"I was hoping you could tell me. His records show that he's a retired Secret Service Agent—one of their best. Highly trained, and like Dennis, an expert in Shaolin martial arts. But his file also has a reference to him being self-employed now, specializing in counter-terrorism and offering himself out as a mercenary for hire."

"Okay, so why would I be familiar with that?"

"His income tax records show that he received numerous payments over the last few years from the Pentagon. Looks like he was on contract to you guys."

Bill gulped. "Not that I know of, Grant. Maybe another division knows about him—I'll ask around."

"That would be great. See what you can find out. I know you guys are pretty secretive about things, but this man's a serial killer, which brings him within my jurisdiction. I'm going to find him with or without the help of the Pentagon. And I'm putting out an APB within the next hour."

"I'll get back to you, Grant. Good work."

Bill hung up the phone and took a deep breath. He sucked it in and held it. Then he took another deep breath using the muscles of his abdomen, breathing deeply, holding it, and exhaling in a slow rush. He gradually felt relaxation setting in.

Then he picked up the phone and rang General Metcalf.

"Metcalf here."

"General, I think I know who's leading the breach at Snow Lady. And we have to sanction him. He can't get off that island alive. Bring out the big guns. He's a force to be reckoned with, I can guarantee that."

"Who is it?"

"An operative named Brett Horton. I've used him many times in the past, and I assigned him to recover the package for us from Lucy Chambers. He's gone rogue—I haven't been able to connect with him for several days now, ever since things went horribly wrong at a rendezvous up in Chesapeake."

"Jesus, Bill. You guys in Defense Intelligence take some serious chances that you shouldn't take sometimes. You hire the most unstable people."

"He wasn't unstable. He was the best. I think he just developed a conscience, and there's no way we can ever predict that sort of thing."

"What makes you think he's raiding Snow Lady?"

"Just that I have reason to believe he knows everything now. And I think he kept the package for himself. And…I've just learned that he's been identified through DNA as being the Washington vigilante serial killer. If so, he's definitely acting on his conscience in a variety of ways. I wouldn't be surprised if his newly-found self-righteousness is being acted out on our Shackleton project."

Bill could hear the General sigh at the other end of the phone. "Well, all that may be true, I don't know. However, we in the military tend to believe it's the Israelis. They'd love to have something they can use to blackmail us into an Iran war. We've tracked some serious hacking into the Pentagon database—traced it right back to the *Mossad*."

Bill could barely control his belly laugh. "Christ, General—that's child's play for someone like Brett. He could easily orchestrate a hack emanating from anywhere in the world. Trust me, it wasn't the Israelis—it was Brett Horton."

Silence.

"General, are you still there?"

"Yes, I'm thinking."

"Have you had any luck getting in touch with Shannon yet?"

"Tried—no luck yet. Cell signals and phone service in general are predictably bad down in the Caribbean. Sometimes we get some dead periods and 'Murphy's Law' being what it is, we have one right now. I have a team phoning down there every few seconds trying for a connection. As soon as I get one, I'll alert Shannon. I hope it's not too late."

"Yes, General, we can both agree on that. But if I'm right and it's Brett Horton, we have to take him out. Full sanction—agreed? Including whoever is with him."

A pause. "Yes, I agree, Bill. We can't afford to show any mercy with this Shackleton thing."

CHAPTER FIFTY

"We won't spend much time here at this next lab. What you will see is similar in scope to what you witnessed at the de-socialization compound. Just a bunch of lethargic Vervet monkeys, sleepy and indifferent." They stopped in front of the glass panel. Fiona was trying to spot something that might be different, but Shannon was right. It seemed to be the exact same scenario as the first lab.

"So, what's different here that we can't see?"

"They're all stupid."

Fiona turned away from the window and frowned at Shannon. "Stupid? What do you mean by 'stupid?'"

"Just what I said. These monkeys have completely lost their ability to think. We modified the alien organisms to rob the recipients of their brainpower. The little buggers barely have enough intelligence to eat. They simply can't function. These guys are sixth generation—and they'll have an average lifespan of only about two years, because they lack the smarts to even just survive."

Brett swore under his breath. "What's the point?"

Shannon chuckled. "C'mon, Doctor Sikorsky. Even a non-military man like you should appreciate how we could use this particular strain of the creepy crawlers. We spray a city, or an entire country for that matter—let's say Japan—and within months the population would be helpless. Their brains destroyed. We then swoop in and take over their industry and infrastructure. It's brilliant. Never again would we have to worry about the Japanese auto industry dominating an industry that we Americans invented. Hell, we were hoping Fukishima would accomplish that for us—you don't really think that the quake caused the tsunami, do you? Anyway, our subsurface nuke didn't do what we thought it would, so maybe this alien invention will do the trick."

Avery turned to Shannon. "Are you insane?"

Shannon scowled. "Hey, you military types gave us our marching orders. Aren't you in the loop, Colonel? I thought you were one of the architects of this little enterprise. I'm surprised that you sound shocked by this."

Fiona could feel goose bumps tingling up her back. She knew that Avery wished he could have taken back what he said. The brutal reality of what they were seeing was working to tear away their cover identities. Avery was clearly starting to forget who he was pretending to be. She could see that he was a bit flustered now, well aware of the mistake he just made.

Brett jumped in. "Doctor Shannon, I think it's obvious that for someone like you who works with the details of these experiments every day, you can get de-sensitized to the realities of them. For us back in our ivory tower worlds, we deal only in the high-level big picture. I think that I can speak for Doctor Huntington as well when I say that the three of us are shocked at how these applications can be used at the grassroots level."

Fiona had to fight back the smile that wanted to creep across her face. Brett to the rescue again. She had never met anyone before who was as persuasive and quick on his feet. She could see Shannon's face immediately lose its suspicious cast.

Shannon turned away from Avery and stared back through the glass wall at the almost comatose monkeys. "Well, that's understandable, I guess. To me, this is just everyday stuff. You folks only get to see and hear about it a few times a year."

He motioned with his hand and led the way further down the corridor, coming to a stop at another glass wall that, like the one with the superman chimps, was shielded on the inside by steel blinds. He pulled the remote control off his hip and hesitated before pushing the button.

"I want to warn you. This is not pleasant—not that any of it has been pleasant so far, but this one is really not pleasant at all."

Fiona felt her knees grow weak. She'd seen enough already and just wanted to turn around and run through the jungle back to Dennis.

"Prepare us."

"These are the mistakes. The cast-offs. The mutants that popped out once in a while in a litter. We knew we'd have some bad crops, but these were the exceptional ones. So, we study these guys and try to understand what it was in the strain that caused them to happen. As long as we can convince ourselves that these bad apples are unique and rare and won't start becoming the norm, we'll be satisfied. We sure wouldn't want this to happen in the human population."

Shannon let his eyes pass from one to the other. "Are you ready?"

They each nodded.

"Okay, then." He pressed the button on the remote and the steel blind folded back.

All three of them gasped in unison.

The immediate thought that entered Fiona's mind was that this was worse than the movie, 'Night of the Living Dead.' The floor inside the compound was covered with feces, with several of the creatures licking and crawling their way through the mess. Fiona thought she could smell it, even though she knew the unit was airtight and any escape of odor was impossible. But just the sight alone brought the notion of the smell to her nostrils and she felt like she wanted to puke again.

She could tell that these animals were monkeys, but only barely. Several had two heads, each with moving eyeballs and flicking tongues. Two heads that were both functional and competing with each other. One creature had two heads that had grown out in a manner that they were facing each other, biting and snarling at each other.

Fiona was startled from her hypnotic trance by a loud bang against the glass. She lurched, and stared at the animal that had tried to break the barrier. It was sort of a chimp, but had virtually no hair on its body—just an ugly gray mass of skin. It had four hind legs and three arms; one arm protruding from its chest. Each limb seemed to be functional, banging on the glass like a grotesque giant insect. Its tongue was too large for its mouth and hung down past its chin. It wiggled and twisted but seemed unable to retract into its mouth.

She glanced over at Brett to see his reaction. She could see he was transfixed by a curious creature that was licking the glass directly in front of him. The thing had three eyes in its forehead, a hole in the middle of its face—presumably a nose—and no ears. Protruding from its mouth were two teeth that were at least a foot in length, reminding Fiona of the illustrations of sabre-toothed tigers. It drooled yellow scum down the glass, and then just as quickly licked it back up again. Then more drool, more licking—Fiona guessed that this was how this beast occupied its day.

Avery was leaning up against the glass, examining several tiny little animals scurrying around the larger ones. They had shells covering their backs like turtles, but they also resembled crabs. Their heads though were clearly Vervet monkey heads—with one difference. They had antennae poking out from their foreheads; quivering, probing antennae that seemed to give the animals their direction. Then Fiona saw why these antennae were important—the animals had no eyes, not even sockets.

Brett coughed and turned away from the window. "Doctor Shannon, close the blinds. We've seen enough."

Shannon complied without argument, but Fiona thought she saw a grin cross his face for just a second.

"Okay, follow me. My office is just down the hall."

There was no hesitation from the three of them as they followed Shannon around the next corner and into a spacious office, a space that immediately struck Fiona as being functional but very cold. It suited Shannon's personality, being dominated by TV screens, computer terminals and a shiny metal desk.

She noticed also that there was a large control panel on the wall equipped with a magnetic keypad and button console. Fiona guessed that this was the main panel for the entire complex, controlling all the security and access doors. She saw that Brett and Avery were taking special notice of this panel as well.

Shannon motioned for them to sit down in the guest chairs that were parked in front of his desk. The chairs were metal as well and matched perfectly with the ugliness of the desk. He sat down in his plush leather chair behind the desk and stared at them.

"Well, what do you think? Did we pass muster?"

Avery cleared his throat before replying. "I think that what you're doing here is both remarkable and shocking at the same time. However, from a military viewpoint, I'm quite excited about the prospects."

"I'm glad to hear that—in fact I'm relieved to hear that. How about you, Doctor Sikorsky?"

"The scientific aspects are fascinating, but I have to say..." Brett was interrupted by the buzzing of Shannon's cellphone. He slipped it out of its belt holster and looked at the screen.

"Excuse me—I need to take this call."

He put the phone up to his ear and said nothing. He didn't have to say anything. Fiona watched his expression change dramatically with each second. She glanced over at Brett and could tell that he was noticing it too. The goose bumps were back and Fiona got a strange feeling; kind of a premonition of impending doom.

With the phone still attached to his ear, Shannon reached his hand under the desk. Almost immediately a siren began screaming throughout the complex and Fiona heard a series of loud metallic clicks, starting with the door to Shannon's office and cascading on down through the corridor.

She knew in her gut that they had just been locked in.

CHAPTER FIFTY ONE

To Fiona, the next few tense minutes went by in a blur. Her eyes were transfixed on Shannon, the angry determined look in his eyes as he was pushing the panic button underneath the desk. His other hand dropped the phone and, in one swift move, yanked open a desk drawer and pulled out a pistol.

Her ears were filled with the wail of the sirens, but not even they were loud enough to drown out the pounding of her heart.

Out of the corner of her eye she caught Brett on the move—lightning fast, he leaped onto the top of Shannon's desk and kicked the pistol out of his hand. Then the foot twisted sideways catching the scientist on the side of his head knocking him to the floor.

Avery was on the move as well—he tested the door; sure enough it was locked. He ran over to the control panel and examined it. He turned to Brett as if to say something about it, then stopped himself and shouted, "Brett, he's popping!"

Brett swiveled around and dove on top of the prone Shannon. He pulled the man's hand from his mouth and rammed his own fingers inside just as the scientist chomped down. "Help, Avery. Scoop it out!"

Fiona had no idea what was going on—she just knew that her two companions were panicked. Brett kept his fingers inside Shannon's mouth and she saw him wince as the man's teeth clamped down hard. Avery grabbed the scientist's hair in one hand and inclined the head backwards as far as it would go, with Brett's fingers still inside. Avery then slid his index finger inside the corner of the man's mouth and made a scooping movement.

"Got it!"

Avery pulled something out of Shannon's mouth and tossed it onto the floor near Fiona. She picked it up and could see that it was a little oval pill, brown in color, and knew right away what it was.

Her Pentagon experience had exposed her to the seldom-discussed topic of cyanide pills. She had never seen one but knew that they were small and coated in rubber to prevent premature breakage. Underneath the rubber coating was a light glass capsule containing the death potion. People who were provided with these pills were instructed to crush them with their molars—after that brain death was quick and the heart would then stop within a couple of minutes.

Fiona knew that agents in the field and air force pilots flying sensitive missions were provided with these pills, in case they were captured and tortured for information. She also knew that astronauts were always provided with cyanide pills in the event that an incident in outer space made it impossible for them to return to earth. Fiona shoved the pill into her pocket.

Brett yanked Shannon up off the floor by the lapels of his lab jacket, and threw him roughly back into his chair. "You're not dying just yet, Doctor Strangelove. At least not until you unlock the door."

Shannon just stared back at him, no expression in his eyes at all—Fiona thought that it was the face of a man who had already decided upon and accepted his own death.

Brett reared his hand back and rammed a finger into the right side of the man's chest. Shannon started to cough as blood began to stream out over his white jacket. "Okay, Shannon, one lung is now punctured. You'll survive, but if I puncture the other one, it's doubtful if you'll last through the night."

Avery was over at the control panel again. He swiped his card across the magnetic pad. Nothing happened.

"Brett, throw me his card."

Brett rummaged through Shannon's pockets, found it and tossed it over to Avery. Avery swiped and they all heard the encouraging beep. But the door remained locked.

"We need his combination now to punch into the keypad."

Brett slapped Shannon's face hard. "I'm not fooling around here, Doc. Give me the combination, now!"

Shannon's face was rapidly turning a sickly shade of white. He coughed up a bit of blood and shook his head. Brett rammed his finger into the man's forehead, just enough to make a small puncture. "I'll put the next one right into your brain, you prick. Give me the combination."

Shannon shook his head.

Brett stood up and rubbed his temples, cursing. "There's no point torturing someone who's already made up his mind that he's prepared to die. Think, think…"

Fiona watched the rare signs of frustration on the face of a man who always had a solution. She could tell that he knew he'd finally hit a brick wall, that this was probably the end of the road. She knew it would be for her and Avery too.

Avery walked over to Brett and rubbed his back. "We need to get behind the desk, Brett. The cavalry will be here soon. We'll just shoot our way through them."

Suddenly Brett slapped himself on the side of his head. "I know what numbers they used, the arrogant pricks!"

He rushed over to the keypad. "Nine, thirty, seventy-seven."

The door clicked open. Fiona shrieked with joy. As they each ran for the door, she asked, "How did you know?"

"That's the same combo that the real Colonel Wentworth used for the safe at his house. And that's the date when the assholes nuked the moon."

As they were going through the doorway, Brett suddenly stopped. "Wait. We can't have him locking the doors again on us."

Brett ran back to the scientist and rammed his finger into his right temple. He toppled out of his chair and lay prone on the floor.

"He'll be out for awhile. Let's go. Get your guns out and switch the safeties off."

With Avery leading the way, they ran down the corridor, back the way the scientist had led them from. They came to a metal door. It was locked. Avery tried his card—nothing. Then he tried Shannon's card. Nothing again. Brett punched in the same numbers—no luck.

"Okay, it's clear that the cards can get us through one way, but don't get us out. Another security measure. If they want to keep people in, they can. Shannon must have an extra code he uses—an exit code."

Fiona shoved the Glock into her waistband. "Let's go back the other way. When Shannon's door unlocked, I could hear the clicking of other doors somewhere in this complex, and that panel in his office looked like the main control panel. I'm sure his door must be on the same circuit as other doors, because I heard them unlocking."

Brett nodded. "Right. We'll head back and take another corridor. We'll find the open doors—if there's a clear way out of here, we'll find it."

The sirens had stopped, presumably when Shannon's door and others had unlocked themselves. In the silence of the corridor now, they heard the unmistakable sound of heavy footsteps…coming from somewhere. Fiona felt her heart becoming heavy in her chest. Breathing in the antiseptic air was causing her to feel nauseous again, but she knew she didn't have the time to be sick now. She pulled her gun out of her belt and held it up in the air as she ran.

Avery held out his hand in the stop sign. He bent over and took off his shoes, and motioned for them to do the same. He cocked his head trying to ascertain where the footsteps were coming from—several hallways led off the main one they were on. It could have been any one of them. They knew they had to go north to get out of the complex, so there were only a couple of options they could take. The first one they tried had been locked, and Fiona could see that the next north corridor was only about thirty feet ahead.

Avery was smart to have made them remove their shoes—they would now hear approaching footsteps but their pursuers wouldn't hear them.

He motioned and they started running again—this time to the comforting sound of the soft padding of their socks.

Avery raised his hand again. They stopped.

He whispered. "Brett, from the diagrams I saw of this complex before we came, I remember how all the hallways connected at different points. It's a labyrinth. There are plenty more labs that we didn't even see today. The corridors on the other side of that locked door back there all connect back to this side from what I remember. So, we could work our way around—do an 'end run.' It may be the only way we can get out of here. Some doors are going to be open, and some will still be locked. We have to find the ones that are on the same circuit that Shannon's door was on. As Fiona said, we heard other doors locking and then unlocking again."

"Yeah, I agree. The problem is, with all the tile and steel in these hallways, sound travels a long distance. Hard to tell where the sounds of unlocking doors—or even footsteps—are coming from."

"Let's just get going. We'll get out of this maze."

Avery started running again, and Fiona and Brett were just about to follow when they saw their first pursuer. About fifty yards down the hall in front of them—a soldier in green fatigues, carrying an AK47, burst around the corner heading straight in their direction.

He saw them at the exact same moment they saw him. Brett yelled a warning. Avery dove to the tiled floor, gun in hand, and slid along the smooth tiled floor on his chest for about ten feet, pistol barking as he slid.

The marine took the blasts from Avery in the chest and he screamed, machine gun bursting towards the ceiling as he fell dead to the ground.

They heard shouts and more footsteps. They seemed to be coming from the direction of the hallway the marine had turned in from. However, there was one other hallway before that one, and without saying it to each other they knew that was the one they had to turn into…and fast.

This time Brett led the way. They half ran, half slid, in their stocking feet along the slippery floor. The sounds were getting closer. They heard yelling now as well and surprisingly, gunfire and some screams.

Suddenly three more green-fatigued figures burst around the corner, but these guys were running backwards, firing their machine guns down the hallway they had just come from.

Then Fiona saw why.

Three gigantic hairy figures burst into the hallway from the connecting corridor and the panicked soldiers fell back against the wall, their guns firing erratically in every direction.

One hapless soldier slid down onto his back, his gun clicking on empty. One of the super-chimps grabbed him by the neck with one hand and twisted and squeezed until his head tore off and rolled along the floor. The creature roared, the blood-curdling sound reverberating along the corridor.

Fiona heard the screams and she was transfixed by the sight. One other soldier who was trying desperately to run in their direction was grabbed from behind and thrown with full force into the wall. He stuck like a blob of jelly against the tile for what seemed an eternity, and then just slid to the floor.

The third marine was holding his own. He had already taken down one of the beasts with his AK47, but then he too went empty. He screamed in agony, turned and ran in the opposite direction. Fiona was startled to see that in less than four steps the two remaining beasts had caught up to him— the speed of the creatures was mind-boggling.

They grabbed him from each side, lifted him into the air and flung him up against the metal ceiling. He fell like a sack of potatoes to the floor and they immediately began devouring him.

The three of them stood frozen in place. What they had just witnessed was horrifying and Fiona knew that they should move, but her feet felt like lead. She looked over at Brett and Avery and was surprised to see that her tough companions were also frozen in terror.

She knew that the two friends had no doubt seen a lot, and done a lot in their lives, but nothing probably compared to this. Human emotions could be suppressed, but they were still always there with everybody—sometimes just under the surface.

Avery awoke from his trance first. He shook Brett and grabbed Fiona by the shoulder. "We have to move."

"I can't lift my feet."

Avery slapped her across the face. "You have to! Make yourself! Find it in yourself!"

Fiona just stared at him.

He slapped her again. This time she felt it, and her feet started to feel lighter.

"Okay, I can do it."

Brett pulled the gun out of her waistband and shoved it into her hand. "This is all we have. Keep it in your hand and don't hesitate to use it. I have extra magazines in my pocket. I think we're going to need them."

They started running again; turning south at the corridor just to the west of the one the marines had come running out of.

Fiona shouted. "Sweet Jesus! Those things are loose! Their doors must have opened when we unlocked Shannon's door."

Brett turned his head toward her as he ran, not bothering to whisper anymore. "There must have been one extra code number that needed to be entered, to isolate the unlocking to only Shannon's door. Looks like I entered the code that opened the labs too."

Avery raised his hand again and they all slid to a stop. He motioned to a recessed doorway. Fiona and Brett flattened themselves against it. Avery jumped into a recess across from them. They waited.

A few seconds later a marine came running past. Out of the corner of his eye, he caught them. He swung around with his machine gun and Brett fired. The young man went down.

Brett walked over to him, bent down, and yanked the gun out of his hand. Fiona could see that the wound was in the soldier's abdomen. He looked up at Brett, stark fear written across his face. He couldn't have been more than twenty-one years old.

Brett said, "I'm not going to kill you, son. Help will be here soon."

Fiona heard the sound first, and turned in the direction they had just come. It was a sickening combination of snarling, growling and claws tapping on the tile.

"Oh, God."

Brett quickly raised his pistol and pointed it down at the head of the terrified young soldier. He closed his eyes and fired. Then he made the 'sign of the cross.'

They resumed their run. Four creatures were closing in, but they knew they would stop at the dead soldier. And they did. They heard the sound of claws scraping against the floor as the beasts slid to a stop. Then the stomach-churning sounds of tearing, chewing and slopping. They ran faster.

They came to a junction, and Avery pointed down the west arm of the next hallway. "I think this will lead us in a big half-square back towards where we first entered. We'll have one more turn to make after this."

Brett yelled. "I agree! Let's just get the fuck out of this nightmare!"

Fiona had been on the track team at her college, and that was a long time ago. But she never remembered having the speed or the stamina that she had right now. Fear had the adrenaline rushing at such a ferocious rate, that she knew she was breaking records. She took the lead, gun raised to the ceiling as she ran.

Another junction—and another marine. Fiona saw him just an instant before he saw her. He began to swing his machine gun in her direction and yelled, "Stop!" Fiona aimed her gun and fired. The bullet went through his throat and he went down.

Brett ran over and pulled the gun out of his hand and threw it to Avery. They now had two AK47s in addition to their Glocks. They were on the move again.

"The next turn is just up ahead! Watch out for any intersecting corridors!"

Avery was running with the AK47 in one hand, the Glock in the other.

They passed the next connecting hallway with only thirty yards to go until they'd have to make their next turn. Fiona started to feel like they were going to make it.

Then she went down.

An arm had shot out from the connecting hall and grabbed her by the leg. It held on as she hit the floor, then swung her around until her head hit the wall. She saw stars, and then she saw the beast. It was crouching over her, a pink grotesque tongue hanging out of its mouth, green drool dripping onto Fiona's face.

She raised her gun hand and realized that the gun was gone. The beast seemed to smile as the freaky arm protruding from its chest grabbed her around the throat and squeezed. She could sense its multiple legs sliding up and around her middle, and felt the pressure as they began to tighten. She couldn't breathe. Its two other arms began to stroke her forehead as the third arm continued its quest to choke her to death. She knew she only had seconds left, and despaired at the thought that her compatriots wouldn't be able to fire their guns as the beast was enveloping her.

Suddenly, two additional legs appeared—they were human and they were wrapped around the neck of the monster. It reared back and roared. Brett's legs crossed themselves around the thing's chest, and she could see them begin to squeeze. The pressure eased on her neck as the beast concentrated on the diversion.

Brett's powerful forearms extended outwards, then sped inward against each side of the animal's head. It was already the ugliest thing she'd seen in her life, but it became even uglier as the head crushed into itself. Its eyes bulged out of their sockets and a huge clump of green slime slid down the over-sized tongue and landed on Fiona's head. She screamed.

The beast fell to the side as Brett slid off its back. It died with a sickening sigh. Fiona struggled to get free—the thing's legs were locked around her stomach. Brett pushed her hands out of the way and simply broke each leg one by one. Then he lifted her up by her arms and shoved the errant Glock back into her hand.

He brought his face to within an inch of hers, and stared into her eyes.
"Block it out. Don't think about it. We have to move."
Fiona nodded.

They ran, turning north at the next junction. They were almost at the exit. Avery pointed ahead as the next junction came into view. One left turn and they would be near the exit.

Avery motioned with his arm to urge them on, and he sped into the next corner, sliding around it in his stocking feet. Brett and Fiona were right behind him, and saw the hairy arm reach out and grab him as he slid.

Fiona gasped as Avery was swung through the air by a seven-foot tall monster. He slammed against the wall sending the AK47 flying, and the beast pounced on him. Avery tried to raise his pistol, but it was swept away by a powerful hand.

Before they could react, the beast tore Avery's right leg away from his body and began to go to work on the other one. He screamed in a way that Fiona never imagined a soldier could scream. She could see that the leg had been ripped away right beneath the hip, and blood and guts were pouring out of the opening. She couldn't help it—she retched.

When she raised her head again she saw Brett. He was spinning, and his foot connected with the creature's head. Fiona heard the crunch of breaking bones, and heard the roar of the beast as he turned in Brett's direction. Brett went into a stance and hit him twice in his gray hairless forehead with his index fingers. The thing looked stunned as blood started gushing out of the gaping holes. He snarled again and moved away from Avery. That's all Brett needed. He picked his machine gun up off the ground and blasted the thing with at least a dozen rounds to the face.

It fell backwards with a resounding thud—Fiona could feel the vibration in the floor. The beast gave a mighty sigh, and died.

Brett knelt beside his friend, took off his jacket and wrapped it around the gaping hole where his right leg used to be. He used the arms of the jacket to tie it around Avery's belt.

He motioned to Fiona. "Help me, Fiona. We'll carry him."

Avery moaned. "No…leave me. I…remember from…the plans. Turn right…at the next corridor…and there's an exit. Go."

"I can't leave you, buddy."

"You…have to…my friend. You…know that. You'll never get away… dragging me."

Brett started to cry, and rubbed his fingers over Avery's forehead, trying his best to soothe him.

Avery smiled. "I love…you…my friend. Go…be safe."

Suddenly, they heard a sickeningly familiar sound. The clip-clop of claws on the tiled floor. They could tell it was close, very close.

Fiona started to shake, her knees felt like they were going to collapse. She looked at Brett and could tell he was in a quandary. He didn't know what to do—for the first time since she'd met him, he was lost. His emotions were getting the better of him. Brett was more human than even he realized.

Avery spoke again. "I…hear them. Go. Now."

Brett lowered his head and nodded agreement.

"Shoot…me…first. Don't…leave me…to them. Hurry."

Brett was sobbing now, tears rolling down his handsome face.

"I can't."

"Yes, you…can. You…have to."

Brett shook his head back and forth. "No."

Fiona rushed to his side and hugged him. "I'll take care of it, Brett."

She reached into her pocket and pulled out the cyanide pill. She held it up above Avery and looked at him with a question in her eyes. He nodded and opened his mouth. She gently slipped it inside, placing it in the corner near his molars. Then she leaned over and kissed his lips. "Goodbye, my friend." The clip-clop was getting louder, and Fiona's heart was beating faster. Avery smiled at the two of them and clenched his teeth together. Within seconds, his pupils rolled out of sight and they knew his brain was gone.

Before they resumed their run, Brett stood at attention and saluted. Then he bent down and picked up Avery's AK47. He smiled grimly at Fiona and mouthed the word, "Thanks."

They ran. The creatures were close. Reaching the next intersection, they slid around it at breakneck speed. Fiona shrieked with joy as she saw the gaping opening of an exit door about fifty yards ahead, the rapidly approaching dusk welcoming them on the outside.

She yelled, "Go, Brett, go! We're almost there!"

Fiona turned her head at the sounds behind her. Two giant beasts had just slid around the same corner and were racing towards them at breakneck speed. Clip-clop, snarling—they announced their presence.

She didn't care—she just ran. Brett was ahead of her and they were mere yards away now. Suddenly they heard a metallic groan and the metal door ahead of them slid shut. Brett slammed into the door and banged it with his fist in frustration.

They turned around together and faced the inevitable. The lumbering beasts were only fifty yards away now, and gaining fast.

Brett handed Fiona Avery's machine gun.

"Wait until they're closer and start firing. Aim for their chests. And don't take your finger off the trigger—just keep squeezing."

With shaking hands, she took the gun from Brett and braced it against her chest.

They both looked down the corridor at the monstrous creatures lumbering toward them—snarling, teeth gnashing, claws clip-clopping on the polished tile floor. It was an ominous sight.

And Fiona wished she had two more cyanide pills.

CHAPTER FIFTY TWO

Bill Charlton wiped the sweat from his brow for the second time in the past ten minutes. The phone in his damp palm made a squeaky noise as he waited for General Metcalf to answer. He didn't enjoy waiting, and he sure didn't enjoy being out of control. Things were not only reeling out of control fast, but there was nothing he was able to do about it.

"Hello."

"General, it's Bill. Where are we on this? You're not keeping me in the loop."

"Bill, we talked just fifteen minutes ago. Cool your jets."

Bill squinted as a salty drop of sweat drained into his eye. "What's going on, General? Talk to me."

"The latest is basically the same as the last time we talked. I had Shannon on the phone and told him about the imposters. He never said a word, but then I heard some scuffling noises, a grunt, and the crash of the phone as it presumably hit the floor. I lost the signal, and haven't been able to connect with the lab again since—either by landline or cell."

"So, we're in the dark."

"Well, we won't be for long."

Bill perked up. "Why? What's happening?"

"I can't assume that the marines at the lab are able to respond. Horton and his team may have eluded them or even taken them out already—if he's as good as you say he is."

"He is."

"So, we have to plan on the basis that they're out of commission. I made a few enquiries after you and I first talked, and the closest marines we have to Nevis are on the island of Puerto Rico right now for some training exercises. I ordered two teams of them down to Nevis."

"How long will it take them?"

"They should be on site right now. I've briefed the leaders. There's no way that Horton and his team would have taken the ferry over from St. Kitts. They would have arranged their own transportation. So, our teams will keep an eye out for a boat that seems to be out of place—it's almost dark there now so there shouldn't be too many boats out on the water. I've told them to keep a particular eye out for any boat that seems to be cruising back and forth, waiting."

"Good. Good. I'm encouraged by this, General. Are they equipped to deal with this?"

Metcalf chuckled. "They are marines, Bill. Get serious—of course they're equipped. We're sending two teams of four. The craft we had available are a 50-foot ASPB, and a 50-foot MK2. And those boats are fast."

Bill blew through his teeth in frustration. "Speak in English, General. What the hell are ASPB and MK2?"

"Sorry. One is an assault patrol boat, and the other's a patrol craft. Both are equipped with machine gun mounts. We tried to load on some rocket launchers but no go. Maintenance was out of date on each of them. So, the machine guns will have to do."

"So, tell me, what are their orders as to the 'rules of engagement'?"

"Elimination."

*****

Dennis looked at his watch. Three and a half hours now since they left the boat—he was already well past the three-hour limit that Brett had given him.

He paced back and forth on the bridge, stopping occasionally to gaze towards shore hoping to see any sign of life. It was so eerily quiet. He knew that if they were racing back he would hear them. Only two cars had approached the pier in the last hour and both had gotten his hopes up, only to have them dashed when they kept on driving.

Dennis picked up the binoculars and scanned back and forth along the beach. Nothing. No romantic strollers, no evening swimmers. He thought this was the strangest island he'd ever been to.

There were no signs of danger either, which reaffirmed his decision to just stay put and wait despite Brett's instructions to the contrary. It was getting dark now; he'd probably see their headlights coming before he heard them.

Dennis sat down in the Captain's chair and cracked open a can of pop.

Then he lit a cigarette, his tenth in the last hour. After having quit for ten years, the last month had driven him to take up the habit again, something he wasn't proud of at all. But he rationalized that if it made him feel better, then it was an essential vice right now.

He perked up at the sound of another car engine, at first faint but getting louder with each second. It was definitely coming in his direction.

Dennis jumped off the boat and stood on the pier…waiting…hoping he'd be hugging Fiona at any moment.

His hopes sunk quickly as an orange and white police car pulled up at the end of the pier. Two black uniformed officers got out and started walking in his direction. As they got closer Dennis noticed both unsnapping the safety leathers on their gun holsters. Dennis was glad that he'd left his holster on the dash of the boat. He would have looked mighty suspicious, even more suspicious than he already did, if he'd had a gun attached to his hip.

He smiled at them as they approached. They didn't smile back. Dennis knew that police officers on these little Caribbean islands were poorly trained, and while they probably earned more than the average islander, their wages were still pitiful.

Most of them earned the real money with 'extras.' Payoffs, extortion. He'd spent some time years ago helping to train a new roster of officers in the Bahamas. After a month, there he was glad to get home, home to where people took their jobs seriously and wanted to work hard. Maybe it was the heat that made them lazy, he didn't know. All he knew was that the only thing they seemed to care about was how powerful their shiny new uniforms looked. They cared only about 'looking important.'

"Good evening, sir. How are you?"

Dennis smiled again—the warmest, most innocent smile he could muster.

"I'm fine, officers. How can I help you?"

"We're investigating a car theft. Did you see anything suspicious here in the last few hours?"

Dennis felt his stomach churn. "No, it's been pretty quiet. I've been here for most of the afternoon. Where was the theft from?"

"Those villas up there." The officer pointed up the hill behind him. "The owner was drugged or something, and his wife discovered him when she returned from bingo."

"That's terrible. Well, at least they can't get too far on this island."

"Well, sometimes they drive them onto large motor launches and take them to other islands for resale. Did you see any large boats beached around here?"

"No, I didn't see anything. Been a quiet day."

The officer that had been quiet so far wandered over to the rails of the boat and peeked in. "Nice boat you have here, sir."

"Thanks. But it's just a charter. I wish I owned it."

The other officer rubbed his chin and cocked his head. "Do you own one of the villas here?"

"No, I don't. Just visiting."

"Who are you visiting?"

"I'm not visiting anyone here. My friends and I are just visiting the island. I'm waiting for them. They're photographers and they decided to take a hike up into the jungle and get some nature photos."

"Trying to snap pictures of monkeys?"

"Sure. And some of your beautiful tropical foliage."

The other officer jumped up into the boat. Dennis dreaded what he knew would come next. "Sir, there's a pistol up here. Is it yours?"

"Yes."

"Do you have a license for it?"

Dennis had a license in his wallet for his guns at home, not this smuggled one. But that license didn't even match the name on his phony passport: 'Frank Cotterhill.' He couldn't fake this.

He gulped. "No."

Both officers pulled their guns simultaneously.

Dennis raised his hands into the air. "Hey, officers, take it easy."

"We'll take your gun, and you can buy it back from us, okay?"

Dennis sighed. So, this was their money-making ruse for the day. "How much?"

"Two thousand dollars."

Dennis shook his head. "I don't have that kind of money with me. I can give you two hundred."

"Sorry, no deal. We'll take the gun, and confiscate the boat as well."

"You can't do that. The gun is just a minor infraction. Take it, but I need the boat to get back."

The officer standing next to him on the dock spread his fingers out over his shirt. "You see this uniform, man? This means we can do anything we want. You're on our island and we're in charge."

"How do you propose I get back to St. Kitts?"

The officer on the boat jumped down onto the dock. "You're not going back, not tonight. We'll hold you until the banks open tomorrow, then you can maybe transfer some money to us for your…um…bail?"

He heard the officer behind him unsnap handcuffs from his waist. He knew the man's gun was pointed straight at his back. His partner holstered his own pistol, and then walked around and roughly yanked Dennis' hands down, twisting them behind his back.

Dennis knew he had no choice. This was an unexpected turn of events, but he had to just deal with it. He looked quickly up the pier to make sure they were still alone. They were.

With his hands still held behind his back, he pulled down rapidly bringing the officer towards him, then reared his head back and smashed it into the stunned man's nose. His hands now free, he spun around and flashed both hands towards the other policeman. One hand knocked the gun free while the other one went palm first into the man's nose.

The other one was struggling now to get his own gun back out of its holster; clearly frantic, fumbling. Dennis leaned back and flung his right foot into the man's gut, sending him flying about fifteen feet in the air. He spun around back to the other guy—he didn't want to kill them, just put them out. His hands worked in perfect unison, one finger jabbed him in the Adam's apple and the other one rammed him in the temple. Dennis pulled back on both impacts at just the last millisecond. The officer went down, unconscious before he hit the ground.

Dennis walked over to the other hapless policeman, who was now trying desperately to scurry away from him on his hands and knees. Dennis kicked him in the gut, turning him face up, then reached down and pulled the gun out of the holster and tossed it over the pier into the water.

The office had his hands up in front of his face, pleading. "It's okay, it's okay! The two hundred dollars is fine! We'll let you go!"

Dennis looked down at him and laughed. "Oh, will you, now? You'll let me go, will you?"

"Yes, yes!"

Dennis leaned over, grabbed the man by the hair and pulled his head up off the pier. Then he reached behind and squeezed at the base of the skull until his pupils rolled cross-eyed. He gently lowered his head back onto the pier.

Dennis moved quickly now— first glancing toward the beach to make sure that there had been no witnesses. Luck was still with him. He jumped up onto the boat and ran down to the lower cabin, raised the hatch and climbed further down into the engine room. He yanked open the door to a utility chest and found what he wanted. Duct tape.

Before heading back up, he noticed the contraption that Desmond had lugged on board. He was surprised to see that it wasn't connected to the engine as Brett had said it would be. It was just standing alone in the centre of the engine room. It had dials and switches and was about three-foot square. He'd have to ask Brett about it—it appeared as if Desmond had neglected to connect it after all. As Brett had said, they would probably need that extra speed that this booster would give them. They would need every edge they could get.

He ran back up and duct-taped both officers' hands, legs and mouths. He found the keys to the patrol vehicle in the pocket of one of them. He was glad that it was a Honda CRV—plenty of room in the hatch for these clowns.

Dennis tossed the first one over his shoulder and ran to the Honda, opened the hatch and laid him inside. Then he repeated the trip for the second officer. The windows were darkly tinted so no one would see inside. He then jumped into the driver's seat and drove the vehicle along the beach road and into a beach club parking lot. It was deserted, and the restaurant was closed. Perfect.

Dennis ran a fast mile back to the boat, cast off the lines and jumped on board. He fired up the Ocean 62's 1500 HP engine, swooped away from the pier, and cruised slowly out to sea. He knew he had to get away from the pier now in case other officers came by to find out what happened to their buddies. He didn't want to leave but he had to. He wouldn't go far. Dennis intended to just cruise back and forth along the shallow coast, keeping an eye out for his three friends.

One friend in particular.

He couldn't leave her. He couldn't lose her. Brett had given him sound advice, for sure: leave the island, jump on the Gulfstream and fly back to Virginia. Then expose this whole mess with what they had hidden in the vault back at the safe house in Norfolk.

That was smart and logical advice. But emotions weren't necessarily smart and logical, and right now Dennis was listening only to his emotions. He loved Fiona; if it hadn't occurred to him before, it sure did now. Sometimes it takes the fear of losing someone to realize how much they mean to you.

Dennis turned on his running lights and then immediately switched them back off again. He saw something on the horizon that made his heart stop.

He shoved the throttle into neutral, and swung the binoculars up to his eyes. About three miles distant were two motor launches—but through the powerful binoculars he could see that they weren't normal launches. These were gunboats, and they seemed to be at full stop in the water.

Dennis was surprised—he wasn't aware of St. Kitts/Nevis having any kind of naval power.

He stared for a full minute, letting his eyes adjust through the lens to the dim light. Then his heart stopped for the second time in as many minutes.

Both gunboats flew flags of the United States of America.

CHAPTER FIFTY THREE

When the beasts were about thirty yards away they started firing. Fiona aimed for the chest of the chimp on her left, closed her eyes and pulled her trembling finger against the trigger. The gun rattled and shook in her hand but she held it steady in desperate determination. Beside her she could feel the vibration of Brett's gun as he fired at the monster on the right.

Then the rattling stopped. The guns were empty.

She felt something slide against her foot and she sensed Brett falling to the ground. Fiona opened her eyes with dread.

"Help me, Fiona!"

At her feet was the creature she had been firing at, blood pouring out of several wounds in its chest. The other one was dead also, draped on top of Brett. The thing was so large all she saw was Brett's blood-covered face peeking around from under its chest.

Fiona managed to lift one side of the bloody mess up—just enough for Brett to get his arms free and finish the job himself. She reached down a hand and pulled him to his feet.

No time to chat. They had survived this last onslaught but more would be on the way. They had to find a way out.

Brett turned around and examined the metal door. "Look, Fiona. This door doesn't have a magnetic reader—just a number keypad. I'm guessing because it's just an exit door. Maybe we'll get lucky." He punched in the same numbers again: nine—thirty—seventy-seven. Nothing happened.

He ran his fingers along the sliding door. It was tight in the track and its edge was completely inaccessible, being a good two inches inside the frame. There was no way this door could be pried open, and they didn't have a tool that would be able to do it anyway. The barrels of their guns were too thick.

Brett moved away from the door and ran his fingers through his hair. "Shit! We were so close!"

Suddenly an image popped into Fiona's head—the little remote combination seeker that Brett used to get inside the villa so they could steal the Lexus.

"Brett! The little remote! Don't you still have it?"

She could see his eyes brighten. He quickly patted himself around his waist and checked his pockets. Then he groaned, leaned back against the door and slid to the floor.

"Oh, God. I gave it to Avery when we got into the car."

Fiona felt like she was going to be sick again.

Brett looked up at her. "We have to go back. It might not even work on this door, but it's all we've got. We have to go back for it, Fiona."

She knew they had no choice. They were running out of time and more beasts would be here soon. All they had left were their Glocks and the magazines were at least half-empty. She gulped and nodded.

Brett jumped to his feet. "We can do this. It's going to be a mess, we both know that. Just don't let it get to you. Tell yourself it's not Avery, that it's just a scene from a horror movie. Detach yourself from it."

Fiona nodded again, her mouth as dry as sandpaper.

Brett cupped her face in his strong hands. "Okay?"

"Yes."

Brett reached into his holster and pulled out the Glock. "Here, take this in one hand and carry yours in the other. I'll need my hands free to search Avery. You'll have to cover me, okay?"

"Okay."

"Let's go."

They climbed over the dead animals and Brett led the way back up the hallway they had come from. Their stocking feet were completely red now, covered in blood from the beastly things. They didn't slide now, being sticky with blood. Fiona thought this was a good thing—better traction if they had to run for it again.

They reached the end of the hall and Fiona could feel her heart pounding in her chest. She knew that as soon as they turned left at this corner they would see Avery. She held both guns high, pointed at the ceiling, knowing without a doubt that she'd have to use them again.

Brett held up his hand and they stopped. He peeked around the corner, and then turned back to Fiona. "Looks like two of them are still there. We're going to have to kill them. Run fast and get ready to fire when we get close.

Be careful not to hit me while I'm digging around for the remote!"

Fiona's knees were wobbling and she wondered how fast she'd be able to run. She sucked it up and nodded.

"Okay, now!"

They rounded the corner side by side and Fiona could see the mess that was Avery forty yards ahead. She remembered what Brett had said and concentrated on pretending that she was not looking at what was left of someone she knew.

Chewing away at Avery's body were two mutant types she hadn't seen yet; two disgusting aberrations of nature.

One had the body of a chimp but its head was cat-like, almost like a cougar. Pointed ears, whiskers. Its claws were enormous and it was busy using them to tear the flesh away from Avery's chest.

The other creature had the head of a wolf, but the body of a Vervet monkey. The head was enormous, totally out of proportion to the little body of a Vervet. And she noticed that its paws were definitely a wolf's paws, not the dainty little human-like hands of a Vervet. Fiona felt acid rising into her throat—she choked on it as she ran.

Brett yelled. "Start firing!"

Immediately after he yelled that to her, he threw himself feet-first onto the tiled floor and slid the rest of the way on his back. His momentum carried him right to Avery's body, and the surprised beasts snarled their irritation at him. The cat-like animal leaped into the air and Brett caught him with a hard foot to the throat. It fell to the side of Avery's body and started whimpering.

Fiona had always been a good shot and she made sure to use that skill now. The cat creature struggled to its feet while Brett began his search of Avery's pockets. Fiona fired twice—one bullet in the animal's chest and the other right through an eye. It collapsed across Avery.

The wolf-like animal seemed confused. It was smaller than the cat creature and probably saw Brett and Fiona as being a threat. But suddenly it seemed to make up its mind and opened its large mouth, baring the largest canine teeth that Fiona had ever seen. It leaped onto Brett and clamped its jaws around his ankle. Brett screamed in pain.

Fiona didn't want to shoot from a distance, as the thing was right there with Brett. She ran up and rammed the barrel against the giant head and pulled the trigger. Brett screamed again. She reached down and pried the dead thing's jaws off Brett's ankle. Not too much damage, but she could see why Brett had screamed a second time. Her bullet had gone down through the thing's head and out against Brett's ankle, grazing it.

"Sorry, Brett!"

He winced. "No sweat. Better than the alternative."

Now that she was standing over him Fiona could see the damage that the creatures had done to their friend. He was unrecognizable. She turned away.

"Got it! Let's go!"

Brett was holding the little remote up in triumph and Fiona prayed to God that it would work. It was probably their last chance to escape from here unless they could find another route.

They ran as fast as they could down the hallway again, turned the corner and went full tilt to the sliding metal door that had blocked their last escape. Fiona thought she could hear the dreaded clip-clop sounds again but she blocked them out of her mind.

Brett used the door as a break against his momentum and, out of breath, pointed the remote at the keypad. They heard it do its little singsong, then a beep. Fiona smiled. Two more singsongs and two more beeps, and the door lurched and slid open along its track.

Shrieking with joy they threw themselves through the open door and drank in the beautifully humid tropical air.

They hugged each other and high-fived.

Then they heard them coming. Three of the beasts were running at full speed down the hallway. Brett pointed the remote at the outside keypad and pressed the button. It seemed to take forever for the three beeps. The door groaned closed just in the nick of time and they could hear the beasts crash into it on the other side.

They were free. And they could see their stolen Lexus waiting for them right where they had left it hours ago.

They jumped in and Brett squealed the tires as he swung the car in the direction of the main driveway. As they approached the metal gate, they could see that it was closed. Through gritted teeth Brett said, "Brace yourself."

He gunned the engine and the swift Lexus rocketed ahead, smashing through the gate with ease. He spun the wheel as they turned down the main highway back toward the pier at 'The Hamilton.'

Brett looked at his watch. "It's been four hours. Denny should be gone by now, but I'm hoping and praying that he didn't listen to a damn thing I said!"

*****

Dennis kept the Ocean 62 as close to the shoreline as he could—with his lights off he had to be careful, but he was able to gain some illumination from the lights of the homes and all the piers. He kept 'The Hamilton' pier in sight, never wandering more than 100 yards away at any one time.

He had the boat on autopilot while he scanned the shoreline with the binoculars. And he alternated that with scanning the horizon as well, keeping an eye on the gunboats. They were still there—in fact they seemed closer now. As if they knew he was there, which he found hard to believe at the distance involved and the fact that his lights were off. But he remembered that he did have them on briefly, so if they were attentive they could have seen him then.

The gunboats weren't hiding. All their running lights were on. They were clearly waiting for something, watching for something.

Suddenly Dennis heard the roar of a car engine and the sound of spinning tires on the dirt road. Someone had just taken a sharp corner.

He pushed the throttle and began moving closer. Then he saw it—a large sedan spinning onto the pier. It drove right to the end, skidded to a stop just short of flying into the water, and flashed its high beams on and off—then on again.

Dennis' heart screamed with joy. It had to be them!

He needed his running lights now. He was afraid to use them but he'd never be able to dock safely without them. He switched them on and rammed the throttle to full. The boat lurched in the water and he set a course straight for the pier. He noticed two people get out of the car and stand on the edge. A man and a woman.

Off in the distance he heard the dull roar of engines. Dennis glanced over his shoulder and could easily see that the gunboats were no longer broadside. Their running lights illuminated the profile of two craft that were now pointed in his direction.

CHAPTER FIFTY FOUR

Dennis slammed the throttle into reverse when he was within fifty feet of the pier, slowing his approach enough to make a slick docking against the thick timbers.

Brett jumped on first, then grabbed Fiona's hand and gave her a swift tug. Dennis didn't wait to exchange niceties—he rammed the throttle forward and the nose of the launch rose into the air. He did a 180-degree turn and headed north towards St. Kitts.

The two of them joined him on the bridge. Fiona hugged Dennis from behind and nestled her cheek alongside his. He turned his head sideways and kissed her. Her face was illuminated by the running lights and he was shocked to see the blood and green slime covering her cheeks and hair. Brett didn't look much better.

Already knowing the answer, he asked, "Avery?"

Brett just shook his head slowly. Fiona started to cry, just gentle sobbing at first but then the tears started to flow in a torrent. She knelt on the floor of the bridge and held her head in her hands. Brett motioned to Dennis to give him the wheel and Dennis knelt beside her, taking her into his arms and rocking her.

"Oh…Denny. You…wouldn't believe…how horrible…it was. And poor Avery. It was…awful."

Dennis held her tighter to his chest. "Shh. Don't think about it. We're going home now."

Fiona wiped at her eyes and started to tremble. Dennis took off his jacket and wrapped it around her shoulders. It was a warm evening but he was afraid that she might be going into shock.

Brett turned his head and looked down at them. "Denny—Fiona was amazing. She is one brave lady."

Fiona lay down on the floor and curled up into the fetal position. "We killed people, Denny. And...monsters."

Denny looked up at Brett with a question in his eyes.

"No time to give you the story right now, Denny. We'll have time later to debrief."

Dennis spread his jacket out more, to completely cover Fiona's body—she seemed to have suddenly faded off to sleep.

He stood up beside Brett and whispered, "You've probably already noticed that we have company out there."

"Yeah, I have. We're going at a speed of forty-five miles per hour right now, but they're faster and they're gaining. I know what types of boats they are, and I know that they're American."

"Will they just want to board and interrogate us, maybe?"

Brett looked at Dennis with cold detachment. "They've been sent to kill us, Denny. But we're not going to let them."

"Brett, I was down in the engine room. That booster contraption that Desmond brought on board is not connected to anything."

Silence.

"Brett?"

"Oh, yeah. Sorry. I was thinking about those boats behind us. Yes, that booster works off a remote transmitter. There's a receiver connected to the engine, so it's all wireless. Once I activate it, the signal is sent and the torque of the engine magnifies."

Dennis frowned. He knew a lot about boats and had never heard of such a thing before. He shrugged. The secret world that Brett lived in probably had devices he could never even imagine.

"Shouldn't we activate it?"

"No. Leave that decision to me, Denny. Trust me. We have to save that until we really need it."

Denny looked back. The gunboats were about half a mile distant. "I think we really need it now, Brett."

Brett glanced behind. "No, not yet. We need to save it until we're along the St. Kitts coast at the closest point to the airport. We'll need a surge of speed then so that we can escape onto land quickly without getting fired upon."

"If we get that far."

"Oh, we will. Those boats behind us have no ability to harm us right now. They're equipped with rear-mounted heavy machine guns, so while the boats are pointed toward us trying to catch us, they're useless. They need to be beside us or in front of us in order to fire on us."

Denny turned around and watched them approach. Then he saw something that caused his stomach to flip. The gunboats were both starting to flank them, moving out in wide arcs. He knew they would give up some approach proximity by doing that, but it was almost as if they had just heard Brett's explanation. They wanted to be able to take a shot at them, broadside to broadside.

"Brett, look what they're doing!"

Brett turned and stared into the dark void behind them. "Shit! They're clever. Okay, the best defense is an offense. Wake Fiona up. I don't want her rolling around. Both of you hold on tight."

Dennis shook Fiona awake. In a groggy voice, she asked, "Are we home yet?"

"No, sweetie. Hold onto the rail beside you—tightly. We're in for a bit of a rough ride. I'll be right here beside you."

He looked up at Brett. "What are you going to do?"

"I'm going to give them what they don't expect. And you're going to help. Open that compartment under the dashboard. There's an Uzi in there. I had it smuggled onto the boat as a failsafe."

Dennis leaned over and opened the cupboard. Sure enough, an Uzi submachine gun was resting there peacefully. He pulled it out, flicked off the safety and slid back the bolt along the top.

"Denny, it looks like you've used one before."

"Yeah, it's an amazing weapon."

"Well, it's going to do something amazing for us right now. I'm going to start a turn into my own arc—toward the boat on the west of us. He's behind us still, so when I finish my arc I'll be pointing right towards his nose. We're going to play a game of chicken with these marines. I guarantee you they'll turn before we do. And when they do, start firing—at the bridge first, then at the machine-gunner as we pass alongside."

Dennis gritted his teeth. "What about the boat on the east side of us?"

"We'll worry about him after. He'll be shocked when he sees what we're doing, and will surely second-guess his own strategy after we're done with the first boat. Might buy us some time."

Brett pulled back on the throttle and started his turn west. A gentle arc, but it was noticeable to the gunboat because it also seemed to slow down a bit. Probably confused. Then as the arc was almost complete Brett slammed the throttle into full and the nose of the boat lurched upward.

They were racing now at full speed toward the bow of the gunboat—dead on. They were only about 200 yards away now and the gunboat started honking its warning horn. Brett swore under his breath, "Assholes!"

He leaned on his warning horn as well and kept going straight toward the nose of the marine craft. Dennis held his breath—the boat gave no sign of turning.

Only 100 yards apart now and both boats were still on a collision course. Dennis held his breath and marveled at Brett's nerves of steel.

Suddenly the game of chicken came to an abrupt end. The gunboat swerved when they were fifty yards apart. It was going to be close.

Brett yelled. "Denny, he's turning to his starboard! Move to our port and nail them!"

Dennis jumped over to the port side, raised his Uzi and began firing at the bridge. Both boats were moving so fast he only had a couple of seconds. But his aim was good, and he could see and hear the tinkle of glass as the surround of their bridge was disintegrated. Several astonished heads ducked down inside.

The two boats were only thirty feet apart as the military vessel's machine-gunner came into view. He was swiveling his heavy gun towards them when Denny let loose. The Uzi rattled and tore the soldier to shreds while his heavy machine gun fired harmlessly into the sky.

As they passed the gunboat, Brett made a sharp turn to his port side and spun the boat in a tight swivel around to the starboard side of the gunboat. Dennis knew he was making a finishing run.

"Denny, hit the bridge again as I swoop by! Take them out!"

Dennis leaned over the port side railing and braced his elbows against the cold steel. He clenched his teeth and waited.

He could see four naïve blurry heads in the bridge as they raced past. They clearly did not suspect at all that their prey had snuck back up on their other side. Denny took aim, squeezed the trigger and watched three of the heads lurch backward and collapse out of sight.

Brett veered away from the gunboat and set his course back directly toward the St. Kitts coastline.

"One gunboat down."

Denny moved over to the starboard side of the boat and gazed into the dark. He saw the running lights of the second boat swooping in an arc to their rear. "He's turning behind us, Brett!"

They were only about 300 yards apart. Brett kept on his course, racing toward the coast.

"Denny, take the wheel. I'm going to activate our little turbo boost now."

Dennis grabbed it and held it on the same line that Brett had set. Brett disappeared down into the hull. In less than a minute he was back. He pointed to a bend in the coastline. "We're going to turn at that point and try to ram our boat onto the beach. Then we'll run like hell."

Brett grabbed the binoculars off the dashboard and trained them back at the gunboat behind them. "Shit! One of them has a grenade launcher!"

Dennis felt the contents of his stomach rise into his throat. "What? Give me those!" He ripped the binoculars out of Brett's hand and with one hand still on the wheel gazed back at the gunboat, which was only 100 yards behind them now.

"I don't see a grenade launcher. I think you're seeing things."

"Trust me—my eyes recognize these things better than yours do." Brett grabbed the binoculars and trained them on the boat again.

"Definitely. We're in trouble big time now."

Denny looked at him quizzically. "Where's this turbo boost we were supposed to be getting?"

"Damn thing doesn't seem to be working, but no time to fix it."

Brett reached into his pocket and pulled out the mini-DVR that his eyeglass camera had been recording into at the lab.

"Take this. Put it in your pocket. You and Fiona dive off the boat as soon as we round that point there. They won't see you if you stay under for about ten seconds as they pass the point. Stay under until they pass. And the DVR is waterproof, so you don't have to worry about it. I'll try to maneuver them around a bit to make it difficult for them to fire the launcher, and detour them away from you guys. Swim to shore and hike to the airport. If I'm not there in an hour, leave without me."

Fiona had moved inside the bridge canopy as Brett finished his instructions. "What are you talking about? We're staying together! All three of us!"

Brett pushed Dennis out of the way and took over the wheel.

Dennis was stunned. He couldn't believe what Brett was proposing. "We're not going to leave you, Brett. We'll fight it out with these guys.

There's an extra magazine for the Uzi in the cupboard. We'll do the same moves again."

Brett grimaced. "It won't work a second time, Denny. We need to protect that DVR first and foremost. You both have to go, now."

Dennis shoved the DVR into his side pocket. He peered through the windscreen. He could see that they were now approaching the point.

He walked over to the starboard side to join Fiona, and gazed down into the dark water. Dennis nodded to her soberly. "He's right, Fiona. We have to go."

Brett yelled back to them. "I'm going to slow it down to half throttle. In twenty seconds, we'll be out of sight of the gunboat. When I say 'dive,' you dive!"

They both stood up on the edge and crouched, holding onto the rail. Denny counted down in his mind. He looked at Fiona. "Remember, stay under for ten seconds—no, let's make it twenty to be safe."

She blinked her eyes and held them closed for a second, seemingly in a daze.

Brett yelled. "Dive!"

They hit the water at the same time. Denny dove downward as fast as he could and saw Fiona right beside him. He motioned to her to aim toward the shoreline. He counted.

At twenty seconds, Denny grabbed Fiona's hand and pulled her up with him. They broke the surface and looked back. They could see the gunboat closing in on Brett.

Denny mouthed, "Go, Brett, go."

The explosion was so ferocious it rattled his teeth. He watched in shock as the Ocean 62 disintegrated into a mushroom fireball, while the gunboat suddenly veered away and headed back in the opposite direction.

Brett Horton was gone. In one sudden horrific moment, he was gone.

*****

They were lying in a grove of palm trees just up from the beach. Not a word had been spoken between them for the half hour they had been lying there. Dennis thought he might have dozed off for a few minutes, but he wasn't sure.

Fiona had her arm wrapped around his chest, her fist clenching tightly to his wet shirt.

He gently rubbed her back and finally found the need to say something.

He leaned his lips into her ear. "He's our hero, Fiona. He saved our lives."

Fiona just sighed, and he could taste the salty tears on her cheek as he softly kissed her. He whispered again. "We have to move soon. Get to the plane while it's still dark. Bring this thing to an end."

Fiona slid off to the side and grabbed Dennis by the hair, pulling him over on top of her. She kissed him hard on the lips, so hard that their teeth knocked together. She bit his lower lip, then moved her mouth to the side and did the same to his earlobe. Her hands swept over his back. She dug her nails in and clawed him. Dennis felt the pain, but it felt good—and oddly necessary.

She was crying—hard now. Dennis could feel her body shaking underneath him, and she arched herself upwards into him in one violent thrust. He was stunned at her sudden power and strength.

He tried to calm her by stroking her forehead. She responded by grabbing his hair again and roughly yanking him closer to her. He looked curiously into her eyes and saw nothing. They were still Fiona's eyes, but they looked dead, lifeless.

She gritted her teeth for a second, then succeeded in pushing out the words she seemed to want so desperately to say.

"Denny, I need you to fuck me. Don't make love to me. Just fuck me. Fuck me the hardest you've ever fucked anyone in your life. Make it hurt. I need to feel that or I swear I'm going to just wither up and die right here, right now."

CHAPTER FIFTY FIVE

Dennis was back in the same old familiar conference room; blinds drawn, no light except for the interrogation-friendly overhead dome lamp. He braced himself for what was to come.

Grant Folsom was sitting at his usual spot at the head of the table, and to his right was Bart Davis. Two things were different this time though. That asshole from the Pentagon, Bill Charlton, was absent. And Dennis was invited to take a seat across from Bart instead of being parked in no-man's land at the other end of the huge conference table. He was starting to get the feeling that this meeting was going to be more pleasant than the last one that took place in this intimidating room.

They each helped themselves to coffee and took their seats. Grant flipped open a file that he had brought in with him. Then he looked up at Dennis and smiled.

"A lot has changed since we last met in this room."

Dennis played innocent, wondering if they'd discovered where he'd been and what he'd been doing. "Has it?"

"Well, you've been away so you missed out on some excitement. By the way, I do want to thank you for staying away from the case like I asked you to. As usual, you demonstrated restraint and respect. And I'm glad you got away somewhere for a while. Probably helped relieve the tension a bit for you."

Dennis clasped his hands together and rested them on the table. "Thanks, Grant, but in all honesty, I got the feeling that I really didn't have a choice."

Grant chuckled. "I guess there's some truth in that, yes. But regardless, you have my thanks."

"Okay. So, tell me what's been happening."

"Denny, I'll start right off by saying that you're no longer a suspect in the serial killing case. You can resume your duties again immediately."

Dennis frowned. "Did you catch the perp?"

"No, we didn't. But there was one more vigilante murder while you were away. The victim was that man that was suspected sixteen years ago of being the killer of your dad. Travis Wilkinson, remember?"

Dennis hoped they didn't notice the lump that he suddenly felt in his throat.

"Yes, I remember that guy."

"Well, he was murdered in a similar venue that your father died in—abandoned warehouse in an alley, chairs set up. The wounds were consistent with a Shaolin attack. Knowing who the victim was and seeing the wounds made us immediately confirm in our minds that you were indeed the vigilante killer as we had suspected."

Dennis cracked his knuckles. "What changed your mind?"

"This time the killer left DNA behind. Wilkinson's fingers were covered in the perp's blood and there was extensive tissue under the fingernails. He must have scratched him very deep—put up a hell of a fight by the looks of it."

Dennis was shaking on the inside from anticipation. "So, you have the guy? You've got him in custody? I'm gonna want to have a chat with him as soon as possible."

"You can't. He's dead."

"Who was it? Did our guys take him down?"

"It was a guy by the name of Brett Horton. He was a Secret Service agent and after retiring he did some contract work. God knows what."

Dennis felt like he'd been kicked in the gut. He was fighting to keep the emotion from showing on his face.

"Yeah, so it was his DNA. I guess he moonlighted as a vigilante. You're off the hook, Denny."

Dennis' curiosity was peaked now. "So, how did he die?"

"It was a boating accident off the coast of St. Kitts. He was there on vacation. Apparently, the boat exploded—initial forensics indicates it was a faulty fuel line. Fitting justice for the guy, huh?"

"Yeah, fitting."

Dennis thought—when the American government wants to cover something up, no one does it better.

*****

"Charlton, here."

"I'm not going to say my name and I ask that you not use it either, but you know who this is."

A pause. "Yes, I do. Why don't we get off the phone and arrange to meet somewhere?"

Dennis grimaced. "No, we'll do this over the phone, if you don't mind."

"Okay, what do you want?"

"You suspect that I have a video, I'm sure. I've emailed some samples to you. When we end this call, check your inbox. I also have tons of incriminating documents—again, samples are sitting in your inbox. Look them over and if you agree that you don't want this horror story made public, you'll want to do exactly what I tell you to do."

"And what's that?"

"First off, I'm going to do a repeat of what one very brave lady did over thirty years ago. A new 'package' will be buried somewhere, with instructions to a trusted source to release everything to the world if anything happens to me, my sister, or my lady friend. Do you understand so far?"

"Yes."

"Secondly, within one week's time I want to read in the papers that the facility down south that we're both well aware of has been destroyed. And I mean completely destroyed, including all things alien that were brought here."

"Okay."

"Do you agree with these conditions?"

"Yes, I do. You have my promise that this experiment will be brought to an end."

"Within the next week, then. I'll be watching. A simple story like a facility far from U.S. soil being destroyed wouldn't normally hit the front page of the Washington Post. But with your influence I'm sure you can make that happen. That's where I'll be looking to see it. Understood?"

"Yes."

CHAPTER FIFTY SIX

Dennis looked across the table at his lovely sister. And he thanked God that she was still in his life. He vowed to himself that they would be closer than ever now, even closer than when they were kids. He smiled as he stared at her—that intense serious look in her eyes, the casual frock-type outfit she loved to wear, her incredible beauty shimmering in the candlelight.

And her cane leaning up against the dining room table.

"Denny, pass the wine, will you? You're hogging it as usual."

Her words shook him out of his trance. Fiona giggled. "What are you thinking, Denny? Mel's right—you do always hog the wine. But tonight, you seem to be lost in space somewhere!"

He laughed. "Ladies, I'm just so thankful for everything. And thankful for you two. I was just thinking of things like that."

Mel smiled. "Aw, that's nice, little brother. Sweet. But, I still want you to pass me the wine!"

Denny got up, grabbed the bottle and walked over to her side of the table. "I'll do better than that. I'll pour it for you."

Fiona took a sip of her wine. "How is the leg coming along, Mel?"

"It's doing great. It's been three months now, so quite the ordeal. The prognosis is good though. Physiotherapy has helped, but I still have to contend with this stupid cane for a while yet. Won't be long though until I'm jogging again."

"That's so good to hear. And you can be thankful that the bullet in your leg kept you out of the action that Denny and I put ourselves through."

"Well, you two have refused to tell me all the details, and I guess I can appreciate that it must have been so horrific that you don't want me to have nightmares. But from what you have told me, I'm glad I wasn't there. It's sad that Brett and that Avery guy died. I never did get the chance to get to know Brett like you guys did. I was already shot and lying on the grass when he first appeared on the scene."

Fiona nodded. "He was a very capable man and I really grew to like and trust him, despite the shadowy world that he lived in. The whole ordeal down on Nevis was indeed a nightmare, and he and I fought our way out of that lab together. Be glad that we haven't shared the whole story with you, Mel. If it weren't for Brett, I would have surely died. At least now I can think back on it without getting panic attacks. I told you how I had to go on anxiety medication afterwards. Took them for about a month. Thankfully I'm now at the point where I can actually talk about it without shaking."

Denny went into the kitchen to make some coffee while the girls continued chatting. As he listened to them he reflected upon how lucky he was. This was the first time since the ordeal that Melissa had been able to join them for an evening.

It was nice to be hosting dinner for his sister. Fiona had quit her Pentagon job and moved in with him a couple of months ago. It was a pleasant and unexpected surprise to discover that she was a gourmet cook. That was one bonus he hadn't counted on. So, he deferred to her on the cooking most of the time now. Tonight, she made roast lamb, slow-cooked for hours surrounded with vegetables, and soaking the entire time in a full bottle of wine. It was delicious. Dennis was looking forward to eating like this for the rest of his life.

But more than that, he was looking forward to loving Fiona for the rest of his life. And life was more precious now than ever. They both knew they were extremely lucky to be alive.

Dennis went back into the dining room with a tray adorned with a coffee pot and pastries. The perfect end to a perfect meal.

Mel was in an inquisitive mood tonight, he could tell. She tapped her long fingers on the table to get his attention. "Denny, did you ever imagine that what mom was blurting out about was something as serious as what you discovered?"

"Well, when she first muttered something about a 'package' and then I found those DOD guys in her room, alarm bells went off big time. But I only started feeling uneasy that day that Barb and I heard her chanting over and over again what we first thought was the word, 'Skeleton.' Then when we realized what she was really saying was the word 'Shackleton' and we found out what Shackleton really was, it started becoming insidious in my mind. After that, one thing led to another…"

Fiona jumped in. "Boy, is that an understatement."

As he was pouring the coffee, Melissa asked another question, one he didn't want to answer. "Denny, do you really believe that Brett was the vigilante killer?"

Dennis sat down, and wrung his hands together. "I guess I don't want to believe it, Mel. But the DNA doesn't lie. We know that at the very least, he did kill that Wilkinson fellow."

"And for a while they suspected you of being the serial killer."

"Yes, they did."

Fiona put her coffee cup down hard, almost breaking the saucer. "Brett was far too clever to make a mistake and leave incriminating evidence. He wouldn't have left his DNA behind unless he wanted to leave it behind. I'm convinced of that."

Mel frowned at her. "Why on earth would he do that?"

"To get Denny off the hook."

Dennis leaned across the table and grabbed a cheese pastry. "But, Fiona, that DNA incriminated him. If he'd lived he would have gone to prison for the rest of his life."

"Denny, I don't think Brett thought he'd survive the ordeal. I think he knew he'd either die that night or shortly thereafter. He would have been a target, and he knew that. Clearing you was his final good deed. And Brett had more of a heart than any of us would have thought, trust me. I saw the way he choked up when Avery was begging him to just shoot him.

"I think he really liked you, Denny. You two were kindred spirits with a lot more in common than just the deadly fighting skills. I think he had a certain self-righteousness and sense of justice about him, just like you have. He believed in doing the right thing. And isn't it telling if the victim that he chose to incriminate himself with was the man suspected of killing your father?"

Dennis rubbed his forehead. He felt a headache coming on. "Yes, that is something, and I have to admit that I've been wondering the same things. But it just didn't seem logical to me that he'd sacrifice himself like that."

Melissa seemed to be able to tell that the conversation was getting to Dennis. And it was probably getting to her too. He was aware of her staring at him, and when he glanced up he could see the compassion in her eyes. After all these years, she still wasn't over the death of their father. And neither was he. He was glad she took the lead to change the topic.

"Let's switch gears here. It all ended up okay, didn't it? The lab, I mean? It was destroyed and the three of us are safe? Aren't we?"

Dennis got up and went over to a cabinet, opened a drawer and withdrew a newspaper article wrapped in plastic. He handed it to Melissa.

"Here's the article from the Washington Post, hon. This was almost three months ago. Read it—you'll see that they complied with my demands. It talks about how a massive fire took the lab to the ground—the Nevis volunteer firefighters couldn't cope. And it mentions how the lab was jointly owned by several American biotech firms and that they've decided not to rebuild. The area will be developed as a wildlife sanctuary. Now, isn't that ironic? A wildlife sanctuary?"

"Was it really owned by biotech firms?"

"I doubt any American company was involved. That was just a cover story for a lab that was owned by the Pentagon and managed by the Centers for Disease Control. It was definitely a public facility, but they would never want to admit that, would they? The public would have asked too many questions—the government would have had to have been accountable for what they were doing down there."

Melissa planted her elbows on the table and leaned forward. Dennis knew that another serious question was coming. "So, why won't you tell Fiona and I where you've hidden the package?"

Dennis felt the headache coming back again. "You know why, sis. It's not necessary. All you need to know is that I've hidden it, it's protected with fail-safe instructions, and that we're all going to be left alone. You don't need the burden of knowing any more than that. All we three have to worry about is just getting on with our lives now."

CHAPTER FIFTY SEVEN

He walked around the perimeter of his kitchen and made sure that everything was in order. The first thing he'd done this morning after waking up, was move all the furniture out of the way. Then he pulled out the old stove and dragged it into the dining room. The appliance guys would take it away when they brought the new one—in just a matter of minutes now. He was excited. Cooking had become a passion for him.

The handsome man walked over to his backyard window and gazed out at the 'Gunten,' the largest mountain peak closest to the city. It stretched 3,200 feet in the air and looked glorious covered in snow. And beyond, only twelve miles away, he could see the majestic Alps reaching for the sky.

He loved Bern. It was one of the cleanest capital cities he'd ever been to, and it did Switzerland proud. With an unemployment rate of only three percent, it was the envy of the world. It was the fourth most populous city in the country at 350,000 people, and he was comforted knowing that ten percent of the population were foreigners just like him. And at least half of those were Americans hiding their money, so he was in good company.

He knew that Bern was rated as one of the top ten cities in the world for quality of life, and this didn't surprise him in the least. Not only was the city historic, but it was also clean and safe. People minded their own business too, which was typical of anywhere in Switzerland. But it did have its share of nefarious people—not surprising considering that the country was a haven for those who wished to escape the long arms of the law...or the taxman.

For the last three months, he had been practicing his German, which had always been pretty good, but not good enough for Switzerland. The main spoken language was a derivative dialect of German, called Bernese German. It required a certain curl of the tongue. He was working on it. And he was confident he would master it. He had to—he would never leave this place.

He was titillated by the knowledge that, only two blocks away from his charming alpine house, Albert Einstein had lived here from the years 1903-1905. Not long, but long enough for him to have mastered his most famous work, the 'Theory of Relativity.' At that time, he had just been a lowly clerk working at the local patent office. He must have had a lot of time on his hands.

The man turned at the sound of the doorbell ringing. He strode across the cherry hardwood floor and cherished the sound of his shoes on the solid surface. He loved the sound of 'solid.'

It was the delivery men. He showed them where the cooker was to go, and then got out of the way as they spent the next two hours lugging in all the pieces and assembling it. When they were finished, he stood back and admired it. A beautiful black 'Aga' cooker, the best cooker in the world, and one of the most expensive. This one had set him back 30,000 U.S. dollars, but it was worth it. He had lots of time to cook now, and he intended to become a gourmet chef. This was going to be his next life, his new passion, and he'd had many lives and passions so far. What was wrong with having just one more? He might even open his own restaurant.

"Sir, we hope you enjoy the new Aga. Have to tell you, we've delivered only one of these before. They're pretty rare."

The man smiled. "Yes, they are. Hey, I can tell that you're American."

The delivery man smiled back. "Yes, I am. And you are too, right?"

"Yes. I had one of these back in the States. But it was so warm most of the year where I lived, that the thing wasn't practical. Since these Agas are on all the time, my kitchen was so hot in the summer I couldn't cook. Had to order out until winter rolled around again."

The delivery man laughed, and his partner smiled. "Well, you'll have plenty of chances to cook here. Hot weather isn't something we're used to. But, it takes some talent to be able to use these Agas. Are you up for the challenge?"

The man laughed. "No problem. I'm actually a killer in the kitchen."

*****

Richard Sterling gazed out of the window of his limousine as it pulled in around his circular driveway. He felt a sense of pride at the majesty of his mansion. He'd worked hard his entire life and he deserved the luxury that he now enjoyed. Life was good in Switzerland, in more ways than one.

And he was glad he didn't have to share any of this with a woman. They just sucked a man dry, and he wouldn't have been able to enjoy his extra-curricular activities if he'd had a woman in his life.

Oh, he liked women for sure. He enjoyed them whenever he got the urge, and he had the money to afford those urges. But his main urge wasn't women.

"Thanks, George. So, it's 10:00 right now, and I think you have a delivery to make to me around midnight, right?"

"Yes, sir."

"And what's his name?"

"Fredrik, sir."

"And how old is this one?"

"He's sixteen, sir."

"Wonderful. Just perfect."

"Indeed, sir."

"Well, I'll see you at midnight then."

Richard walked up the steps, opened his front door, and stepped into the massive foyer. The first thing he noticed was that there wasn't the usual beeping from the alarm. That's strange, he thought. He didn't remember turning the system off. Sure enough, the light was red. Oh, well—old age creeping up on him. He must have forgotten. He punched in his codes and reactivated it.

He hurried upstairs. He was anxious to get onto his computer and get all horned up before his boy showed up later. The young lad was under the impression that he'd be doing computer work, entering data into a financial database. Good money for a sixteen-year-old boy. And his parents had no reason to be suspicious—Richard did live in the most prominent area of the city. He chuckled to himself as he thought back to how many visitors he'd had in the last few years, and only three of them had resulted in charges.

Money sure talked, especially in Bern. It was a wealthy city, and for those envious people who didn't have wealth, they would do almost anything to blend in to the culture of privilege. He was a testament to that. Greedy parents who had been more than willing to drop the rape and molestation charges if he paid up. And he paid up, no problem. He viewed it as just like paying a parking ticket. Violate the law, and then just pay the fine. Then just do it all over again. Ha!

He turned on the computer in his office. The damn thing would take about five minutes to boot up, as usual. He had so much stuff on there, it was running really slow now. He needed to splurge and buy himself another one—then he could spread his stuff out over two computers. That would be perfect.

He headed back downstairs. Time to make himself a sandwich and build up his energy for later. And it would be something for him to eat while he was gazing at the beautiful naked boys on his computer screen. There were a couple of new sites he wanted to check out tonight. Yes, this would be one hot night for sure.

Richard opened the fridge and grabbed some bread, butter and cold cuts. Before he had the chance to pull his head back, the door slammed against it.

Then he was in the air—he felt strong hands grabbing him under the arms and tossing him backwards against the sink like he was a sack of garbage. He staggered to his feet and then promptly stumbled forward face-first onto his terrazzo kitchen floor. He felt dizzy. But he still managed to look up.

The man was dressed in black, from his head to his toes. His face was hidden behind a matching balaclava. He stood with his hands on his hips, looking down at him. He seemed tall, but not too tall.

Richard knew he had to bargain. He was good at bargaining. Decades in the investment banking business had given him skills beyond compare.

"I have a vault in the house. What do you want? I'll give it to you, just name it."

The man laughed. "I want your life, you perverted piece of shit."

"What?"

"You heard me. Get up."

Richard grabbed the edge of the kitchen island, and pulled himself up. "This doesn't have to be messy. I can make you a rich man."

"I'm already a rich man."

Richard suddenly had a thought. "Are you one of the parents? Didn't I pay you enough? Just name it—I can give you more."

He jerked back as a finger came racing towards him in a blur, striking him right in the middle of his chest. He looked down and saw a red patch beginning to form on his tailored Givenchy shirt.

Richard glanced up at the black figure, shocked at what had just happened. He was starting to feel faint. He heard himself asking, "Why?"

"Because you're human filth."

Richard felt his knees starting to buckle. He struggled to remain standing just as a matter of pride. He tried to talk but the words wouldn't come. The man in black leaned in to him, so close that Richard could feel his moist breath seeping through the woolen balaclava.

"You sick little fuck. You know what? None of us have much time left, but I'm going to make damn sure that sick little fucks like you don't hurt any more people during whatever time we do have. So that's why I'm here. And that's why you're going to die tonight."

Richard couldn't help himself. He started to sob. Then he screamed in horror as he watched the blur of two fingers racing toward his forehead.

CHAPTER FIFTY EIGHT

It had been another lovely dinner and Fiona was so tired she went to bed even before they'd had a chance to think about dessert. Tonight, they'd had a nice romantic pasta dinner together—washed down with a 1998 Chianti. Dennis thought he remembered that being a good year, but it didn't really matter. It had tasted great, regardless.

He knew the wine had gone to Fiona's head, but more than that—even though she would deny it—she was still having a tough time dealing with the horror of Nevis. And the death of Brett. It would take time. Dennis would give her all the time she needed, and more love than she could have ever imagined. She was his treasure.

He filled his coffee cup and headed up to his study. It was only 11:00, too soon for him to hit the sack. He sat back in his leather chair and opened a case file. This case involved a string of burglaries throughout the Georgetown area of the city, his area. He had a particular interest in this one for that reason alone.

Dennis was about halfway through the file when the phone rang. Strange, he thought, to get a call this time of night.

"Hello?"

"Hi Denny. You know who this is, but don't say my name."

Dennis felt like he'd been caressed by a ghost. His heart began pounding in his chest at the exact instant that his hand went numb. The phone slipped from his grasp and crashed to the floor.

He froze for a few seconds and wondered if perhaps he'd fallen asleep and simply been dreaming. That notion was dispelled quickly when he heard the familiar voice calling out his name from down on the floor.

He reached down and picked up the phone.

"Uh…where are you?"

"Can't tell you that."

"I don't know what to say. I'm stunned."

"Denny, take a look out your window and tell me if you can see the moon tonight."

Dennis glanced outside—it was a clear night and the moon was half-full.

"Yes, I can see it. It's nice and clear."

"Good. Take another look, towards the south pole of the moon at the lower right-hand corner of the semi-circle. Tell me what you see."

Dennis looked outside again. He stared hard. There was something. He put the phone down and aimed his telescope. Puzzled, he picked up the phone again.

"It looks like there's a little chunk missing—or it's a shadow? I don't really know what I'm looking at."

"A chunk is missing. It can only be noticed when the moon is half-full. That's when the missing section stands out. When it's full, there's too much illumination to see it."

"Do you know this for sure?"

"Yes, I do. The spot you're looking at is pretty much bang-on where the Shackleton Crater is. When they nuked it, that section of rock became fractured and it weakened over the decades. Those so-called meteors and fireballs that have been seen on several continents recently weren't meteors at all. Sure, the information given to the Press identified those things as meteors. But I have inside information. The rock debris recovered from the impact sites; they're moon rocks. They've been positively identified. But the public will never know this of course."

Dennis took a sip of his coffee, and then winced. It had gone cold on him. He walked over to his water cooler and poured himself a glass. If he was going to drink something cold, he wanted something that was meant to be cold. He guzzled it.

He half-whispered into the phone. "The moon's fucked now, isn't it?"

"In more ways than you might realize. I'm sure you've been puzzled, like I've been, about the weird weather patterns over the past few years— the fierce hurricanes, early tornado seasons, abnormal tides, complete islands disappearing, brutally hot summers, bizarre winter storms. Not to mention volcanoes going into overdrive everywhere including the middle of the ocean, an incredible increase in earthquake frequency, and unexplained animal and fish deaths."

Dennis was starting to get a sick feeling in his stomach. A sense of foreboding was beginning to engulf him, and his eyes began to get blurry. He knew his blood pressure was rising.

"Yeah, I've been paying attention to all of those things."

"Well, Denny, you and I both know that the moon affects the earth in serious ways. Without it we'd be doomed; if it was farther away from us we'd be doomed; if it was too close we'd be doomed. Where the moon has historically been, has maintained a sort of equilibrium for us."

"Yes." Dennis braced himself for the words that were coming—he didn't know what those words were going to be, he just knew they were coming.

"When they nuked the moon, it became destabilized—irreparably. It's moving much faster now and its orbit is much tighter. The public wouldn't notice anything; most people never look up at the sky anyway. They take our moon for granted. And it's normally about a quarter million miles away from us, so even a reasonably tangible difference in its distance wouldn't be noticed. Not yet anyway."

"Spit it out. What are you saying?"

"I'm telling you this because after everything that's happened I feel you deserve to know. Enjoy life, get things in order, treasure the world such as it is."

"Again, spit it out!"

"The moon is 20,000 miles closer to us today than it was a decade ago. Within about ten years we're going to get hit. It'll keep coming closer until earth's gravity suddenly just sucks it in.

"Denny, our moon will become the largest asteroid mankind has ever recorded. Except that no one will be alive to record this one. It will be an extinction event."

His heart was pounding. A burning pain shot through his chest, up through his shoulder and down his left arm. Dennis' thumb hit the 'off' button on the phone and for the second time in the last few minutes the poor little instrument crashed to the floor.

Dennis staggered over to the water cooler, popped an aspirin, and sucked back the refreshing liquid. Then he splashed some on his forehead, and promptly lowered himself to the floor fearing that he might just keel over at any second. Dennis took some deep breaths and relaxed for a few minutes until the chest pains subsided.

He'd had these before, a long time ago. After a battery of tests, his doctor had reassured him that they were just stress-related; no damage done to his heart. That was just after his father's death. Well maybe it was just stress again, but he decided he would keep the aspirin close at hand anyway until the reality of what he'd just heard sunk in.

Feeling much better, he stood up and walked back to his telescope. He re-focused it back on the moon again and just stared. Under his breath he cursed, "Jesus Christ."

Suddenly he felt her from behind, nestling in close to him. She wrapped her arms over his shoulders and clasped her fingers across his chest. He could feel her head resting against his back and it felt wonderful, comforting.

"What are you looking at, Denny?"

He licked his dry lips. "Oh, nothing, sweetheart. Just enjoying the view."

She gently pressed one knee up between his legs and sighed. "Why don't you just come to bed? I can promise you that the view is even better in there."

He turned around, took her into his arms and hugged her tightly. "That's a promise I'm going to hold you to for the rest of your life."

ABOUT THE AUTHORS

Peter Parkin was born in Toronto, Canada and after studying Business Administration at Ryerson University, he embarked on a thirty-four year career in the business world. He retired in 2007 and has written seven novels with co-author Alison Darby.

Alison Darby is a life-long resident of the West Midlands region of England. She studied psychology in college and when she's not juggling a busy work life and writing novels, she enjoys researching astronomy. Alison has two daughters who live and work in the vibrant cities of London and Birmingham.